John is a thirty-one-year-old suburbanite and part-time member of the human race. He was educated in most areas of the media only to leave university and end up having nothing more to do with it.

He spends his daylight hours sitting behind a desk, then going home to make funny voices for his daughter, Lara's, fat giraffe, Calvin.

When not writing satire, science-fiction, or reading Mr Men books to Lara, he can be found helping his pub quiz team out in the movie round or being outbid on eBay.

OBSESSION

John Conway

OBSESSION

Vanguard Press

A CIP catalogue record for this title is
available from the British Library.

ISBN 978 184386 430 1

Vanguard Press is an imprint of
Pegasus Elliot MacKenzie Publishers Ltd.
www.pegasuspublishers.com

First Published in 2008

Vanguard Press
Sheraton House Castle Park
Cambridge England

Printed & Bound in Great Britain

Dedication

To Lara Catherine Conway

Acknowledgements

Thanks to all those who helped, encouraged and motivated me to keep writing, especially:

Mr Biggs, Joanne Salter, Teresa Weston and Jayne Watson, for their inspirational teaching.

Andrew England, Lara Kelly, Paul Shelock and Shelley Smith for all their help, proof-reading and support.

Mum and Dad for everything.

Chapter 1: Name in Lights

Okay, I admit it; I am a bit nervous as my luxury limousine pulls up at the police roadblock to Leicester Square. I originally chose my tuxedo because it looked like the black one George Lazenby wore in *Diamonds Are Forever*. But I've just realised I've been sitting on a cigarette butt all the way here and now have grey ash marks all over my trousers.

"Oi, mate, wake up, we're here!" shouts my faithful driver. His words make me take a deep breath. I'll bet every budding young starlet had a few butterflies the first time they were greeted by screaming fans along the red carpet.

Robert DeNiro, Scarlett Johansson, David Bowie – they're already inside the Odeon and now it's my turn: Doug Morrell – novelist, social commentator and most importantly, other half to beautiful television personality Donna Trayhorn.

You're a star, I remind myself. And you're just as good as the rest of them – better in fact. And in a few moments, you'll be inside with dear sweet Donna.

"Are you getting out, mate, or what?" my driver goes on. "You haven't fallen asleep again, have you?"

I ignore his insubordination and compose a suitably harsh email to his employers for tomorrow morning. I only nodded off because I've been working a full day at Parcel Plus, delivering stupid garden/ornaments to ungrateful old women./Besides, I was too excited to sleep last night thinking about this premiere. Luckily I didn't wake Mum when I was throwing up at 3 am. Hopefully she'll have cleaned it up by the time I get home./

A burly security guard wrenches open the limo door while I check my reflection in the glass separating me from the driver. Yes, I'm certain my hair isn't thinning, like that spiteful tea lady said. But of course Donna doesn't care and that's the main thing

13

– she loves me the way I am. I hope she's wearing something classy, like that little off-the-shoulder minidress she wore to the *Reality TV Star of the Year* Awards Ceremony – which she should have won.

I step out onto the red carpet and a primate in a suit, posing as a security guard, says something to me. I don't listen, as I'm too busy taking my first breath of celebrity air – it's like being born again. Born into a wonderful world of glamour and excitement, where only the beautiful exist and everyone has their name in lights. The crowd cheers and I'm almost too flustered to tell if they're chanting my name or not. I check my inside pocket for pens – I don't mind signing autographs, but only if the person promises not to sell them on eBay the next day.

"Mate, if you don't have a pass, you're going to have to turn around," grunts the security guard.

Who the hell does he think he his? I'm Doug Morrell and I shouldn't even need one of those tacky bits of laminated paper to get through. In my thirty-one years on this planet I've never been so offended as I am right now.

"I've got a pass," I say to him indignantly, making sure I only use words with one syllable. He doesn't look like the type who could handle any more and I doubt he's ever read a book in his life. That would also explain why he doesn't recognise me – he certainly wouldn't have read any of my books.

"Let's see it then," he growls in something that I guess could pass for English. I reach inside my pocket again, but get distracted by all the cheering. This is the happiest day of my life, but where did I put that damn pass? I hear cars sounding their horns and look up to see the ape eyeballing me with a raised mono-brow.

"Listen, Titch," he snarls. "You and your clapped-out old banger are holding up the line."

14

"I have got a pass!" I tell him again, as you have to show these people who's boss. "And I'll have you know I'm only one inch shorter than Tom Cruise! I'll bet you'd let him in!"

"Tom Cruise doesn't have a comb-over – now where's the pass?" he says, sniggering.

I would cut him down to size for that one, but I'm too busy fumbling in my pocket with all those pens to find the pass. Madonna and Guy Richie had the right idea – just ignore the fans – the useless proles will buy your music anyway.

"Just let me through, will you?" I say with a sigh.

"No, you could be a terrorist," he says robotically.

"Do I look like a terrorist?" I reply patronisingly. "I'm here with Donna Trayhorn!"

"Who?" says the Incredible Hulk.

"From the TV show *Voyeur*?" I point out, but before I can list all her other achievements, we're rudely interrupted by a driver from another limo.

"Excuse me, mate," he shouts from under a peaked cap in an overly cockney accent. "But I've got Johnny Depp on board and your – vehicle is blocking his way."

"Right, that's it, you don't have a pass; so get back in your minicab and piss off..." the ugly guard says as he puts a hand on my shoulder, creasing my jacket's lapel. "I think you want the seventies night down Old Compton Street."

"Excuse me," I say in a firm voice. I don't shout as I don't want the journalists to hear, "I'm also a media commentator as well as a writer, you know?"

"Then you should have written out a pass," the insolent lump remarks while the other driver gets out and starts mouthing off again.

Wait, I remember now! I put the pass on the top of my limo's little computer-thingy that tells you how much the fare is.

So, I clasp Kong's hand with my own vice-like grip and throw him aside so I can open the car door and lean in the back.

"I believe Donna Trayhorn is waiting for me," I say smugly when I climb back out and wave his precious little pass in his face.

"Oh, right," he says as he tries to focus on it. "You're one of that reality TV lot – no wonder I haven't heard of you – go on then, go find the rest of the fifteen-minuters."

Why don't you go back to swatting biplanes off the Empire State Building? He's going to get one hell of a scathing entry on my website when I get home. I hope he logs on to www.myspace.com/douglasmorrell tomorrow morning and finds out what I've written about him.

He waves me through and I leave the sound of car horns behind. At last I'm on my way down this luxurious red carpet. I don't get too upset about the little mix up, after all, I am a writer and a good writer turns every situation to his advantage. Perhaps I could use this encounter in my next book?

Secret Agent Doug Holster steps out of his shining black sports car – its engine still purring from winning the Monaco Grand Prix the day before. He's treated to a rapturous round of applause from the crowd. But to Holster film premieres have become a bore. However, he knew that he had to attend at least one a week in order to keep his secret identity hidden – that he was only a handsome millionaire philanthropist playboy during daylight hours, while at night he was the world's most secret and deadly weapon against evil.

A hideously mutated security guard leapt forward, blocking his path with a pair of those things with a chain between two sticks. Little does the poor sap know how many similar henchmen Doug had dispatched only the night before while raiding Doctor Death's Isle of Man hideaway. After an

unimpressive display with his mock-oriental weapon, he layed a
hand on Doug's tuxedo.

"Touch me again lumpy-boy," the dashing secret agent
hissed. "And you're a dead man."

The guard recoiled as he felt Doug's manly breath scolding
his scaly hand and let go. His tiny brain had just made the wisest
decision of his life.

"Doug!" a hapless female voice shouted from the crowd.
"Help me!"

I continue down the red carpet listening to the cheers and
spot a young girl with her hair in pigtails giving me the eye. As I
approach she takes my photo with her camera phone.

"Hey, baby!" I cry as I make her day by winking at her
while using one of my most charming smiles. She turns and
giggles with her mates like a schoolgirl – Mum always said my
humour made up for everything else. Actually, I really do hope
she is over sixteen – I didn't bring my glasses in case they
reflected camera flashes.

There aren't as many autograph hunters as I'd expected, but
at least that means my pens are safe. I might even get to return
them to the stationery cupboard at work tomorrow and no one
will any the wiser. I reckon the crowd must have been briefed by
the organisers not to bother celebrities for autographs.

I smile graciously and pose for the flock of paparazzi in
front of the cinema entrance. Perhaps I'll be shown in
tomorrow's Arts section of *The Times* rather than the tabloids.
I'll borrow work's communal copy and cut out the bit about me.

My Donna will be in there by now. She's incredibly stylish,
but without being trashy. Yet the press still try to invent a
catalogue of lies about her, even using badly airbrushed pictures
of her topless on holiday. Of course I was the first to debunk
them on my website donnaTisthebest.org.uk.

But right now I've given the photographers enough for one night and head inside. The film will be starting in about ten minutes and I want to get to my seat so I can make sure no one taller than me obscures my view. Despite the strongly worded email I sent to my local *Empire* cinema, I'm still barred for causing a disturbance during a showing of *Basic Instinct 2*.

Tonight is the premiere of yet another mindless action film – *The Last Day on Earth* – I doubt we'll be seeing its name at the Oscars, but I'd better show my face inside. Besides, Johnny Depp has arrived behind me, and the fool's even stopped to sign autographs. He doesn't realise that by saturating the market with his scribbles, he's driving down the price of a true autographed copy. That's a well-observed piece of social commentary – I'll have to try and remember it so I can upload it to my website tomorrow after work.

"Pass please, sir," says another hulking lump in a bow tie, standing between me and the Odeon's entrance.

Where do they get these people from – Rent-an-Ape? This one's even bigger than the last. I don't protest as I'm not one to make a scene. Besides, if I get too angry it'll bring on another nose bleed, so I obligingly hand him my pass.

"I'm afraid this pass is no longer valid, sir."

His words nearly bring the blood pouring from my nasal passages and I seriously contemplate suing. This imbecile will be hearing from my solicitor first thing in the morning – or rather when I get back from the depot as I'm on early shifts tomorrow.

"I demand to see the manager!" I shout in his face.

"Busy," is his one-word reply, proving my theory about how security guards can't form complex sentences.

"Well, the Event Organiser then," I say. I want to speak to an organ-grinder as I've had it up to here with monkeys.

18

"She's with Keanu Reeves," he says as a colleague of his ushers Johnny Depp straight through.

"Hey, Johnny!" I shout, giving him a nod and a wink for old time's sake. "Tell Donna I'll be inside in a minute, yeah?"

He's with his wife, so he obviously doesn't have time to chat right now, but I'm sure we'll catch up later. It's interesting to note that he's actually not as tall as he looks on screen. He probably wears boots with big heels, but then something else hits me.

"Wait a minute, he didn't show a pass!" I point out to the thug in the tux.

"He – is Johnny Depp," the tattooed hooligan replies.

"And I'm Douglas Morrell, so will you get out of my way?" I say unflinchingly as I push past him into the foyer. I head towards Johnny, thinking this would be as good a time as any to ask him if he'd consider taking the lead in a screenplay I wrote back in college.

But the meathead behind me barks something into his radio and three thugs in suits appear between me and Johnny. I don't know how I stop my nose from bleeding as they grab my arms and legs and "escort" me through the lobby. I'm no pushover, so these thugs must have been on steroids to fend off my ferocious attacks. They were lucky they had the element of surprise on their side as they carry me kicking and screaming past Johnny, Kylie and those kids from *Blazin' Squad*.

"Donna!" I scream. "Donna, where are you? Tell them – tell them I'm with you!"

Sadly Donna must have already taken her seat and she doesn't hear me being dragged through the building. Before I know what's happening, a flashback of my schooldays enters my head and I find myself flying through the air. Only this time I don't land in the girls' changing rooms, but some dirty back alley that reeks of what a Chinese takeaway has thrown out.

19

I land on my elbows in a puddle that's made up of sweet and sour noodles. Just because those skinheads are over five foot three they think they can pick on the little guy. By the time I get up, two of them have jumped back inside and the third is getting ready to bolt the door behind him.

I know no celebrity should ever say this, but under the circumstances, what else is there to do?

"Do you know who I am?" I scream as he leers at me from the doorway. Of course his minuscule mind resorts to the lowest form of wit and he simply replies, "Uninvited."

Oh, yes, very funny. Move over Jim Davidson, we have the wittiest doorman in Britain here.

"I'll have you know that my pass is as good as everyone else's," I remind him. "Would you do this to Jordan?"

"The passes were changed at the last minute due to a security scare," is his feeble excuse, "and for the record, the only thing you have in common with Jordan is you've both got the same size tits!"

"I am proportionate to my size!" I yell as I feel my nose starting to tingle. "You let me back inside this instant!"

"New passes were issued to everyone."

"I don't think so somehow," I point out. "Passes were clearly not issued to everyone, as I didn't get mine! And more to the point, what are you going to do about my tuxedo?"

I explain that it's on hire and who is going to pay for the cleaning costs that are rapidly mounting up? How can I mix with the great and good, smelling like a wok?

Finally, I get through to him and he nods understandingly; his face now solemn and deep in thought. I knew the prospect of legal eagles swooping down on him faster than you could say GBH would stop him in his tracks. He reaches into his pocket and takes out his wallet; from there he produces a small business card and hands it to me.

I look down at it, but before I can take in the tiny printed words, he slams the door and I hear bolts sliding across. What does he think he's playing at? I squint down at the card: it's for some dry cleaning company in Soho.

I find myself alone in the alleyway with only eight dead henchmen for company.

Doug Holster dispatches the henchmen with ease: their unskilled punches and kicks easily dispatched by years of hand-to-hand training from the British Secret Service on how to dispatch people. Upon searching the corpses and dispatching their clothes, he finds that Doctor Death must have taken the biological weapons schematics with him. The door to the subterranean compound begins to pound – more guards are attempting to break down the barricade – Doug doesn't have time to dispatch them too and speaks into his watch.

"Colonel, this is The Crow. I was set up – he knew I was coming. I've got heavies hurling handbags left and right and I need evacuation. Tell the chopper to come down on my signal."

"I don't care if your wife is doing her Tuesday night Tesco's run. I've changed my mind, all right?" I say into my mobile phone to my driver. "Not that it's got anything to do with you, but I just decided this particular premiere was too low-key for my public persona. So, yes, I do need picking up now."

"Sorry, boss," the rude little man laughs down the phone. "You booked me to pick you up at four in the morning, not ten minutes after I've dropped you off!"

"You come down on my signal this instant!" I shout.

"You what, where are you then?" he asks.

"Three degrees north of Skull Citadel," I mutter, not wanting enemy agents to hear.

"Eh?" he blathers.

"I mean – the alley next to the *Odeon*," I snap. "You know, round the back. And stop laughing – I can hear you!"

"Look, boss," he scoffs. "I've got another job to go to and the best I can do is come down – on your signal – at nine-thirty."

I hang up. What am I supposed to do for two hours until then? Stride into *Chinawhite's* nightclub with a pork ball hanging out of my top pocket?

I end up getting home just after ten. The film will be finishing about now and everyone will be going on to some swanky club with the paparazzi hot on their heels. And to think I had to get the tube home! I'll bet Keanu Reeves didn't have to spend his evening getting pestered by drunks on the London Underground asking him, "Do you work at the *Golden Dragon* takeaway?"

I unlock the front door to my Hillingdon flat quietly. I told Mum not to wait up as she worries about me. I once caught her reading one of my copies of *Star* magazine and immediately wanted to know whether I was indulging in drugs and wild orgies. I told her I'd never get mixed up with the Primrose Hill mob and that seemed to pacify her. Besides, I wasn't in the mood for a lecture, not after she'd gone and bent the spine of three issues.

I go into my bedroom and look up at the poster of my Donna on the ceiling – she smiles down at me with her breasts cupped lovingly together. She also gazes longingly at me from the two laminated posters I bought from *Poundland* – the ones that take pride of place on my wardrobe. My bedroom light isn't on and I can't make out the other photos, cuttings and clippings all over my walls. I hope she's not too disappointed I didn't make it. It's so lonely at the top.

I should try and sleep as I have to get to the depot and load my van by seven. In a few short hours I'll have left the glitterati behind and I'll be back to driving around outer London delivering people's stuff from *Amazon*. And I'll bet half of them don't even have the courtesy to wait in for me.

Yet I decide not to sleep just yet as I have to sort out that fiasco at the *Odeon*. I turn my computer on to be greeted by the image of Donna on my desktop: she's modelling a line of white *New Look* lingerie. I think it's amazing how *Rimmel*, or one of the other big make-up companies, hasn't used her in one of their promotions yet. I call it snobbery because Donna found fame on the reality TV show *Voyeur* rather than the catwalk.

I posted my feelings regarding that travesty on my website. It's head and shoulders over the other Donna Trayhorn fan site, and whoever started up her *Yahoo* group has long since lost interest. I only wish I knew which timewaster bought the rights to donnaT.com as he's only put up a holding page. If he's not going to use it, what's the point of hanging on to it? I did briefly speak to him once via *MSN Instant Messenger*, but the conversation didn't last long – it was along the lines of:

Steely_Doug9: hi m8, I run the official donna trayhorn site. its much better than urs. u want 2 sell it 2 me?

Majorjon101: ok. i cant b bothered 2 keep it. not since she got evicted 3rd from voyeur

Steely_Doug9: ill give u £10 via paypal 4 it.

Majorjon101: it cost me £200 just 2 register it! >:o(

Steely_Doug9: i wont go higher than £15.

Majorjon101 has left the conversation.

Since then, he seems to have blocked me and won't reply to my emails. But of course since *Metropol Industries* picked up Donna's contract, they bought the rights to donnatrayhorn.com. I'm glad they're behind her now, as she needs professional backing. I check it every day for updates, but it too is only a holding page with a box where you can subscribe to her official mailing list. I entered my email address weeks ago, but didn't

23

get anything back. At first I thought it was a glitch, so I entered my other sixteen addresses, but still nothing. However, I'm not disheartened as I know whatever she has planned will be fantastic and she'll make sure I'm the first to hear about it.

I check my *Hotmail* account, but there's still nothing from Donna. I know she's busy, but at least a brief "hello, how are you?" would be nice. But then, I've waited thirty-one years for something nice to happen, I suppose a little longer won't make much difference. Please don't tell me the trash can has automatically deleted the email I need. No, here it is:

Congratulations, you are the winning bidder on: two tickets to The Last Day on Earth Premiere.

I knew it, there's no mention in the eBay listing about changing tickets at the last minute, nor them being non-refundable. Seller "*crazy_hippie_dude10*" is going to be finding one pretty nasty email waiting for him when he logs on.

If he doesn't refund my money by Friday and offer me some form of compensation for my emotional and financial suffering, he can expect to find one hell of a negative rating gracing his eBay account come Saturday.

I send him my list of demands and go to bed, but I still can't sleep as I'm too angry – that and the drugs coursing through my system. I knew I shouldn't have taken so many pills in the back of the limo. I took an entire strip of *Pro-Plus* tablets as I thought I'd need them to give me the energy to stay up past ten-thirty. I should probably go back online and look up the plot to *The Last Day on Earth* on ruinedendings.com, just in case anyone at work asks me what it was like. Not that I can normally be bothered to talk to them. In fact, I have a good mind not to return those pens to the stationery cupboard tomorrow. Let's see how they like that.

Chapter 2: Deep Undercover

I'm up early, but I'm not in a good mood. I was sure I'd have dreamt about Donna last night, but instead I had some twisted dream about being fried in a giant wok for so long, I lost all the hair on my head.

Why movie bosses insist on holding premieres on a Tuesday night is beyond me – don't they know some of us have work in the morning?

Mum's not up when I leave, and I'm at the depot early to load the parcels into my van. What a writer has to put up with to get to grips with his character. Sometimes I wish that my arch enemy, Doctor Death, ran a nicer empire which I could infiltrate. Sadly, supervillains rarely consider the working conditions of their henchmen and hired goons. So, until such day as I can bring down his evil regime, I'm forced to pass myself off as mild-mannered delivery driver, Douglas Frederick Morrell.

Once my first bestseller hits the shops and I'm recognised in the literary community, I can tell work where to go. But in the meantime I console myself with the knowledge that when I get home the Internet will be teeming with gossip and pictures of Donna. Once I've found them, I'll upload them to my site and see if I can knock out a few chapters of the book.

Maybe today I'll come up with a name for it, but how do you sum up your life's work in a few words? If I was being honest to my readers, the title would be a chapter in itself. I'm even starting to contemplate sending the opening chapter to an agent, as that's the first step to having a little bit of Doug in every lounge throughout the world.

Of course I have to be careful though. I read on the Internet about how a bloke from Luton wrote the screenplay for *Star Wars*, then made the mistake of sending it to an American agent who just so happened to have George Lucas on his books. I think that serves as a lesson to us all.

As I walk into the loading bays I see one of the dolly birds who works in the offices upstairs tottering down the steps in a short skirt and heels. Her name's Anna and she's neurotic.

"Hi there, sweet thing," I say seductively from across the bay.

But she's still acting like a spoilt child and completely blanks me. I watch her walk up to another driver called Matt Tyler who does the same shifts as me. And to think I once thought she was attractive with her black roots showing through her peroxide-blonde hair. Of course that was before she reported me to the management for supposedly harassing her. Typical woman: gives me the eye for months then when I show an interest, she blows cold on me. Like I say, totally neurotic. But how else would you expect a Supervillain's moll to act?

I suppose I should be grateful my arch nemesis Doctor Death isn't around. He uses the alter ego "Henry Jeffries" when he walks among us. He fools the proles I work alongside by pretending to be a humble office manager. However, this insignificant import/export business merely acts as a cover for his quest for world domination. If he thinks he can beat me by sitting behind a desk and clicking a mouse then he's gravely mistaken. And on top of that he has incredibly hairy ears. Why he can't run an electric razor over them like everyone else is beyond me.

I watch as Anna giggles and laughs with Matt, before he pats her saggy behind and she wobbles back upstairs. I notice she doesn't call his blatant groping "harassment". Unfortunately, after Matt's stopped sexually assaulting her, he comes over.

"Hey, Doug, how's it going?" he says while I try not to stare at his abnormally small head.

"Fine," I yawn as I hurl the last of my parcels into the van.

26

"I'm surprised to see you in today," he says, laughing. "I thought you'd be hung over after your big night out! So, when's the next premiere, and can I come?"

Damn it, why did I even show him my pass – except to see his look of jealousy when he realised I was going to be hanging out with celebrities.

"They'd never let you in," I point out.

"You're probably right," he replies as he hides his disappointment, before faking interest and adding: "Come on then, how was it, mingling with the great and the good?"

"It was okay," I say casually. "I might go to another one, I might not. It was all a bit shallow for my liking."

"Yeah, I'll bet," he says, nodding, clearly seething with envy. "So, spill the beans. Did you see anyone famous?"

"See anyone? He can't even see over the bar!" yells a coarse voice from across the loading bay. We both look round to see another of Death's henchmen, Frank, and his idiotic mates grinning at us. He deliberately meant me to hear that, but I choose to ignore his pathetic attempt at humour.

"Oh, you know," I say with a sigh, "the odd familiar face here and there. I was chatting to Johnny Depp about…"

"Johnny Depp? No way!" Matt rudely interrupts me.

"Huh? Oh, yeah, we were chatting about our current projects.

He was asking me if he could star in a little something I've been working on…"

"No way!" he shouts again, not only reaffirming his lack of vocabulary, but interrupting me for a second time. "I'll bet you and your other half had a great time?"

He's so jealous it's amazing. How many celebrity parties has he been to? He spends all his time in *Royals'* nightclub in Uxbridge. It's incredible how some people can waste their lives boozing and taking drugs in dives like that – the last time I heard it was filled with underage drinkers. He's twenty-six now; when I was his age I was midway through a screenplay about Nazis from the future breeding dinosaurs to enslave mankind.

"Doug?" he says. "Did you take what's-her-name – that girl you're seeing?"

As if I'd take Hannah to a showbiz bash in the West End – she's only a primary school teacher. Could he really see her exchanging witty banter with Quentin Tarantino? I can just picture it: Quentin talking about how he's persuaded Laurence Fishburn and John Travolta to reunite for the sequel to *Pulp Fiction*, and her coming out with something about little Billy doing his first finger painting with his feet.

"I didn't take her," I point out, which shuts him up good and proper.

"Oh, I see," begins Matt, "you two haven't…"

He deliberately doesn't finish his own question, implying we might have split up. I remind him that she isn't the only woman in my life and that I went with someone else.

"Your mum?" shouts Frank from across the room.

"Come on, Frank," says Matt quietly. "That's not nice."

Yes, ha-bloody-ha, good one Frank, you're just so amazingly funny, aren't you? What a pity the tattoo of a dragon on your arm looks more like a seal cub.

Donna has had more than her fair share of supposed ex boyfriends inventing lies about her for the benefit of the press. But I value our relationship too much to sink to sordid kiss-and-tell stories, and I would never openly discuss our love. But seeing as Matt needs cutting down to size, I feel that Donna wouldn't mind if I name-dropped a little.

"Actually, I went with Donna Trayhorn," I say, smugly.

"Who?"

It doesn't surprise me that he hasn't heard of her as he's not exactly one for having his finger on the pulse.

"Do I take it you haven't actually heard of the biggest reality TV show ever: *Voyeur*?" I say in a deliberately patronising tone.

"Er – yeah," he says with a daft look on his tiny face. "Why?"

Using simple words, I summarise Donna Trayhorn's cultural input on society.

"Oh, her!" he exclaims. "Yeah, she's quite fit. Is she the one you've got all those pictures of in your van?"

"I keep some tasteful keepsakes of our relationship with me during the day," I say casually, "for sentimental reasons."

"There's more soft porn in his van than on *Channel 5*!" Frank cackles to one of the other brainwashed clones Death breeds in hell's test tubes.

"Don't worry about him," Matt says in a simpering tone. "He's harmless."

"I'm not worried about him," I say, indignantly. "After all, which one of us has Donna?"

"Okay," says Matt slowly, obviously lost for words. "Yeah, she's a nice looking girl. I remember her now. Didn't she get evicted third from the *Voyeur* house?"

"That's doesn't matter," I snap. I can never understand why people are so obsessed with when she was evicted from the show. "I spent my evening with her, all right?"

"No way!" he says for the umpteenth time. I would elaborate, but I fear I've already said too much, so I quickly change the subject.

"And what did you do last night?" I ask. No doubt he spent another night staggering round some seedy club.

"Oh, nothing much. Me and a few mates went to see Radiohead, at the *Hammersmith Apollo* and…"

It's at this point I say goodbye as some people only want to talk about themselves.

*Doug Holster had successfully infiltrated Doctor Death's
parcel delivery firm. Little did this army in overalls know a
lethal weapon in human form was walking among them.*

*Holster used his mind powers to tap the pin-headed
henchman for information and in a matter of seconds he
willingly handed over the confidential documents our hero had
demanded. Now deep within the enemy's bosom, his glistening
manly eyes scanned through the reports in the hope of finding
something he could pin on Death.*

*"Curse the evil fiend," he said to himself through his
gritted pearly-white teeth. There was nothing that could link the
mad doctor to that terrorist attack on Amersham Old Town. A
million questions raced through his head: was this another set-
up? Did Death know he was coming? How did Matt's head get
that small?*

And why aren't there any bloody pictures of Donna in
today's magazines? I'm parked outside the newsagents reading
the papers and all I can find is yet more on the Primrose Hill
mob. It's not until I open up the *Daily Star* that I see a picture of
my Donna. She's dressed in a classy black micro skirt and
matching boob tube, while giving her trademark flash to the
camera. I'll cut this one out for the scrapbook when I get home.
At least she got some exposure thanks to *Metropol Industries*.
They produce *Voyeur* and dozens of other classy reality TV
shows. In fact I could see myself ending up working in their
London towers one day. Perhaps I'd be in my own penthouse
office where I continue to write a string of international
bestsellers. After I've bagged a couple of Pulitzer prizes and run
that hack John Grisham off the road, perhaps Donna can retire
and come and work for me. She could look after our three
children: young Hillingdon, Ickenham and baby Luton Morrell –

as I hear it's fashionable to name kids after where they were conceived. Then I could just sit back at my computer and write the next instalment of my futuristic spy thriller while she brings me cups of hot chocolate and muffins. Anyway, what does it say about her in the *Daily Star*?

And proving that you can still flog dead horses, media mogul Peter Carter dragged another ex-reality TV starlet from the celebrity scrapheap to accompany him to the premiere of The Last Day on Earth. Judging by the shameless grab for publicity it looks like Donna Trayhorn, 21, still hasn't given up on her singing career.

This is what's wrong with modern journalism: they're desperate to pigeonhole people. Haven't they ever heard of multitasking? It is possible for people to be able to do more than one thing. So what if Donna was a contestant on *Voyeur* – does that mean she's going to be one forever? She was only inside the house for three weeks – the public clearly saw she was meant for better things and voted her out.

As for not giving up on a singing career, her first single reached number thirty-nine. Don't the press know that if you go into Woolworths, the music chart starts at a hundred and goes all the way to number one? In any healthy society a top forty single would be applauded, but it seems there are only two chart positions in today's music industry: number one and failure.

I calm myself before my nose starts to bleed and decide to never buy the stupid *Daily Star* again. Not unless they print some sort of formal apology – or perhaps another picture. I begin to compose an email to the newspaper when I receive an alert from Skull Island.

31

"Greetings, Holster," sneered Doctor Death into Doug's in-car communicator.

"Great Days of Thunder!" gasped Holster heroically when he found his arch nemesis was on to him. Doug's lightning-quick mind raced faster than a pervert searching Google for porn when he realised Death had intercepted the signal he was transmitting back to base. If Death knew the importance of this and somehow network-jacked this frequency, he could discover the true identity of every British Secret Agent in Middlesex!

Holster had to stall for time before he could implement the jamming equipment.

"Doctor Death, I presume?" the steely agent said casually, as he sipped a chilled glass of Lucozade Energy Tonic while cruising down one of London's most fashionable parades.

"I hope you enjoyed the little reception I put on for you last night?" cackled the mad Office Manager.

"I hope their widows aren't too upset?" The agent chuckled, wittily enraging his adversary.

"You haven't been to number thirty-two Cliffton Gardens yet, have you?" the office-bound psychopath continued as he tried to bait the fearless stallion into a trap. *"I have a little surprise awaiting you there!"*

Doug's ultra-cool exterior had tricked this insane fiend into revealing where his deadliest of sleeper cells were residing. Knowing Cliffton Gardens is across town, Britain's finest used his onboard mapping system to pick up Death's multiple roadblocks standing in his way (along with speed cameras and bus lanes).

"My life is one big surprise, you evil fiend," Doug hissed as he performed a three-hundred-and-sixty degree turn in a disabled parking bay.

"What was that?" Henry says over the speaker phone.

"Oh, nothing," I reply. "I'm just going through a tunnel, so the signal will be cutti…"

I initiate the jamming software I designed myself and hit the "Call End" button on my mobile. I don't have time to exchange witty banter with mass murderers who spend all day designing forms for their army to fill in.

"Curses," I say out loud as I forget to keep the jamming software online and Doctor Death calls straight back.

"Damn tunnels, eh?" he says with an insane cackle, as he tries to bewitch me with his hypnotic tone.

"Yeah, and I got stuck behind an OAP on the way – I don't see why we need traffic-calming measures while there are still old people on the road," I mutter.

"Yes, people should be culled at fifty-five, that's what I say," Henry admits, showing his true colours.

"Anyway, you don't know what the traffic's like this time in the morning," I sneer – let's see him argue with that. His silence tells me I've won.

"Your van was one of those that had satellite navigation fitted, wasn't it?" he replies.

My god, they've bugged me. His spies could be following me every step of the way. He knows damn well my van has satellite navigation.

"Yeah, but it only tells you the fastest route, it doesn't make allowances for traffic," I point out. I outwit criminals before brunch.

"Press the second red button down on the right, Doug," he says.

What second red button down on the right? I look at the digital readout thing sticking up on my dashboard. It's not like I asked for it to be fitted in the first place. I'm a free spirit – a maverick – I do things my way and to hell with the consequences. I'm not one of his drones who needs some know-

33

it-all computer telling them where to go. If the computer is so clever, let's see it deliver a parcel all by itself. I see his red button, but he must think I'm stupid if he assumes I'm going to press it. I can tell it's linked to an explosive device somewhere on my vehicle.

"Doug?" he goes on. "Are you still there?"

No, I've jumped out of the cab while it's still moving. Of course I'm still here; where does he think I am? I activate my fireproof thermals and press his beloved second red button down on the right. I hold my breath as the flames engulf me and the on-screen map changes to show there's not a traffic jam for miles.

"It was explained at our last team talk," he rambles on. "Would you like a refresher cour…"

"Oh, no," I cut him off with, "not another tunn…"

This time I press the off switch and jam him for good, also saving countless innocent lives in the process. I lock and load my weapon and head for his Cliffton Gardens hideaway. It's a warehouse built on an abandoned American Indian burial site near Acton, but more importantly it's not too far away from Donna's mum's house. Her parents are divorced and like me she doesn't see her dad – we have so much in common.

I'm parked down the street from Donna's mum's house. She lived there right up until after she went on *Voyeur*. Once her singing career took off, her management thought it better to move her into a flat in the West End. I don't blame them – there are a lot of dodgy people about these days and this house is a bit too on view for my liking. The only problem is that it's so difficult to park outside. You'd think traffic wardens would have better things to do than victimise me. Even though I'm in a big green and yellow delivery van with the company name plastered down the sides, they still try and harass me. I have to put up with a lot to sit in the same street a living legend grew up in.

Her mum's a wonderful woman and so youthful-looking for thirty-six. You'd never catch Gloria Trayhorn out of the house without make-up. I reckon she must bleach her hair at least once a week to stop the roots from showing through, not like that bimbo back at the depot. The last time I saw Gloria going to the shops, she looked good enough to be a model in a *New Look* window – miniskirt, heels, sovereign rings and ankle bracelet – the works.

The front door opens and a man leaves, but Gloria shuts it quickly. I wonder if he was one of those God-awful journalists. Won't they ever leave this poor family alone? I decide to take his picture with one of my digital cameras.

The hunky Holster's manly black Ferrari remains invisible outside the Indian burial ground thanks to its onboard cloaking device. There he uses sophisticated surveillance equipment to capture the image of the weedy mystery man and wire it back to base camp in a matter of seconds. Soon the backroom boffins have uploaded the photograph to their central databanks and confirmed his identity as one of Doctor Death's hoodlums.

"Dammit," snarls the gallant Holster as he thumps his strapping fist down on the dashboard.

Death's man has obviously been pumping Gloria vigorously for information and there's nothing more he can do for her. All the masculine hairs stand up on the back of his muscular neck and he suddenly gets a bad feeling about this place. Then an enemy agent appears out of nowhere and pounces on Doug's car. Could Death have developed a cloaking device of his own?

"Excuse me, but I'm delivering a parcel here!" I say to the traffic warden.

"Yeah, yeah, yeah," the hobgoblin says smirking, as he slaps the ticket on my windscreen.

"Well, what do you call this then?" I say as I point a masculine finger at the firm's logo on the side of my van. "I'm a delivery driver for God's sake!"

Or at least you think I am – you minion.

"I could have ticketed you the last two times I walked past," he shouts back. "Now get out of here before I call the clampers."

I console myself with one last picture of the ceiling fan in the upper bedroom. I've looked at that fan a lot in my time. After all, that very room could have once belonged to Donna.

I arrive back at the depot at half past two, happy with the day's intelligence gathering. I unload all the undelivered boxes, throwing in a hand grenade for good measure, and sling them on the conveyor belt which takes them back into the sorting bay for some other mug to deal with.

"You all done for the day, Doug?" an annoyingly familiar voice says from behind me. I spin round to be confronted by none other than Doctor Death himself. I cover him with slugs from my weapon, but my load goes right through him. The maniac cackles insanely and I realise this is only a hologram of the biggest threat to North West London the world has ever known.

"Yeah, that's it for now, but I'll be back. We have unfinished business to discuss – you and I," I answer. "I got tagged by one of your men."

"Sorry?" he asks as his image flickers slightly.

"What? Oh, nothing, I got a ticket," I say.

"Not again," he sighs when he realises he has to employ yet another henchman to deal with the paperwork my heroics have caused him. Wait till he finds out where I've placed that hobgoblin's head!

"I was only outside the place for two minutes – honestly," I protest. "You don't know what it's like out there. You don't know the truth! You can't handle the truth!"

"Okay, right. Tell you what, just drop it off upstairs before Friday and one of the girls will take care of it," he says while smiling and revealing his yellow pointed teeth, "but you did get them all delivered, didn't you?"

"Yeah, all done," I say, making sure I hold the van's back doors open so he can see there isn't a single parcel left. "The Dougster doesn't go back for sloppy seconds."

"Yeah, nice metaphor," he says, slowly, trying to baffle me with science. "I'm taking my most trusted assassins to the Rat and Parrot around five; you can join us – if you dare!"

So, this is how he infects minions with his nefarious brainwashing techniques. The only time his type and mine will ever meet is on the battlefield when the final outcome between good and evil will be decided.

"We'll be there!" shouts some meaningless drone from across the loading bay.

"Great, see you later," he replies as he rubs his hands together at the thought of stealing another soul. "Join us, Doug! One of us! One of us! You haven't been down the pub with us in ages."

And you have hairy ears, but I don't keep on about them. I hate you, your ears, your rotten little pub and the way you keep trying to take over the world. I'm never setting foot in that seedy dive alongside the scum of the universe. Besides, they all sit on ridiculously high barstools at even higher tables and my feet don't reach the floor.

"I think not," I say to the hologram, while trying not to stare at the two furry caterpillars it has balancing on each ear. "Duty to Queen and country calls."

"Okay, no problem," he says with a shrug as he realises my will is not to be broken. "We'll be in there till about seven if you change your mind."

I won't.

"And we're going to the quiz again next Tuesday if you're interested?"

I'm not. While working deep undercover I once infiltrated that high-profile casino among a gaggle of his pawns. The mass brainwashing rally was held at the Dog and Duck and Death's High Priest – also known as "The Quizmaster" – threw the most ridiculous questions at us all night. Fortunately I was operating at a higher level and, using reverse psychology, decided not to answer a single one. I knew it was all a ploy to find out who was the most intelligent among us and bump us off first. I left blanks for every answer in the news, history and geography rounds. I might have answered a few if they'd bothered to put in a reality TV section, but Death never was one to be realistic.

Besides, the constant attention I was receiving from his harem of floosies kept putting me off. They seemed more interested in making eyes at me than trying to guess the connection in the link round. I finally told them that as they were so completely out of their depth on matters of knowledge, they might as well go home.

But as luck would have it, I made my escape before I succumbed to their charms. I went home early when some drunken bimbo on Matt's arm knocked her wine all over my face. By the time I came back in a clean shirt, they'd all left.

But of course the Dougster had the last laugh as I took all the pens home that they were using to write the answers in with. No wonder they lost.

"I'm on recon in the badlands next Tuesday," I tell the demon in office manager form.

"Okay," he says. "Just sign here for today's run, will you?"

A droid wheels in and hands me one of Death's precious clipboards and pens and I watch his hologramatic form start rooting around in the back of my van. I keep sniffing in an attempt to prevent a nosebleed from coming on.

"Are you all right, Doug?" he says with a cackle, as he leans back out of my van.

"I'm tougher than a thousand tantric trolls."

"Yeah, but…" he trails off with as he touches his nose. "Oh, never mind. That's quite a collection of posters you've got in your van, isn't it?"

Curses, he's found out about my love for Ms Trayhorn. If he lays a tentacle on her I'll…

"I'll see you at the pub, Henry!" a voice shouts from across the room which I recognise instantly as Frank's, "after you've finished looking at DM's soft porn collection!"

"DM?" I protest.

"Yeah, will do," replies Henry before turning to me and raising an eyebrow in parallel with his furry ears, "Your initials, surely?"

"What, oh, yes," I mumble as an image of being back at school clears from my mind. I haven't been called Danger Mouse since then.

"See you later then, Henry," Frank drones on. "Bye, Penfold."

"What was that?" I snap.

"Oh, nothing, don't worry about it, Doug," Henry says, laughing, even though nothing was funny. "This Donna is a nice looking lass, but remember, the van is technically company property, and some customers may take offence at your – tastes."

Doug Holster has been captured. Early intelligence that the base had been long since abandoned has proved woefully

39

*inaccurate. It is in fact teeming with enemy agents. Doctor
Death thinks he has the defiant Doug right where he wants him
and now intends to use his treacherous tentacles of terror to
extract tricky titbits from our hero.*

*"So, Mr Holster, we have you at last," he sneers. "And
soon, we will have the delectable Ms Trayhorn here too begging
for mercy over a pit of my most hungry mutant squids."*

*"You'll never get me to stop loving her," Holsters says
defiantly.*

*"You say that now," he cackles. "But we'll see how
beautiful you still think she is when we've put black Sellotape
over all her rude bits!"*

His insane laughter echoes throughout the volcano.

The thought of Henry drooling over my Donna almost
makes me physically sick and I have to resort to sniffing again to
stop the blood from flowing. I stuff his clipboard back into the
droid's claw and slam shut the rear doors of my van.

"Anything else?" I say in such a stern voice that even his
cowardly hologram backs off.

"Only that you've signed your name D Holster," he replies
fearfully as he evidently sees by the look in my eye that I'm not
to be messed with. "But that'll do."

It'll be the last words he ever reads.

"Er, Doug?" he says as I spin round and blast the robot to
pieces with the secret weapon I keep hidden beneath my belt.

"Next?" I say as I'm obliged to turn back and look at him.

"Have you got my pen?" he asks, while scratching one of
his hairy ears.

"No," I say with an innocent shrug. "I gave it back to you."

And I don't much care for his tone, let alone the accusation.

40

"Did you?" he says as his fleecy ears bristle. "Yeah, you probably did – blimey, I'd lose my own plutonium if I didn't sleep on it!"

Then his image flickers and disappears and I wonder what evil deeds he's plotting from the depths of hell. Little does he know I can track him from his Biro that I now remove from my sleeve and place safely in my inside pocket.

The lab will be able to take a sample of his DNA from this. He'll never be able to go ahead with his diabolical cloning programme while I still have breath left in my body.

Chapter 3: The Burden of Talent

It's just gone three in the afternoon when the side of Hillingdon mountain slides open and I park my Ferrari in the garages next to my block of flats.

"There's a message waiting on your answer phone from one of your many gorgeous ladies," my secretary purrs as I hang my Parcel Plus jacket on the hook in the toilet. "She wants you to call her back."

"Oh, so you didn't delete this one then?" I smirk, knowing that she's secretly madly in love with me. I know the poor girl can't help the way she feels, but I wish she could try and at least pass on a couple of messages from my admirers.

I could marry her. I probably should. She's young, attractive, smart – everything a man could wish for – but she's not Donna. So I put my dinner in the microwave and go straight to my room. I'm sure the only reason publishers haven't been kicking my door down to get my book is because she hasn't passed on their messages for fear of losing me. Maybe I should sue her?

I shut my bedroom door and seal it by wedging a chair against the handle.

"Mum, I'm home!" I shout, but she never hears. I swear if she gets any more senile then I'll put her in a home once and for all. "Why isn't my dinner ready?"

I see if there are any new assignments from The Colonel in my inbox. Perhaps the lab has come back with a few leads on Doctor Death?

"Fifty per cent off Viagra," reads the first email, then two more offers for a loan with no interest for the first six months and the inevitable "get your penis enlarged" proposition that I now delete without even reading. Those products are a complete waste of money and customer aftercare is non-existent. I can't see the compensation email from *crazy_hippie_dude10*. I don't know why I use the Internet sometimes – all it is, is a breeding ground for weirdos and perverts.

I'm always careful about opening emails as they could be from enemy agents trying to steal my ideas, or worse still, trying to find out where my penthouse is. I heard that if you keep a piece of junk mail on your screen for more than four seconds, the government can find out which websites you've viewed. They also hack into your computer and steal your files. Luckily I'm smarter than them and never save any of my work to disk. I only keep it on the screen while I'm typing, then copy it onto a notepad in Biro.

Sadly, I don't get a chance to check on Donna yet as the phone goes and my secretary is in tears because it's one of my women.

"Doug, did you call my number again?" asks Hannah – the primary school teacher who actually thinks we have a future together. She doesn't even bother to ask how my day went before selfishly steering the conversation back to her. "Do you know what kind of day I've had?"

This is the second time in a week she's rung. Does she have to fill in pointless forms all day? All she has to do is make sure she has the same amount of kids in the afternoon as she did in the morning and read them a story about kittens.

"Well, I'm quite busy too actually," I say when I can get a word in.

I have to run some searches on Google for Donna's name.

Doug Holster regrets being so generous with his contact number. The Colonel has already run his balls through the bacon slicer for mixing business with pleasure, but what was he supposed to do if women insisted on falling at his feet?

43

Holster generously listens to her desperate plea for attention. It's the decision every spy dreads – boost a sad and lonely woman's confidence by spending the evening with her, or save the world. A lesser man would have only chosen one, but Doug is too generous to be a lesser man.

"I'm going down the Rat and Parrot," I say before getting rid of her. I suppose artists must suffer for their talent and it's times like this that I wonder whether J R R Tolkien had all these interruptions when he was writing *Lord of the Rings*? If he had to put up with the distractions I have to, those Hobbits would never have left the Shire.

I watch a few taped episodes of Donna on last year's *Voyeur* and ignore any more phone calls as they're bound to be from Hannah begging to see me. She's so obsessed, it's sad. I know we've been together for nearly two years now, but it's not like we're getting married or anything.

I get back to my computer to find that sadly, my true love still hasn't emailed me back. I notice I've got a new member to my forum and I make a point of emailing every newbie to welcome them to the leading Donna Trayhorn fan site. I introduce myself as the webmaster and leading media commentator for all *Voyeur*-related issues, plus tell them of all the things I can ban them for.

I check her official site, but there's still nothing new. She's obviously far too focused on her career to update her online journal, or even create one.

After I upload my new photos, I dash off a quick email to her about how excessively heavy handed the security staff were at the premiere last night. I'm sure she'll use her influence to see that those apes get what's coming.

I wake the next morning annoyed that I didn't dream about her for the third night in a row. Instead, I had some bizarre dream about my Auntie Eileen chasing me down the street repeatedly asking if I'd like some sweets. I kept telling her the ones I wanted, but she didn't listen and could only ask me the same question again and again. I suppose the most annoying thing is that I don't actually have an "Auntie Eileen" and why did she keep calling me "Willy"?

I cast the vision of her warty face aside as my mind is impervious to Doctor Death's subliminal mind-manipulation techniques – as proved at the last team bonding weekend. Some of us are simply free-spirited rebels who cannot be tamed by authority. I didn't even apologise when I let a co-worker fall flat on the floor instead of catching her during that game of trust. I wasn't about to put my back out.

I arrive at Death's Delivery Depot late – my head filled with images of mad aunties – and pay for my lapse in concentration. I find myself surrounded by a thousand enemy henchmen brandishing Ninja warrior swords, bazookas and the latest issue of *GQ* magazine.

"Doug, you're famous!" shouts Frank, exposing his yellow teeth with an ugly grin.

Doug Holster dramatically draws his own deadly shining Samurai sword and holds his mighty weapon aloft. One by one he dispatches Death's dastardly deformed dullards in a suitably grisly fashion.

He stands over their severed bodies and picks up what's left of the magazine filled with secret orders from their lifeless corpses.

"It was all just a gross misunderstanding," I point out, stunning them into silence.

This is what's known as "lazy journalism" – where readers send stuff in and the magazine publishes it. Some clever dick

45

obviously thought it would be funny to send in a camera-phone picture from the other night showing me being dragged out of the cinema by security.

"I like the caption," says a driver who looks like Ann Widdecombe, but with more stubble.

"Yeah: *Know This Loser*?" Frank says taking great delight in reading it out for all to hear.

I don't give them the chance to pursue the matter any further as I initiate my cloaking device and disappear in a ripple of energy.

"You okay, Doug?" Matt says the moment I turn my cloaking device off. He taps on the window of my cab and I unlock the driver's side door and get out. "Why have you locked yourself in your van before you've loaded up?"

He must have arrived even later than normal and hasn't seen the slanderous propaganda. I choose not to tell him, but instead spin a completely believable lie.

"There was a snake among my parcels. It must have come in from abroad," I say.

"A snake – Jesus – I can't help you with that one. If it was another spider I could have squashed it for you," he says as the deluded fool checks the packages still waiting for me to load up. "It's all right; I think it's gone now."

By eleven I'm parked outside the newsagents scanning today's publications for news of Donna. I was duped into buying *FHM* magazine with the promise of "new pictures of reality TV stars". However, it only has interviews with the so-called "winner" of *Voyeur*.

I go straight round to Donna's mum's place, and stay there for most of the morning until Gloria returns holding grocery bags.

Intrepid superspy, Doug Holster, was taking time out from thwarting the forces of darkness in yet another blistering conflict to meet his vivacious female contact. The golden sun glinted off her gold tooth as she lit up a Benson and Hedges cigar while striding elegantly down the road in her knee-high boots. His steely eyes met with her steely thighs and he held her tightly in his masculine gaze and exposed his perfect teeth with a smile that would moisten the coldest of female hearts. Yet something was wrong. His contact let her shopping fall from her sovereign ring-clad hands as she spotted him. Her luscious pink lips opened wide as she pointed her finger in his direction.

An inhuman screech consumed the terraced houses, shattering parking meters. Only Doug's toned physique saved him from the sonic boom erupting from her snarling face as he dived back into his Ferrari.

His strong finger quickly flicked a switch igniting the turbo engines as he sped away. The electromagnetic shielding on his Ferrari prevented further laser fire from penetrating his vehicle. He listened to blast after blast thumping against his car's armour plated chassis and breathed a sigh of relief as it held out against the onslaught.

The situation was far worse than he had imagined. Could Death really have made a pact with those nefarious aliens, the Bodysnatchers? Could he really be selling out the whole of humanity to a race of intergalactic space zombies?

I return to the depot to find Doctor Death has resorted to a smear campaign in the press against our humble hero. The picture in *GQ* has been blown up to A3 size and plastered all over the loading bays in a callous attempt to unite enemy ranks against me.

My Samurai sword makes short work of every last one of them and I'm soon using the offending bits of tabloid lies to wipe the side of my Ferrari. A lesser man may even report them for bullying like I used to with the boys at school. But I decide to pick off Death's minions before going after the man himself. I slide the remaining copy under Henry's door with a yellow post-it note attached reading:

Please find enclosed the kind of lowbrow humour your drivers are displaying. Matt started it.

I expect the insane madman to feed these unruly subordinates to his pet sharks over this. Or at least sack them.

Later that evening I swap my inconspicuous Parcel Plus uniform for a set of casual slacks in which to infiltrate the Rat and Parrot. I find Hannah there already. She must have been waiting for me for hours. She's sitting in a booth talking to a cackling gaggle of female impersonators while I stand over by the bar and consider making conversation.

"...and when I'd turned round, Ellie had only gone and painted Maxwell's face purple!" she exclaims. I fear it may be too late for her as her mind may already have been overpowered by Death's Intelligence Draining device. I try to let my mind wander, but I cannot help but be sucked in to her mind-numbing chatter. "And when Ellie's dad came to pick her up in his Range Rover, he wasn't too happy about paint getting on the seats!"

She thinks she's had a bad day? She should try cleaning fruit stains off the side of her van before she returned to the depot. And I'll bet the editor of *GQ* doesn't even have the guts to answer my email. Earlier I pointed out to him how "losers" don't attend film premieres and how many had he been to?

"...Ellie's dad's a lovely man, very well turned out," she dribbles on. If I wasn't driving, I think I'd have forced myself to get drunk by now. "As I was putting newspapers on his seats, he was saying how he works up in London and..."

"Does he wear a suit?" I shout over at them.

"Excuse me?" she asks as they all look over in my direction by the bar.

"He's not an agent, is he?" I say seriously and I swear one of the things next to her even has the audacity to ask who I am.

She doesn't answer and only rolls her eyes while her dippy friends giggle.

"God, he's in here again," the one with the leathery face says. Who's she calling "he"? She knows full well who I am.

"You should be careful about who you talk to," I'm forced to remind her, as people keep walking in the gangway that separates us. "Don't let them lull you into a false sense of security and then tell them about my book. That's how it happens."

"Yeah, that would be a shame!" laughs Leatherface. "Please, Doug, why don't you come over and tell us about your masterpiece?"

I ignore the whispers that follow and stay put while casually sipping my Archers and Lemonade – careless talk and all that. I lean on the bar and let them get on with their meaningless lives. I catch a few looks from her friends – they're obviously jealous of her, but at least they're attempting to hide it. Occasionally I train my highly sensitive ears back on their conversation.

"He reminded me a bit of my dad," Hannah drones on. "Well, from what I can remember of him."

Here we go again. And she doesn't understand why I don't join in. I wondered how long it would be before we have to hear about how her dad died nearly twenty years ago. You really would think she'd be over it by now. At least he has a genuine excuse as to why he doesn't contact her. She should try having a father who lives on the other side of the world!

"I hear you're a famous author," a stunning barmaid purrs seductively at me out of nowhere while she leans across the bar

49

in a low-cut top. "I hear you get invited to all sorts of A-list social events."

I should only ask her for another drink and leave it at that, but I look over at Hannah and see she's now talking to that idiot Matt and his cronies. Two of us can play that game. So I flirt outrageously with this fine specimen of womanhood who's now pulling a pint of John Smith's for someone else.

"Yeah, all the publishers want me," I say casually while she gives some loser his change. "In fact, most people want me."

She gives me the eye as she giggles nervously. Her delicate hand starts to quiver, letting the foamy head on the bitter spill over. It runs down on to her fingers and she begins to suck each one sensually, before whispering in a husky voice, "I think I'm beginning to see why."

"I have loads of agents interested in my work..." I start, but the poor girl's rushed off her feet and she darts down the other end of the bar to serve some drunken lush.

"Yeah, it's hard when everyone wants a piece of you," I say with a sigh as I make my way down the bar towards her so I don't have to shout.

"Yeah, I'll bet," she simpers. "Your girlfriend is so lucky to be going out with a man with such a huge talent."

I look back at my supposed girlfriend, Hannah, as she tries to hide her dull and dismal existence by laughing and joking with freaks. She doesn't have much in her life – she works all day chasing horrible kids and spends her evenings helping the Salvation Army before coming here. What kind of a life is that?

Seeing me is the highlight of her week. I suppose I don't mind giving her a reason to live. I think of Hannah as a kind of helpless child, lost in the world and in need of guidance.

"I don't exactly have one serious girlfriend," I say to the petite little thing as I run my fingers through my thick hair. "How about you, do you have a boyfriend?"

She blushes as I hold her in my steely gaze. Then she stammers nervously at my blatant come-on, but unfortunately her shift finishes and she has to go.

"Look, mate, do you want a drink, or not?" says the barman who takes over from her. He has ridiculously long hair. He's obviously a homosexual.

I don't like his tone. Little does he know he's speaking to a man whose name will one day be alongside Tolkien, Andy McNab, Brett Easter Ellis and the lucky cow who wrote about that little wizard. One day my name will be splashed across the world and the people at school who mocked me will remember it and wish they'd treated me better. Sometimes I almost want to send my work to a publisher so I can speed up the day when the name Doug Morrell becomes synonymous with success rather than laughter.

"All right, Doug. What are you doing over here all on your own? Do you want a drink?" Matt asks as he appears out of nowhere next to me. That's the problem with having an enemy with such a small head – you don't see him coming.

"Double Archers and lemonade," I say. "And I'll have one for later, if that's okay? Oh, and two packets of crisps – the expensive ones; the bags the cheap ones come in are half filled with air."

He owes me more than that for what I have to put up with from him every day. The reason I choose to stay at my job is because it provides me with an endless source of inspiration and subject matter for my book. To write about real life and make your characters believable, you have to live with them. Death's delivery firm is littered with the dregs of humanity – meaningless losers with no hope of reprieve. By working alongside such creatures, I can study them in their natural environment and use their character traits for my own purposes.

If I have seen further than most, it is because I have stood on the shoulders of idiots.

"No Donna with you?" he asks with a slight smile while I gather up my drinks in case he steals one.

"She wouldn't be seen dead in a place like this," I snap. "I think you could learn a lot from her."

But of course he doesn't answer and stares blankly at me with one tiny eyebrow raised.

"There are few people throughout history who can truly inspire and teach others the way she can," I go on.

"Yeah, poor old Jesus pales into insignificance compared to Donna, eh?" he says with a sigh as it slowly sinks in.

But I don't need a sermon to go with my Archers and Quavers. The only thing I admire about that publicity seeking hippie was the way he knew how to manipulate the media to his advantage. That man went around doing exactly what he liked and got away with it without so much as a bad word said against him. Mr Holier-than-thou-Christ overturns a load of tables in a reputable establishment and everyone worships him. Yet as soon as Liam Gallagher trashes a bar, he's labelled a thug.

"I think Donna is slightly different to him though, don't you?" I say condescendingly.

"If you say so," he replies and I'm glad we have that one sorted out. "Doug, if you don't mind me asking, why do you like her so much?"

Chapter 4: Stupid Question

"So, what is it that made you choose Donna? After all, you've had thousands of female admirers throwing themselves at your feet throughout your hugely successful career." the simpering female journalist from *Hello* magazine asks.

I don't answer immediately. Instead, I make myself comfy next to my beloved wife, Donna, on the drawing room's leopard skin sofa in our country mansion. I tenderly put one arm around her and we gaze into each other's eyes, clearly in love.

"That's quite a question," I eventually reply to the journalist, who has blatantly been giving me the eye throughout the interview.

I've lost count of the amount of times I've tried explaining about Donna. Only last week I was in the Post Office showing an old lady a printout of her online biography, but she still didn't understand. The trends of popular culture seem to be a bit much for the elderly. In the end she said she had a migraine and hurried home, leaving her pension book on the counter.

"But why do you like her so much?" the journalist asks again, fluttering her false eyelashes.

"As I said on the Biography Channel, I admire her as a woman," I reply honestly as my dear wife Donna giggles sweetly in my ear.

"Yes, she is a woman," the journalist says as she cocks her tiny head to one side and tosses her hair back over one shoulder. "It's such a change to see a celebrity couple so genuinely in love, but why choose Donna? After all, before you married her, you were linked with Britney Spears, Kate Moss, Davina McCall this list goes on!"

"The truth is that she actually chose me!" I reply as Donna and I share a private joke that goes way over the journalist's head. "I distinctly recall that it was on day two of *Voyeur* when I could tell that she was actually looking directly at me from within the studio house. I felt we connected on a deeper level and, before long, my heart leapt with every cheeky glance. At first I thought I was imagining it and, in the end, I had to ask her: why do you keep giving me those looks? Then, believe it or not, only two episodes later she started singing a cover of some band called Placebo's hit "Because I Want You Too". How do you explain that?"

"Delusion?" the journalist comes out with in an ugly voice that makes her sound like a man.

"Oh, give it a rest," says Matt as Frank joins us at the bar. "Go waste your money on the fruities again, will you?"

The look I give Frank makes him wither and melt away.

"I suppose you could call that destiny," continues the journalist, shrugging, but I can tell she doesn't believe me. The way she's been looking at me tells me she'd do anything to split us up and have me for herself. I smell a trap and consider my next answer carefully as she turns her attention on my innocent bride. "And, Donna, what is it you admire about your ravishing young husband, Doug? Is it his rippling body, or just the thick locks of hair on his head?"

"She admires me because of the similarities in our characters, experiences and how we behave socially," I add, on my wife's behalf as I sneer at the journalist. "But being able to relate to someone isn't necessarily a reason to like them. For example, I've had many friends over the years who I've hated."

"And how similar would you say you are to the fictional hero, Doug Holster, in your best-selling novels?" she blathers on.

"What do you mean, fictional?" I can't help but snap. Then I remember my security team is at lunch and I can't be bothered to eject her from my estate, so I let that one slide.

"And what do you think motivated you to such dizzying heights?" she rambles, seemingly not bothered I'm not answering all her trick questions.

I bite down hard and force myself not to say "revenge". I also suppress the desire to get a dig in at various pupils from my old school who used to make fun of me. How nice it would be to take out a full page spread in a national magazine with a picture of me and Donna under the headline "Who's laughing now?" Instead I spin her some completely believable line about wanting to entertain and educate the masses.

"Thank you, I think I have enough. I'll let the beautiful couple be now," the journalist twitters once she's finished taking notes. "I should be making a move – I have to write a piece on how Hollywood is moving one of its biggest studios to Hillingdon."

"Looks have nothing to do with it," I remind the shallow woman as I grab her thick arm and prevent her from leaving. This interview ends when the Dougster says so! "People should look beneath the toned legs, perfectly formed stomach, bronzed complexion and wonderful brown hair on my head and see the real us. Like me, Donna's kind, intelligent, thoughtful and stands up for what she believes in, even if people judge her for it."

"Right," is the only thing Matt mumbles and I realise he's drunker than I thought. "I should probably be getting back to the others now. Come over if you feel like it."

I nod and let him go. People don't want to know the truth. That's why I felt it was my duty to start up a website for Donna. It took a while for people to find the site, but as the months went by, like-minded individuals were drawn there. Now we have almost a hundred members, not including the ones I've had to ban for disrespectful behaviour.

"You see, I'm not like other men…" I tell the reporter from *Time* magazine. "Other men only take an interest in Donna's exceptional career because she's attractive. But this only proves how shallow the male population is. Personally, I prefer the term supporter over fan. If people are only fans of Donna because of her looks, then they're admitting they only like her exterior. These people can't possibly be fans of her personality. To be a supporter you have to admire what she does and how she does it. I support Donna because she stands up for what she believes in, the way Martin Luther King did for blacks."

"Look, mate, you've got two drinks in front of you," says the barman with the girlish hair. "Please stop waving me over if you don't want anything."

I wish I could ban imbeciles like him the way I ban people on my site. He's probably coming on to me. I don't know who I hate more: his kind who don't appreciate Donna, or men so driven by testosterone, they only saw an attractive girl on a reality TV show. I, on the other hand, observed a rose stuck in a house of thorns.

"But wasn't she only on the show a couple of weeks?" asks the reporter, proving her lack of knowledge surrounding popular culture.

"To some it might look like the other housemates won by evicting her after only three weeks, but really it was a release for her," I say. "She was only just beginning to open up when she got evicted. The angel was free from her cage and undamaged by the long weeks of suffering at the hands of the other revolting contestants."

I remember the night like it was yesterday: I'd blown Hannah out and taken a cab to the compound in London where the *Voyeur* house stands. I would have liked to have been among the official crowd, but the bouncers were in a particularly fascist mood and wouldn't let me in.

"I'm gagging for a shag!" I heard Donna shout into the microphone, while talking to the show's hosts Ray and Ford during her exit interview.

I admired her courage to say what she wanted rather than answering any of the questions they put to her.

"I love you, Donna!" I yelled at her limousine as it drove past me once the show was over.

Later that night I was waiting for her in her hotel room. I'll never forget how beautiful she looked as she came out of the bathroom dressed in a long virginal, flowing white negligee.

"I've waited for three weeks for this moment," I said to her.

"I'm glad I've got you to look after me," she replied as she planted a kiss on my forehead. "I want you to hold me forever. You do know that all those kiss-and-tell stories about me were made up."

"I know," I said with a sigh. I knew she wasn't like that. "And Hannah means nothing to me."

"Good, I've been saving myself for you," she let slip, and I felt more honoured than I ever had in my life.

"Let's just cuddle on top of the sheets," I whispered as we lay back on the king-size bed.

"I'd like that," she said with a grin. "We don't have to have sex until you're ready."

"You never told me about this," says Matt as I clamp my hand on his shoulder and stop him following the other girls into the ladies' toilets. I grin as I watch the last of the women in his group bundle inside and slam the door in his face.

"Do you think I made them jealous?" I say with a laugh as we now stand alone.

"I don't know, mate," he says with a depressed sigh. "Tell you what, I'll just pop in there and see if I can get them to come out – on my own. This time, you just stay here and I'll send someone back for you when I find them."

Matt's so stupid – he'll do anything for a nice pair of legs. I never saw him again that night. I waited outside the ladies' toilets and even though I could hear Hannah and her friends inside for the next forty minutes, I decided I couldn't be bothered to wait.

I found Matt in the loading bays the following morning, but he said he was in a hurry when he saw me coming. I tried to tell him that if the evil megalomaniac was working him too hard, he should report him to the Personnel Department, but he's too far gone to the dark side to listen.

The suffering of a soul in servitude to a sinful sultan sent shockwaves through spunky superspy Doug Holster. Could this slave of a slave driver be severed of his ties to Doctor Death?

Holster fixed the pin-headed one with a steely stare and, using his colossal mind powers, waved one hand in front of the minion's face in a daring attempt to pull his strings away from the puppet master who was pulling those aforementioned strings that were holding him so tightly in an evil vice-like grip of a Titan of terror.

"Listen to my voice," the Holster said firmly.

It worked. The servant of the evil one stayed and a spark of sense sparkled in his sanity.

"But according to the papers, all your beautiful wife did was talk about sex for the two weeks she was on *Voyeur*," continues the witless journalist as she tries to rile me into dropping my guard and saying something controversial.

"Three weeks!" I remind her. "And she didn't constantly talk about sex – the show was just badly edited. If she didn't have much to say then it was down to nerves – she was on a TV show that's watched by millions. And look at the nut-jobs she was in there with. Donna isn't the shy type. You must have seen the tasteful glamour shoots she's done since leaving the house? She's a very confident girl who was put into a very difficult situation and handled it brilliantly."

"It must be amazing to have such a perfect relationship," the journalist simpers. "But I've taken up enough of your time, so I'll just leave you two lovebirds alone now."

"Oh, yes," I reply as I get up and block her path. Then turn to Donna, "Any chance of a cocktail, my dear?"

As my stunning wife obediently scurries off to our poolside bar, I think back over our relationship. It is indeed as perfect as it could be. Of course, it was slightly marred by some of Donna's contractual obligations after she left the show. She was the prize in an Internet auction where people could bid to have dinner with her in aid of testicular cancer.

It wouldn't have been so bad, but I was outbid on eBay at the last minute. Why the auction had to end at four in the morning was beyond me; only oddballs stay up that late. I had to go to work the next day and was fast asleep by three. Then, when I checked my email the following morning, I found "Big_Daddy69" had won.

I was so mad, it took nearly two hours for my nose to stop bleeding and, on top of that, I was late for work. I had to sit at my computer screen with a bung up my nose. Of course, I got the last laugh when I was interviewed for the hit TV show *Room 101*.

"And your first choice for *Room 101* is…" the interviewer begins, "…Big_Daddy69!"

"Yes, indeed," I say as I sit back in my chair opposite the chat show presenter. "I feel that these sorts of losers should be gotten rid of once and for all. I mean, does society really need the type of people who surf the Internet late at night outbidding people on eBay?"

"I don't think they do, Doug," he replies with a serious nod.

"If that's the highlight of their life, they should go back to sitting by the side of railways taking down train numbers!"

The studio audience howls with laughter and the interviewer obediently banishes Big_Daddy69 into the bowels of *Room 101*.

"I must have missed that episode," mutters the journalist. "With that kind of wit, you should get your own show."

"No, I've said my piece," I muse. "Always leave the public wanting more, that's what I say. Now I've consigned Big_Daddy69, my old workmates, everyone I ever went to school with and that wide boy who calls himself my brother to *Room 101*, I think there's little else left for me."

"I hope I'm not included in your banished workmates, am I?" laughs Matt out of his tiny mouth.

"You bought me a drink last night," I say begrudgingly as I skate round the issue.

"I bought you nine," he replies, proving what a liar he is.

"Wasn't Donna upset at being voted out of the *Voyeur* house after only two weeks?" the journalist goes on. "And how does she feel about Jason, who eventually won the show?"

"I'm so sorry, I wasn't listening," I say as I flick through the hundreds of photographs *Hello* Magazine's official photographer has taken of me and Donna. I still can't decide which ones I want published. "Oh, I see. Jason – what can I say, but he was gay. And as we all know, gay men get a cult following. He may be classed as good looking from the tabloids' jaded perspective, but only because the media has distorted the public's perception of what's considered handsome. I mean, you'd say I was good looking, wouldn't you?"

"I don't know how to answer that, Doug," says the journalist nervously, proving that at least she doesn't need glasses.

"Exactly, but only because you know what I'm really like, yet if the media saw me walking down the street, they wouldn't allow me on the front cover of *Vanity Fair*," I point out. "Jason may have won the show in name only, but he doesn't exhibit Donna's post-modern, radical feminist behaviour. In fact, in a way I too am a feminist. I believe women have almost as much use in society as I do, and you can quote me on that."

I'm glad Donna is a feminist. As long as she doesn't turn into one of those hairy-legged ones who feels she has to emasculate herself to be equal to men.

"Right," Matt says as he looks round at the other drivers who are laughing at him. He looks pained. His skin obviously isn't as thick as mine. If Frank's relentless taunting is getting to him that much, he should report him. "Anyway, I'd love to hear more about post-feminist theory, but these parcels won't deliver themselves."

"They won't if they're in Doug's van!" sneers Frank. "What do you do all day? No, wait, I've seen the inside of your van, I don't want to know! Oh, and why did you sign a despatch note: D Hamster?"

Once again I must rise to a higher place over his crudeness.

The unflappable secret agent, Doug Holster, always smiled politely, just before he drew his Water PPK and dispatched his adversary with a single bullet and a witty quip. In a flash his big gun was pointing at Doctor Death's henchman, The Seal Cub, and he was about to shoot right in his face.

A quick squeeze of his thick trigger later and he was no more and Doug was got ready to race across town in his sports car. As he strolled past the lifeless corpse, he tore that ridiculous tattoo from his arm with his bare hands. Now all that remained was the witty quip.

"Sticks and stones..." I sneer at Frank, before getting on my way.

Chapter 5: Knockers

I infiltrate the base early today and slip below Doctor Death's radar. Normally the final confrontation between hero and villain would be atop of scaffolding, overlooking Los Angeles, but that image of me being circulated has sped up Death's demise. My brilliant plan works perfectly and catches him completely unaware. The office is almost empty and only the cleaners gaze in awe as I stride towards my destiny.

"Ah, Doug," Henry says as I kick his office door open and throw the head of one of his underlings on his desk. "You're in early today."

Typical maniacal type – obsessed with timekeeping.

"I take it you know why I'm here?" I ask, but before he can answer, I carry on. "It's over, you hear me? This futile conflict ends here and now."

"Um, okay," he mumbles. "I take it this is about the picture?"

"I've fought my way through all manner of fiendish traps and inventions to get where I am today. You won't take me down so easily," I state, firmly.

"I assure you, no one's trying to take you down, Doug," he begins. "I'm sure there was no malice meant by it, it's just a bit of harmless fun between drivers."

My face is stoic and expressionless. The artificial lighting above us casts my foreboding shadow across his desk. I watch as he squirms helplessly like a worm on the end of my mighty sword.

"Right, I can see you're not laughing. Yes, I'm sure I wouldn't be if I was in your shoes. Look, I'll find out who the culprit is and make sure they don't do it again, okay?"

No, it's not okay. You can't try to enslave humanity and then say, "Oh, sorry about that – I won't do it again." I'm here for blood. I'm here for vengeance. I am Doug Holster and someone is going to pay.

"You said it was Matt who circulated the picture?" he asks as his furry ears prickle. "All right, I'll have a word with him."

"You won't get the chance," I sneer as I pull a concealed length of cheese wire from my pants. "You'll be dead before…"

With Death helpless as a newborn kitten, Doug moves in to plant the killing blow. One quick tug of the cheese wire around his arch enemy's neck and the world will be safe again.

"Please, Doug!" begs the Doctor, now on his knees and sobbing like a girl. "Don't do it! Have mercy!"

"Like you had mercy on the people of St Albans when you detonated that neutron bomb in their branch of WH Smiths?" I say.

But suddenly a secret hatch slides open and in one desperate attempt to save his worthless hide, he summons a Romanian Sloth Demon from the bowels of hell to come to his aid. What can Doug do? Stay and complete the mission, or let the Demon from the seventh plain of hell finish him off at the same time?

"Oh, sorry," says the swarthy cleaner as she pushes a hoover through the door. "I thought there was no one in here."

"It's all right, Sara," says Henry. "We've just finished."

And that was the story of how Death lived to fight another day. While the hell-spawned demon and I did battle, the evil Doctor dived into an escape pod bound for the burger wagon in the car park.

"Next time, Death," I say as I watch him fly into the heavens towards Joe's greasy spoon, "next time."

Back in the loading bays the god of irony decrees that this is the one day Matt isn't too out of his head to roll in some time after nine.

"All right, mate?" he shouts as I climb into my van. I'm not his mate and never will be.

"Good morning, Matt," I say politely, not wanting to sink to his level. I would have greatly liked to rub my little conversation with Henry in his face, but I think I'll play it cool for now. "I think Henry's looking for you."

"Is he?" he says, blissfully unaware of the hailstorm that awaits him. "Okay, cool, I'll catch up with him later."

Then came one of those awkward silences in conversations where you only want to stick a fork in the tiny head of the person eyeballing you. I get this sort of moment often enough with Hannah, so I really don't need it at work too. I switch the engine on and turn the radio up full blast, but unfortunately Matt doesn't take the hint.

"So, how's Donna?" he asks.

Can he be trusted to keep it a secret? What if he went to the papers about us? How would Mum cope with a press pack on our doorstep clamouring to get exclusive pictures of her only worthwhile son? It could well spell the end for me and Donna. On the other hand, I do want to stick our love up his arse.

"Donna's fine! I'm going to see her today actually," I announce loudly, as I take a photo of her from my glove compartment and show him. It was one of her first shoots for *Nuts* magazine after she left the house. But I cropped her from the surroundings and had her digitally added to a tasteful Middle Earth landscape from the third *Lord of the Rings* movie.

"I definitely think her pictures are more along the lines of art over simple magazine shoots. Of course the online community would have my Adobe Photoshop efforts condemned as fan-art but it's more than that. Donna's pictures inspire me to create things in her image. Through her art, I can find my own – you could say she's my muse. I noticed her ability to transcend mere reality TV to high art in a lot of the footage that was shown of her time in the *Voyeur* house. The beautiful way the shots were framed showing her sitting alone in the garden, or alone in the lounge, or alone in the bedroom while the rabble that infested the house cackled on regardless."

"Either that, or they all hated her!" yells Frank from across the loading bays. "What's her name, Donna from *Voyeur*?"

If that man spent as much time getting a competent tattooist as he does listening in to private conversations, he might not be quite such an unbearable buffoon. Also, he thinks that just because someone goes on a reality TV show, they lose their surname for a double or triple barrelled alternative like "Idiot from *I'm a Celebrity*" or "Untalented from *Pop Idol*". If he was on my forum, he'd have been banned long ago.

"Donna Trayhorn!" I correct him while ignoring the cries of: "who?" from his Neanderthal cohorts. I explain to Matt that she and Metropol have entrusted me with looking after her online promotional campaign since our love had blossomed. But for the sake of the media we're keeping things under wraps to avoid press intrusion. I can tell he's jealous by the way his cheek twitches as I walk away.

A quick stop to pick up today's periodicals and I am indeed with Donna – or at least her old house in Acton. I park a little way down the street out of respect for her mother's privacy – and because all the spots outside her house have been inconsiderately taken. I wait a good hour and a half before a guy leaves her house and gets into his car, allowing me to pull my van down a bit. Looks like her mum's had a Sky Digital dish fitted since yesterday – I'll get a picture of that for the website.

Nothing about Donna in today's publications, only a snobby piece in *The Mail* pontificating how reality TV is affecting the public in a negative way. Typical: when something becomes popular, people try to knock it down – that's so British.

Unfortunately Donna didn't visit her mother's house today, but just being there allows me to return to the depot feeling a little bit more at ease with the world. I want to slip in and out of the loading bays as quickly as possible, but the fascist security guard on duty wants to check every parcel I've returned. This strung the ordeal out long enough for me to see both Henry and Matt coming down from the offices, laughing and joking. It's heartening to see your supposed boss take your claims of harassment in the workplace so seriously.

"You all right, Doug!" Matt yells across the loading bays, obviously forgetting he isn't in a club right now and doesn't need to shout. I mutter a reply and hope he gets the hint that I don't fraternise with the enemy. Sadly, he never was that bright.

"I wish I could get my drops done as quickly as you," he rambles as he bounds over. "So, how was Donna then?"

"Perfect." I reply. What else could I say about our time together?

"See ya, Lucas!" Frank's grating voice hollers across the bay.

"Take it easy, Bear!" Matt shouts back as he waves to the idiotic driver who's leaving.

"Lucas?" I say. "Why did he call you that?"

"Oh, you know," he mumbles, "only a bit of harmless fun – everyone's got a nickname around here!"

"But why does he call you Lucas?" I ask again. Obviously my first question was a little too complicated.

"Well," he begins, "because my first name's Matt, so…you know, Matt Lucas – from *Little Britain*?"

He then proceeds to do the most embarrassing impression of one of the characters from that show. I would say which one only his rendition is so appalling, I haven't got a clue who he's meant to be. I can't help but smirk as some of the other drivers have even noticed him making a fool of himself.

"Very good," I sneer. "But I left my nickname in the playground thank you very much."

"Oh, right," he says, "what was it then?"

I'm certainly not going to tell him. I had to move schools to get away from that unfounded label.

"Well," I say, cunningly changing the subject. "At least I don't have a nickname at work."

I watch him shuffle nervously from foot to foot.

"I don't have a nickname here, do I?" I demand to know.

"No, no, no," he says quickly, "don't be silly."

Doug Holster hadn't saved the world more times than he'd trimmed his toenails by falling for such tall tales. He could smell an untruth in a bad Chinese takeaway and he wasn't going to let this patsy get off so lightly.

He grabbed the turncoat's minuscule head between his thumb and forefinger and thrust it down a toilet bowl in the gents – paying careful attention to pick the one no one had flushed this week.

"Please!" screamed the collaborator pitifully. "I can't tell you! They'll kill me if I tell you!"

"And what do you think I'm going to do to you if you don't?" Holster hissed in his sopping wet ear. The trembling pinheaded traitor began to cry as he caught sight of the colossal black nightstick in his captor's strong hands and the sadistic gleam in his eyes.

"Oh, it's just a character from *The Simpsons*," he finally replies as he cracks like an egg on a hot tin roof.

Interestingly enough, on the rare occasions I've watched such trivia, I could always empathise with the little girl of the family, Lisa. I saw a misunderstood genius surrounded by incompetent morons.

"Oh, sorry, Hans!" booms Frank's voice across the room. "I didn't see you there!"

"He wasn't talking to me, was he?" I ask, sternly.

Matt changes the subject back to my film premiere again, but I don't let him get away with it so easily.

"Well," he stammers, "it's just that some of the guys call you Hans Moleman. You know – the funny little guy with the big glasses from *The Simpsons*?"

"But I don't wear glasses!" I protest, "Well, not big ones anyway."

"See, there you go," he says, "see how stupid it all is?"

I agree, and decide that I'll let him know more about what really went on at the premiere the other night. He's suitably humbled once he realises how many famous people I know. He even takes it in when I tell him about the terrible misunderstanding between me and the security guards over the passes. I give him a brief run-down of the film's plot, but I don't go into detail, as my time with Donna was far more important than some stupid movie. Then I regale him with the story of the limo ride to the club and which celebrities were there.

"Cool, I'm glad things are working out after all that stuff with – you know?" he finally says, amazed at the speed I live my life. "How do you do it?"

Wouldn't everyone like to know? But I'm not about to divulge the secret to my success so easily and tap my nose cryptically.

"Oh, right," he says, then proceeds to wink. "I do some of that sometimes. How much can you get a gram for?"

Is he talking about drugs? I don't have time for them – only losers and emotional cripples need narcotics.

As I leave for the day, I face the fact that Henry has a severe problem keeping authority among his staff. I may have to go over his head if I'm going to see that Matt gets what's coming. I wonder what the managing director would think if he knew one of his employees – the face of the company – is doing drugs.

When I arrive home I don't bother talking to Mum. She's still in one of her apathetic moods and won't come out of her bedroom. Just as well – all I'd get is how bad the arthritis is in her hands and how hard she finds it lifting pots and pans. Little does she appreciate that I've been lifting heavier things than a frying pan all day.

I use the time to ring Hannah's mobile and hang up so she'll see it's me and call back. When she does, I'll take her to the pub or something. But in the meantime, I scan my forum and find I have to ban an idiot called "bootyguy6" yet again. I banned him as "bootyguy", then "bootyguy1" and so on. Every time he reregisters with the same email address, but a slightly different username. I would let him stay, but I've warned him countless times about referring to parts of Donna's anatomy as "flange".

Hannah phones back, but we don't talk for long. I'm not going to drive all the way out to her house just to pick her up. She can meet me in the Rat and Parrot.

When I get there I find she's unfashionably early and talking to one of her friends again. At least it means I don't have to put up with the drivel she spouts all night.

"You'll never guess what Gregory did in art class today…" she rambles on to one of her air headed mates who looks like a melted Teletubbie. I can only shake my head as I watch the two of them in the pub's booth, exchanging pointless anecdotes.

Not more stories about little Gregory again! Why doesn't she marry him if she likes him so much?

"…but how could I tell an eight-year-old that his ghosts looked more like Klan members?" she goes on. I think there was a middle bit, but I'd stopped listening.

I order an overpriced sandwich from the pub's menu and eat it at the bar as I wait for my opportunity to steer the conversation back to me.

"I've been so busy lately, what with the parent-teacher evening coming up," she drones on. "And then helping Mavis out in the evenings…"

"Mavis?" I say when I can finally get a word in edgeways. "Who's Mavis?"

She and Tinky Winky look over and glare at me.

"She runs the choir," the one with the purple aerial on her head snaps. "Not that it's any of your business."

Cheek! Oh, yes, the fat one. I remember seeing a photo of her taking up an entire stage.

"She's having a terrible time lately," Hannah continues. "Her husband died thirty years ago!"

Seeing as that statement didn't make sense, I decide it doesn't warrant a reply. I notice she gives the furry one her credit card to go to the bar and buy some Tubbie custard. She can buy me one later. Seeing as she's so flush with money, perhaps she could use her Mastercard to book me tickets to be in the crowd of next season's *Voyeur*. She could make it a belated birthday present, seeing as she completely forgot to get me one again.

The Teletubbie with the red handbag waddles back with a round of drinks and Hannah starts up again.

"My church is having a little musical gathering soon."

"Oh, right," replies Tinky. "That's nice. Is your man taking you?"

"No, sadly not," Hannah says, with a wistful sigh. "He's working."

70

I'll bet the crafty cow meant me to hear that as well. So what if I told her I was going to London to see a publisher?

"So who are you going with?" asks the Teletubbie in drag.

"No one," she replies. "But I'm meeting Gail and Marcus there."

"Who are Gail and Marcus?" I shout, but I don't think she hears.

"Marcus works for Metropol Industries on *Voyeur* and Gail..." Hannah natters on.

The word Metropol focuses my attention like no other could. She never told me she knew anyone there. In that case, I may have to reconsider her offer and join her for an evening of watching overweight women shaking tambourines.

Chapter 6: Sex, Lies and Teletubbies

"Of course I'll come," I say to myself, immediately making her start banging on about how she has nothing to wear.

That could only come from a woman's mouth. There she is standing at the bar wearing – you guessed it – clothes, and she tries to make out she's some sort of vagrant.

"Right, I'll be leaving now! Bye, Hannah, bye, Po!" I shout while making my exit. Now all that's left to do is wait. Sit out the two weeks before I can meet these Metropol employees and get free tickets. How am I going to last two weeks?

Doug Holster hated waiting. He was a man of action, not discretion. He hadn't joined the Secret Service to sit behind a desk and he certainly didn't enjoy spending his days on surveillance duties.

Time passed as he posed as a humble worker in one of Death's supposedly reputable businesses. He made sure he didn't mix with the other henchmen so as not to arouse suspicion. As luck would have it, they were a tight-knit bunch and seemed more than happy to leave him to his own devices.

So he spent his days watching their comings and goings. Little did they know that while they laughed, joked and ate their Kit-Kats, their downfall was being logged and plotted from within.

I have decided to keep a third diary. My first details mine and Donna's movements. I figured it would be worth making a few notes to save time employing a ghost-writer for my autobiography. The second is of my dreams, or to be more precise, dreams about Donna, and now I have a third. This one chronicles what is said and done to me at work. It'll come in handy when I present it to our CEO at a board meeting.

I try to avoid Matt as much as possible, but this morning I'm forced to call him over as there's a spider in my van.

"There you go, mate," he says as he throws the ugly brute out of my cab, clearly loving his new-found power. "Evicted like a *Voyeur* housemate."

"Thank you," I mutter, before blasting the offending arachnid with my twin pistols as it scuttles across the loading bay floor.

I spend my evening deleting defamatory posts from my message board and checking Donna's official site. I did email her the other day, but only received another standard automated response. She must be putting a lot into her new material not to answer me.

I did get an email from Hannah though, although it was actually from her Internet service provider saying something about delivery notification failure. Modern technology isn't all it's cracked up to be.

The waiting game was playing heavy on Holster's soul and he needed something to take his mind off the battles that lay ahead. He decided to take advantage of the "no Congestion Charge at the weekend" rule and drive into the centre of London to spend some quality time with the delectable Ms Trayhorn.

How he longed for the day this bloody struggle would be over and they could be together forever on white sandy beaches. Yet while evil stalked the streets, he was dedicated to a life of serving a thankless public. There would be no statues of Doug erected after a hit man's bullet finally found its mark. Only a few tears from Ms Trayhorn and a moving speech from The Colonel about losing the finest secret agent the world has ever known.

*He drew up in his Aston Martin outside her Clerkenwell
pad. She wasn't home just yet and he strolled over to the paper
shop opposite to browse through a copy of the Financial Times.
As he checked his stocks and shares something caught his eye:
an enemy agent prowling near his car. He didn't have the
patience to diffuse yet another bomb while driving, so he drew
his Walter PPK and glided over.*

"Don't touch the car!" I sneer at the former concentration
camp guard who poses as a doorman to Donna's block.

"Look, I've told you about this before," he says in a thick
German accent. "You're not to park here and only residents are
allowed inside, limey-pig-dog!"

I'm dealing with a pro here. This isn't some wet-behind-
the-ears assassin who can be bought off with a twenty pound
note and a slap in the face. When I tried before he acted like I
was trying to bribe the Lord Chief Justice and threatened to call
the police.

I'm almost tempted to get a photo of him, not for the site,
obviously, but just to annoy him. As he puts his hand over my
lens I want to tell him to go back to 1940s Germany, but I don't.
Instead I take a deep breath and swallow my pride.

"You couldn't pass a message on to Donna for me, could
you?" I say, before gritting my teeth and adding "please?"

"I am a servant of the Secret Fire," he screams as he waves
his staff at me. "You shall not pass!"

He's obviously a man who takes his job way too seriously.
All he is in fact is a biological door closer. Tesco's have
eradicated the need for someone like him with automatic sliding
doors – his time will come.

Little does he know that I eat the Secret Fire's servants for
pudding and take a step towards him. He vanishes in a cloud of
smoke. I knew he would – his type are all hot air. I complete my

mission and take multiple pictures of Donna's flat with my digital camera.

"Right, that's it," he screams from inside the communal lobby. "I'm calling the police!"

Doug's work here is done. He's captured all the evidence he needs and pulls out a grappling gun and aims it high above the two-level Kentucky Fried Chicken restaurant. While sirens roar and Nazi guards pile out of every doorway, Doug soars up into the night sky out of their reach.

Concealing himself behind a giant illuminated Colonel Sanders, he sets up his mobile transmitting device ready to send his information back to base.

I cross the road and enter a smelly phone box. I know it will do me no good to make enemies so close to Donna, no matter how miserable they are. I look back at the apartment block, safe in the knowledge that somewhere up there is Donna's life. I can see myself living with her there one day. Besides, once I'm in there we can fire the old git anyway.

"Oi, mate!" slurs a drunk as he bangs on the phone box window. "Hurry up – I need a piss!"

I try not to think about what my shoes are standing in. I'll get Mum to clean them when I get home.

"Are you going to be in there all night?" says some little girl wearing too much make-up. "I need to make a call!"

"I don't care!" I snap, as I know she's lying. How many people go out for the evening without a mobile phone these days?

But I'm concentrating so hard on jamming my foot against the phone box door that I miss my chance with Donna. Across the road I see the Gestapo doorman in his silly top hat shutting the door of a limo just after a shapely leg has climbed inside. I could recognise that leg anywhere and barge past the commoners outside as I run towards the car.

"Donna!" I cry, but her limousine turns the corner and I'm left with only three blurry pictures of her rear number plate.

Sunday morning comes and I check my inbox to find that idiot "Big_Daddy69" has sent me another stupid email in a pathetic attempt to wind me up:

I see you've got more pictures of the ceiling fan in Donna's bedroom. Did I tell you I've seen that fan close up? It was the time she was riding me like a jockey after I took her to dinner! We went back to her mum's and I took her up the...

I couldn't read any more of his feeble lies and deleted the mail before I could finish it. At least I had a news alert from Google. Despite failing to recognise my website as the top Donna Trayhorn fan site, I have to concede that Google is a reasonable search engine. Its automated news alerts save me countless hours sifting through celebrity newsgroups for information.

This morning it diverts me to some fantastic shots of Donna from last night. Obviously she'd hit the town to promote her forthcoming musical reinvention and had performed an impromptu photo shoot for the paparazzi in the back of her limo.

She looked fabulous in a low-cut, white minidress and matching heels, finished off with an elegant pearl necklace. It seemed she put on a bit of a show for the photographers before she left the car. This latest batch of images really bring out the different range of emotions she's capable of conveying. I upload the photos to my site, making sure all the nudity is covered up to protect my younger members.

It's fair to say that with such images of womanly perfection in my head, completing my book's first chapter is going to be impossible. I had thought about turning it into a film script; that way it would save a lot of time what with Hollywood making almost every book into a movie. Yet all I can think about was that dress – that dress – Donna in that dress. It's still on my mind as I go to the newsagents and check the Sunday papers and find her playful frolics have made the entertainment sections.

You have to admire Donna's awareness of the media. She knows the tabloids are only interested in sex and plays up to it. That's what's known as being astute, not slutty as the caption under one picture suggests. When was the last time the newspaper reading public got bored with sex? Sex keeps people in the limelight for longer and Donna knows this. I'll scan these pictures in later for my members. After all, her use of nudity is more of a political statement; a way of empowering herself over the lecherous male public. But I have to admit that dress really is something else. Actually, that gives me an idea regarding Hannah's so-called lack of things in her wardrobe.

During the week I manage to successfully avoid Hannah by telling her I'm busy working on the first draft of a screenplay based on my book. I don't need to talk to her anyway as I've sorted out her little problem of what to wear to the church function.

I also note two further incidents in my "Work Insults Diary". One of the drivers has been whistling "Creep" by Radiohead twice while I've been around. The second came from a driver who I caught making a paper aeroplane out of an old magazine that featured Donna. How would he like it if I folded up a picture of his mum and threw it across the depot?

Most of the other drivers are so intimidated by me they merely scurry away when they see me coming. I catch Matt getting out of his van and decide to rub more of my antics with Donna in his face.

"That's cool," is the gist of his replies while he seethes with envy. "I saw her in the papers over the weekend – she's looking pretty hot!"

"And I saw her much closer than you," I say, with a knowing smile.

"You're kidding? She looked amazing in that dress," he goes on, "you were with her Saturday night?"

Of course I was, and I tell him about the limo incident in full detail and how we were out clubbing till the small hours.

"You dark horse," he says, bitterly, "what did you take to keep you up all night?"

That proves how the worm will eventually show its true colours. He's so jealous of me he thinks everyone is as low as he is. He believes the whole world's on drugs.

I make my excuses and walk out, ignoring the comment from one of the tarts in the office about why he even bothers to talk to me.

The weekend was just about sufferable. First a message from work asking me whether I'd like to do some overtime. Luckily I don't need to as I still have the money *Hello* magazine paid for mine and Donna's wedding rights. Besides, I'm too busy posting my views online regarding Donna kissing a fellow reality TV contestant in a club. Sadly my social commentary is interrupted by Big_Daddy69 popping up on messenger.

Big_Daddy69: i shagged Donna! i shagged Donna!

Steely_Doug9: ive told u b4 – ur banned – go away

Big_Daddy69: u 4got 2 block me on messenger!

Steely_Doug9: im doing that now

Big_Daddy69: i joined ur site again

Steely_Doug9: no u havnt

Big_Daddy69: i have and u dont know wot my new username is!

Steely_Doug9: ill find u and ban u. i know who u r

Big_Daddy69: who am i then?

Steely_Doug9: im not telling

Big_Daddy69: who r u then?

78

Steely_Doug9: im a writer, media commentator and webmaster of donnaTis thebest.org.uk and u well know it

Big_Daddy69: can I ask a question then mr writer?

Steely_Doug9: ok

Big_Daddy69: y r u such a loser?

Big_Daddy69 has been blocked from your contact list.

He's the loser, thinking he can wind me up. Once my nose stops bleeding, I get back to checking the stories about Donna kissing a girl called Orac, if you can believe that's actually a woman's name. She was another contestant on *Voyeur*, but the two didn't get on. Orac kept picking on her all the time, complaining about her singing at night, or eating too much during the day – she was never happy. Then when Orac came out of the house on week five, she was offered a fitness video. You can always tell the reality TV rejects as they always do work-out tapes. I know for a fact that Donna would never stoop so low. Apparently the two of them have now been spotted by Metropol photographers kissing in a club. This is a great way for Donna to publicise her new music, plus it proves what a nice person she is by forgiving someone who wronged her.

The press have tried running her down saying she's now bisexual. Little do they know that she's merely cleverer than Fleet Street hacks.

I decide I'd better check my site's members in case Big_Daddy69 has joined again. I couldn't find him, but I did spot "bootyguy8" who I banned immediately. I think he's a bit weird actually, as it was because of him that I had to start blurring out the house numbers of photos of Donna and her mum's properties. The guy is obviously obsessed and he keeps emailing me asking for the name of her road. It's people like him who Donna needs to be protected from. People like him aren't right in the head.

Chapter 7: We Need To Talk

"we need 2 talk," reads Hannah's text message.

Well, no, obviously she feels the need to talk, but I'm fine, thank you. Besides, when I see her at the pub, all she seems to do is talk to her friends – and about her, never what I want to talk about. I'm still going to that church do of hers tonight and what a great way to spend a Saturday evening it's going to be.

I expect all those messages I haven't listened to are about what time she wants picking up. I don't see why she can't get a cab down there like any normal person; after all, it is she who wants to go. I hate listening to messages on my mobile phone. At least when I'm famous I won't have to. I'll employ a pretty personal assistant to do the monkey work for me. Of course she'll probably end up falling in love with a powerful and successful man like myself and Donna will get jealous. Then I'll fire her and get another one.

It's late Saturday afternoon and I've been sitting at my bedroom desk since noon. I've been writing solidly all day and I've had a most productive time. I haven't actually written anything yet, as you should never try and force creativity. Instead I've superimposed a photo of Donna standing in front of the Hollywood sign. That's where we'll be one day – that's our true calling.

People say reality TV stars' appeal dries up once they've left their show, but I don't think so – there's always the exception to the rule. I truly believe that one day Donna will be up there collecting a Best Actress Oscar at the Academy Awards.

I think I'll call it a day now on the book as I don't want to rush things, plus chapter one is almost completed. A solid beginning can be built on anytime. The new series of *Voyeur* will be starting soon and I can't stop thinking about opening night. Past guests often turn up at these shows and it would be a good chance for me and Donna to catch up.

But in the meantime I have to deal with the depressing reality of Hannah's church do. I suppose I made her day by agreeing to go. I just have to be careful her cult doesn't try to get me drunk and sign my life away. If they think I'm going to be getting down on my knees in front of some all powerful, egotistical, megalomaniac; they've got another think coming. I'd rather kneel before Rupert Murdoch; at least he genuinely bestows happiness on the masses through his quality television schedules.

I finally relent and call Hannah back to see what time I'm meeting her at God's house.

"Look, what's up, why do you keep calling me?" I say when I'm diverted to voicemail after five and a half rings. Then I hang up as this is costing me money and start combing my hair forward ready for tonight.

Doug Holster walked into the casino and made all heads turn. He was dressed in the finest tuxedo tailors had to offer. As he moved through the crowds of gambling addicts, more than a few wealthy women in expensive ball gowns made eyes at him. But now was not the time to play, he had business to attend to.

He had hired an expensive escort girl for the occasion to make it look like they were just another well-to-do couple out for a good time. He spotted her across the room and considered asking the agency for his money back once the assignment was complete. Ignoring the harlot they had sent him, he helped himself to a tall glass of the finest complimentary champagne and picked out the contact he was here to meet. Marcus's hair was slicked back and his lilac-tinted sunglasses obscured his sea-green eyes. His wife could be a model: her long black

81

*flowing hair cascaded down around her shoulders as she swung
it back and forwards provocatively as he approached.*

"You must be Marcus," I say using my most charming
smile as I shake his hand and kiss his ring. "You've probably
heard of me – the name's Morrell, Doug Morrell. I'm a friend of
Hannah's."

"Oh, so, you're the young stud we've been hearing so much
about?" jokes his gorgeous wife.

"Guilty!" I say, as I raise my hands hilariously as if
surrendering.

They think it's side-splitting and laugh hysterically, only
trailing off when some fat women start banging tambourines on
stage.

"We haven't seen Hannah yet," Marcus says as he stops
laughing. "Where is she?"

"Around," I say casually as they look about the room, but
she's obviously got lost among the coffin dodgers and cream
cake guzzling grannies.

"Hannah tells us you're a media pundit," states Marcus.

"Guilty, again!" I cry, to another burst of spontaneous
guffaws.

"Boy, are we glad to find you then," says Marcus when he's
stopped laughing, "Metropol needs a guy like you to add his
voice to *Voyeur*."

"I'm your man!" I say and we all share another hearty
chuckle.

He shakes me warmly by the hand and I ask what my duties
will be.

"Interviewing new contestants, letting us know what you
think, you know – if they've got what it takes to make it after
they've left the show."

A big, ugly octogenarian starts warbling on stage.

"Not like her then, eh?" I joke.

"Exactly!" replies Marcus, "sort the wheat from the chaff."

"She's too fat for TV!" I continue as Hannah comes up to me and leans on my shoulder lovingly.

"Doug!" Hannah says, gently. "Don't say things like that about your auntie Eileen."

"I beg your pardon?" I say as I turn towards the stage. Oh, God, she's up there bouncing on a pogo stick.

I open my eyes to find I'm face down on my keyboard and it's nearly dark outside. The strain of writing all day has obviously taken more of a toll on me than I'd realised. I can feel the imprint of the "caps lock" key in my forehead. This church trip better be worth my while and I still haven't done my hair right.

Later that night I arrive at the hall. Hannah is sitting at the end of a row of cheap plastic chairs which look like they've been borrowed from her school. Normally I'd sit next to her, but I can see straight away that she's wearing a pair of beige trousers and a navy blue blouse, as opposed to the dress I spent £39.99 plus delivery on from As Seen On Screen.com. Women are never happy – they moan that you never buy them anything; then when you get them a trendy white minidress from an online site dedicated to selling clothes and accessories that celebrities have worn, they don't wear it.

If it's good enough for Donna then I don't see why Hannah didn't wear it here. Now I can understand where the phrase "my wife doesn't understand me" comes from.

Sadly there is no complimentary champagne in tall glasses, only juice and tea in polystyrene cups. I help myself to some squash and empty a tray of biscuits into my pocket. I've been standing at the back now for nearly an hour watching group after group of smiling simpletons shaking maracas on stage while praising the Lord's name. It amazes me that there are even kids as young as sixteen up there. You'd think they'd be spending their evenings doing something constructive like trying to audition for the next series of *Chart Icon*. Oh, great, now the living dead are taking the stage.

"Aren't they wonderful?" a female zombie wearing what appears to be a tea cosy on her head says in my ear. "Did you know Mrs Gronk is eighty-five and she still plays the clarinet?"

"Badly," I add. Then I sever her head to stop her biting the Reverend and creating a plague of the undead before the raffle has been drawn.

"Excuse me, but is there a Marcus here?" I say to a passing tramp who's getting ready for his big moment on stage playing the triangle.

"I think he'll be along later. His wife Gail's not too well; she's had to go into a wheelchair and…"

I tune out and hope beyond hope that Hannah didn't take the dress out of the packet so I can send it back within fourteen days.

On stage the completely unlovable old bag squeezes the life out of a lump of wood she calls an instrument and the crowd goes wild. They don't have a clue what proper music is. How many acts have topped the charts in the last three decades playing The Lord is my Shepherd on the paper and comb?

Finally, I spot some old bloke pushing in yet another old girl in a wheelchair. This lot really are the wild ones, but this time Hannah waves at them.

Doug Holster focuses all his mind powers on not succumbing to the mass brainwashing techniques the cult is using. The vile harpy on stage continues her murderous yowling, but little does she know that years of Secret Service training has made Holster immune to her bewitchment.

While she warbles to the masses, he removes another plate full of poisoned Rich Tea biscuits. If he can do nothing else this evening, he can save the lives of the congregation when their evil leader tries to embark on a mass suicide pact once he's packed up the tombola table.

A mechanical whirring makes Holster spin round towards the main entrance. He sees his contact Marcus has been captured by some half-human, half cyborg female impersonator. Her wheels roll round as she controls her metal transportation device via a joystick in one clawed hand. Doug knows he must be careful as he eyes up the many other buttons and readouts on her built-in computer panel. One false move and her tank-like lower half would unleash a volley of rocket-propelled grenades on his position.

The audience hasn't realised that the old codgers on stage look as if they're about to run out of breath, so I head towards Marcus and his wheelchair-bound wife. I could tell he wasn't like the others as he's smartly dressed in a suit and appears to be the only person in the room – apart from me – without a flute in his trouser pocket.

"Good evening, the name's Morrell, Doug Morrell. Hannah's better half," I say with a friendly smile. "I'm so delighted to meet you."

"Doug? Oh, yeah, I think she mentioned something about you," he replies warmly, as he shakes my hand. "Nice to meet you too. This is my wife, Gail."

"Yeah," I say to her, before turning back to him. "I'll bet it must be great working for a huge media empire like Metropol Industries. You know, I can see myself working there some day. Did Hannah tell you that I'm not only a writer, but a media commentator with my own website?"

"Um, no actually, she just said you're a delivery driver at Parcel Plus who…"

"Do you have any contact with the publishing side of Metropol," I add. "Or do you just work on *Voyeur*?"

"Well, I used to work on *Voyeur*," he replies. "But it's Gail here who…"

"Used to?" I say. He better not have left.

"Yes, I asked for a transfer away from reality TV," he says, as if that should make it all better. "So many shallow people there, I couldn't take it. I work in advertising now."

"But, you still work for Metropol, right?" I ask.

"Oh, yes," he rambles. "But it's Gail who…"

"So, do you still have any contact with the reality TV department?" I ask him again.

"I still have a few friends there, yes," he replies, and I breath a sigh of relief.

"So you're a bit of a writer?" whatever his wife was called butts in.

With the pleasantries over, I ignore her and usher Marcus over to a table well away from the main seating area. I want to get him alone so we can talk shop. I start to lead him away, but unfortunately he seems to insist on bringing the cripple.

"Reality TV, eh?" I laugh once we are sat down. "Where would we be without it?"

"Heaven I expect!" he quips wittily. He is obviously a man of many talents. I haven't laughed so loudly in a long time.

"No, but seriously," I say once I've calmed myself down. "It really is the best reflection of society we've ever had."

"If that's the case I fear for our children," he replies. I don't know what he means by that, but I'm sure it is hilarious so I laugh respectfully.

"It must take a lot of bravery and hard work for a contestant to make it into the *Voyeur* house," I say once I've stopped crying.

"Either that or we take the ones the nut houses can't handle!" he cracks. He really is a card.

"No, but seriously, look at Donna Trayhorn…"

"Who?" he asks, playfully.

"Nice one – who!" I joke, the two of us getting on famously. "She was the real winner of last season's show and decided to leave the house on the third week to pursue her true calling."

"Oh, her," he says, being serious for a moment.

"Yeah, so like I say, take Donna Trayhorn for example…"

"I wish someone would!" he interrupts. Sometimes people forget that there's a time and a place for humour. But I have to agree, there are a lot of lecherous males who would like to take her.

"Have you done much writing lately, Doug?" his wife croaks from somewhere. Her butting in completely makes me lose my train of thought, which sadly allows Marcus to change the subject.

"Gail's a writer too, you know…" he says, as if I care.

I try to hold back from smirking out of respect for Marcus. What has someone like her got to offer popular culture? I guess it would be harsh of me to point out to the old girl that the days of writing poetry about your cat have long since gone by. Still, I'll bet it's about the only thing that keeps her going. Handicapped people can't do an awful lot as it is.

"…and a publisher," he continues.

My heart skips a beat. I think Matt must have sneaked in and slipped one of his pills into my orange juice as I come over all light-headed. Had I been standing up I may well have fallen over.

87

"Is your book ready to be given to the world?" the old crow cackles as she rubs her twisted fingers together greedily. I don't say a word as I stare her out. I can see the pound signs lighting up in her eyes like they do in those old cartoons.

"It's a trap!" Ms Trayhorn yelled as she was dangled from the ceiling by her wrists over the casino's roulette table. Her cry alerted Doug to the danger he was now facing. This whole evening had been a set-up. This fiendish cult weren't only after his soul, but his life's work too.

But they hadn't bargained for Doug's steely resolve holding up to their mind reading metal witch and her cauldron of tea. She wanted to rule the world and steal every innocent person's mind for her own. Then when her vile hands were clasped round every bank note ever printed, her criminal cranium planned "redistribution of wealth to the poor". But the vicious necromancer hadn't counted on Doug Holster showing up to thwart her plans.

"Join us!" she whispered, seductively. "Join us and you can have anything you desire, for I work at Askew Publications in London."

"Join this!" Doug snarled as he pointed both barrels of his twin pistols in her wrinkled face. This is one man who will never be a charity case. If she was truly as all powerful as she claimed, she would know that Doug Holster received offers every day. Not to mention publishing requests for his signed underwear.

"You can't hide your secrets forever, puny mortal," the wheelchair-bound vulture cackled insanely. "I'll take a look at it for you."

"I don't think so," he retorted as he squeezed both triggers and shot his load over her face.

88

"Oh, bless him, he's just shy!" chortles the old woman to her poor brainwashed husband on a leash. He laughs sycophantically, but I'm not about to be emotionally blackmailed. A book is never truly finished, even after it's gone to print.

I need to turn the conversation back towards Marcus, and fast. I can see what's happened here – a clever, witty man has been forced to quit his job on *Voyeur* for a profession which was no doubt dictated to him by his scheming wife.

"Holster is not shy," I point out to Marcus through gritted teeth.

I decide that if I'm to complete my mission, I'll need to get Marcus away from Medusa. I play the tactical retreat card and leave them to mingle while I choose to see what the toilets look like. Nearly half an hour later, she finally lets go of his strings and I leap into action and home in.

"I am taking tickets to *Voyeur* and to the after show party," I say firmly as I hold eye contact. "You can either profit by this or be destroyed. It's your choice, but I warn you not to underestimate my powers."

Then I point out my mother isn't feeling too well and I have to get back. Of course the moment I make a move on him, his wife on wheels comes in for round two, but I tell her in no uncertain terms that she will never take my book from me. This time I think I get through to her as the two of them walk off straight away.

As I leave the hall, I look back at the people inside. I see the way they clap and applaud every single honk coming from the living dead on stage. It amazes me how deliriously happy they pretend to be. I don't think I've been to church since I was at school, and that was only because I was made to. It's sad the lives some people lead. I wave to Hannah and make my exit.

Chapter 8: This Year's Crop

Voyeur – possibly the greatest show on TV, begins again in only five short days. It's amazing how it can still remain as fresh and intuitive on its fourteenth series. Ever since it started I was hooked, as I felt it was about time a television show really involved the viewers and let them shape how it evolves. Not only do I personally take credit for weeding out the useless contestants by phoning in, but I'm one of the top five posters on the official *Voyeur* online message board.

Last season while Donna was on the show, I used up all my holiday time staying home watching the live feed. Of course when she was callously evicted after only the third week, I found myself with little to do for a fortnight. This season, I again intend to watch the show and offer my insight on the character traits and motivations displayed by this year's crop. And point out that none of them will come close to the impact Donna had on the series.

I'm expecting membership of my site to pick up again. The re-ignition of interest in reality TV should spark a wave of people remembering Donna. Chances are it will also be a good thing for her upcoming single. I'm guessing she'll make an appearance on one of the daytime shows like "*Voyeur Exposed*", "*Voyeur Unplugged*", "*Voyeur Uncut*", or "*Voyeur Plus*". But I do wish Marcus would hurry up and get me those tickets. I've rung Hannah from work every day now for two weeks and she never seems to return my calls. She didn't even have the decency to send me back my dress and when I saw her in the pub, she even threw it at me! I don't know why I bother with her sometimes.

By way of an apology, I let her take me out to dinner in the Rat and Parrot. However, we sit in near silence and I get so bored, I can only think about getting home to watch an old episode of *Voyeur* starring Donna. I try and attract the acne-coated schoolboy posing as a waiter, but to my horror I accidentally catch the eye of Matt and his buddies. He's obviously half-cut and, although I do my best to hide us, he weaves his way over to the bar.

"Hey, Dougy-boy, how's it going?" he says, slurring his words.

I don't answer, but sadly Hannah starts giggling like a twelve-year-old.

"All right, babe!" he yells as his octopus-like tentacle shoots out round her neck. "What's the matter? Are you all right?"

Hannah whines and moans to him. If he only knew what she was really like! Then he whispers something to her and looks down the bar at me for some strange reason.

"We were just going!" I tell him firmly.

"What, already? It's not even nine! Come to Royals nightclub with us. You'd love it," he dribbles on, before starting to do some ridiculously vulgar attempt at dancing.

Hannah of course finds it hilarious and so do his drunken mates. What a shame poor Matt doesn't realise they're not laughing with him, they're laughing at him.

"Come on, Lucas!" yells Frank from across the pub. "We were only supposed to be in here for one."

"Yeah, coming, Batman!" he shouts back.

"Why do you call him Batman?" Hannah asks with another childish giggle. "He doesn't look like Bruce Wayne."

"Nah, it's because he hates the Penguin!" Matt blurts out, before glancing at me nervously.

"I said we were just going," I remind them both as I put my coat on and leave them and their lowbrow conversation well behind.

As we walk to my car Hannah is so quiet, I barely notice her. But I don't feel like an awkward silence right now and take the opportunity to explain how *Voyeur's* selection process works, but she doesn't understand. And she wonders why I don't invite her to any of the live shows with me.

I get to work Monday morning, still thinking about when Marcus will get me those tickets. I don't notice Matt coming crawling up to me.

"How's it going, Doug?" is his opening gambit.

"Fine," I reply without really looking at him – I'm too busy throwing the parcels into my van.

"And how's Donna?"

I knew it; he's fishing for gossip. Whatever I let slip here will doubtless appear in the *News of the World* this weekend.

"She's good," is my most neutral of replies.

"That's cool," he says as he thinks up his next move, "it's turning into a regular *Notting Hill* tale, eh?"

"I beg your pardon?" I blurt out. "What on earth do you mean by that?"

He then starts trying to explain the plot to the film *Notting Hill* where some Hollywood film star played by Julia Roberts falls in love with a lowly bookshop owner played by an idiot with silly hair.

"I have seen the film, you know?" I remind him and I hated it. I remember that was the one where I had an eyelash in my eye and I couldn't concentrate on its wafer-thin plot. "What's it got to do with me?"

"Well, you know, she's a celebrity and he's…" he blathers, "oh, never mind – how's the book coming along?"

"Very well actually," I inform him, "someone from Askew Publications in London is very interested."

"Smart," he says bitterly, "do I get an autographed copy?"

"If you buy one," I say under my breath as I get into my van and slam the door. From my cab I watch him lumber across the depot. He strikes a lonely soul when he hasn't got his mates or drugs for company.

I watch as some little tart from Human Resources totters over to him in her high heels and low-cut top; she says something that I can't catch, before looking in my direction. Our eyes meet and I do believe she's giving me some sort of dirty look. Matt shakes his head and shrugs, before leading her away. I drive off. I can't help it that I don't want to associate with people like him.

I visit the newsagents to see what's written about Donna, but for some reason the press have decided to go with stories concerning the new *Voyeur* contestants who might or might not be on the show. I chuck the magazines in the bin and drive to Gloria's. Gas men are digging up the pavement outside her front door as there are bollards round a hole. I take a picture for my site as I feel it's my duty to keep Donna's fans up to date.

While I'm outside I read an article about Jack Nicholson wanting to take a year off making mainstream Hollywood films. It suddenly occurs to me that this might be the ideal time to send him the script adaptation of my novel. It's not quite finished and I'm still trying to decide whether the main character should be called "Doug Steele" or "Doug Holster", but I think he may find it interesting. I picture him playing Doctor Death and perhaps Whoopie Goldberg as that vindictive old cow in a wheelchair.

But soon Henry is on the phone wanting to know why some old biddy hasn't received her garden gnome. You'd think she'd be grateful I hadn't delivered the eyesore. Plus the damn thing put my back out when I humped it into the van. Reluctantly I figure I'd better get Ms Swann her precious lump of rock, but not before I've been to the café for something to eat. I always seem to get hungry outside Donna's mum's place – it must be the excitement.

I get back to the depot late as Henry kept calling and insisting I get a signature from every single client. Again, it was up to me to point out that if a customer was out, then it was a little bit difficult to get them to sign for a parcel. Faced with such unquestionable logic, he finally gave in and stopped ringing every five minutes.

Matt is already back as I drive into the loading bay and he sits huddled in a corner having tea with his cohorts. He waves, but I ignore his superficial gesture. It's time he learns that he's not as popular as he thinks he is.

I climb out of my cab and overhear a snippet of their conversation.

"…I can't believe it's come round so quickly…" one grease monkey drones.

"Twelve more weeks of that shit on TV," says another one.

"Tell me about it," pipes up Matt. "At least I'm not missing anything on telly when I'm at the pub!"

"I hate bloody reality TV," the fourth ape splutters as bits of a Mars Bar drop from his mouth. The others agree. I don't.

"If you don't like reality TV," I state loudly, "then you obviously don't like real life!"

They look at me as their tiny minds try and comprehend advanced semantics. Then they stare at one another and start laughing nervously as not one of them can answer me.

"Yeah, nice one, Doug, that's why we love you," says Frank as he holds up a chocolate bar. "Do you want a Penguin?"

I don't know why the others find that so funny, but I tell him I've already eaten in the café and again in *Burger King* before I got back. I don't want their ten day old leftovers. I'm going to put a stop to this once and for all.

"He's not here right now," the Managing Director's bimbo-secretary with a fake tan bleats at me from behind her desk. No wonder this company's in the state it's in when the management can't even be bothered to stay at work.

"Hello, Doug," says Henry from behind me. "What are you doing up here this late?"

Was that supposed to be some sort of dig at me? Either way, I wasn't about to rise to it – I know that's what he wants.

"I wanted to talk to our Managing Director about Matt," I say, "but seeing as he finds it too hard to sit behind a desk for eight hours, you'll have to do."

"Okay," he replies, slowly, "what's up with Matt?"

I keep my Works Insults Diary on me at all times and by rights I should add the schoolgirl behind Mr Bateman's desk for her insolence. I was under the impression receptionists were supposed to smile and be polite.

"I have evidence of a vicious campaign of hate, orchestrated by Mr Matt Tyler, directed at me without any form of provocation whatsoever," I say in a loud clear voice for all the office staff to hear. I ignore the snigger from the kid, who's now started doing her nails.

"I see," says Henry guiltily as he scratches one of his hairy ears. He doesn't like the rest of the office knowing he has a problem with his staff. "Would you like to step into my office for a little chat?"

No, actually, but I don't think I have a choice.

After much discussion behind the soundproofed door of his office, the upshot of our "little chat" was that "Frank did it".

Apparently Matt had nothing to do with the posters of me and it was all down to Frank. I don't know what that man has against me. About the only time I've ever spoken to him properly was when he reversed out in front of me and I crashed my van into his Lexus.

95

As for the songs being hummed about me, according to Henry, whistling isn't banned by company policy and therefore isn't a dismissible offence. He obviously hasn't heard the lyrics to Creep by Radiohead, a situation easily rectified when I recite them from my diary.

"Coincidental," is all he has to say about that; the same goes for the dirty looks from the typing pool. He also says he's already spoken to Frank and told him to leave me alone. Hello? Doesn't that sound like something a primary school teacher would say? I think it's fair to say that my faith in human nature has taken an extreme battering today, or should I say my faith in competent management?

I've heard enough as it seems that the chiefs have no control over the Indians. I turn to walk out, but Henry decides he hasn't finished.

"Oh, while you're here, there was one more thing."

This better be good.

"About your application for duty manager…"

My application for duty manager? I'd forgotten all about that. I applied for the position a couple of months ago after I heard some of the drivers discussing the improper activities they got up to with women in the staff toilets. I wrote on the application form a most detailed list of all the people I'd fire when I got the post, but I never even got an interview.

"What about it?" I ask, curiously.

"Well," he begins, not looking me in the eye, "we've decided – after careful consideration, that your skills aren't best suited to management issues. We'd prefer to keep you on the front line so to speak, you know, customer facing and all that."

Yes, I know exactly what he means – keep the workers down at all costs. He goes on to say that they're looking for someone with "people skills" whatever that means. However, I know the real issue is that he is afraid I might actually shake things up in the offices and kick a few backsides into shape.

Doug Holster returned home to his luxury penthouse London apartment. He was relieved he hadn't invited any of his girlfriends back as he needed some "me" time. He thought about the events of the day, how his boss, The Colonel, had begged him to give up field work.

"But Doug, you're too important to us," he pleaded. "A bullet could have your name on it at any time! We need you to coordinate our base and run things from here. I'm not going to last forever, you know? Who will look after Britain once I've gone?"

Doug smiled. He liked the old boy who muddled his way through the country's safety, but he still couldn't bring himself to trade in his trusty pistols for a pen and spend the rest of his days sitting behind a desk. He was still too young for that. Maybe he'd try a desk job when he was in his eighties.

From his mini-bar, he poured himself an Archers and Lemonade – stirred, not shaken – and looked at the life size portrait of William Shatner he had hanging above his fireplace. Captain Kirk never traded in command of the Enterprise to become an Admiral. The two men were kindred spirits. He admired the work Kirk had done for intergalactic peace. Kirk was a role model in Holster's life. He was a man who wasn't afraid to punch a woman and could despatch a Lizard Man with a single chop.

I don't go home after work. Instead, I go back to Gloria's and park up. Being here makes it all better. I think I will take some holiday next week or maybe the week after. That way I can stay at home and monitor the new housemates. *Voyeur* may be without Donna, but anything's better than being at work with

97

that bunch of losers. I'm getting hungry again, so I switch on the radio to take my mind off my rumbling stomach. A voice from the radio says:

"…now do stick with us through the latest offering from *Voyeur* reject, Donna Trayhorn, with her new single Game For You. Coming up, right after these important messages…"

My heart skips a beat. It's finally out. I can't believe it. I'm actually going to hear her first single since she changed record labels. And what did he mean, "reject"?

Chapter 9: Elliptical Allegories

Still no official release date for Game For You, but since
Monday, I've heard it on the radio twice! Even though it was
only a demo version, I have to say it was absolutely fantastic. I
can only guess as to how good the finished track will sound. I
feel it is my duty to inform the other members of my site about
Donna's new sound:

*Donna's background in popular dance culture is clearly
visible in Game For You – the first track from her as yet untitled
second album. Her love of clubbing and dancing shines through
her music, not only in her performing, but also her song writing.
Despite not being credited as a writer, her influence is visible
for all to see.*

*Both the lyrics "wide open in your bed" and "sharing your
tongue with your sister" certainly speak directly to the masses
and move them deep inside. Not only do they make us think of
the profound nature of the piece, but touch us at a higher level of
climactic understanding and sometimes even both at once. The
dichotomy between soothing and unsettling is perfectly conveyed
in lines like "your sister, your brother or your dog," or "falling
for your fingers". Her upper-middle-class roots are displayed
like a landscape in the chorus when she talks about "the
brooding hole is her past meets with the hole down below". This
concords with the equally unnerving elliptical allegories of "I've
seen your father's one too".*

*It's all here: Donna's writing conveys a mature acceptance
of (and tolerance of) the world's foibles and a desire to influence
people's attitudes and make them more aware, compassionate
and tolerant themselves; musically this is often expressed by a*

languidly wistful and hypnotic quality that proves somewhat deceptive.

Five out of five stars.

I can't wait until it's released. I've checked her official site and it's been updated for the first time since March. Apparently Game For You will be released on album, vinyl and mini-disc – I'm going to buy all three – I suppose I'd better get a mini-disc player and some record decks while I'm at it.

You'd think the track would be downloadable via the big music websites, but for some unknown reason, none of them seem to have it yet. Probably Metropol don't want to let it fall into the hands of the snivelling music pirates. In the meantime, I've recorded it off the radio with an old tape recorder and I'm playing it non-stop wherever I go.

I booked the next few days off work so I can watch the new series of *Voyeur* in peace. I've told Mum to go out for the day and let me have the television in the lounge.

It's the opening night and before the show starts I quickly send a sample scene of my screenplay to Jack Nicholson via his official website. Donna's tape plays on the stereo and the phone is off the hook in case Hannah decides to ruin the atmosphere. I don't dwell on the fact that if Marcus had come up with the goods, I might even have been attending the opening night. But I suppose he could still come up with a ticket for one of the daytime shows if Hannah pulls her finger out and hassles him.

The show starts with the two hilarious presenters – Ray and Ford – doing their banter to camera while the crowd cheers behind them. Once they've done their bit, it's time to introduce the ten contestants. As they step out of their limos, I can tell immediately that not one of them is a patch on Donna.

1. Max – the obligatory bloke who's supposed to be good looking, but his ears are way too far down his face for my liking, not that the screaming teenage girls seem to care as he passes them on the way in.

2. Gemma – the obligatory thick one – she said in her interview she doesn't care what people think of her. Why do they all say that?

3. Karl – the obligatory gay hairdresser – what's the betting he'll win? Half the winners of this show have been gays.

4. Susie – the obligatory loud one – she'll probably be out once the press get stuck into her. She also said she didn't give a – bleeped expletive – what people thought of her.

5. Paul – the obligatory old one – out first week, you mark my words. Old people have a better chance of survival in a hospice than on a reality TV show.

6. Bertha – the obligatory fat one – to double the cliché they even found someone with a fat sounding name. Coincidentally, she also claimed not to give a – bleeped expletive – about what the press or skinny girls think of her.

7. Blaze – the obligatory black man with the made-up name – no ethnic contestant has ever won *Voyeur*.

8. Lisa – the obligatory quiet one – she'll make it to the end, but she won't win – they never do. But despite coming across all sweet and innocent, she also had to state in her audition tape that she doesn't care what the others think of her and will say what she thinks to them.

9. Cuthbert – the obligatory posh one – they'll hate him and then vote him out. I don't know why he even bothered to audition.

10. And finally Kat – the obligatory fit girl – I guess she's supposed to fill the void that Donna left, but as I predicted, she doesn't even come close. She's got eyebrows that seem to stop halfway over her eyes. Weird. I was too busy looking at her eyebrows to listen to whether she cared what people think of her, but I think we have to take it she said that at some point.

I stay up to watch the live feed after the show has finished. I can't make out what they're doing all the time because the producers play "crowd noise" and "bird-song" whenever contestants talk about people on the outside. In fact, Lisa went to bed before I even heard her voice.

Not much happens during the night. They all go to bed at gone eleven – you certainly wouldn't have got that last year. I remember by that time, Donna had already gone topless in the shower and made a play for that ungrateful inbred Bryan. I watch them throughout the night: a couple get up to make drinks and go to the toilet, but that's about it.

I'm quite tired when morning comes, but Mum still won't bring me breakfast no matter how many times I call for her. Just as well; last year I was watching the live feed all night and she came down and started accusing me of "talking to one of the players in my game called Auntie Eileen."

I was forced to once again explain that *Voyeur* is more than a TV show. It's about life, blah, blah, blah. But I've long since given up trying to get through to her. I'm pretty sure I wasn't talking to Auntie Eileen last night though, although that might explain why I stopped taking notes between about 3.30 am to half past five.

The live feed goes on till midday, before going off air for a couple of hours until two. This gives me a much needed chance to catch up on my website and post my thoughts and opinions on this new lot of fame-hungry wannabes.

I post my opinions on both my site and the official *Voyeur* message board. I actually feel a bit sad at the amount of seemingly prepubescent teenage boys who have developed a strange fascination with Kat after only one night. I do my best to point out her unfortunate eyebrow affliction, but I doubt it will do much good. Would you believe someone has already trademarked both katmartin.com and katherinemartin.com?

I use the two hours to correct many other forum users on simple facts, such as how reality TV is not just about titillation and mindless, passive entertainment, but is in fact a window on the world we live in. Not forgetting that Donna is head and shoulders over Kat and her freakish eyebrows.

Suddenly an instant message window pops up out of nowhere.

Agent_Orange999: hi m8

Steely_Doug9: hello? Who r u?

Agent_Orange999: an agent representing a publisher. ru writer and media commentator doug morrell?

Steely_Doug9: yes y?

Agent_Orange999: we want to publish ur book

Steely_Doug9: omg thats amazing. u wont regret this, its going to be a sure fire bestseller + ive already started work on a screenplay. do u make films 2?

Agent_Orange999: yeah

Steely_Doug9: cool, i was thinking either jack nicholson or john travolta as leading men

Agent_Orange999: sure, i no them both. i will get them signed up. wot about a female lead?

Steely_Doug9: well, this may sound funny, but have u heard of donna trayhorn from last series of voyeur?

Agent_Orange999: yeah, shes gr8, ill call her up

Steely_Doug9: thats brilliant, i cant wait 2 meet her. thank u so much

Agent_Orange999: thats ok, i want 2 c her again. did u no I shagged her after i totally outbid u on ebay!

Agent_Orange999 has been blocked from your contact list.

He thinks he's so funny, but I knew it was him all along. I suppose that's the problem with having my email address on my site – any idiot can add you to their contact list. But *Voyeur's* live feed is about to begin, so I don't have time to go out and get Saturday's papers. The flat needs more milk anyway, so I write out a list of things I need Mum to get and leave it on the kitchen table. Plus a sub-index of the magazines and papers I buy, and more importantly the ones I've blacklisted due to unfavourable coverage of Donna.

I watch the live feed into Saturday evening until the next break. I'm not impressed as it seems this series is simply "the Kat show". I've lost count of the amount of airtime dedicated to the little girl with the hairy forehead. I'm actually quite relieved when the show shuts down for a couple of hours as I'm not sure how much more I can take of her feeble attempts to hog centre stage.

I don't post too many comments on the boards during this gap. And worst of all, Mum hasn't even touched the list of papers I wanted, so I have to go out and get them myself.

Nothing much to report. most publications go with shameless self promotion for this unworthy bunch of new contestants. Friends and relatives sink to new depths and sell the most intimate of details regarding the contestants' personal lives. This to me is proof positive of what self-obsessed losers these people really are; it seems that every one of them has had a threesome – or more!

Of course last season wasn't any different. Blokes who barely knew Donna were making out they'd slept with her. It was disgraceful how the press lapped it up on no more than their say-so. I turn page after page of endless tripe about this season's contestants' "horny sexploits in Ibiza" until finally I think I see light at the end of the horizon.

My oasis in an otherwise barren media desert comes in the form of a most tasteful paparazzi shot of Donna in *The Star* newspaper. She's leaving a West End restaurant wearing a delightful pink PVC miniskirt and matching see-through blouse. My heart lifts to think that there's still room for quality journalism in today's press. Then I read the snippet of writing underneath:

On a roll. After netting his first goal for Watford FC last Saturday, Championship footballer Wayne Moore, 20, has netted his very own reality TV girlfriend, Donna Trayhorn, 22. The pair were spotted canoodling in a trendy London bar over the weekend, and have been on a string of dates ever since.

From my heart lifting, I can feel it crashing down through the floor. My mouth dries up completely and after what seems like an eternity, I have to physically remind myself to breathe.

Half an hour later and I still haven't left the bathroom. I can tell my nose isn't going to stop bleeding for a long time. A thousand thoughts rush through my head, yet every one of them comes back to a singular question: how could she do this to me?

My nose stops bleeding at eleven o'clock, or at least that's the time I decide to stuff enough tissue paper up my nostrils to allow me to make it to my computer. This time I'm not about to offer commentary on that new bunch of riff-raff as I think I'm entitled to answers.

My first port of call is Donna's official website, which I email immediately demanding she explain herself.

Sadly no one's online from my website. I private-message a few trusted members like "Davros666", asking whether he's heard anything about Donna getting a boyfriend. Maybe I shouldn't have banned bootyguy again as he hasn't rejoined in over a week.

I post messages on my site, asking members for their support during this difficult time. Then I check back a few minutes later, but no one's replied. I turn instead to the official *Voyeur* message board knowing that the true fans must be online somewhere on a Saturday night.

I'm not wrong. I check other posts from little kids saying how fit Blaze is and find they were only posted a matter of minutes ago. Despite being blatantly wrong, I don't even feel the need to correct them. In fact, I actually feel a sense of relief to know I'm not alone. I feel I'm back with my own people, those who will understand.

Unfortunately there are only eleven dedicated message boards for this series of *Voyeur*: one for each contestant, and one for "general" topics. I post on all of them.

Dear all. It has come to my attention that the press have been circulating vicious rumours concerning Donna Trayhorn and her alleged relationship with a footballer. I would be grateful if you could forward any information to the webmaster at donnaTisthebest.org.uk. Many thanks – Steely_Doug9.

I press the "post" button for the eleventh time and sit back at my computer. Every few minutes I refresh the pages and check how many people have read my post. A few hours later and a total of twenty-nine comrades have viewed my new topics, but as yet no emails.

Doug Holster stood next to his Aston Martin as he looked out over the sea from the highest cliff top. As the sun set, casting orange rays down on the ocean, he threw a single red rose into the murky depths below.

Ms Trayhorn was dead. He had been forced to kill her himself. He had failed in his mission to rescue her from Doctor Death's grip. His nemesis had returned her to him, but only as a robotic clone who tried to knife him in the back when he asked her to iron his tuxedo.

The hardest thing he'd ever done was pull the trigger and splatter her metallic brain across his new ironing board cover. Perhaps it was true what The Colonel had said, about how people like him are destined to only ever be married to serving the public.

Ms Trayhorn's name was added to the list of women he had loved and lost and now consigned to memory. A lesser man may have hurled himself off into the water below. But Doug is less to no man.

By morning I've just about run out of tears and Kleenex, but I'm still asking the question, how could she do this to me? And I'm also no closer to getting an answer. The last time I checked over two hundred people had read my posts. I click refresh again.

"This post has been deleted by a moderator."

And not just one post, all eleven. I email the site straight away and tell them what I think of their power-crazed little moderators. I then receive a standard reply telling me *Voyeur* message boards are for discussing this year's contestants only, and to please stop emailing. I feel another nose bleed coming on.

Perhaps it's times like this I should immerse myself in my work and make Donna see what she gave up when I'm winning yet another award.

I know when the cameras are on me and pretend to look nervous in my seat at the Awards ceremony. I give my tuxedo a quick dust down as this prize is in the bag. Stephen Fry stands behind the podium on stage and speaks into the microphone.

"And the winner of this year's Doug Morrell Outstanding Award for Literature goes to…"

Dramatic pause while he opens the envelope. I look behind me at the other novelists also up for the award. They don't stand a chance.

"Doug Morrell!" he shouts, "for the ninth year in a row! Well done, Doug, old chap!"

I knew it. I shake the hand of a few pointless well-wishers and hangers-on before shoving my way through the crowd. I wave indiscriminately at the press before climbing the steps to the stage.

"Congratulations, Doug," Stephen says, but I keep my distance in case he leans in for a kiss. Instead, I shake his hand in a manly fashion. "And here to present your award is your Auntie Eileen! And she wants to know would you like any sweets, Willy?"

Damn it, I nodded off again and missed half an hour of the live feed and now I'm starving. Perhaps I should have taken those damn sweets she was offering. Right now I'm tired and very hungry as I didn't eat dinner last night. And seeing as it's started to get light outside and Mum's still in bed, it looks like I won't get breakfast either.

I can't even concentrate on *Voyeur* as I'm too upset. I feel like my life's been turned upside down and there's nothing I can do about it. I haven't even been back into the lounge to look at the paper again – it's still lying on the floor where I threw it.

Finally I relent and pick up sheet after sheet of *The Star*, looking for the offending article. Maybe it'll look different in the cold light of day? I read it again, this time line by line.

On a roll – what does that mean? That's meaningless – simply tabloid-speak when they're looking to fill column inches. What has rolling got to do with a footballer or Donna?

After netting his first goal for Watford FC – Watford Football Club – now I don't claim to know much about the so-called "wonderful game", but I do know that Watford aren't exactly up there with Manchester United, Arsenal or Wigan.

...last Saturday, first division footballer Wayne Moore – he has a name like a chav – *20* – twenty years old? He's younger than she is! Something smells fishy here.

...has netted his very own reality TV girlfriend – typical of the press to lump Donna in with the reality TV crowd, conveniently forgetting all her other achievements when they're trying to belittle her.

Donna Trayhorn, 22 – I knew it. This story can't be right. Not only have they fabricated this entire romance to go with a picture of her standing next to him, but they've got her age wrong again – I know for a fact she's only twenty-one years old.

The pair were spotted canoodling in a trendy London bar over the weekend – I'd like more evidence of this. Where were they spotted canoodling, and by whom?

...and have been on a string of dates ever since – I doubt it. Donna is supposed to be promoting Game For You, not dating. This whole story is nothing but a pack of lies.

Feeling reinvigorated by this discovery I immediately post my findings on my message board – adding a comment warning people about the draconian moderators on the *Voyeur's* official site. Then I go to the shops as there are Sunday papers out there. I feel sure they will shed some light on Donna's true intentions.

You'd think that a celebrity romance would almost certainly make the front pages. Every little thing David Beckham and that failed singer do seems to be dissected by the world and his wife. However, I can't see Donna and that football bloke anywhere. In fact, until I catch sight of a bleary paparazzi shot of Donna's breasts cupped together in the back of a limo, I think she isn't in the papers at all.

There's not much written about them, but I suppose this is one of those occasions where a picture is worth a thousand words. At first I think the hands around Donna's breasts are her own until I notice the chav-like excessive sovereign rings that adorn the chunky fingers. They belong to Wayne. I look my love rival square in his gloating eyes as he sneers at me from behind Donna. I can see the smug smile on his face. What is he hoping for by doing this – an eight-page centre-spread in *Hello* magazine? He's using her, plain and simple – exploiting her good nature and playful ways to climb higher on the celebrity ladder. I'll bet he isn't even a particularly good footballer. That other article said he'd only scored one goal; how's that going to get him into the British football team?

Chapter 10: Understanding

A week later and I haven't been to work even though the holiday days I booked off have come to an end. I've come down with some sort of bug that prevents me from going in.

I haven't eaten much, and I've been throwing up a lot. I think I may have lost so much blood from my nose I may require a transfusion soon. The blood loss, combined with my lack of appetite, has been making me feel tired. I don't think I have the strength to load a van, let alone drive around London. Hannah has been constantly ringing me, but I'm not in the mood to speak to her. She didn't talk to Marcus like I told her to, so I guess we've nothing to say to each other. I've been watching *Voyeur* throughout the night. At least some of the contestants have perked up a bit and have started arguing, apart from Kat that is.

She's been the model of self-restraint throughout the entire show. It's funny: after I've watched her for a few days, I've almost completely forgotten about her hideously deformed eyebrows. But of course just when the public starts to like a contestant, the producers have to try and play God. She's barely been seen on the show for the last few days, and they're focusing on the possible relationship between thick Gemma and posh Cuthbert. Oh, and old man Paul was first evicted, just as I predicted. I should run one of these shows, I really should.

No one has yet got back to me about Donna and what's-his-name's relationship. If she wants to be used like that then I have no sympathy for her. You'd think that if she was going to embark on some high profile celebrity relationship, she'd choose someone worthy, someone who can help raise her profile, such as Brad Pitt or Robbie Williams.

I go online sometimes and find that some of the other members on my site have been discussing it, but I carefully delete any posts which mention that second-rate footballer.

Still no email from Donna and I check her official site for some form of public apology. I feel that after all we've been through I'll give her one last chance to redeem herself. So I email her official site again pointing out that this man is merely exploiting her for his own twisted gains and that a relationship such as this can only be self-destructive. I hope when she reads it, she thinks hard about my words.

However no sooner have I pressed the send button, when she suddenly appears online.

Donna_honey_girl: hey babe, sorry 4 not telling u personally

Steely_Doug9: donna? is that really u?

Donna_honey_girl: yeah its me hun, i read ur post on ur site, don't worry. im only doing this 4 the publicity

Steely_Doug9: u r? thank goodness, i knew that the press had blown it completely out of proportion

Donna_honey_girl: waynes a loser unlike u and i dont luv him, i luv u sweetie do u like my new song?

Steely_Doug9: totally! its amazing, were u thinking of me when u wrote it?

Donna_honey_girl: yeah, thats right, will u go out and buy 5000 copies 4 me baby?

Steely_Doug9: yes, certainly. anything u say.

Donna_honey_girl: thats so sweet. how can i ever repay u?

Steely_Doug9: mayb u could pick me up in ur limo and we could go out?

Donna_honey_girl: sure, but u know i cant sleep with u

Steely_Doug9: of course, ur promoting ur single. people need to believe ur either single or in a high profile relationship with that footballer

Donna_honey_girl: no, its because I'm shagging big daddy after he totally outbid u on ebay!

Donna_honey_girl has been blocked from your contact list.

Bloody hell, why doesn't he just piss off and leave me alone?

"Doug, glad you made it!" says Matt as his pin-headed frame sits opposite me in the pub.

"Are you going to buy me a drink?" I say, as it was he who suggested I come down to this grotty little hovel.

"Sure, when's it's calmed down – it's a bit busy up there," his tiny mouth wiggles. "It'll do you good to have a night out, what with Donna and everything."

"I don't want to talk about her!" I snap. "She's dead to me!"

"I know, it hurts, huh?" he rambles and I get the horrible feeling he's going to start talking about one of his past relationships. "Still, plenty more fish in the sea, yeah?"

"Hell, yeah," I almost splutter. Who does he think I am, some sort of loser who can't get a woman? "I've got more women after me than publishers!"

"That's the spirit!" he says, as he smacks me on the shoulder. If it wasn't for the fact he was about to buy me a drink, I'd punch his lights out for that grievous bodily harm. "So, who have you got your eye on – one of the girls at work?"

"Don't be stupid," I reply. "You know how weird that lot are around me."

"Oh, blimey, yeah," he mutters, as he covers his whole face with one hand. "I forgot about all that ugliness."

"If I'm going to start dating again – and that's a big if – it would have to be someone on my social scale," I point out.

"Right," he says, slowly. "Doug, do you mind if I ask you something?"

Yes, probably, but before I can answer, he asks anyway.

"Why is it so important to be famous?"

His blatant impertinence knocks me backwards and I'm too offended to reply. So, naturally, he goes on.

"I mean, once I read about Victoria Beckham and how she couldn't go out to the shops because of the paparazzi getting in her way!"

Lucky cow.

"I mean..." he goes on. "How could anyone actually want that? That sounds like hell to me! You wouldn't want that, would you?"

Yes. Yes, I would. I want that more than anything else in the world. I want my image to be splashed all over the papers and magazines so those evil shits who used to mock me at school will know they couldn't keep me down forever. I want my name to slowly seep back into their consciousness and I hope it burns their tongues when they speak it.

"No, I guess not," I reply.

"Doug," barked The Colonel as he arrived at the Secret Service's Head Office. "This is your new partner, Kitty-Kat."

Doug's eyes rolled over the figure of perfection standing in front of him. Her long slender legs, encased in a tight, but respectable green miniskirt, tapered up to her hourglass figure and bright yellow office jacket. Suddenly he found he couldn't even remember the name of that android whore.

"The name's Holster, Doug Holster," he said coolly.

"I know," she giggled. "I've heard all about your exploits. I've been so looking forward to working on you, really I have!"

"You're at the top of the queue, baby," he smiled graciously.

"Is it true how big your weapon is?" she said as she went so weak at the knees, he had to catch her in his strong arms.

"In five minutes you'll know all about it," he said as his manly mouth kissed hers.

"I'll step outside," said The Colonel respectfully. "Try not to disturb my paperwork too much."

I'm spending my time on *Voyeur's* official forums. The over-zealous moderators didn't notice me rejoin under a different username. I'm sticking up for Kat more and more as, after the initial cries of how attractive she is have died down, people have been saying she's boring. I disagree. For a start, most of her critics are female and therefore feel threatened by an attractive girl with a brain.

I've started to imagine what Kat will do once she wins *Voyeur*. I wonder what sort of platform it will give her to propel her to the next level of the celebrity ladder. I haven't heard her sing yet, but I'm sure any reputable studio could work around that.

I've decided that perhaps me and Kat are suited. She isn't as loud as Donna, but she has a quiet charm about her, and she's not that bad looking, nothing that a good going over with a pair of tweezers wouldn't sort out. I'm trying to imagine her on my arm attending an awards ceremony. How would she conduct herself while we chat to the critics about Shakespeare and Dickens?

As Kat naturally survived the first eviction, I decide to take a second week off work. Although I feel better and even have forced myself to eat, I want to be at full strength when I do return to work. I look up Kat's biography on the *Voyeur* site and find she's from Woking, just south west of London. She lives with her parents in a nice detached four-bedroom house, not like the old terraced dump Donna comes from. Driving down there to see her might pose a problem, unless I ask to transfer my drop-off area to somewhere a little further afield. Still, I have seven

115

more weeks to sort out the finer details, as I'm confident she'll win.

I don't feel like I'm doing anything wrong by contemplating seeing other people. It seems that Donna feels like an open relationship is the way forward, so what's good for the goose as they say.

I'm sure that with such angelic looks, Kat wouldn't find it hard to make her way into the papers and magazines. As I browse the publications, I find pictures and stories about Kat, which I tear out and put up in my room. I soon find space by relegating some of Donna's more trashy poses to the dustbin. One item in the snobby *Mail* mentions how this new crop of reality TV stars will spell the end for last season's batch. Perhaps there's a grain of truth in that? Donna only seems to have been able to cling on to fame by hanging off the arm of some Watford hooligan. I find two more pictures of "the happy couple" as the press has dubbed them, but I still don't like the way he's looking at me. I have a good mind to drive to Watford and give him a piece of my mind while he's training. He's not the relationship type. You can see it in his eyes. He'll use her then dump her and it'll be up to me to pick up the pieces. I've heard about the sordid activities footballers get up to: the ones who aren't being gay in the showers are out prowling countryside car parks for sex with strangers.

I also spy an item in the entertainment section about Jack Nicholson starring in no less than three upcoming indie films. It would have been nice if he'd let me know he had something lined up. My nose starts to feel damp inside. Then my mobile ringsg and I'm too flustered to check who it is before answering it.

"Listen, Doug?" Hannah snaps and I click the "off" button before stuffing the phone into a drawer. The evening edition of *Voyeur* will be starting soon.

Again, Kat steals every scene, for the little time the producers bother to show her. Under normal circumstances, I would send the programme makers a strongly worded email regarding how they were portraying the contestants. But seeing as most of my email addresses have now been banned by the fascist moderators at *Voyeur*, I think I'll bite my tongue for now.

The following morning when the live feed finishes, I go back to my computer and seriously start looking into the prospects of starting up a *Yahoo* group dedicated to Kat. It might not be a proper website, but I feel the need to communicate with people on my level. I want to talk to those who can see the witty and interesting girl whose true character is being stifled by the idiots she's been placed in the house with.

Unfortunately there's already a *Yahoo* group started by a strange man calling himself "Mr_Kiplings_Mistress", not to mention the *MSN* group about Kat started by "Neo". These must be kids with ridiculous names like that. I join both groups with the knowledge that they'll soon lose interest and offer me the post of moderator.

It's Wednesday and my home phone rings. As *Voyeur* is just beginning again, I consider not answering, but it could be a publisher begging to sign me up.

"Hi, Doug, it's Henry," a voice on the other end says.

"Yes?" I say feebly. I'm still not feeling great; I think I may be coming down with stress. I read in *Heat* magazine that signs of being under stress were constant tiredness and a highly pressurised job.

"How are you feeling?" he asks with false politeness. In other words he wants to know when I'm going to deliver his precious parcels.

"Not too good," I tell him. Fortunately he can't hear *Voyeur* on TV, as the contestants are obviously talking about drug taking, so the producers are courteously playing birdsong over the footage of Susie snorting a line of salt off the kitchen table.

"Oh, I'm sorry to hear that," he blatantly lies, "you take as long as you like off. We can handle things here."

I somehow doubt that.

"Do you reckon you'll be back by next week?" he asks.

"I'll try," I say. But I'm seriously thinking of booking a meeting with one of those stuck-up cows in Human Resources to let them know about the harassment I'm getting.

About the only thing that makes me want to get back to work is the fact that I know what a mess everything will be in when I finally do.

"Don't worry about your route, Doug," he goes on. I wasn't. "Matt's handling it in your absence."

Typical – Pinhead to the rescue.

"He's not using my van, is he?" I ask. The last time he used it, I found a half eaten sandwich on top of a picture of Donna in my glove compartment.

"Err, no." Henry replies, but he doesn't sound too sure. As I say a firm goodbye, I'm filled with a sudden urge to get back to work as soon as possible. But right now the birdsong has ended, so I think I'll just watch what they get up to until eight this evening.

Thursday morning and the nominations are in: Susie and Kat. I can't believe Kat is nominated again. Susie came as no surprise as she's been mouthing off for days, but what possible reason could anyone have for voting Kat out? Boring, apparently, but only because she's never allowed to blossom.

I'm straight on the home phone dialling and redialling the 0845 number to keep her inside as it's far too expensive to do it from my mobile. Sadly that's another good reason to return to work as I can use the phone in the loading bays.

I'm not happy about Kat being up for eviction, and my mood isn't made any better by Hannah bothering me again. I've only just turned on my mobile phone and she rings, supposedly to find out how I am.

"Look, I'm ill, okay?" I protest.

"Isn't that the truth!" she shouts. "Will you get it through your thick hea…"

I hang up. If she asks me why, I'll make up a completely plausible excuse. That's one of the benefits of being a writer – creativity comes easily. I'll say there was a spider on my leg and when I tried to brush it off, I accidentally hit the call-end button.

It's now half past seven on Friday morning. I've been up all night watching the contestants celebrate fat Bertha's birthday: they gave her a cake – like she needed one. Now the housemates have been asleep for three hours, but I know the show's producers won't let them lie in much after ten. This means I can go into work and make a few phone calls to save Kat from eviction.

I arrive in the loading bays slightly before eight and I'm starving as Mum didn't cook breakfast. I thought the drivers on early shifts would already be loaded up and out, but to my amazement and horror, Matt is still here.

"Doug?" he stutters, "I thought you were ill?"

"I am," I point out. "I just came to get something out of my cab."

I notice my van is parked at the wrong angle. I open the door to see Matt's flask inside. I also spot dried up rings on the dashboard where he must have left cups. He comes over, still looking guilty.

"I see you've been given my van?" I say.

"Yeah, well, seeing as you weren't in, and it is one of the biggest," he replies, like size actually matters.

"I've been here the longest. Why shouldn't I have the biggest van?" I ask, but he doesn't reply and still looks furtive.

"How are you getting on without Donna?" he asks as he can't look me in the eye.

"I don't want to talk about that harlot!" I inform him and I tell him where to go. So he leaves his copy of *The Sun* and slinks off. I take the opportunity to use the loading bay's phone to make sure Kat stays in the house. I have to laugh to myself as I press the redial button for the fiftieth time when I read a most interesting article. It has a picture of that arse Wayne Moore leaving Hatfield Magistrates Court after being caught in possession of a gram of class A drugs.

I suppose I still feel for Donna during this difficult time as I knew this day would come. I said before he'd lead her down murky paths that would distract her from her true calling, but did she listen? I sent her more than one email explaining what would happen if she got mixed up with him, but again, nothing. Part of me wants to drive to Gloria's house and see if she's there, but does Donna deserve my shoulder to cry on after what she's put me through?

I stop redialling before the first batch of drivers returns at ten and leave the warehouse. I guess the housemates will be getting up about now and I should be getting home.

Saturday morning comes and I'm feeling a lot happier after saving Kat from the chop last night. The presenters Ray and Ford said it was close, but I don't believe them – they always say that to get more people to vote. Susie was thrown out of the *Voyeur* house and suitably booed like all the other evicted contestants.

"Hello, my darling," I say to Kat when she appears on the screen.

I notice she's started giving me the eye. I can tell she's interested by the way she keeps looking at me.

"Hiya!" she once said after I'd said hello to her at the beginning of an episode.

A little shudder almost ran down my spine when she answered me.

"You heard me!" I exclaimed.

"Yeah," she giggled, before adding: "I'd love a glass of juice."

"I'd like a glass of juice too!" I shouted. That really was uncanny how she knew I was just about to get a drink. It's little touches like that which forge a relationship.

The live feed finishes at eight then resumes at ten, but the moment it comes back on, my mobile rings. I wasn't going to answer it, but I don't want Mum to get it and put off a potential publisher.

"Yes?" I say into my mobile.

"Look, Doug, we need to talk..." says Hannah's voice on the other end.

What does she want this time – money, a lift somewhere, or just more clothes?

"...I want you to stop calling me and..."

I hang up. The bloody cheek: asking me to stop calling her by calling me. I don't need her anyway, I have Kat now. I can't wait to see her face when I stride into the Rat and Parrot in a few weeks time with the winner of *Voyeur* on my arm. I feel justifiably proud of sticking it to Hannah, and treat myself to a stroll down the shops to pick up today's papers.

"My Nights of Passion with Kit-Kat!" greets me on the front of *The Sun*.

Some loser has only gone and sold his story about an alleged affair with Kat. I stare at his ugly mug on the front page as he pretends to look sorry for himself. He's claiming that he was her secret boyfriend and she had the name "Kit-Kat". This was apparently due to her being able to do something involving four fingers, but I'm not quite sure what he means by that as we all have four fingers on each hand.

I know he's talking nonsense as I've read her contestant profile and she'd clearly stated "single" by "relationship status". He claims that she's only done that to try and win "the single male vote". Now, I would have said he was simply being bitter because either she never had anything to do with him, turned him down, or just plain dumped him. Then I turn the page and see the photos.

I worry about the state of women today and how they'll let themselves be degraded by unscrupulous men. He's filmed them engaging in what I believe the press refer to as "sex acts" in the back of a boat while they were on holiday in Spain.

I look at her naked breasts staring back at me as cheap wine drips down her chin. Is this really the kind of girl I could take to an evening of literary awards? A top author like me standing next to someone who's been filmed making improper use of a life ring?

I feel gutted. I don't know why I bother with women in the first place – look what happened to John Lennon once Yoko got her claws into him. I should concentrate on my career and to hell with the lot of them.

"So, Doug," Jonathan Ross begins as I make myself comfortable on his chat show sofa. "What's a handsome guy like you doing staying single all this time?"

"I'm leaving all the girls for you," I quip and the audience rolls around in fits of laughter.

"Well, that's very nice of you, but seriously, let me run some names by you: Jennifer Aniston, Julia Roberts, Halle Berry and Donna Trayhorn. Just a handful of the beautiful ladies you've been linked to, so why did you turn them all down?"

"None of them really fitted the bill to be honest," I muse. "Most women seem to be impressed by drug taking footballers – and that's just not me. Either that or they have so little character judgement they'll indulge in sordid role-play with a man so shallow he'll sell their story at the first given opportunity."

"But Doug – what about Julia Roberts?" asks Jonathan as the screen behind him changes to those paparazzi shots of me throwing the blubbering actress out of my London bachelor pad.

"She's a rotten cook," I state.

"Say no more," he replies with a nod.

"I suppose I'm just a guy who's married to his career," I say, to which the audience respectfully applauds.

"And what a career it's been," he adds, clearly green with envy.

"Plus I look after my elderly mother in between crossing back and forth to Hollywood," I add. "I don't know where she'd be without me."

"I don't know where any of us would be," he goes on with a sigh, while he reflects on my colossal accomplishments. "Do you think you'll ever find Miss Right?"

"I could have married my childhood sweetheart – Hannah Mathews, but she went all weird on me. In fact, I think I'd better call her and find out."

From my bedroom, I ring her mobile, but in typical contrary style, she's switched it off. That annoys me as it isn't like she's at work; she's probably only shopping – again. I wait a while and compose a suitable message to leave on her answering service.

"Hi, this is Hannah. Please leave a message after the tone and I'll get back to you."

"Yeah, hi, Hannah, it's Doug – Doug Morrell," I say to her machine. "Look I'm – I'm sorry about the other day and how

123

you felt you needed to hang up on me. And has Marcus come back to you yet about the tickets? Could you let me know as I can make it to the eviction on Friday. Thanks, bye."

Of course what with Kat's antics, I now feel I have every right to boo her when she comes out, if I bother to show up. I imagine how low she'll feel when she's evicted from *Voyeur* and I haven't turned out for her interview. If Marcus does get me the tickets, I can sell them on eBay.

I contemplate switching on *Voyeur*, but decide against it. This lot of fame-seeking parasites will have to do without my viewing figures for today.

I check my phone, but Hannah still hasn't got back to me. I really am at a bit of a loss as to what to do. What do other people do on a Saturday?

I've banned everyone I can on my site for talking about that leech Donna's got stuck on her. I'm not about to give them any more publicity by uploading their photos, and I certainly don't feel like sticking up for that hairy-eyed freak Kat on the *Voyeur* message boards.

The television in the corner of the lounge looks different: all dull and lifeless without the birdsong and expletive-bleeping of *Voyeur's* live feed.

Hannah still hasn't rung me back by the evening. In the meantime I check my emails, just in case there's a fault on her phone and she's mailed me instead. She hasn't.

Also there's nothing from Donna. She's obviously too busy lusting after that junkie to read any of my wake-up calls.

I do however have an email from a bloke who owns the rights to www.voyeurkatisfit.co.uk. I forgot I'd emailed him asking to buy it and, although the price he's asking is reasonable, there's no way I'm going to help that mono-browed slapper any more. I tell him what he can do with his domain name.

Now it's Sunday and neither Hannah, nor Donna have got back to me. I sometimes wonder why I bother with women who don't understand me.

Chapter 11: Buses

Monday morning comes and I return to work. My only fear is that Mum will touch the video, as I'm recording the whole of *Voyeur's* live feed. Not that I'm going to watch it on principle, but I thought I'd better just in case I need to know something in an emergency.

I checked my email before arriving at the depot early, but found nothing from either woman. I knew Matt wouldn't be in yet and I was going to take this opportunity to throw his rubbish out of my van before loading up. It's not my fault if his ipod breaks when it hits the floor.

As I near my van I see two men in suits walking away and heading upstairs to the offices. I don't like the look of them and keep watching in case they come back.

"Oh, you're back," a horrible voice yells across the depot. "We thought you'd left us for Hollywood!"

"They haven't sent me the air fare yet," I reply as Frank lumbers up dragging his knuckles on the ground.

"You going to load up, or what?" he says as he rudely leans over my shoulder into my empty van. "Or can't you fit any parcels in with all that Donna Trayhorn porn in there?"

"It's not porn!" I remind him as I remove a picture of Donna's face on the body of a female elf in a leather bikini waving a broadsword at an Orc, "Since when was this porn?"

Frank uses both brain cells to scrutinise the high-art mock-up of Donna's epic struggle against the media – represented by General Leerious: high commander of the Black Claw armies.

"Which one's Donna?" he asks.

"Oh, for crying out loud!" I shout, realising I am dealing with the stupidest man alive. "She's the female one! Since when did she have green skin and horns?"

I watch as my cutting put-down sinks into his tiny mind. His mouth twitches uncontrollably and I honestly think he's about to cry. But I don't have time to stand here explaining what a real woman looks like to this loser.

"I'm not talking to you," I say as I snatch the artwork from his dirty fingers.

"What was that?" he replies.

"I said I'm not talking to you!" I yell, as he finds it impossible to comprehend.

"Pardon?" he says.

"Look, I know you're finding this very hard," I say, with a sigh. "But I'm not talking to you."

"So, what are you doing now then?" he asks, but all I can do is shake my head. Even some of his own tribe are laughing at his stupidity.

"I'm telling you I'm not talking to you," I say, almost smiling at his lack of brainpower.

"Okay, that's cool," he says, taking it better than I expected. "I don't blame you – careless talk and all that."

He turns and walks away.

"Hang on!" I shout after him, sticking to words of one syllable. "What do you mean, careless talk?"

"I think…" he begins, before trailing off, "I heard someone say those two men in suits were literary agents. Apparently they were looking for something in your van, but couldn't find it. Anyway, I thought you weren't talking to me?"

"Never mind that," I snap. "What do you mean?"

"Oh, nothing," he muses. "It's just the less I know about all your projects, the less I can tell anyone. You saw them, didn't you? They were looking through your van and asking questions about your manuscript."

Oh, my god, they've found me. I'll bet Big_Daddy69 put them on to me. Did I tell him I was writing a film? No, surely I wouldn't have been so careless. Perhaps they've been monitoring my emails and intercepted the scenes I sent to Jack Nicholson? That would explain why he never got back to me!

"Doug?" I hear, and turn to see Frank looking at me. "You all right, mate? You've gone white as a sheet! And that's one hell of a twitch you've developed!"

Work drags by. It's eleven o'clock and I'm getting some old fart to sign the electronic delivery slip with his jittery hand. I look down at the squiggle that's supposed to pass for his signature. I don't know why Henry is so obsessed with getting them to sign for their goods as I could have signed it for him.

This job is doing my head in, so I park up in a local NCP and go to an Internet café in case I've got email waiting. I haven't, but at least I can claim back the five pounds parking fee from work that the crooks in the NCP charged me to leave my van in their smelly, graffiti-clad dump.

I have more drops to do, but I can't be bothered. I dump each package outside what is probably the house or flat door and make my own mark on the computer screen. I sit in my cab and phone Hannah. I'll bet she loves this – me doing all the chasing.

It's off again. I don't see why she can't keep it on during lesson times. I phone back and tell her answerphone how immature I think she's being by ignoring my calls.

I'm on my way back to the depot when my phone goes. I look at the screen to see who it is, but I don't recognise the number, so I pull over and answer.

"Hello, Doug?" Hannah's quivery voice says on the other end. I knew she'd come crawling back eventually.

"What?" I reply and she goes on to tell me how she hadn't had time for us recently because she's been visiting her grandparents in Yarmouth. Her granny apparently had a funny turn when she choked on a pomegranate. Then her granddad got run over by a Salvation Army ambulance when it came to help.

It was something like that anyway as I gave up listening pretty quickly. But the upshot is she doesn't want me to contact her for a while during these apparently traumatic times.

We part on good terms and I decide I should play the part of dutiful boyfriend by saying how sorry I am.

"I accept your apology," I say maturely. "I'm very sorry for your loss. And sorry about earlier, okay? I really am sorry, but at the end of the day, it was your fault."

Hannah must have gone through a tunnel as her phone cut out. She's probably driving up to Yarmouth to watch her grandparents lie in a hospital bed. I would offer to come, but I hate hospitals – too many people lazing around feeling sorry for themselves and living off taxpayers' money. If I have a spare moment, I'll pick up some leaflets from the doctor on euthanasia and drop them through her door.

I return to the depot and catch Matt drooling all over a creature in a short skirt in the middle of the loading bay. I speed up, but unfortunately they see me coming and jump out the way. I ignore the dirty look the one in make-up gives me. If people insist on standing where vans drive, what do they expect?

She leaves quickly and doesn't even say hello. I want to leave too, but everyone's best buddy Matt comes fawning round me. It must pain him to realise that not everyone thinks he's wonderful.

"All right, mate?" is his usual opening gambit. "How's life?"

"Fine," I reply as I get ready to leave.

"Heard anything from Donna?" he asks in a strange tone.

"I think that's between me and her, don't you?" I snap at his blatant nosiness.

"Yeah, I'm sorry," he says. And so he should be. "I see she's single again?"

129

I speed to the newsagent and buy up what's left of today's papers and go straight to *The Daily Star*. Matt, being the classy sort, reads that rag and had seen a story inside about Donna. I turn straight to the entertainment section and spot a paragraph aptly titled "Life's Loser". It reads:

You know you're down on your luck when you get dumped by an ex-reality TV star. After scoring his first goal for his club, the success must have gone to Wayne Moore's head, not only did he get a suspended sentence for possession of a class A drug, but media whore Donna Trayhorn has only gone and chucked him. Their agents both say the split was amicable, but my sources tell me that it was her who initiated the break up.

She's seen my email! There's no other explanation for it – she's read what I had to say and taken it to heart. I go straight home to email her back and say what a brave and courageous decision she's made. I feel I should let her know that I'm not bitter and that I still have room in my life for her, but only if she's willing to make sacrifices.

On my first draft, I concentrate on her recent diversion from her career. For example, if she was one day going to crack Hollywood, having parts of her body fondled in public was not going attract Steven Speilberg, Quentin Tarrintino or Uwe Boll. However, after proof-reading my initial words, I feel I dwelt too much on the physical aspect of her infidelity. She is an attractive girl and I'm not unreasonable enough to realise that other men find her desirable. But if she wishes to attract the male record-buying public, it may be beneficial to act like she's single, at least until she's cracked the US market.

I'm pleased with the second draft. I feel I've suitably put my point across in a firm, yet fair manner. I had to make sure that she knew I wasn't happy about what she did, yet I felt we

130

could still progress. As I'm about to send it, my mobile goes off: it's Hannah, so I don't answer it.

As the weeks go by I continue to comment on *Voyeur*. The bird with the funny eyebrows seems to be surviving a few evictions, as I said she would. I put it down to manipulative editing, plus the fact her sister sold a story to the press denying whatever it was a couple of blokes had claimed she had gotten up to. When I get to the studio to go on *Voyeur Uncovered*, I'm ushered to the front of the audience to sit opposite Ray and Ford.

"The only reason she's still in the house, is because she's got lucky. The viewers obviously still have room in their hearts for a sympathy vote."

The crowd in the studio applauds my intuitiveness.

"You know, mate," Ray says, before turning to Ford, "I've never thought of that, have you?"

"No way, mate," he replies, before turning back to me. "That's a fascinating insight, Doug. Do go on."

"Well, Ray," I begin, then realise I've got the two cockney scamps mixed up again. "The problem with people like Kat, and today's youth in general, is that they're taught to want fame and fortune without having the necessary talent to accomplish their deluded goals."

This time I get a cheer from the audience. While the camera isn't on me, I look round at some of the nicer girls among them, I was sure one of them keeps giving me the eye. I turn and see her touch her hair, which as everyone knows, is a sure sign that she's trying to make herself look attractive for me. What a shame I'm taken.

"Don't stop, Doug," says Ford, desperate for me to carry on.

"Well, it's just youngsters expect to be able to run riot through their teenage years – take as many drugs as they like, sleep with the world and his wife – then wonder why these stories come back to haunt them when they enter the public domain."

I was referring to the headlines of debauchery on the massive screen above us.

"You see," I muse, while keeping Ray, Ford and the crowd on the edge of their seats. "I'm a writer, and have been ever since I can remember. And, like many writers, have suffered at the hands of people who didn't understand my work. First it was the other kids at school…"

The audience lets out a collective "aw" in support, but I'm not looking for sympathy, I'm here to enlighten.

"Thank you, thank you," I say. "But you see, I ignored them and one by one they gave up throwing things at me through the library window."

"You deserve a medal for what you must have been through," says Ford as he puts his hand on my knee. I move my leg away as I've always considered that these two were a little bit too friendly with each other. I decide to turn the topic of conversation from me to *Voyeur*.

"I know," I say with a sigh. "But as I've said before on almost every message board I'm not banned from, Kat is not, and will not ever be a patch on Donna Trayhorn. Look at everything Donna's managed to achieve since leaving the show. Does Kat really deserve to win?"

"Let's ask the audience," Ray says, turning to the crowd.

A collective "no, Doug", is the answer, proving my point entirely.

"And does she have what it takes to stay in the public eye for the long run?" I add.

Again, Ray and Ford open it up to the crowd, who back me up wholeheartedly.

132

"All she does is flirt with Max," I continue. "I mean, is he really what society considers attractive? The man's eyes are too far apart and he has facial bum fluff masquerading as a goatee beard. It makes him look like the love child of Thunderbird puppet and an Oompa Loompa!"

The crowd roars with laughter as I'm on fine form.

"I think we can all see that now, Doug," says Ray, with a nod.

"If only Kat was more like Donna, eh?" adds Ford.

"And cut!" shouts the director, before I can steer the conversation rightfully on to the love my life. Pity, it was just getting interesting.

Now the cameras are temporarily off, I overhear a couple of girls in short skirts and skimpy tops pointing at me and giggling. Part of me wants to go over there, but before I can, Ray turns to me.

"You know, Doug," he says. "We could do with a straight-talking man-of-the-people on our team. This series of *Voyeur* ends on Friday, but another one is due to start in a few weeks; would you want to be a regular feature on the show?"

All my life I've known that when I finally got inside Metropol, they'd see how much of an asset I could be. I'm about to answer "yes, of course I will" when a warty voice from behind my right shoulder distracts me.

"Hello, handsome," it says.

I'm sure it's that girl who keeps giving me the eye. I turn to look, but find Auntie Eileen has her face pressed right up against mine.

"No, Auntie Eileen!" I shout. "Not now! Stop touching me!"

She bursts into fits of deep throaty laughter and as I recoil, I realise it's not Auntie Eileen at all, but Frank. His ugly mug is

133

leering in through my cab's windscreen while I'm parked outside the newsagents.

"Oh, Doug," he says, with a laugh. "You've called me a lot of things in my time, but never auntie! What the hell are you doing, sitting here all morning?"

"I'm having my lunch!" I shout, before rolling up the window.

"For two hours?" he says through the glass. "I drove past here at eleven o'clock and you were parked up looking at your women's mags. Don't you have deliveries to make?"

I ignore his question and drive off.

"Why do I even bother with this job?" I ask myself as I cruise the streets. I should just be allowed to stay at home and write, like I did throughout my teenage years. That had the added bonus of racking up a completely scandal-free existence. I can't wait for those reptile-like journalists to start trying to dig up dirt on me. They won't be able to find a single ex for a kiss and tell double-page spread. I'm sure there'll be a few girls who I've bumped into along the way who will exaggerate our relationships for financial gain, but they'll soon pipe down when my lawyer gets hold of them. If the so-called celebrities of today truly wanted fame and fortune, they should have lead better lives when they were young.

I take the long route to my next drop as I want to pass through "Dukes Way". It's a long road filled with five-or six-bedroom mansions, one of which even has a swimming pool. I like to check for "For Sale" signs outside in case I want one.

I return home to find a rather nasty email from Metropol Industries waiting for me. It says something about my IP address being logged and if I rejoin their forums once more, I will be "reported". Who to, they don't say. But I don't have time for their idle threats, just because they know I'm right when I say that this year's contestants aren't a patch on Donna.

I still haven't got an email back from her and I can only assume she's chewing over the pages of my previous correspondence – that and promoting her new single. I haven't heard Game For You on a single radio station for nearly three weeks now, and I've been listening constantly.

I heard through the grapevine at work that Hannah's grandma took a turn for the worst the other day and died. I'm sure she would have wanted me there, but I don't like funerals, so I've had my phone off all week. I left a message on her answerphone to comfort her. I mentioned that if an old person is ill, they wouldn't want to be hanging around upsetting people by becoming a burden, they'd want it to be over and done with.

Then *Voyeur* finished and Kat won. I didn't bother watching much of the live final, as I was too overjoyed when Donna got back to me:

Hi Doug Morrell,
Subject: Greetings from Donna Trayhorn!
You asked to be notified with the latest news from my official site and I wanted to send my love to you and all my fans to thank you for your support over this past year.
It's been a hectic time for me what with promoting my upcoming single "Game For You", but I'm pleased to say three different versions will all hit the shops on Friday 16th June, hope you all help me out and buy a copy!
I'm currently taking a short break in the south of France, enjoying the sun, and working on a few projects, which I look forward to sharing with you in the not too distant future.
Much love,
Donna xxx

Doug Holster returns to his country mansion after a hard day's killing terrorists. The only thing that goes through his head is how much Archers to put in his lemonade, but as he nears the front door of his colossal mansion, his hawk-like eyes open wide. His front door is ajar – someone is inside!

He draws his twin pistols and breaks the front doors down in a single kick, before somersaulting through the entrance hall and taking up defensive positioning behind an antique vase the Queen gave him. His finely tuned nostrils twitch as he picks up the smell of a roast coming from his kitchen. The servants were all in bed. Who could it be boiling a turkey in his kitchen at gone midnight?

With cat-like finesse he tiptoes down the corridor and blasts open the kitchen door with his guns. As bullets bounce off saucepans, playing a tune that sounds like God Save the Queen, Doug flies through the air landing between the Sainsburys carrier bags.

"Ms Trayhorn!" he exclaims as he sees his fallen love, Donna. She's wearing one of his shirts and little else while she cooks his midnight meat.

"Oh, Doug," she whimpers as she falls into his muscular arms. "I've missed you and your thick head of hair so much!"

"But — you're dead," he cries. "How can this be?"

"No," she sobs. "Doctor Death cloned me from my DNA, then wrapped it around a cyborg endoskeleton and sent it back through time to kill you!"

"I knew it," Doug snarls as he held her quivering frame tightly. "Doctor Death will die!"

I'm delighted Donna's alive and I feel like I have something to live for again. Also three versions of Game For You are about to be released and she has asked for my assistance personally. I'm going to make it my mission to buy as many copies as I can to help her get to number one.

I've come to the conclusion women are like buses: one minute there's not one in sight, then three come along at once. From the clip I did see of *Voyeur's* live final, I was sure Kat was trying to patch things up between us by giving me the eye again.

But Miss Eyebrows will have to find some other mug to leech off. I'm far too busy now Donna has publicly renounced her misguided ways and looks like she's taking things seriously again. It's just a shame my life is once again marred by Hannah's constant phoning. I haven't answered any of her most recent calls. Why should I? She never bothered getting me tickets to *Voyeur*.

Chapter 12: Nasty Donuts

Voyeur is over and I feel like something is missing in my life. If it wasn't for Donna's single being released soon, I really don't know what I'd do.

I've been thinking of all the seasons of *Voyeur* that have come and gone, including the Celebrity ones, and more than ever I realise just how bad this one was.

During her exit interview Kat said she wanted to be an "ambassador for youth". I can only hope that children all over the world don't aspire to be like her. She is the textbook example that you can now be famous without brains or endowment. Follow your dreams; forget your talent.

"Let me explain why she shouldn't have won."

"Mate, I've really got to go," says the seventeen-year-old in a boiler suit as he shuts my cupboard door. "I've got three more house calls to make before midday. I've got your electricity readings. Now, if you'd just give me my torch back, I'll be on my way."

I hand the rude meter reader his precious torch and allow him to leave my flat. And to think he had the nerve to claim to be a fan of *Voyeur*. That's the problem with society: they'd rather accept things at face value than discuss what's wrong with our culture.

"Kat's vain, overconfident and shallow. If this girl was a chocolate she'd probably eat herself. What's sexy about a girl who spent most of her time lazing around on a sofa that was almost as orange as her skin? She had the emotional depth of a puddle!"

"Who's Kat?" says the old crone.

138

Old people shouldn't be allowed to live on their own once they get senile. I get her to sign my portable computer screen for her parcel and leave.

"When Bertha asked Kat what her best features were she replied: my flat stomach. Talk about rubbing it in, just because Bertha's the size of a house, doesn't mean you have to draw attention to it twenty-four hours a day. The fat bird hid it well, but I could tell she was mortified."

I wait for Mum to answer, but when I turn round, I see that she's snuck out of the room when I was trying to index my recorded episodes of *Voyeur*.

"So, do you think she deserved to win the show?" I ask.

"Oh, it's all fixed anyway," laughs the security guard.

"You what?" I reply, taking a step back.

Then a limousine drives up to the front of Metropol Towers and I'm forced to step back from the main gate to allow it through. I watch as the gates slide open effortlessly and it heads towards the two shining black towers dominating the London skyline. One day, I'm going to be in one of those limos heading through these gates.

"Who was that?" I ask the man guarding Metropol's mammoth car park.

"Some glamour model," he says as he presses the button to make them glide closed, shutting me and him on the outside.

"Oh, so what was that about *Voyeur* being rigged?"

"Christ, I thought everyone knew," he replies. "The producers pick a winner before the programme's even started! Don't you read the papers?"

I'm shocked. How can a Metropol employee actually say such a thing? Talk about biting the hand that feeds you.

"Look, mate," he goes on. "It's Saturday night and I'm getting paid to be here. What are you hanging round for?"

"I told you," I say to him again. "I'm waiting to see if Donna Trayhorn turns up."

"Who?"

Cue the detailed explanation of Donna's contribution to popular culture and society.

"Oh, her," he says as the penny drops. "She hasn't been round for ages. I didn't even think we were representing her any more."

"Well, you are," I say through gritted teeth. "So, do you think they fixed it so that Kat won?"

"Wouldn't surprise me," he says with a shrug.

That would certainly explain a lot. I'll bet she slept with every producer just to win. Thinking back to her audition tape, she did say how well she gets on with people. I must be the only one who can read between the lines. No wonder she also said she stood a good chance of winning in week five.

"I think her and Matt would get on well."

"Who's Matt?" asks the guard.

"An idiot I work with," I explain. "Would you believe he's so stupid, he thought Blaze was going to win. Could you imagine if he met Kat? There isn't a room big enough to fit both their colossal egos in at once!"

"You know, I really think Donna isn't going to show tonight," says the hardworking guard. "I guess you should be getting along now, yeah?"

"No, no, I haven't got anywhere else to be," I tell him. "How intellectually challenged was Kat? Or should I say – as thick as a brick? Did you see the episode when she said 'it don't matter' as opposed to 'it doesn't matter'? Plus she thought the 'K' on her National Insurance card stood for 'Kat'!"

"I didn't see that one," he mumbles as another car drives in.

"Oh, I thought you said you never missed it?"

"Well – er – I meant I only saw a few of the shows," he replies.

"I've got them all on video, if you want to borrow any?" I say, ready to educate the man on what he missed. "Have you ever been to my website?"

"No. Look, I really better be getting on now."

We look down the road, but there are no other cars coming towards the main gates.

"What time does your shift finish?" I ask.

"Not soon enough," he says, with a tired sigh.

"I know what you mean, my job drags too," I laugh. We really are two of a kind. "I'll bet you couldn't believe the press claimed she was the only nice girl in the house. They must have been watching an entirely different show to us! They obviously didn't see her tactical behaviour by suddenly becoming all chummy with Cuthbert, simply because he survived an eviction. And that's the sort of person who wants to be an Ambassador for Youth!"

The guard mumbles something into his radio and I realise I don't even know his name.

"My name's Morrell," I say. "Doug Morrell – author and media commentator – did I mention I have my own website?"

"Yes!" he shouts excitedly.

"Would you like the URL?" I ask. "Have you got some paper and a pen?"

"No," he says as he desperately looks up and down the perimeter fence – ever vigilant for danger.

"What about that notepad in your booth?"

"That's for company notes only," he says, slowly. "I'm not allowed – err – to write anything personal on it – the management wouldn't like it, you know what I mean?"

I knew exactly what he meant. He too must have someone like Henry constantly breathing down his neck.

"Sorry, I didn't catch your name?" I ask.

"John," he answers, quickly.

"John?" I query. "But your badge says Karl?"

"Oh err yeah, right – management hasn't got round to getting me one with my real name on it yet."

Typical, he's like the brother I always wanted, as opposed to the one I never speak to.

"Do you want to go for a drink later?" I ask.

"Lenny!" he shouts, and I see a couple of other security staff walking towards us through the car park. John then turns to me. "Sorry, mate, I've got to go and – err – check out the studios."

"No problem," I say. "Can I come?"

"I'm afraid not."

"Oh, right," I say disappointedly. "When's your next shift?"

"I don't normally work here, I'm normally somewhere else."

"Fair enough," I say, with a nod. I'll bet the poor guy doesn't know where he is from one day to the next with middle management making the rules. "Do you want my phone number?"

"I'll get it off your website," he says as he hurries off and the two other guards take his place.

"Right you are," I shout after him. "Have a good evening, John!"

"Hi there," I say to Lenny and his friend. "My name's Morrell, Doug Morrell – writer and media commentator."

"Yes, we know," exclaims Lenny, with delight. Yes, that's right, I've seen him before – we're old friends. "You're round here all the time, now fuck off!"

I can't believe it's Saturday night and I'm forced to spend the evening in my car. I have to park more than a hundred yards away from Metropol's main entrance otherwise those two Nazis said they'd call the police and have me done for loitering.

I tried to get them to call John back, but they said he'd "died suddenly after being eaten by a giant manatee". Lying gits. Then when I tried giving them my business card to pass on to him, they said that they had enough toilet paper and if I tried to throw one over the fence again I'd be charged with littering.

So I sit in my car in looking at a sleazy photo shoot with Kat in *Nuts* magazine. And she still hasn't bothered to pluck her eyebrows. This shoot should have been for Donna.

Now, I dream about what Donna got up to in France. I know she's back as I've seen a photo of her falling out of a taxi outside Kudos in Leicester Square. That's the third day in a row she's made the press. Yesterday she was in the back of a limo outside Ethos in Camden, and the day before there was one of the those dreadful "up-skirt" paparazzi shots of her thong, taken outside Bar Maxims in Soho. I'm glad she's getting noticed again, especially in the face of such adversity from the lesser deserving "celebrities".

Sadly, the press are so blinkered that they only print positive stories about the latest contestants. When they mention Donna, they claim she's "all washed up". But it's not long before her single comes out and they do say the darkest hours are before dawn.

A few days later and I hear Hannah is home, but I haven't seen her yet. She doesn't know I've taken a couple of extra days holiday. It's good to take a break as somehow I don't feel rested from my weeks off work. Now I can finally get away from the pressures of the job and spend some quality time with those around me. I expect when some people book time off work, all they do is lie around in bed all day, but not me. I was up at seven this morning to post my application for *Top of the Pops*.

I meet the postman by the box and hand him the envelope, making sure he doesn't fold it when he puts it in his sack. I always like my applications to arrive in mint condition, even making sure I sprayed a trace of Old Spice on the paper for when Donna opens it. No wonder she hasn't been home recently – she's been doing a lot of work for charity. Apparently, she's going to donate ten per cent of her single's profits to a "worthy cause" – as far as I know she hasn't said which, but you can bet it's not some fly-by-night charity who only gives money to foreigners.

I can't wait to be in the crowd and cheer her on. At least now I know why she was going out with Wayne. It's a well-known fact that celebrities often fake relationships when they've got a product to plug. Look at Tom Cruise – he even went as far as to get someone pregnant to promote *War of the Worlds*.

I've been sitting outside Donna's mum's place for nearly three hours now. I know Gloria's in there as her friends keep coming and going every hour. Hopefully I didn't miss Donna arriving when I popped round to the corner shop to get some donuts.

I reckon it's only a matter of time before she comes home to see her mum before going on tour. I've already called the big venues, not that they were much help. Wembley Stadium refused to let me know when she'd be playing there. The Birmingham NEC wasn't much better – they simply told me to "ring back at a later date", and the Milton Keynes Bowl told me to "please stop calling" and then hung up.

It's gone midday and I've already eaten an entire bag of donuts. I suppose I could hop across the road and get some more. I could be here a long time.

I return to my van as quickly as possible with two more bags. Luckily no limo passed me on the way there and back.

Another one of her mum's friends leaves, but I don't take his picture as I've got an entire online folder dedicated to "friends of the family".

Doug Holster pulled up outside Ms Trayhorn's stylish Acton apartment. As he looked up at her bedroom window, a wry smile crept across his face as he saw her ceiling fan gently rotating through the window. He knew that fan well. He'd helped her put it up when she moved in.

As the delectable Ms Trayhorn was undoubtedly up there making herself even more attractive for him, he thought he would give her an extra treat. As he pressed the button on his dashboard next to the one marked "Missile," a mirror descended and he ran his fingers through his thick black locks of manly hair.

"Damn that oriental hit man," he hissed as the mirror revealed more than he bargained for. Although his hair was looking immaculate and thick, he realised that while decapitating a henchman outside Costcutters, he now had blood down his tuxedo.

Typical – you bite into your donut and the jam oozes out of the other end and goes all down your front. I'd better go easy on these donuts as I've already had two out of this bag. My mobile rings and I can see by the readout that it's a transmission from Death Island. They'd better not be planning to take over the world on my day off. I switch the radio on to mask their signal.

"Hello?" I shout into my phone while some dismal track by Westlife blares out. "Sorry, it's a bit noisy here! I'm in the pub!"

"Doug? It's Doctor Death," announces Henry, typically unaware I knew it was him, thanks to his name coming up on my phone. "How the devil are you?"

145

Talk of the devil more like. I dare you to ask me to meet you on top of the abandoned cathedral for the final showdown today of all days. Even if you are offering double time.

"Fine, bit busy right now," I shout back over the fat five's awful rendition of Uptown Girl.

"So I can hear – sounds like quite a party?" he cackles.

"Yeah, you wouldn't believe it, sorry, one moment – mine's a pint please, Cheryl – sorry about that, just getting another round in. You don't want me to work, do you?"

"No, Mr Morrell, I want you to die!" he screams, before adding, "well, I was going to ask, but I get the impression you're in no fit state to drive!"

Doug Holster saves the world yet again.

"Doug?" he goes on. "Which pub are you in, exactly?"

A true agent knows never to reveal his location to his nemesis. Why doesn't he just ask me to jump into a pit of mutated scorpions?

"The King's Nose," I say, quickly, throwing him completely off the scent. "Why?"

"Oh, nothing, I thought it sounded like Chiltern FM that's all."

What? Oh, shit, the bloody adverts have come on.

"Was that Linda Barker I just heard?" Doctor Death scoffs before communication is blocked by my scrambling system.

With Death hunting for me on completely the wrong side of the island, I have another donut to keep me going. Every agent knows that each meal could be his last.

Two hours of surveillance and still no Donna. I expect her mum told her about all these friends coming and going all day and she decided not to pop by. Still, at least I managed to get photos of them leaving for our central intelligence database.

I only have one donut left and I feel a bit sick now. As my stomach turns, I contemplate the possibility that the despicable

Doctor Death has put something in them. I shouldn't eat this last one, but they go hard so quickly and I did pay for them. I can't bear to see it going to waste. Maybe I could offer it to Donna's mum as it might be a good icebreaker? Although, then again I might seem like a bit of a weirdo – knocking on her door in the middle of the afternoon offering her the last donut in the bag. What would Doug Holster do? What would a rebellious free spirit do in times of turmoil? I decide to live a little and devour the last donut.

By three o'clock I haven't moved. Hannah has rung on my mobile. I knew who it was as she keeps withholding her number. I didn't answer though as she's so clingy. My stomach turns and I probably shouldn't have eaten that last donut. I feel so queasy I don't even bother taking a photo of a butch woman who goes in to see Gloria. She'll never make it onto the front cover of *Hello* in those tatty old dungarees!

I think I'm going to be sick. Next time I come here all day, I'm going to bring some indigestion tablets. Oh, my god, there she is – there's Donna!

What do I do? She's walking down the street. Her bleach-blonde hair is covered by a red baseball cap and she's wearing some classy, oversize sunglasses, but it's definitely her. That was the same disguise as she wore when she went shopping in Ickenham High Street on the third of March.

Come on now, you can do it. I'm shaking. My hand has just about got the strength to pull the handle and open the car door. I've been dreaming about this moment for years, or at least it seems that way. I've rehearsed this meeting over and over again in my head and so I know what I have to do.

My feet hit the tarmac and I take a deep breath. Should I say I'm the one who loves her? Then I remind myself she already knows that as I've been emailing her site ever since it was created.

She gets her door keys out to go inside as I lock my car. Soon, I'll be in her mother's house for the rest of the day and we'll probably end up taking Donna's limo to the city and...

"Bleugggggh..."

I'm staring down at the white lines in the middle of the road as I hold my stomach and puke up half of the two dozen donuts I've been eating all day. I then complement the first barrage of vomit with a second, even larger puddle.

I catch Donna's eye and she gives me a strange look as she watches the semi-digested chunks of pastry and jam dribbling down my chin and settling on a cat's eye. The last thing I see is her frantically scrambling to get her keys in the door. A few seconds later I hear it slam loudly. I throw up again before my nose starts to bleed.

Chapter 13: Working Men

"There you go, Doug," Gloria says as she puts down a glass of water on her lounge coffee table and hands me an indigestion tablet. "You take two of those and you'll feel much better."

"Thank you," I reply, politely. "That's most kind."

"Not at all, Donna will be down in a minute," she says with a smile as she sits next to me.

"Excellent," I say with a satisfied grin. "I'm very sorry about the vomit outside. The baker I bought them from has promised to come round and apologise personally."

"And so he should," says Gloria, indignantly. "They ought to consider themselves lucky you don't have them closed down – selling products that are past their sell-by date. You should send them an email first thing tomorrow morning and…"

The front doorbell rings.

"That'll be him now," she says. "I hope he's brought some form of compensation for you."

A few seconds later she comes back into the lounge.

"Sorry, Doug," she laughs. "False alarm, it wasn't the baker at all."

"Who was it then?" I ask.

"As a matter of fact it was your Auntie Eileen – she wanted to know would you like some sweets, Willie?"

I've failed to have a dream about Donna three nights in a row now. I wake up in the morning and look at the poster of her on my ceiling and to make matters worse, there's a spider on it.

Mum won't touch them, so I'll have to wait for a neighbour to come round and throw it out of the window in a glass. I shut my eyes and resume thinking about how much I hate my life. Thank you God, thank you so bloody much. My meeting with

Donna ruined by you for no reason at all. What did I do to deserve that? I saw the way she looked at me – she was disgusted. Probably thought I was some sort of vagrant staggering across the road to bum some spare change, or even mug her. What if she thought I was a criminal?

No, she would never think that. She knew who I was, but she was focusing about her career – what if there was a photographer present? What if on the eve of releasing her hotly anticipated new single, she was pictured with another man? It would be a media disaster! I could understand her not wanting to be seen in public with me, especially as I was feeling off colour.

I have three more days due to me as holiday and I can hardly bring myself to go and sit outside Gloria's. But I doubt Donna will return until after the tour, unless of course she becomes a tax exile. I heard at the height of the Spice Girls' fame they could only live in Britain for thirty days a year. What if I had to pack up my job and go travelling with Donna?

But I'm cheered up by an email from the BBC saying that they've agreed to send me two tickets to be in the audience of *Top of the Pops*. Of course I won't need the second ticket as Donna will already be there.

There are nine days before I have to be at the studio. I did think about setting off tomorrow to make sure I get to the front of the queue, but I think that's a bit excessive. At least I have plenty of holiday time left to spend updating donnaTisthebest.org.uk.

In the meantime, I continue to watch as Donna promotes her single. She's been using the media to get photographed leaving venues around London in the early hours of the morning. I suppose the usual route of promoting via pointless radio and TV interviews didn't appeal to her.

It's amazing that she can party so hard yet remain so beautiful. There was a great picture of her in *Now* magazine wearing the tiniest black top with matching miniskirt. You could tell she'd taken a long time over her appearance as the press were flocking round her. Of course out of all the pictures they chose to print was the one where her nipple popped out. I made sure I blurred it out when I uploaded it to my website.

I've decided it's time for me to finally enter the spotlight and head to the trendy West End clubs to catch up with Donna. As I wander round Soho, I'm taken aback by how hard it is to push my way through swarms of seedy paparazzi infesting the area. I do wish the Government would do something like pass a credible law that protects people from weirdos and dangerous types.

"Seen anyone interesting, mate?" a nasty cockney voice says in my ear as I stand across the road from Chinawhites, camera at the ready.

I turn and come face to face with a human reptile holding an expensive looking camera.

"Go on," he hisses. "Who've you got?"

"I'm not one of your lot," I reply without looking at him. "I don't lead such a sad existence."

"You what?" he says, clearly rattled.

"Look at you," I go on. "Scooting round bars on your mopeds hoping to spot someone famous. I've heard Russell Crowe is inside Chinawhites and if he catches you, he'll show you what for!"

"Oh, piss off, shorty!" he sneers and saunters off.

They say the truth hurts and I shout after him that it's no wonder he can't find any celebrities if that's how he speaks to them.

"Tom Cruise only looks tall because he's on a big screen!" I add, but he's gone and I regret not shooting him dead with my twin pistols when I had the chance. He wouldn't be missed; his kind are merely leeches who have nothing better to do than pester their betters.

Later, I overhear photographers talking about reality TV contestants and Donna's name comes up. I'm about to defend her honour when I catch a snippet of their conversation which leads me to believe she's inside Bar Maximo's right now.

I get there in record time with both my digital cameras at the ready, plus magazines in my bum-bag. But as soon as I arrive, one of these cheeky parasites has the nerve to tell me that this bar is "his patch".

"I work for bleeping Top Shot, mate!" he snarls, using colourful language.

The "Top Shot News Agency", or as I call them "every celebrity's antichrist", has photographers who behave like wolves. They're famous for chasing down and humiliating celebrities by using their long lenses. I remember when they followed Donna to a beach in Ibiza a few days after she left *Voyeur* and took disgusting topless pictures of her. Then, to add insult to injury, the press insinuated that she'd initiated it all to keep herself in the public eye. The moment I hear the words Top Shot, I can't hold back any longer.

"You're scum," I tell this one, "why don't you do a proper day's work and leave these people alone?"

He squares up to me, and I realise he's actually quite a big bloke – almost five foot ten. I stand my ground as he and his cronies surround me. Little does he know I've dispatched worse hired goons than his pitiful band of ruffians.

"What did you just say?" he growls.

"I said that your type are scum and should leave these poor hardworking celebrities alone," I say after taking a deep breath.

He looks down at me and I can feel his eyes running up and down my body. He knows I'm an adversary not to be messed with.

"And who should I be photographing?" he finally says, with an evil toothy grin, "what about a film star, like you?"

At least he recognises that I am indeed someone, but I have to correct him on one thing.

"I haven't actually starred in any films yet," I say. "I write them, and would only consider appearing in one if the part suited me."

"Oh, I'm sorry, mate," he says as he realises his mistake and backs off. "I thought you were one of the goblins from *Lord of the Rings!*"

Some people nearby overhear and start making wooing noises, obviously trying to stir up even more bad feeling between us.

I'm about to point out that there were no goblins in *Lord of the Rings*, only Orcs, when he proves he's a true bully and takes to his heels and runs. In fact, they all do, and I find myself the only one left standing in the street.

"Oi, you!" shouts the doorman from Bar Maximo's once they've gone. "Come here a minute."

I go over wondering if he too wants a piece of the Holster rammed down his throat.

"Nice one, mate, here's a little something for your troubles," he says as he offers me a twenty pound note. "I've been trying to get rid of that lot all night!"

Of course seeing that cowardly photographer run was reward enough, but I decide it would be rude to decline his money.

"That showed them, eh?" I say, choosing to adopt a slight cockney accent, as I often do when dealing with working men.

"Huh?" he grunts. "Nah, while that lot were surrounding you, Russell Crowe was able to slip out."

I don't quite understand what he's on about, but he is only a doorman, so I don't expect deep and intelligent conversation.

Still, I feel we're bonding in a kind of "odd couple" style relationship.

"Kurt, I don't suppose Donna's in there is she?" I ask him, after reading his name badge.

"Who?" he replies. Obviously being so professional, he doesn't disclose celebrity whereabouts.

"Donna Trayhorn," I say with a wink, but he keeps up the act of not knowing who she is. It seems like he isn't about to let on until I mention she was once a reality TV contestant.

"Oh, her," he finally says. "She left about an hour ago."

I go home, stopping only once outside her apartment block.

"Has Donna come back yet?" I ask the Nazi in the top hat on her front door.

"Right, that's it," he starts ranting. "I'm calling the police on you!"

"No you're not," I say with my most charming of smiles, then hand him the twenty pound note. "Here's a little something for you, now, has she come home, or not?"

"No, she hasn't," he says, through gritted teeth. It's amazing what a difference a little money makes. "I won't call the police this time, but don't you come back round here pestering the residents."

"Of course I won't," I say with another dazzling smile. Little does he know that when I move in there, he'll be long gone! That's worth twenty pounds of anyone's money.

The week drags by and there are now only two days until I meet Donna at *Top of the Pops*. I even decide to see Hannah in an attempt to make the time pass more quickly. As I go inside the pub I spot her car outside. She's with Matt and his horde by the bar. They're green with envy about my trip to the BBC and I pick up their catty remarks about me mixing with "teeny-boppers".

Even the girls in the office are a bit jealous. Three of them came up to me with an old Westlife poster and pen asking me to get it signed.

"Westlife are a constructed band with no drive, soul or talent of their own, plus on top of that they mime all their alleged hits," I point out to one little tart who I don't even know. I hand back her tacky poster, but slide the pen inside my pocket when she's not looking.

"Aww," she bleats, with a little pout. I knew social commentary would be wasted on people who wear false nails and too much eyeshadow. "You know, I'm surprised that you're not in a boy band, you've got the looks!"

The two girls behind her are obviously taken aback by my verbal dexterity and giggle. I'm sure one is giving me the eye. I must use some more long words in my next sentence to further prove my intellectual sophistication.

"I have no interest in being part of some record company's mouthpiece which only appeals to the lowest common denominator," I say with a sigh before running my fingers through my thick, wavy hair in a sign that I'm flattered by her attention.

"That's a shame," she coos. "What about some sort of long-haired death metal group?"

"That's not really me," I say, after considering the prospect. "I couldn't go around headbanging all day as it would bring on a nose bleed."

I think one of the other girls is definitely interested as she copies me and runs her fingers through her hair. It's a pity she's so ugly, otherwise I might be more interested.

"Doug," the girl with the poster and talons purrs. "Could you do us a favour—please?"

Now she's interested as well. She says "please" in an over sensual manner and flutters her eyelashes at me. I'm totally in here. Sadly, I can do the favour, but nothing more as I'm obviously bequeathed to Donna.

"Of course," I say with another one of my captivating smiles.

"There's a spider on Sue's desk and we're all really, really afraid of it. We were wondering if you'd get rid of it for us?"

One spider against the lives of millions? As much as Doug Holster could have blasted the radioactive arachnid to high heaven, he felt it was more important to tackle the problem at the source. If Doctor Death was dabbling in diseased DNA, he could create anything.

"Girls," Holster said reassuringly. "When the shit goes down, you make sure you've got your skirts pulled up. Sound the evacuation alarm. I'll handle this."

"But, Doug..." one said as she gripped on to his tuxedo cuff. "It's huge!"

"I've heard that before," he smiled. "Now, let me do my job."

Luckily the office was having a fire drill and the spider seemed not to like the bell. While people line up in the car park, I take the opportunity to use an office PC and find out the phone numbers of the two nicer girls who wooed me. Sadly, I only get one before the staff return. But at least while I was at the desk I managed to pick up two more pens (and one of them was brand new).

I don't go to Donna's mum's today. I'm not embarrassed as I know they'd realise those mouldy donuts were to blame. I'm too busy picking up the latest issue of *FHM* magazine. It's the annual bumper edition where they list the top hundred sexiest women.

I put Donna in first place, not even bothering to fill in spaces two through ten. I also put up a notice on my website advising Donna's fans to do likewise. I'd even set up thirty new email addresses to register my online votes, not to mention the small fortune I've spent on previous issues of *FHM* to collect more voting forms. Donna will be so happy when she finds I've got her in the top hundred.

I come home from work at midday, after calling Doctor Death and saying I've got a tummy bug.

I read *FHM* backwards, starting at number one. I didn't really think she'd make it that far, but you never know. But by the time I reach number twenty I'm a bit concerned, as she still isn't there. Instead there are only a load of Hollywood bimbos and drunken socialites. I pass number fifty and rack my brains as to why I still haven't seen her, then eighty, ninety and still nothing! I can't understand it, but then I see who is at number ninety-two.

"Marge Simpson".

A yellow cartoon character with a towering mop of blue hair is the ninety-second sexiest woman in the world. It's then I realise the *FHM* poll means nothing any more. Gone are the days when it actually stood as a true reflection of beauty. I skim through numbers ninety-three to a hundred, but Donna isn't there.

The editors of *FHM* are going to be waking up to a strongly worded email first thing tomorrow morning. At least that's one good thing about taking the day off – I can choose my words carefully. I'll make them feel about as small as I did to that paparazzi. I'll let them know their game has been rumbled.

It's dark outside by the time I press "send" and I sit back in my chair, pleased with the overall tone of my mail. I think I put my case across in a mature and adult manner – which is more than I can say for their rigged poll.

Chapter 14: Money Well Spent

I'm finding it hard to contain my excitement as I stand outside studio four's entrance at BBC television centre. In under an hour I'll be watching Donna live.

According to my ticket stub, recording starts at seven, but I've been here since eight this morning. I wanted Mum to ring work and tell them I had a stress-related viral condition, but she wouldn't, so I ended up doing it myself.

However, as I stand here, I find I'm not concentrating on the joy of catching up with Donna, but on how much I wish the security guards would leave me alone. I don't know what it is with security firms these days; you give them a peaked cap and a badge and they become honorary Gestapo officers. I explained to the guy on the morning shift that I was queuing for *Top of the Pops*, then again to the bloke who took over from him at lunchtime. Now another new guy has started his stint on the door and I've had to go through the whole rigmarole with him.

Still, who'll be having the last laugh when we get inside – the whining kids queuing behind me, or me – the man who's been here all day and gets ushered straight to the front?

A pretty young woman with a clipboard and headset bounces out of the building and comes towards us.

"Hello, everybody!" she shouts to break through the childish chatter behind me. "My name's Louise and I'm the stage manager for *Top of the Pops*."

She's cut short by a huge cheer from the kids.

"If you'll all file in and head down the corridor to your left, we can get you in to watch some of the rehearsals."

Her words her like music to my ears and she removes the red rope blocking my way into the building and I take my first steps towards Donna.

158

"Oh, you'd better let your kids go first," she says to someone. Then I feel her bony hand coming to rest on my shoulder and realise she's addressing me.

"Excuse me?" I blurt out.

"Are those your children behind you?" she asks with an ugly smile.

I just look at her. I'm not laughing and her mistake sinks in.

"Oh, I'm sorry," she stammers, "I thought you were – oh, never mind. Do you mind letting the kids in first?"

"Yes, I do as a matter of fact," I say sharply, while wondering how such a clearly incompetent girl has become a stage manager. "Do you know how long I've been queuing for?"

"Since eight this morning!" a man's voice shouts from nearby and I scowl at the leering security guard.

"I've been waiting here since eight o'clock this morning to see Donna Trayhorn," I point out.

"Who?" she asks, "oh, yeah, wait I know – the reality TV girl. It's just we normally let the kids in first, they…"

"Excuse me, but this lot only turned up within the last hour!" I state.

"I see," she mutters under her breath, "I'll see what I can do."

"Come on!" shouts someone from behind me and I turn round to see the brats are all looking at me. I ignore them, just like I did at school.

"We want to see Charlotte!" a little girl shouts. Then her Neanderthal dad chimes in.

"Get the hell out the way, will you?"

I ignore him too. School taught me about dealing with the pack: ignore them and they'll leave you alone – a tactic I used at all four of my secondary schools. I look Louise in the eye and she smiles uncomfortably. I can feel another victory coming my way.

159

"Okay, go through," she says, as she bends to my iron will. I don't thank her; she's probably only really a work experience kid pretending to be the stage manager. I simply march past her and on towards Donna. My pace quickens so I don't have to listen to what the rabble behind me are accusing me of. Kids weren't like this when I was their age; they used proper words like "detest" and "despise", not like the ones they're shouting at me now.

An hour later and I'm in the studio, but only barely. I took the centre spot at the front of the stage surrounded by screaming chavs. I thought that would be the worst aspect of the evening, but I was wrong.

First the producer came up to me and asked would I mind retreating to the back of the crowd as I was blocking the view of a four-year-old. Again, I was forced to explain how long I'd been queuing and perhaps if these little darlings were that desperate to be on TV, they should take off their hoodies and let the cameras see their delightful acne clad faces.

After about twenty minutes he finally saw sense and left me where I was. I'm not sure why he was so bothered about having the brat-pack up front anyway. All they kept doing was pushing forwards and bumping into me.

The show was late starting, probably due to the blatant mismanagement by the staff. The kids were getting restless and kept shouting things at me, as if for some reason it was my fault. Finally the director came down from the control room to talk to me. I was a little taken aback by the fact he was flanked by no less than three burly security guards.

"Look, mate," he said, like I was actually his friend. "You're going to have to move back out of shot. This is a kids' show, and we need youngsters up front."

I had no choice but to explain yet again about how long I'd been waiting for this show to start. This time I even went as far as waving my ticket in his face to prove that I had as much right to be here as the unruly rabble surrounding me.

"Let me see that," he snapped as he whipped the stub out of my hand. "This ticket does not guarantee a reserved seat," he read off the back before stuffing it back in my hand.

"I don't care," I stated, "first come, first served."

"Please don't make a scene, Sir," he said, quietly. Apparently I was no longer his mate.

"I'm not going to make a scene if you'd pull your finger out and start this bloody show!" I shouted for all to hear.

The next thing I knew he nodded at his three meatheads and they took hold of my arms and dragged me out of the crowd and finally dumped me unceremoniously at the back of the room. This was thought to be hilarious by the little kids baying for my blood. It was amazing how a spot of mindless violence suddenly cheered them all up.

So, here I am at the back of the studio. I think they'd have thrown me out completely if it wasn't for the fact I threatened to email the Director General and tell him about this incident. I can barely see the stage now as there's a lighting rig, two fixed cameras and about a hundred screaming Muppets jumping up and down in front of me. I hope the cameras pan across and get a shot of me letting viewers see that not everyone is enjoying this stupid show. Let the world know that this whole event is merely a piece of carefully staged propaganda. Would you believe that the supposed stage manager even has to go around with a sign saying "applaud" every time an "artist" comes on, just to get a reaction out of these people?

They're like little robots; they let the media dictate who and what they're supposed to like. It's like: "Here's a rap star – you like him, so whoop and cheer like a pack of screaming buzzards". And they do!

"Okay everyone that was great!" Louise yells into a loudspeaker at the hooded army. I'll bet she wanted to be a children's TV presenter, but failed the audition. "Now, if you'll all turn to your left and look at stage five, you'll see the lighting guys getting ready for Donna Trayhorn!"

"Oh, yes!" I bellow, proving some of us don't need a loudspeaker to get our point across. Everyone looks at me and I wave sarcastically, pointing out I'm still here. Sadly my actions prove how unfair life is – I stand at the front and nearly get thrown out, then twenty little yobs hurl drinks and coins at me and no one dares say a thing.

"Um, yes, well. She'll be out in five, so get ready to give her a big *Top of the Pops* style welcome when she does!"

Of course we will Louise. Some of us don't need to be told when to applaud and when not to.

It's fair to say that the next five minutes were the longest in my life. In fact they seemed more like forty-two minutes and sixteen seconds, which turned out to be the exact elapsed time before Donna arrived on stage. Her fashionable lateness was commendable and well worth the wait.

For a start she looked radiant: dressed in a black leather miniskirt and thigh-high boots. Her top was low cut, yet extremely tasteful and elegant, only allowing the audience a glimpse of her amazing braless figure when she leant over to sing directly to her fans in the front row. In fact her performance blew me away so completely that I almost forgot that I should have been one of the lucky ones up there. I won't dwell on how I failed to be as close as I would have liked, as once I had my glasses on, I could make out her writhing around on the stage pretty well.

I can definitely see this single silencing her critics once and for all. You could tell it had been produced by some of the biggest names in the music industry. I can't wait till it hits the

162

shelves later next week, as it'll be one hell of a vehicle for her to launch an international tour with.

You can tell she's got music in her blood: when she was on stage you could only liken the way she worked the crowd to Freddie Mercury, or maybe even Elvis. The way she used every inch of space to full effect was truly inspiring. She even imitated rockers with an impromptu stage dive, but combined grunge with the sensuality of Madonna's oozing sexuality. She fluidly mixed the edgy, hard-hitting rocky feel of Another One Bites the Dust with a more upbeat underground dance, techno-fusion kind of feel. I can see Game For You becoming something of a club anthem.

But like all the best things in life, her performance was cut way too short. It amazes me how the producers will give airtime to established artists who don't need it, yet the ones with genuine talent have to fight for every second. Still, she'll have the last laugh; I was there and I saw the reaction she got from the crowd. Easily led sheep they may be, but at least they seemed to be able to appreciate her art. Of course I made sure I cheered the loudest after she'd finished and I'm sure she heard me, even if I was behind a camera's dolly.

I leave as soon as she departs the stage as I'm not in the mood for staying and watching whatever manufactured pop puppets are supposed to be "headlining" the show. I dart round the back of the studio as during the day I had successfully infiltrated the base and acquired its technical schematics. The backroom boffins had wired me the exact location of the stage door.

Just as well I get there when I do, as the paparazzi are already starting to congregate. Luckily not too many and I'm able to get to the front pretty easily with my camera at the ready.

"Oi, mate," a voice says from behind me. "Don't I know you from somewhere?"

163

I look round to see a slimy looking guy in a black leather jacket eyeing me up suspiciously. If his lizard-like features didn't give him away as paparazzi, his overall creepiness and the sniper-style sight on his camera did.

"I don't think so," I sneer.

I can feel his eyes burning into the back of my head, so I take a deep breath and turn round. Sure enough, he's still looking at me quizzically. I don't speak immediately, as the only thing I wanted to say involved various expletives about his dirty profession.

"Yeah," he says slowly, as he drew his lips back to form a smile which showed his missing teeth. "I know you: you're one of the new breed, aren't you?"

"Excuse me?" I say with raised eyebrows, "I most certainly am not."

I turn away again, not actually knowing what I'd just denied I was part of. But I feel him coming closer and tapping me on the shoulder.

"Yeah, yeah," he says quietly, still with an evil leer plastered across his mug. "Hey, don't worry; I've got no problem with freelance paps. I was one myself long enough!"

I don't believe it; he actually thinks I'm one of them. I'm so paralysed with rage that I can't even bring myself to put him straight. What possible reason could he have for likening me to the paparazzi?

"I saw you outside O'Neils in Leicester Square a few weeks back with your camera," he continues. "Get anyone good?"

Oh, right, yeah I was outside there a week last Tuesday.

"No," I say begrudgingly, still reeling from the insult.

"Unlucky, mate," he says, as he nods knowingly, "I know how you feel. Damn private security firms are ruining us, eh?"

I don't answer. The good men and women of such firms are all that stand in the way of this sorry excuse for a man. In fact, I can't even believe I'm being civil to him.

"Who you here to get then?" he asks.

As if I'm going to tell him, and let him pip me to the best shots. No wait, that's me thinking like a pap. I'm not like him – I shouldn't have to hide anything.

"Donna Trayhorn." I say, firmly.

"Who?" he splutters.

I check to see she isn't coming out and then educate this primate in the ways and lives of celebrities. I do my best to enlighten him, but as I feared, he's way too set in his ways to be able to take in any new information.

"Oh, her," he interrupts, rudely. "But she's rubbish!"

"Excuse me," I interject, still not giving up on correcting his jaded viewpoint. "But I think you'll find that at the end of the day it's the up-and-coming celebrities that will ultimately sell copy. People know what Kylie Minogue looks like – people like her are old news."

He gives me a strange look. I think I may have actually got through to him.

"So, I take it they don't know your face?" he asks, curiously. I'm about to say something when he beats me to it. "Hey wait, that's not an insult, I'm just saying – you know – I've been in this game for years and every bouncer in London knows me. What I'd give to be like you – just another face in the crowd."

If Donna comes out now and I'm stuck talking to this imbecile, I'll never forgive him.

"I could put some work your way if you're interested?" he continues. "I'd make it worth your while."

I turn to face him, my mouth dropping at the sound of his words. He actually thinks I'd stoop so low as to stalk hardworking celebrities for money?

"Two hundred for a good shot," he whispers.

Two hundred pounds for one picture – that is a lot of money. With that sort of cash coming in, I could afford to buy the rights to donnaT.com! But wait. Who exactly does he work for?

"All right," he says, "I can see you're not some wet-behind-the-ears amateur. Three hundred for a decent snap, yeah?"

"Three?" I blurt out before I can properly weigh up the offer.

"Okay, three-fifty, but that's my final offer."

My mouth seems to have gone dry, so I just nod.

"Good man," he grins. "It's no problem, Top Shot are paying."

Top Shot? Work for those amoral shysters? Even three hundred and fifty pounds isn't worth working for such criminals. Nothing could get me to work for them – nothing.

"Yeah, if you come and work for us and you're not a face, we can get you in places – you know what I mean?" he says quietly.

"In places?" I query.

"Yeah, but, keep your voice down, eh?" he says, as he hushes me. "You know, get you inside clubs, hotels, apartment blocks – that sort of thing."

"You mean people's homes?" I say, in a slightly warmer tone.

"Well, if push comes to shove," he says, trying to back peddle. "But mainly we're after drunken celebs or them sunburnt in bikinis, you know the sort of thing."

"And apartment blocks?" I say, wanting him to confirm this part of the prospective deal.

"Sure, sure," he says, keeping one eye on the stage door. "Whatever."

I smile, suppressing telling him what I think of his employers. Suddenly we feel the weight of the press pack surging forward as the stage door opens. I find myself caught in a frenzy of strobe lighting as camera flashes go off all around me. The slimebag I was talking to joins the baying mob and I find myself slowly being jostled to the back. I make out several burly minders pushing the paps out of the way as they clear a path for – actually I can't see – are all celebrities so small?

A limo pulls up behind me and I find myself gazing down on what look like four teenage boys wearing too much hair gel.

"Who the fook are you?" the one at the front says in a thick Irish accent. But before I can answer I spot two bouncers converging on my position as it dawns on me that I'm currently standing between Westlife and their ride. The last thing I see before my backside crashes down to the floor – courtesy of the angry leprechaun in front of me – is the pap I was speaking to urging me to get a picture.

My finger hits the button on one of my cameras as I sit in the dirt at Westlife's feet. I don't get up immediately as the four band members bundle past me into their limo with their entourage. I'm not happy, but it could have been worse – Donna could have seen me get pushed over. I feel a hand grab me roughly under the arm and "help" me up. My new best friend – the leering pap – is grinning at me.

"Hey, good one," he says. "They obviously didn't clock you as a pap – we sue 'em if they touch us! Oh, please tell me you got a good one of Kian there."

Once Westlife have scampered off, the mob goes back to flocking round the stage door. While I dust myself down he introduces himself as Jeff, or "Raptor" as he boasts his friends call him. I'll call him Jeff.

I quickly realise this sudden introduction was merely a ploy to get my camera off me and look at the picture I'd taken.

"Holly shit!" Jeff exclaims as he stares at the picture of Kian on my digital camera.

I snatch it back while he rubs his greedy little hands together, practically drooling.

I look at the screen – I don't see what's so amazing about it – a slightly blurred extreme close-up of Kian's ugly face.

"Look at his eyes!" he hisses, gleefully.

I do just that. Strange, for such an extreme close-up you'd think you'd be able to tell what colour his eyes are, but no, they're entirely black, as if he has only pupils in his eye sockets.

"How many pills must he have taken before he left, eh?" Jeff says, laughing.

Perhaps he said it too loudly, as the other paps' radar must pick up things like that. Like meerkats, they begin to look round and scurry over to see the image on my camera.

"I'll give you a hundred for that!" the nearest one shouts directly into my ear, making it ring slightly.

"Two hundred!" another one cries, followed by what can only be described as a bidding frenzy for my camera's memory card.

"Hey, hey, hey!" interjects Jeff as he steps between me and the mass of lizard-men. "He's already contracted to me!"

Suddenly I find myself being dragged away from the pack by Jeff.

"Something tells me you've got a knack for this sort of thing," he smiles. "We'll call it five for that one, Okay?"

Five hundred pounds for a picture of a stoned Irishman? I can't imagine who that would be of interest to, but obviously Jeff seems to think he can find a buyer. He immediately pulls out a lead from somewhere ready to upload my picture on to his laptop.

"Show me the money!" I shout and he looks slightly taken aback, but then smiles with those horrible teeth again.

"You drive a hard bargain er, mate?" he says, before adding. "What's your name?"

I could introduce myself as Doug Morrell, novelist and media commentator, yet I feel that if I'm going to infiltrate the seedy world of Top Shot, I need a cooler "handle".

Iceman? No, too blatantly Top Gun. Jet? I think she was a Gladiator in the early nineties. Neo? Not likely, some kid uses that handle on my message board and I don't need to copy. What about, Doug Black? No, might be perceived as racist. What I need is something that sounds cool, yet reflects my devotion to Donna.

"Call me – Trayman Rose," I announce, proudly. I don't know where the Rose bit came from, but I'm sure it adds to the overall effect.

I can tell Jeff's impressed as he looks at me speechless. It must be like Clarke Kent taking off his glasses and revealing himself as Spiderman.

"Trayman Rose, huh? Okay," he says, as he stuffs the lead back into his pocket and takes out his wallet instead. It's packed with notes no smaller than fifties. He counts out ten and hands them to me. I'm so taken with their crisp, fresh feel that I hardly notice him snatching my camera and scurrying round a corner muttering something about a blue Lexus round the back.

I suddenly become aware that I'm displaying a huge bundle of cash in a public place and quickly stuff it into the inside pocket of my jacket – the one with a zip.

"What's all this on my hands?" I say out loud as I see the white powdery substance the notes have left on my fingers.

I was about to take a sniff when I hear the chugging engine of a taxi rattling near me. None of the photographers have moved, so I consider going and getting my camera back from

Jeff. I'm just about to set off after him when I swear I spot Donnar about to get into the cab!

Like Murphy stated in his law, if it can go wrong, it will. I was so busy wiping the flour from my hands that I took my eyes off the stage door. In that time she had got past me and into the cab before I could get to her. Trust her to be cleverer than the paparazzi and not bother with a traditional limo.

I was so overwhelmed by the money that I didn't even notice a single flash bulb go off. So here I am, watching Donna's stocking-clad leg folding into a black cab as she gets ready to leave before she noticed me.

I have no camera and nearly panic before realising that I still have the magazine clippings for her to sign. With speed I never knew I had, I sprint towards the cab as the door begins to shut, my hands searching my inner pocket for the clippings. My fingers fiddle with the zip as I make a beeline towards her car. I take hold of the clippings and pull them out, but in doing so dislodge my hard-earned cash.

The eternal dilemma: do I turn round and try to grab the notes before they blow away, or do I leave them and make it to Donna.

Easy come, easy go – donnaT.com will have to wait.

I bang on the cab window and she looks at me. She actually looks me in the eye and I can truly feel the connection. I know she feels it too.

"Donna, I love you!" I shout as I press the clippings up against the window.

But they don't stay there long as she's been too clever for her own good. Her deliberate stealth means she's forced to rely on an ordinary member of the public to drive her away from the relentless photographers. The over-zealous cabbie puts his foot down and it roars away in a cloud of exhaust fumes which make my clippings join the fifty pound notes in the wind.

"Join my fan club!" I hear her shout as the taxi zooms away.

That was to me. She's finally admitted she wants me to be part of her life. I knew this day would come and I well up inside. I turn back towards the stage door and the other paparazzi are looking at me guiltily. My money is nowhere to be seen and I smile warmly, which provokes some confusion among them.

I walk away in a bit of a daze and bump into Jeff who has come back to return my camera, but I wander off. What's five hundred pounds when you have what I've got?

"Where are you going?" he asks.

"Over here," I reply, my mind on other things. I don't really know where I'm going.

"What about your number?" he shouts. "I can put some work your way!"

I don't answer. Who needs work when you have someone like Donna? I'm not even fazed by Charlotte Church coming out of a fire exit ahead of me wearing dark glasses.

"Voice of an angel," I say out loud, too happy even to dwell on the fact that she achieved fame in the confines of a greedy faceless record giant. Or even that a mere kid had received top billing on tonight's show.

"What was that?" Jeff asks.

"Huh? Oh, nothing," I say, dreamily, "Only Charlotte what's-her-name over there."

I feel the wind on my face as I gaze into the night. Then realise it wasn't the wind at all, but Jeff sprinting by. I think some camera flashes go off in front of me and an angry Welsh voice shouts something most unladylike. You wouldn't catch Donna using such obscenities.

Another white limo speeds past me and I set off into the night. I can't remember where I parked my car.

"Damn, you're good," Jeff says as he catches up with me. "You've got a sixth sense!"

I think I give him my number before I go home. Money well spent.

Chapter 15: Licensed to Pap

Top of the Pops appears on television the following night. At least I don't have to fight to get to the front of the TV like I did at the stage. Mum must have been in her room watching Coronation Street.

More "shouty-shouty" presenters introduce the show and there's no mention of Donna. I'm guessing they aren't about to blow their trump card so quickly. A hip-hop artist was first, if you can actually call hip-hop "art", and to think I'm bothering to record this whole show.

Westlife are on next and the crowd of simpletons goes wild just like they were asked to. I have to say this is the first Westlife performance I've ever enjoyed. For once I overlooked the fact they were miming as they pranced around the stage. Instead I concentrated on today's copy of *The Sun* and *Closer* magazine: both featured my photo within their pages. The text speculated on what "medications" Kian had been taking during his energetic dance routine. A spokesperson for the band stated that he'd had a bad cold and sometimes cough medicine can make your eyes go like that.

Next come two more hip-hop artists with unpronounceable names, then the top twenty count-down and finally Charlotte Church. No Donna.

I'm not upset, not for me anyway, but Donna has been robbed. All the hard work she put into her performance has been for nothing. She's been replaced by some overweight Irishmen, three acts who used words like "bling" and "hoe" and a Welsh schoolgirl. Is this really what we pay our licence fee for?

I have a good mind to boycott the BBC. I get out of my seat and rewind the video ready to record over this abomination. I then go straight to my computer to look up the *Top of the Pops* website. I spend hours surfing the BBC's site getting all the email addresses I can with which to "cc" my complaint to. For some reason the Director General's address had been left off completely.

When I finish it's dark outside. I could go to bed, but I need to find that fan club Donna spoke of. She distinctly asked me to join it, and yet I can't seem to find a single mention of it anywhere. It goes without saying I check her official site first, but still nothing, not even an email from her, which is more than I can say for that crowd at *FHM* magazine.

I found this threatening little number waiting for me when I logged on:

Dear Mr Morrell,

Thank you very much for your email yesterday and we are sorry if the opinions of the rest of the world do not match your own warped views.

By all means talk to your MP about holding a public enquiry into the way the voting system works within our organisation. Perhaps while you're talking to him, you can bring up the little matter of the thirty separate online votes you cast for Donna Trayhorn. Congratulations on registering thirty completely different email addresses with which to cunningly throw us off the scent with, but for future subterfuge, it may be worth filling in a different name and address with each registration.

Believe it or not, we set up this poll; therefore we are actually aware of the terms and conditions of organising such an event, in fact, we wrote the Ts and Cs ourselves. If you had bothered to read them, you would see that in section 1.2 was a little piece about "only one entry per person. Anyone found to be using multiple entries will have their votes discounted."

Bearing that in mind, we have been instructed by our solicitor not to reimburse you for the time, money or emotional trauma you claim to have suffered by not getting the decision you desired. Nor shall we be offering compensation to Ms Trayhorn, who as yet, has still not come forward to demand any.

If you wish to take this matter further, please feel free to take it up with our legal representatives.

Yours sincerely,

The FHM Management

P.S. If Ms Trayhorn really is a personal friend of yours, as you stated so many times, perhaps you should ask her when her nationwide tour starts.

I'm never buying *FHM* again.

It's hard to return to work after my time with Donna the other night, as now nothing seems to matter any more. It's like I'm living in a beautiful dream. I've been in such a good mood I could almost let Doctor Death live after he masterminded the sacking of Torquay.

"So, Holster, we meet again," he sneered as the superspy breezed past the bodyguards in his throne room. "How fortunate our paths should cross right now as I have a little favour I wish you to do for me!"

"I'll never turn to the dark side!" Holster retorted as he drew his twin pistols.

"You don't have a choice, deluded fool!" crowed Death, "for it was I who allowed you to know the secret location to our forest base, it was I who allowed you to steal the shield code and it was I who let you think you'd foiled my diabolical plans! For

175

while you were running around thinking you were saving the world, we kidnapped your Ms Trayhorn again!"

"Fiend!" Holster cried. "What have you done to her?"

"Nothing, yet!" laughed Death as he rubbed his hands together. "But if you don't get every customer to sign for a delivery, there'll be hell to pay!"

I don't dwell too much on how I should have killed him when I had the chance, but despite his tyranny, I can still find room in my heart to smile. I throw today's parcels in the back and blast my way out of his base before his robot attack dogs can get my scent. From Gloria's Acton safe house, I pull the bullets from my body and breathe a sigh of relief at surviving another day in hell.

Doug had taken a break from his hard day's espionage and was browsing a luxury car lot in an upmarket London suburb. His Aston Martin had been a faithful old workhorse, but from all the action it had seen, its chassis was now more lead than metal. As he glided through the rows of expensive yellow Audis, he beckoned an employee over.

"All right, mate," said the underling. "You got a delivery for us?"

"How much?" said Doug, pointing to a convertible.

The little man laughed nervously as he could see his customer was obviously a man of impeccable taste. But before Doug could use his celebrity status to demand a free test drive, his communication device went.

"Curses," he said under his breath. "He knows where I am."

"Is that parcel for me, or what?" asked the lackey in the car lot.

How did it come to this? The world's most feared spy being forced to run errands for his nemesis. Doug bit his lip and handed over the drop to Death's undercover man, then got him to sign for it and left.

I really should get my book deal sorted out. That way my PA can screen all my calls and stop Hannah bothering me at work. I return to my van and listen to the radio hoping to find a station that still plays Game For You, even if I do have to ring them up and request it yet again.

Sadly I can't find a single one that still has it on its play-list. I return to the depot and unload my undelivered parcels, but while I do, I have the misfortune of being spotted by one of Death's most trusty henchmen.

"How was the trip to the beeb?" Matt asks.

"Fine," I say, not bothering to turn my head all the way round to look at him.

"I didn't see you in the crowd the other night," he goes on.

Oh, big hunky clubber you are, eh – staying in on a Friday night to watch *Top of the Pops*.

"I let the kids stand at the front, so they could have a better view," I inform him.

"Oh, fair play, mate," he says as he nods. I'm not his mate. Why do so many people think I'm their mate? "What happened to Donna's song?"

"Too raunchy," I sigh, "she's going for a more mature audience, not right for pre-watershed broadcast. But I was talking to her last night and things are going brilliantly for her. You wouldn't believe how favourable some of the early reviews are of her work."

"Oh, right," is all he says to that. "Have you read *The Mirror* today?"

I hadn't and so he shows me what I've missed in his tea-stained copy

Lost all Concept of Reality by Midnite's Keeley Kline

Madonna did it. Britney did it. Christina Aguilera does it all the time, but sadly Donna Trayhorn's name is not one I'm going to be adding to that list. Why is it that when a singer (and in Donna's case I use that term lightly) suddenly wants to try and be taken seriously, they dress up like a second-class dominatrix and expect us all to believe that they've suddenly come of age?

I feel it is my duty to inform the readers of the spectacle Donna made of herself when she appeared on Top of the Pops the other night. Most will be unaware of her laughable attempts at reigniting her pop career as the show's producers quite justifiably cut it from the final edit.

For a start, she was visibly drunk on stage, which at one point caused her to hit the deck faster than her career seems to be doing. But if you're thinking how did that affect her voice? I can tell you: not in any way. But that might have had something to do with her song playing on even when her lips weren't moving – or provocatively licking the microphone that she was supposed to be singing out of.

Mistress Trayhorn, as perhaps she is now going to be called, topped off her performance the way every true artist should – by exposing her left breast and showing the world her Ratner's nipple ring. Classy love, classy.

Still, it's not all bad news: we're sure that whatever Ms Trayhorn was paid for her "strip-show to music" she can now probably afford to buy a decent whip and pair of handcuffs. From what I've read on the cards in London phone boxes, she could make anything up to three hundred pounds an hour for her time.

178

Oh, and the song was awful too. Little wonder no reputable radio station will play it.

From the confines of a work toilet cubicle, I wait for the blood to stop dripping from my nose, and reflect on Keeley's "review". Never have I read such a bitter, one-sided character attack on someone. I don't see Keeley out there singing or dancing, or writing the next Shakespearian sonnet. What does she do? Sit behind a desk in London Docklands running down true talent. I've never liked the Mirror's "Midnite Girls", or Britney Max, Keeley Kline and Sarah Large, if you believe those are their real names. All they do is bitch about women who are better looking than they are, and don't they even know how to spell "Midnight"? If I ever met any of them I'd...

"Hello?" I say gruffly into my mobile as the damn thing waits for the worst time to ring.

"Doug?" a man's voice says on the other end. I don't recognise it. It could be a new hit man Death has only just got on the payroll. "Or should I say Trayman Rose? It's Raptor, we spoke the other night."

I'd almost completely forgotten about him. What the hell does this leech want? I mutter something back, but right now I'm more concerned about not getting blood on my uniform.

"Up for giving some celebs a good stalking?" he laughs. I can tell he's relishing in the prospect of upsetting people. I even think my nose is bleeding harder just through talking to him. I was about to tell him what he and his stalking buddies could do with their precious cameras, when he continued.

"Show the world what they're really like, eh?"

His words have a profound effect on me and for a moment I can almost see where he's coming from. As everyone knows, most celebrities are hardworking; leading noble and decent lives, while pursuing unassuming and admirable goals. Then there are

179

the others. The ones who thrive on the scandal and publicity, the types who need their fix of exposure to make them feel alive. Or those who get a tiny bit of power and use it to run others down – like Keeley Kline for example.

"It's good to hear from you, Raptor," I say. He is indeed one of Death's men, but he seems blissfully unaware of who I am. "Let's talk targets."

Later I sit at my bedroom computer deep in thought. For tonight I go into battle. Not to do harm for harm's sake, as I'm not like the other sleazy photographers, I'm different, I'm a crusader. Like the masked vigilantes in the comic books under my bed, I shall slip undetected through the night, seeking out and punishing those who have used their powers unwisely.

And tonight's target shall be Keeley Kline. In a few short hours I will be out there in the heat of battle. Raptor has arranged for me to get into the Coconut Club after hours. It's going to be used as the venue for an after show party for yet another of Metropol's action blockbusters – *The Last Plain* or something. All three Midnite girls will be attending, and I shall be too. I need to plan my strategy and don't dwell on that email I got from some trumped up BBC secretary. I won't go into details as my nose has only just stopped bleeding, but it was along the lines of Donna's performance wasn't shown due to lack of audience participation and problems with the sound.

Audience participation – that's a joke. I was screaming and shouting louder than anyone all the way through her track. Personally, I think it was more down to the producer's lack of understanding as to what viewers want to see.

Raptor is also well behind my plan to expose the sordid world of tabloid journalism with the simple truth of photography. In fact, when I told him, he said that was so good, he'll "have to write that one down". Maybe not all of Death's men have been completely brainwashed?

180

"Just out of interest," I asked him earlier. "Have you ever photographed Donna Trayhorn?"

"Not economical enough!" he said, when he'd finished laughing.

I knew what he meant: he's only interested in the ones who act up for the camera and show off. Donna is far too classy to sink to those levels.

Later that night I'm standing in the club with half a packet of *Pro Plus* tablets inside me. If you'd been delivering other people's goods all day then clubbing all night, you'd be on hard drugs too! I've been here for hours now, but no one told me the celebs wouldn't start arriving until after midnight. I can see me having another upset tummy tomorrow.

I now know why Raptor didn't want to risk trying to get inside himself; on my way in I saw another pap being chucked out because he'd previously troubled guests. When the bouncer frisked me, he was so taken up with rummaging through my packet of travel tissues that he didn't bother checking my other pocket which contained my camera.

"What are these for?" he grunted.

"I get nosebleeds, okay?" I said, firmly. "And unless you want blood all over your precious dance floor, you'd better let me keep them!"

Finally he just rolled his eyes and shook his head, before letting me through. I'm guessing Raptor stayed out front, snapping his quarry as they arrived. I have to say the thought of him out in the cold pleases me as I order another free Archers and lemonade.

I don't recognise anyone yet, apart from some weather girl who spent her time eyeing me up and then passed out on a three foot high speaker. I was halfway tempted to get an "up-skirt shot". But I decided I wouldn't bother, even though I'm sure she was the one who forecast bright sunshine the day my car broke down on the M25. I got soaked walking home.

The moment the clock strikes 12.30 am celebrities suddenly appear from every nook and cranny: big stars, little stars, hangers-on, management, personal security guards and even the odd footballer. I watch press packs and fawning journalists move from one supposedly famous face to the next, all desperate for a juicy morsel or clever soundbite. The male journalists try to be all matey with male celebrities, whereas the girls simply flutter their eyelashes and lean forward a bit. Tarts!

I'm not sure what I'm supposed to do here. Judging by all the signs, photography without prior consent is "strictly forbidden". There's no way a movie star is going to embarrass himself in front of the world's media. Then I notice Keeley Kline.

She's leaning on the shoulder of that bald cockney bloke from *Snatch*. I guess she thinks that because he's recently split from his other half, he'll divulge anything to a nice pair of legs; although, I feel I should point out that Keeley has nasty fat ankles. How am I going to get close enough to pour a drink down her padded cleavage?

I move over to where she and the other two Midnite bitches are and observe them laugh hysterically at whatever pearl of wisdom Jason what's-his-name has come out with.

But an hour later and I'm back at the bar with the memory card in my digital camera still unused. I've been watching the Midnite girls work their black magic all evening, moving like a pack of giggling banshees from one A-lister to the next and milking them for all they're worth. Little do their victims know that by tomorrow these three harpies will have completely distorted everything they've said for the benefit of their tawdry column.

182

A man comes to the bar to get a drink next to me and I realise I'm standing next to British film director Paul W. S. Anderson. I've been waiting for this moment for a long time.

"Paul!" I say, as he turns to me. "My name's Morrell, Doug Morrell – author and media commentator. About that last film of yours…"

"Hey there, buddy," he says, sounding more American than I thought he would as he takes an empty glass. "What's up?"

"I felt it kind of lacked the social commentary that some of your contemporaries are displaying. Take Tim Burton for example, he creates mood and atmosphere with every inch of the screen. The characters have depth and complexity, which I just couldn't see in your last picture."

"What are you talking about?" he says, eager to learn where he went wrong.

"*Zombie Crypt: Dead By Dawn*," I remind him. "What exactly was the central character's motivation to go back inside the abandoned mines?"

"Er, not to get torn apart and eaten by the living dead I expect," he replies.

"Well you see, that's where you're going wrong," I sigh. "I've seen zombie films which convey direct social and political messages. Did you know that George A Romero's *Land of the Dead* was an attack on the Bush Administration?"

"You don't say," he replies, as he puts another empty glass on a tray.

"Perhaps your lack of insight contributed to its poor showing at the box office?" I continue.

"You know," he says with a nod. "I think you could be right; maybe you should write all my films?"

"Well, if you insist!" I say, slightly flattered.

"Great!" he says with a grin as he loads up his tray. "Tell you what, you give the catering company a call and pass on your scripts and I'll make them for you. In the meantime, I have to get these empties back to the kitchen."

He walks off across the dance floor with a stack of dirty glasses then disappears into a door marked "Kitchen: Staff Only". I realise he was actually only a waiter. Pity, Paul WS Anderson really needs to be told; maybe I'll email him when I get home? Hopefully he'll be more approachable than George Lucas was when I emailed him a list of all the things wrong with his new *Star Wars* trilogy and my offer to rewrite *Episode I* (well someone had to). In the meantime, I order another drink.

A little later and some of the stars have left; if I'm going to get any pictures I'd better do it fast. How do all these people manage to stay so fresh faced and full of energy for so long? They can't have done a proper day's work in their life. I turn to the barman and order again, but by now he seems to know what I want. I still don't think he deserves a tip though.

"Scuse me luv, you got a napkin back there?" a female voice says in a thick, ugly Brighton accent.

I look across to see one of the Midnite girls leaning on the bar. The barman looks round, grimaces and shakes his head. All I can think about is that if he did have a napkin, he'd better not give it to her before serving me.

"Sorry, but I don't suppose you have a tissue or something, do you?" she continues, but this time in my direction.

Perhaps fate does play into my hands after all. One third of my enemy has been delivered to my doorstop. I guess now there's nothing else to do but tell her what I think of her scummy little column.

"It's not for me," she goes on as I open my mouth, "it's for my mate!"

She gestures beyond the dancefloor and I see Keeley Kline smiling at me from across the room. One of her badly manicured hands dabs her nose, while the other one waves at us.

"That's Keeley Kline?" I stammer.

"Aww you know us already, that's so sweet," she simpers, "the poor girl shouldn't have even been out tonight, she's got a terrible allergy. I don't suppose you have a hanky or something she could borrow?"

I smile through gritted teeth and reach into my pocket to take out my travel tissues. I make sure I only remove one, but her scrawny claw-like hand shoots out and, before I can stop her, the cheeky cow takes the entire packet. She then plants a quick peck on my cheek and speeds off back to her infected friend.

I can do nothing but watch as Keeley dabs her bulbous nose with first one, then all my pocket tissues. I wish I'd sprinkled some anthrax on them now, and where's my Archers and lemonade?

"Barman!" I shout at the clearly disinterested man in a waistcoat behind the bar. He doesn't turn around, and I'm about to shout again in a sterner tone, when someone taps me on the shoulder. I turn round to find not one, but all three Midnite girls standing in front of me.

"Thanks for these, sugar," Keeley giggles like some sort of fourteen-year-old schoolgirl, before throwing the now empty packet of tissues on the bar. "You okay?"

"Yeah," I say, defensively. She probably wouldn't be interested in how bad my day had been after some old lady had a go at me claiming I was six hours late.

Right, here goes: time to tell her what I think of her spiteful and twisted tongue. I open my mouth, but she beats me to it.

"You don't look it, babe," she says, as her two fellow harlots grab me by each arm, "you look like you need a little pick-me-up, come with us, we'll sort you out."

All the things I wanted to say go completely out of my head as I find myself being dragged across the dance floor flanked by the three of them. I don't know what to do and am about to mention that my nose is about to bleed, when I see where we're heading.

The ladies' toilet door looms ever closer. Are they really going to try and take me inside? Surely not: there's a big, ugly bouncer on the door for a start – like he's going to let us all just waltz past.

A few seconds later and I find myself inside a ladies' toilet for the first time since the other boys at school locked me in one overnight. The bouncer didn't bat an eyelid, and even held the door open.

"Have you got any?" one of the Midnite bimbos asks.

I'm too taken aback by the amount of men in here to answer.

"Aww," she goes on, "don't worry, sweetie, Britney's still got some you can have."

And with that, they lead me down the brightly lit room, tapping on cubicle doors as they go. One swings open and as we look inside we're greeted by what I can only describe as a woman performing a "sex act" on a man. I can't see her face, but under the circumstances I'm quite glad. The man, who's standing with his back to us in the cubicle, turns round and gives us the thumbs up.

"Whoops," Keeley laughs, "sorry, babe!"

I think I know that man's face. Isn't he a singer? Didn't I read somewhere he was gay?

"Wasn't that…?" I stammer.

"Yeah," giggles Sarah, "but don't worry, they'll be finished soon. Between you and me, I've heard he's a wham-bam, thank you ma'am type."

"Or thank you, Sir," hisses the other Midnite trollop.

"I heard that!" the man shouts from within the cubicle, before making loud moaning sounds.

186

"Told you," says Keeley in my ear, "we can go inside in a minute."

I'm not sure I want to go in there after what's been happening behind the flimsy wooden door, but as it happens I don't have to. Another toilet door opens a few stalls down and I'm frogmarched into that one instead. Once inside, the door is firmly bolted, the toilet lid put down and the girls position themselves with great expertise around the bowl. You might wonder how four people manage to fit inside a regular size toilet cubicle. I do too, but these three seem to have had plenty of practise.

As one of the girls helps Keeley empty a little packet of white powder onto the lid, another one turns to me.

"We've seen you standing by the bar looking bored," she says as she flutters her eyelids at me, making my knees go a little bit weak, but that was simply the Archers. "We thought you could do with a little something to lift your mood."

I know exactly what she's referring to – class A drugs.

"Now," she goes on as she rubs up against me to move closer to the toilet seat, "you look like a man who's been keeping his eye on things. Seen anything we should know about?"

I watch Keeley take out a rolled bank note and prepare to inhale a neat line of powder.

"Yeah," I say with my first genuine smile of the evening, "I think I may have a few scoops up my sleeve. Let me show you."

They all giggle and I pay close attention to the powder disappearing up Keeley's nostril. Then I reach into my pocket for my camera. Keeley stops inhaling and waits for what I have to say.

"Ladies first," I say with a charasmatic grin that sets their hearts a flutter.

187

Keeley continues to snort. She may need this kind of pick-me-up, but I don't require drugs to fuel my high-powered body. With a simple press of a button, I get very high on life.

The three little strumpets are left open-mouthed as I press the button a second time in case the first one doesn't come out.

"What the bloody hell do you think you're doing?" the nearest one screams.

"That's for calling Donna Trayhorn awful," I state proudly, "she's got more talent in her little finger than the three of you put together. That'll teach you to mess with the Holster!"

And with that I turn, unbolt the door and make my way out. That singer bloke in the other cubicle is still groaning loudly, so as I pass, I stop outside his door as those moans sound way too fake for my liking.

Kick, bang, click.

The startled pop star looks at me aghast before the woman starts screaming.

"That's a keeper that is!" I say with a smile as I leave the toilets.

I'm not worried he might try to chase after me. It would take him too long to do up all the buttons on those ridiculous leather trousers he's wearing. I've had enough of this orgy of flesh and I want no more to do with it. Was it any wonder Donna didn't attend a gig like this?

Chapter 16: Uncharted Territory

Oddly enough, the next day my pictures make every newspaper apart from *The Mirror*. I pick up a copy to find that some junior nobody has been given the task of writing the Midnite girls' column today. It was largely dwelling on the story of how an eminent pop star, who everyone thought was gay, was caught with his trousers round his ankles and a young blonde glamour model with "a mouthful" – the paper's words, not mine.

Raptor's pleased with my work and I receive a nice bundle of notes for my troubles. I'm off sick today as I couldn't rid the world of Doctor Death due to a tummy bug. Besides, even if I was to launch a full scale assault on Death Mountain, I wouldn't have got much done. Donna's single Game For You is released today and I have to buy as many copies as I can to get her to number one.

I go straight to HMV to buy their entire stock, but would you believe it, a supposed "leader in the field" fails to have a single copy. At first I thought their delivery must be running late, but on closer inspection I see that both Charlotte Church's and Westlife's crap new singles have arrived. I insist on waiting at the front of the checkout queue until it arrives. I demand to speak to the manager as I'm not about to be fobbed off by some spotty kid doing a Saturday job on a Wednesday. Unfortunately the manager isn't available and I'm told to try one of the smaller independent music shops, before being thrown out by two ruffians posing as security guards.

"You're barred, mate!" one of them grunts at me.

Barred from a music store? I've never heard anything quite so ridiculous in my life. They don't have to bar me. I certainly won't be coming back here. Who'll be laughing when people start asking where Donna's new single is? I can see a strongly worded email hitting the HMV head office first thing tomorrow morning.

Only a faceless market leader like them would say something so condescending. They know full well that their presence in our high street has forced the smaller stores to shut down. It looks like I'll have to go into London if I'm going to buy her CDs.

When I get there, I find our capital city filled with kids, even though it's supposed to be a school day. I go round all the Virgin Megastores, Tower Records, WH Smiths and Woolworths, even begrudgingly going back into an HMV. But by the end of the morning I only have a total of thirty-two copies. All I keep getting from kids behind tills is:

"Why don't you try downloading it?"

Do they really think I'd be buying all these copies if I could simply download the track from the comfort of my own home? In my case I would, but I was asking on behalf of all her fans who didn't have the luxury of an Ipod. It wasn't on any music download site, and I spent an entire evening searching through them. And to think some misguided pundits keep banging on about how downloading music is the future.

I return home slightly before six, but I had expected to come home sooner as I was sure I'd never be able to walk round London carrying bagfuls of compact discs. As it's happened, I've returned home with two carrier bags full, which equates to a grand total of fifty-four CDs.

I go straight online and post an entry on my site about my haul. I hope it will pave the way for all like-minded supporters to do the same. I texted Mum from London and told her to put my dinner in, but her mobile was conveniently switched off. I suppose I have to face the fact that as people get older, the more selfish they get.

I open a can of soup and upload the photos I took of Donna's mum's house. I'm very happy with the way this lot turned out – you can really make out the detail on the men's faces as they leave.

The following Monday and I'm back at work, not that I needed to be as I still have plenty of money left over from the payout Raptor gave me. I had expected it to have been used up on Donna's single, but I suppose in that respect, I got lucky.

It was a sight no man had witnessed since Hitler's rallies. Thousands of brainwashed troops lined up obediently to salute their criminal mastermind and leader, Doctor Death.

Among the crowd, Doug Holster had no trouble slipping in unnoticed as Death addressed his minions from high up on the loading bay gantry.

"Comrades," the madman cried. "Doug Holster and his band of freedom fighters have thwarted our plans for the last time. We must make sure our bid for world supremacy suffers no further setbacks. It is my sad duty to announce that there are still some citizens still thinking and acting under their own free will, as opposed to under our glorious fascist doctrine!"

While the crowd cheered in unison, Doug loaded a casket of illegal weapons into a tank and prepared to make a break for it.

"There are some people out there still not meeting delivery targets!" he cried as he shook his fist and threatened his hapless slaves with a "motivational team day".

But it would take more than a bonding weekend with his hired goons and crazed psychopaths to scare Doug. He loaded the last of the missiles into his tank and climbed into the turret.

"We have a traitor in our midst!" screamed Death from the gantry. "And if we can't locate him, I will have to talk to every last one of you individually!"

191

*"Not for much longer," Doug grinned as he prepared to
ram his way out of the loading station. But before he could put
the caterpillar tracks in motion, Death's top man, Pinhead,
dived in front of his vehicle – his eyes wild with manic anger.*

"You all right, mate?" Matt says, cheerily.

"I have to go," I inform him as I shut the van door, but
sadly the window is open.

"How was the premiere the other night?" he asks as he
leans on the side of my van eating a sandwich. He'd better not
get any crumbs in my cab.

"It was good," I tell him as I start the engine.

"Yeah? Cool," he begins, "see any stars?"

I reel off a list of the great and good I'd been mingling with
only a few hours ago. I'm not one to name-drop, but when
someone is so blatantly in need of being put in his place, I really
can't help myself.

"So when's Quentin Tarrintino going to pitch your script to
20th Century Fox?" he asks, green with envy.

"When he gets the chance," I muse, "he's got a few projects
of his own to work on first, but that suits me. Gives me a chance
to fine-tune it, plus I only had a rough draft on me at the time."

"Wow," nods Matt.

And with that I leave him to ponder what it must be like to
be me. I hope I haven't made him too depressed.

Once I'm out and about, I park up in a little patch of waste
ground behind the newsagents while I go through this week's
copy of *Zoo* magazine to check out the singles chart. I'd spent
the weekend posting on message boards telling Donna's
supporters to buy as many copies as they could in order to pip
Westlife to the post, but to my horror, my rallying cry must have
fallen on deaf ears.

Not only does Game For You not make the number one slot, it doesn't even make the charts at all! I'm so angry I hurl the ridiculous lads' mag out the window and stuff cotton wool up my nose as I can feel a streamer coming on. In between changing the bungs in my nostrils, I can only console myself the Welsh kid beat Westlife to number one.

I sit here for a while, too angry to drive. I'd probably run someone over and end up being convicted of road rage. And it would all be Westlife's fault. I can't believe that Donna went through all those gruelling promotional activities for nothing. How must she be feeling now? I wonder if she'll be returning home? Maybe she'll seek comfort at her mum's? I set off right away, or at least as soon as my nose stops bleeding.

I sit here waiting for the blood to stop. I have enough time to leaf through a few other papers and spot a three line piece in *The Star* entitled "The Game's Up":

Hard luck to Donna Trayhorn, who's single "Game For You" failed in its bid to break into the top hundred. Metropol claim that lack of radio airplay and a negative publicity campaign from the press are to blame. However rumours are circulating that her single has been inadmissible in the official music charts, due to reports of "buying in teams" operating in the capital over the weekend.

I think people are intelligent enough to know who to believe on that one: a reputable company like Metropol, or a newspaper who delights in running others down. I know for a fact Metropol would never stoop so low as to buy back its own records in order to secure a higher chart position. Besides, I was out all Saturday and I didn't see a single person buying a copy of her song.

I race across town not even bothering to remove the cotton wool from my nose and park up outside her mum's. As I switch the engine off, a great sense of relief sweeps over my body, as if it was me who was finally home. I'm sure it's being here that makes my nose stop bleeding.

This place always acts like a muse for me. I've had almost a dozen amazing ideas for my book while sitting here, and now I've come up with a great way of helping her in these dark times. I'm always reading about celebrities making secret deals with the paparazzi to photograph them in supposed "natural" poses. Now if Donna was to let me shoot her while taking a stroll in the park and feeding the ducks; that would surely make the glossy magazines. Maybe I could even get a few shots of her signing autographs for some of her younger fans. I dial Raptor's number.

"Raptor, it's Doug," I say into my mobile.

"Who?" he replies, I think he's in a meeting.

"Morrell, Doug Morrell!" I remind him, "Trayman Rose?"

"Oh, yeah," he says, after a slight pause, "how the devil are you, big man?"

"Not bad, thanks, mate," I reply in a forced jovial tone which matches his own. Sometimes it can be good to get down with the common man. I consider ending my next sentence with something like "dude".

"What can I do you for?" he asks.

"Well, my man," I begin, "I was thinking of doing a piece on Donna Trayhorn as she's…"

"Who?" He interjects and I'm again forced to remind him of her contribution to the entertainment industry.

"Nah, nah, nah, nah, nah," he says and I think I hear him yawn. "She's last year's news; bring me something fresh for God's sake!"

I point out that he may well regret that decision, but one by one, my valid points fall of deaf ears and we go our separate

194

ways. I can't see me contacting him again. And to think, I was about to refer to a commoner like him as "bruv" the way they do in *Eastenders*.

I return to the depot and unload the parcels back on the conveyer belt, but I'm not happy. The press may well have sunk Donna's singing career with their lies and by the time I get home, I'm too wound up to eat – not that Mum's bothered to cook for me again.

Still no email from Paul WS Anderson about whether he's taken on board my comments about his last films. So I scour the internet for anything on the buying-in conspiracy. But besides the online version of the story, I can find no evidence to back up the press' account – as I predicted.

I go to my own site to post about the newspaper's foul play, only to find someone had already beaten me to it.

"the_antlion" had posted a link to *NME* magazine's official site on the message board. I click it straight away and find a review of Donna's upcoming album "Selling Soul". I suppress the rage for not finding this information myself. Then read what the apparently esteemed music critic Brian Warner had to say about a preview copy Metropol had sent his magazine.

Now I try not to be overly negative in my reviews, but we're talking about Donna Trayhorn's musical capabilities here, not her body parts, which I am afraid to say are her only asset. How anyone would consider buying this album and enjoying it for its musical content is beyond me. And why is her new record label Metropol so obsessed with trying to flog dead horses? Managing Director Peter Carter, or "Supreme Overlord" as some of his ex-employees have dared to refer to him as, has enough money to promote every new band in the world, yet he still puts his efforts into promoting ex-reality TV stars. Sure, we all thought Donna was fit when she was prancing round on Voyeur dressed in stockings and suspenders, but as any sane person knows, the appeal of a reality TV contestant expires about 0.8 of a second after they've left the show.

Come in Donna Trayhorn, your time is up! But if you're unlucky enough to read the press pack that accompanies her new album "Selling Soul", Metropol tries to convince us that Ms Trayhorn's first single "Game For You" is, and I quote, "a return to form". I'm sorry, but correct me if I'm wrong, but didn't her first effort only make the top twenty. No? You're absolutely right, it peaked at number thirty-nine before disappearing into obscurity. And for a jolly good reason – it was rubbish!

Continuing Metropol's propaganda, which incidentally would make Josef Goebbels proud, it points out that her album is an "evolution of dance-culture mixed with underground urban flavours of Brit-pop". I'm sorry, but does the poor work experience kid who wrote that actually have the faintest idea what he's talking about? Has he even heard her caterwauling? This awful, awful CD is by far one of the WORST records I have heard in all my years as a music fan and human being. This steaming pile of pointless capitalist elevator music isn't worth the plastic it's printed on. And to think good pro-tools and major studio money has been used to package this cowpat.

And who did Metropol find to play the backing instruments? Not a real band surely? Perhaps they simply stuck a few microphones in a school's music lesson after the pupils had spent the lunch hour sniffing glue behind the bike sheds? Not one of the "band" – and I can only use the term loosely – is playing their instrument with any kind of skill or passion, then Donna just whines over the top of it. That's it, seriously, nothing else, she just whines to sounds.

Okay, so I doubt in my lifetime I'm ever going to see an ex-reality TV star with their name on a star on the Hollywood walk-

196

of-fame, but I'm not saying they're all completely useless. Some of them have gone on to present TV shows, albeit short-lived ones, but there is a use for them in society. Donna, you're not a bad looking girl. If you're that desperate for fame, stop trying to sleep your way to the top of Metropol and model for a lingerie catalogue or something. Oh, and when I say model, I mean tasteful shoots highlighting decent clothes, not getting your tits out in the gutter of a London nightclub whenever photographers happen to be present.

There is real talent out there, Mr Carter. If by some miracle you ever read this, you have the money and you have the power, please use it wisely and find someone with at least a little fingerful of talent. Promoting this sorry attempt at music only keeps true artists from people's stereos.

Once my nose stops bleeding, I finish an email to both Brian Warner and the editor of the *NME* stating how I will never ever buy their cowpat of a magazine. Not that I've ever bought it before.

Chapter 17: Common People

Now being a media commentator, I do confess to knowing more than the average person about how the media works. Yet there are still times when it manages to amaze me. Posh Spice can release nails scratching down a blackboard to a drum beat and record labels lap it up. Yet when Donna releases an album which is clearly on a higher plain than your average listener, she gets berated for it.

I shouldn't dwell on Posh, but as I sit outside the newsagents on a rainy Monday morning, I find the papers are full of yet another one of her reinventions. How many can she get away with? This week she's going to be a fashion pundit, until that falls through like all the rest of her ventures, then what – a prize gardener?

I skim over anything dedicated to her, but by doing that I find I'm skimming through the entire publication. What with wars, famine, diseases and a new series of *I'm A Celebrity, Get Me Out of Here* planned, what does our press choose to report on? Bloody Kat the human eyebrow and ugly Max have announced their engagement.

Getting engaged is a sure sign that the photo shoots have dried up. I guess they're being advised by some unscrupulous agent how they can make a few bob out of selling the wedding rights to *OK* or *Hello* magazine before they disappear into obscurity.

Once I find there's nothing left in the papers, my next stop is Gloria's place. I sit outside trying not to get too upset thinking about Donna all alone in her big London apartment. I hope she's reading the email I sent her the other day as I expect that should cheer her up.

I look at my mobile phone: it has three bars of signal, but no missed calls. I added my mobile number again to the bottom of that email, but I suppose her phone lines are tied up with urgent talks with her agent. Perhaps I should finally let her have my home phone number? But then I can just picture her calling me for a late night chat and waking Mum. Nothing would kill our relationship quicker than having her shouting down the phone while we're trying to be romantic.

Recently I've been sending flowers to Donna's London pad with messages of support on them. Perhaps I should drop some off at her mother's house by way of a change, just in case that evil doorman has been taking them home for his wife.

I see Gloria opening the door and looking out at me in my car. She smiles warmly before beckoning me inside. I hurry across the road and give her a hug.

"Get your thick head of hair in here this instant!" she says playfully.

I leave my shoes on the "Welcome" mat and follow her into the living room.

"How's our Donna?" I say with a grin.

"All the better once she sees you here!" her mother laughs. She's got such a great sense of humour. I'm so lucky to know the family. "Go through, she'll be back in a minute."

I make myself comfortable in their lounge on one of the reclining chairs and wait for her mum to come back with the tea.

Instantly she returns with her best china and all the biscuits that I like. She sits on the arm of my sofa and pats my knee warmly.

"Now, you tell me everything that's been happening in your life."

While we wait for Donna, I recount my struggle with unscrupulous agents, all champing at the bit to steal my book from me.

"And when will it be adapted for the big screen?" she asks, overwhelmed by my success.

"Well, now I have Brad Pitt, Tom Cruise and Steven Speilberg on board, it should only be a matter of time before it opens the Cannes film festival." I muse.

"Donna's always wanted to go to Italy," her mother says, "I think you've made the right choice picking her as your female lead. She always had a thing for Brad Pitt when she was a teenager."

"Brad's dropped," I say quickly.

"Good call," she nods.

We hear the living room door open and Donna's six-inch stilettos being removed in the marble hallway.

"Doug!" she shouts. "I love you, Doug!"

"I love you too," I reassure her.

"That's the first time anyone's said that to me when I'm dressed like this!" chuckles a man's voice, gruffly.

I open my eyes and see a hobbit dressed as a traffic warden leaning in through my van's window.

"You what?" I say.

"I said..." Bilbo goes on, "you'll have to move your van or I'll be forced to ticket you."

"But I'm delivering!" I point out to the obnoxious little underground-dwelling troll.

"Yeah, right," he grins, exposing razor sharp teeth, "I've been up and down this street three times in the past half hour. You've been sitting in that cab with your eyes closed! Come on, move along."

"But I'm not blocking anyone in, or..." I begin, but the miserable munchkin points to a new sign a little way down the street.

"Residents' parking only," he cackles, clearly loving the feeling of power that comes with the job.

200

I don't say anything as I turn the key in the ignition and pull away. The council will be getting an email from me as soon as I get home. It's high time the Government learns they can't keep oppressing the common man.

"Does this mean you don't love me any mo…" I hear as I roll up the window and drive off.

I can't wait to get home. Some other mug will have to deliver the parcels I didn't get round to. I feel like a lifeline to my very soul has been severed by some money-grabbing town planner. I write the email and press send, but it brings me little comfort. All I can think of is not being allowed to park outside Donna's house.

"Raptor, hello?" I say into my mobile. "What do you mean, who's this? It's Doug!"

"Who?" he says. I think he must be drunk.

"Morrell, Doug Morrell!" I remind him.

"Oh, right. Trayman Tulip?"

"That's right," I say. Maybe he's not drunk after all. Perhaps he's watching a sitcom. I can hear a load of people roar with laughter after I finished speaking.

"Fancy going to another premiere?" he asks.

"No," I say firmly. One orgy of flesh and narcotics is enough for me. "I was thinking, what about exposing unscrupulous town planners or traffic wardens in your next feature?"

The conversation doesn't last much longer. He's very busy and although he appreciates my novel approach to freelance papping, he thinks the general public are more interested in Angelina Jolie than blokes in peaked caps. I sometimes wonder how a man like him got so high up in Top Shot.

During the next week, work was about as much fun as the last series of *Voyeur* – I could still drive past Donna's mum's house, but it wasn't the same. I didn't see a single person come or go all week. I can only hope that my members aren't too disappointed.

I roll out of bed mid-morning for the Sunday papers and find the *News of the World* has gone with:

"*VOYEUR STAR'S MOTHER GAME FOR YOU TOO!*"

My heart skips a beat when I see a photograph of Donna's pretty, smiling face next to her mum at the bottom of the page. My hands are trembling as I read it.

An exclusive News of the World investigation reveals how bisexual Gloria Trayhorn, 37, mother of ex-reality TV dropout Donna Trayhorn, 23, entertains a wide variety of both men and women at her two bedroom council house in North London.

While Donna shamelessly flaunts her assets for free to any paparazzi with a spare roll of film, Gloria is selling hers. For a mere fifty pounds, a lucky punter can enjoy hand relief, oral, or intimate body worship behind the closed doors of her unassuming terraced house. Or, if the discerning lady or gentleman wants to really push the boat out, he or she could go all the way for a nice round hundred.

It's still unclear whether Donna herself has become involved in the family business, but one Stockbroker from West London has claimed to have paid her up to a thousand pounds to meet him in his luxury hotel room.

Gloria's sordid secret first came to our attention when a string of photos depicting her "satisfied customers" was first published on a website for all to see. As yet, Donna has been unavailable for comment, but in a statement issued by her management, Metropol Industries, they said the rumours were merely hearsay and that she is too busy promoting her – aptly titled – new album "Selling Soul".

So while Donna sells her soul, her mother was busy offering to sell our undercover reporter the "time of his life" in

Donna's old bed. They eventually settled on a price of eighty pounds for her to smear piccalilli on various parts of her body, while she spanked him with a rubber chicken. It was at that point in the transaction, our man "developed second thoughts" and decided to leave.

It goes on, but I can't bring myself to read such lies. I think I know Donna and her family well enough to know what they're really like. My mouth is dry and I put cotton wool up my nose in anticipation of the oncoming downpour.

I turn my computer on to be once again greeted by my desktop image of Donna's wonderful pouting face. I can see by her eyes that she isn't the type to have anything to do with a life of vice, let alone have a close family member who'd do something like that.

Strange, ninety-six new email messages are in my inbox.

The first has the subject line "you're ruining my life you…" and I won't repeat the obscenities that are then used to describe me and my mother, not that I'm sure what she has to do with this.

Out of the ninety-six messages, over three quarters are from delusional men who claim that I am somehow responsible for the break-up of their marriages. A few more are journalists wanting "my take on the story", while the rest seem to think that I should have Gloria's phone number, address and "price list".

Those were the only ones I replied to, stating that I would never betray Donna or any member of her family by disclosing personal information about them to strangers.

Then the first of many instant message windows pops up.

Paul_Durkin11: what have i done to you?

the_oracle_lives: im going to sue u. take my f@*king picture down from ur f@*king website right now fetish_lverman: do u no if gloria does nipple torture or enemas?

I blocked that lot straight away and I'm seriously thinking of taking down my instant messenger handle from my site.

Whos_the_man401: have u heard all these terrible lies about donna?

I will of course answer genuine supporters of the family.

Steely_Doug9: yes, its disgraceful

Whos_the_man401: they reckon she charges a grand for a shag

Steely_Doug9: dont believe the lies. its just tabloid rubbish

Whos_the_man401: yeah, dont worry, i no its rubbish

Steely_Doug9: how come?

Whos_the_man401: coz she shagged me for free after i totally outbid u on ebay!

Whos_the_man401 has been blocked from your contact list.

I hoped he was dead. I take my messenger address off the site and check my message board to find comments which were along similar lines. I feel like I'm living in some sort of parallel universe that doesn't make sense. I need to talk to Donna face to face and have this out with her. I immediately dash off an email to her official site with my mobile number displayed in big letters at the top and "urgent" in the subject field. Although I feel a little bad for pressurising her at such a sensitive time, I feel we need to talk badly. Not only because I'm sure there are many things she needs to get off her chest, but because I feel this may affect her celebrity status. We've all heard the old cliché about how "all publicity is good publicity", but right now I'm not so sure.

Monday morning comes and still no mail from Donna, so I go straight round to Gloria's.

I phoned work to let them know my upset tummy had come back. Since reading the fraction of that hideous article, I have been feeling physically sick.

I park outside the house and almost feel like a heroin addict who needs his fix, not that I'd ever do drugs as only losers use them. Being here brings me comfort in this world of chaos. This is the only place I feel I truly belong in, apart from Donna's London flat of course. All the curtains are drawn and I'm sure there are other men watching the house from cars parked nearby. I take a deep breath as I stand outside the front door as this is it, the moment I've been waiting for.

Sometimes it takes a crisis to bring people together and cement a relationship. I'm certain her mother is in there.

"Pervert!" a woman's voice shouts from somewhere nearby.

I look to my right and see an ugly woman wearing a blouse that's way too tight, leaning out of her badly painted front window. For a minute I'm quite taken aback by this unprovoked attack and also by the roll of loose flesh hanging out between her lower buttons.

"Excuse me?" I gasp.

"We don't want your type around here. Why don't you just piss off?"

I'm not going to stand for being spoken to like that on a public pavement, so I march straight up to her with a good mind to slam her tacky window in her greasy face.

"I don't know who you think you are, but I'm here to see Gloria and it's got nothing to do with you."

"Yeah, you and all the rest," she sneers as she points behind me.

I look round and see at least three different men sitting in various cars; one seems to be taking notes, while the other two have digital cameras. They'd better not be taking my photo. That's an infringement of my civil rights.

"She's a personal friend," I tell flabby.

"Oh, yeah," she says with a false sense of superiority. "Gloria's such a friendly person! Maybe if you slip your hundred quid under the door she'll meet you in a nice hotel?"

"I don't have to pay for that sort of thing," I snap, disgusted with her innuendo, "a woman's never made me pay for it yet!"

She doesn't answer and I know I've won a moral victory as she leans back in her tawdry house leaving me alone in the street. Or at least I would be if it wasn't for those suspicious looking men in cars who are still watching me like a herd of vultures. I can't stay here as my oasis of purity has been defecated in by ink straight from the pens of twisted journalists.

I would dearly love to drive into London and speak to Donna personally, as I feel this huge misunderstanding is being blown completely out of proportion. However, being a Monday I'd have to pay that awful congestion charge and I'm not about to sit next to those smelly types who use public transport, so I return home.

Once there, I put on some old tapes of Donna while she was on *Voyeur*. I check my mobile phone – it still has a full battery – but only two bars of signal.

"Please ring, will you?" I plead to Donna on the TV as I can almost feel her pain in these troubling times. Then I realise I think I may have sounded a little bit too pushy.

"I'm sorry," I say to her on screen immediately.

My phone rings.

I don't take in the number on the display, as I don't want to waste my time reading digits in case she rings off, but it's definitely a London number.

"Donna?" I say.

"Um, no," replies a man's voice, "it's Raptor, but funny you should say that, as I think I owe you an apology."

Yes, I think you do.

"What for?" I ask.

"About Donna!" he laughs. "I don't know how you do it, but you just seem to hit home run after home run. How did you know she'd become so hot?"

"Donna's always been very attractive," I point out, slightly put out that he seemed to think that she wasn't.

"Yeah, yeah – good one," he says, "but seriously, look, after that clown went and put photos of those perverts going to see her mum, Donna's become pretty sought after. That's when I thought of you."

I don't answer immediately. I'm not sure what to say, so I listen.

"Look, you seem to know a lot about her. Where do you reckon she's holding up?"

"Will you pay expenses?" I ask carefully.

Chapter 18: Service With a Smile

The following day I still have an upset tummy and type out a letter from Mum to send to work that tells them I won't be in.

I pull up outside Donna's London apartment in my bright yellow Audi 600 sports car and press the button that puts the black leather retractable roof back up. The Nazi doorman scurries over and tips his hat obligingly. He opens the driver's side door and I step out in my Levi boot-fit jeans and brand new Marks & Spencer shirt.

"Good afternoon, Sir," he says without looking me in the eye.

I don't answer and watch as he shuts my car door gently.

"Do you have any luggage I can help you with?" he goes on in a disgustingly sycophantic tone.

Slowly, I remove my lilac John Lennon-style sunglasses and flash him a smile showing my perfect teeth. I watch as one by one the muscles in his ridiculously long face relax before hardening again into his usual frosty look.

"Oh, it's you," he mutters.

"Yes, it's me," I say triumphantly, "and I've left my glasses case in the glove compartment; be a good little man and get it for me."

It is with sheer ecstasy that I watch his long head slump as I make him reopen my car door and lean in to check my glove compartment.

"Er, mind the upholstery, please," I say as I make sure he doesn't sully the PVC leopard skin interior.

"It's not in here," he grunts, before begrudgingly adding "Sir."

"Oh, that's right, silly me – I had it here all along," I laugh as I pull the case out of a pocket in my Levi 801s. "Shut the door now, please."

"Excuse me, Sir," he says as he goes back to the building's main entrance.

It's amazing how differently people treat you when they think you have money. All the times I've been sitting outside this block and he's looked at me like I'm some sort of rodent.

I place my John Lennon style sunglasses back on my nose and look over the lenses as he holds the door open for a couple of men in overalls carrying out a tasteless zebra-skin sofa. Little does he know that I'll be walking through those very doors in a moment.

I allow the overall-clad commoners to pass as I walk to within feet of entering Donna's building, but he spots me.

"You're not coming in," he barks. "I don't care what car you're driving."

I don't answer; instead I put my black mock leather briefcase down and take out a business card which reads "Dean Philips – Insurance Specialist" and hand it to him.

He looks at it, then up at me.

"Number nine is expecting me," I say softly as I gesture to the intercom. "Go on, be a good little boy and buzz me in – then I might think about giving you some sweets."

Reluctantly he moves over to the intercom and presses the button for apartment nine. I wait patiently, savouring every moment before he has to swallow his pride and give me access. Another commoner in overalls leaves the building carrying one of those god-awful lava lamps and a stupid singing fish you buy in Clintons card shops for someone you don't like.

"Miss Jones?" the disgruntled Kaiser says into the speaker, "sorry to bother you, it's Alan at the front door, there's a Dean Philips to see you, something about insurance?"

209

"Oh, right," a woman's voice crackles, "send him up."

What's left of his smugness fades and his long head droops so low, his chin almost touches the ground.

"Go on up please, Sir."

"Why thank you, Alan," I say, not forgetting another one of my best smiles as I march past him into the building. The childish part of me would say something, but I'm proving that I'm metaphorically bigger than him by remaining calm and polite.

Once longhead closes the door behind me I begin my work. He may think my real name is Dean Philips – door to door insurance salesman providing cover for all your household needs – but he's wrong! I'm really Doug Morrell, author, media commentator and crusader against celebrity injustice. Thanks to Raptor slipping Miss Jones a few quid to say she's expecting me, I now have complete access to this entire block, or, more importantly, Donna's flat.

As I stand in the lift ascending to the dizzy heights of her third floor apartment, I imagine her sitting on the end of her bed, hopefully not crying, but quite upset and waiting for me to arrive. We have much to discuss, not just about the media smear tactics and how we can rebuild her career, but how the two of us can take our relationship forward. While I was watching old *Voyeur* footage earlier, I could almost hear her crying out to me for help. Little does she know that I'm now only a few feet from her door.

I get out of the lift and follow the sign towards her flat, only to be confronted by an open door. I'm more than a little concerned for her safety, as you never know who might walk in.

As soon as I have taken a picture of the front door for my website, I go straight inside.

"Only the chest of drawers in the bedroom now, Tariq!" a man's voice says from what I guess is the lounge.

I walk down the empty white hallway, not even stopping to take pictures of the kitchen through an archway to my right. I enter the deserted lounge and see another man in overalls packing a load of stuff into a cardboard box and sealing it with masking tape.

"Who are you?" a man's voice says from behind me.

I turn and am confronted by yet another man in overalls standing before me.

"Never mind that," I say, "who on earth are you?"

"We're clearing out this place," he replies as he folds his arms and tries to make himself look bigger than me, "you got a problem with that?"

"But Donna Trayhorn lives here!" I state in a loud voice as the swarthy man with the cardboard box walks past me.

"Who?" the ogre grunts.

I take a deep breath and look Shrek square in the face, then launch into an explanation of just whose flat his dirty great swamp boots are standing in.

"Look, mate," he says, rudely interrupting me, "I don't care if the Pope used to live here, she ain't here now and we have to clear it out by four as there's a viewing then."

"Where's Donna?" I demand to know, "what have you done with her?"

"She's already been packed in one of the boxes downstairs," he smirks.

"Which one?" I shout, before realising this was some sort of troll-like humour. I stand there seething, too angry even to warn him he'd better not damage any of Donna's tasteful possessions.

"Right, if you don't mind, we've got to get this lot into storage," he says, before walking towards the door.

"But what about Donna?" I ask.

He turns and shrugs, then leaves me alone in her apartment.

So, here I am, standing in the place I've always known I belong, yet somehow it doesn't quite meet my expectations. I wish I could have seen it fully decorated, with all the cute little touches she must have added to turn it into a home. I spend a while walking round the two-bedroom apartment, taking photos of each room from every angle. The kitchen is small, and although modern, slightly grubbier than I imagined. I hope she fired her cleaning lady. I can't quite tell which bedroom she slept in, as both are equally small, but one smells more of perfume, so I figure it must have been hers. I lie on the floor where she had the bed. I know I'm in the right position, as it's where I would have put it, and the two of us do tend to think alike.

While I lie here looking up at the ceiling, I try and imagine why she moved out. This is a lovely little place and the two of us would have been very happy here. At first I put it down to that nasty piece of work on the front door – Alan. I'll bet he's made her life hell while she's been here. Then I remember all the negative exposure. For the sake of a few unsubstantiated headlines, an innocent working girl has been forced to leave her home.

There's nothing in the spare room's fitted wardrobes, but when I open a bedroom cupboard, I see an old cardboard box on the top shelf.

Did she forget this? Or did those arrogant apes in overalls not see it? Maybe she left it for me to find?

I can hardly believe my luck as I take the box back into the lounge and sit on the floor to see what she's left me: paperwork mainly, plus a few old bank statements and letters. I would like to say this lack of professionalism by the removal men amazes me, but sadly I find it only too believable of the lower classes' work ethics. These bank statements are clearly marked "Private and Confidential" and yet they leave them behind in an empty flat when they know people are coming round in a matter of hours.

I scan down the paperwork and can only assume Donna must have many bank accounts in which she distributes her wealth, as this one appears to be almost empty. As I turn the pages, I find her rapidly descending into the red, before going over her overdraft limit altogether. But I suppose with all her promoting, she didn't have time to keep an eye on every single one of her accounts. Either way, I know one thing:

"She'll want these back right away," I announce as I hear my voice echo round the empty flat.

I would rush them straight round to her, but I decide it would be a considerate gesture if I was to reorder them all, as they seem to have been simply stuffed into this old box. Again, I hope the cleaning lady got what was coming to her.

While I fold each page neatly, making sure one side never overlaps the other in an unsightly fashion, I come across not one, but two bonuses.

The first is a small, but dusty see-through plastic bag containing a five pound note, a small make-up mirror and a Tesco clubcard. This shows Donna couldn't be in financial difficulties if she had money tucked away like this. Plus it means she'll be even more pleased when I return these precious items to her, as I can imagine her embarrassment when she gets to the check-out and finds she can't get the points on her clubcard. Then finally there's the make-up mirror – I don't claim to know a lot about women, but I do know that the best ones make an effort to look good for their men, and she'll be livid to lose such a valuable possession.

The other thing I found at the bottom of the box was a letter from her cousin Linda. This made especially interesting reading:

Hi Donz, haven't seen you in ages. Can't believe that spotty little cousin I used to force to eat earwigs is now so famous! Do you fancy coming over to stay sometime? I've told all my friends about how you're my favourite cousin and I'd love to take you out for a night on the town to show you off.

You're welcome to come and stay at my place whenever you like, just give me a couple of days to let my friends know you'll be stopping by. And of course feel free to bring along any hunky celebrities you might know!

Luv Linda xxx

It warms my heart to think that in these stressful times Donna can rely on her family for support. But most importantly, the letter includes Linda's address. This gives me an idea.

I return home to upload my new pictures, knowing my members will be delighted for such an intimate look into their idol's personal life. Halfway through the file transfer process, I'm interrupted by my mobile ringing.

"Trayman Rose my man – talk to me!" Raptor yells.

"What about?" I reply, knowing that the two of us probably have very little in common.

"Well – I just thought I'd ring you up out of the blue to see if you'd like to go out for dinner sometime, some nice little intimate restaurant where we could…"

"You what?" I cut him off with, "I'm already seeing someone, thank you very much!"

I didn't think he was like that, but it seems he's become so completely besotted with me, that I've turned him into a gay.

"Don't be so bloody daft," he snaps, "what the hell do you think I want? You took my car and a wad of money this morning and we got you into what's-her-name's place – what have you got for me?"

I don't know whether I'm relieved or not to find out he doesn't want to date me.

"Oh, don't worry," I reassure him, "I've got the goods."

"Yeah? Fantastic, did you get something juicy for me?" he asks and I think I can almost hear the drool running down his chin.

"Yeah, totally," I say, truthfully, "do you want me to email them over?"

"Do reality TV stars have longer shelf lives than pears?"

I think he must be on drugs.

"Yes, please, Doug," he finally says, before hanging up.

I send him across the files before settling down to watch some reruns of *Voyeur* – safe in the knowledge I've had a most profitable day.

Sadly I'm not destined to enjoy Donna's rendition of Gwen Stefani's "What You Waiting For?" as my mobile goes again.

"Are you taking the piss?" Raptor says on the other end without even having the courtesy to say hello and how are you? "What the bloody hell are these?"

"The inside of Donna's apartment," I state clearly. "Did you not read the filenames?"

"Yes, of course I read the bloody filenames, but I thought "lounge_left.jpg" just might actually have had a picture of Donna in it, preferably slitting her wrists in a fit of depression!"

"That's horrible!" I say, disgusted by his lack of compassion.

"Oh, you know what I mean," he mutters, but I'm not sure I do. "Look, I've phoned round the papers and I know that none of the other agencies have been able to get a picture of her or her old dear. I thought you were supposed to be an expert on these people? Don't you have any idea where they might be?"

"Have you tried her cousin?" I say, casually.

215

"Cousin? I didn't know she had one," he says, "we've tried most of her friends, but they don't know where she is. Even went as far as tracking down her dad, but she isn't with him."

"How can you be sure?" I ask, intrigued as there is always very little mentioned on the web about her father.

"Because he's in serving eight years for armed robbery, all right?"

Okay, so that explains that. No wonder she never talks about him; I'll bet she's glad to be shot of him. If he'd been her role model, who knows what she might have ended up like?

"Anyway, never mind about that. Do you know where this cousin is?" he goes on.

I have Donna's box right next to me; there's no way I'd let her possessions out of my sight. I gently lift Linda's letter from the inside and check the address.

"My services don't come for free you know," I say, with a smile.

Chapter 19: One Track Mind

Donna's cousin Linda lives in Ruislip, which luckily is down the road from me. I think it's funny how Linda says in her letter that they haven't seen each other in ages when they live so close. Still, I'm sure Donna will explain why when I meet her today.

As I pull up in my Audi 600 and park outside the newsagents, I spare a thought for all those people out there going to meaningless jobs they don't enjoy. How lucky I am to be doing something that genuinely thrills me.

Doug Holster is back on the case. After storming into The Colonel's office, slamming his twin pistols down on the desk and threatening to walk unless he was taken off surveillance, he's finally been given a field assignment – and what a return to form.

After being captured by Doctor Death, the edible Ms Trayhorn had managed to bribe a guard and escape. Now she was afraid for her life and holding up in unknown whereabouts.

But who would reach her first: the armies of evil, or the love of her life – Doug Holster? Doug's first port of call was the seedy strip club WH Smiths.

I leave the newsagents in the high street and sit in my sports car reading stories about Donna. It's worth pointing out that the stories were just that – about Donna – not actually interviewing her, or her mum, or indeed anyone who she'll ever class as a friend again.

The papers make a drama out of a crisis and most of them find it hilarious to link Donna's song "Game For You" with headlines like "On The Game". Some practically infer that it's Donna who's selling her body, rather than her mum. Not that I truly believe such poison. Unlike the press, I'm blessed with an open mind and am going to wait and see what Donna has to say before I reach my balanced and rational verdict.

They even make up some garbage about Donna being "thrown out" of her London flat by Metropol because it was a company-owned property. There was one story in *Now* magazine with the headline "Star's Anguish Over Mother" which, to the layman, might sound like it was printed with Donna's consent, but of course it was based on merely a "close friend" of the family who naturally wishes to remain nameless.

I don't know about her anguish over her mother, but what about the anguish of being stalked by an unscrupulous media twenty-four hours a day?

I arrive outside Linda's house, but it seems that none of her neighbours has a job, as they've taken up every residents parking bay in the street. I park in an extortionate NCP car park round the corner and hurry straight back to her road.

Her house is an end-of-terrace building on the corner of a street situated on two main roads. The front of the house faces Freeman Gardens and seems to be kept adequately maintained, although someone has taken the brass numbers off the front door and today's mail is still sticking out the letterbox. The side of the house runs along White Avenue and is basically only a wall where some ignoramus has sprayed the word "slapper" on it. All the curtains are drawn and I launch my first reconnaissance mission by walking up and down both streets.

I check every car, but there are no scumbags waiting to prey on innocent victims for a callous media. I have found a new home.

Occasionally someone comes out of a front door, but years of Secret Service training allow me to blend in perfectly. Sometimes I bend down to tie my shoelace, other times lean on a lamppost while pretending to text an imaginary friend. It's no wonder I'm where I am today – I'm so good at my job.

I feel my heart beat faster as I near Linda's front door on my latest pass. With one smooth flick of my hand, I reach out and grab the envelopes sticking out the letterbox and disappear under cover of daylight to read them. Safely round the corner, I open the first correspondence and read about an introductory offer of a free DVD if Linda subscribes to renting at least three "Top Title" movies a month. I feel like I'm getting to know her almost as well as Donna.

My radar-like hearing picks up the sound of a door opening around the corner and, like a lion breaking cover, I pounce.

The woman who comes out of Linda's front door could be any age as she's fat. The excess flesh on her ample frame masks her appearance almost as well as the designer shades I'm wearing hide my true identity.

"Linda?" I ask.

"Who are you?" she replies, while halfway inside a waiting taxi.

"I'm a friend of Donna's," I say in a firm, yet friendly voice; after all, this portly lump could one day be a bridesmaid at our wedding. But obviously she'd have to slim down first if she was going to appear in any of the pictures we sell to *OK* magazine.

"Um, er, Donna's not here right now," she stammers. Bless her – loyal to the last.

"It's okay," I reassure her, "we go way back. She asked me to bring round the last of her stuff from her flat."

"Are you getting in, or what?" a gruff voice barks from the taxi's cab.

I see the grubby little driver is talking to Linda. I open my wallet and produce a fifty pound note and hand it to him.

"Stay," I say firmly without taking my eyes off her. She swallows hard, clearly impressed with my confidence.

"You can give her stuff to me, if you like? I'll make sure she gets it," she says while she plays with her horrible hair flirtatiously.

"It is of quite an intimate nature," I point out, "I really think I should give it to her personally, if you know what I mean?"

"Oh, all right," she says, dejectedly. "It's just, she's not up yet – she's having a lie in. If you come back later you can give her the stuff – sorry, what was your name?"

"Morrell, Douglas Morrell. But you can call me Doug."

"Doug Morrell?" she says, "she's never mentioned you."

"That's cool, I run her website and promote her online campaigns," I inform Donna's chunky relation.

"Oh, right. Look, I better go," she says, "we're fresh out of Tequila in there and I'm down to my last bottle of Jack Daniels."

"You're going shopping?" I ask as I tip my shades down slightly to hold her gaze.

"Uh-huh," she nods.

I hand the little man in the taxi another fifty.

"Thank you, but we don't need you after all."

A little later my Audi pulls into Tesco's and I can feel every trolley-pushing customer gazing at us in awe. They're probably wondering what a classy guy like me is doing with a fat chick taking up all the room in my passenger seat. It's terrible how shallow some people are. She taps me on the leg.

"Sorry?" I say.

She mouths something.

"Beg your pardon?"

The cheeky blob actually has the audacity to touch my stereo and turn down a remix of Game For You I have blaring out of the customised speakers in the back.

220

"I said, don't you think we should put the roof up? It's starting to rain!" she cries.

I smile. A drop of water on my leather interior doesn't bother me that much. But I oblige and press the button to make the roof slide over our heads, then turn Game For You back up full blast.

After Linda's paid for the parking, we enter the store. She's clearly impressed as I regale her with stories about Johnny Depp reading through the script I sent him and how I'd advised a top director on the content of his film. She hangs on every word, but then she's fat, so she's probably not used to successful men paying her attention. I suspect she'll remember this day for the rest of her life. I lead her straight to the drinks aisle and begin to fill her trolley with what I think Donna would like.

"Champagne," I say as I place another crate into the trolley.

"I think Donna would be happier with a bottle of mentholated spirits right now!" she laughs.

Although Donna's situation is clearly no laughing matter, I resist the temptation to correct her for her lack of sensitivity.

"So," I say through gritted teeth, "what was Donna like as a child?"

"Horrible!" she jokes.

I laugh loudly and repeat the question.

"She always wanted to be famous I suppose, that's why we never saw much of her."

And why would anyone not want to be famous? I think this shows how focused she was even at such an early age.

"And I'll bet her mum was right behind her all the way," I say, awaiting the correct answer this time.

"Behind her?" she laughs. "Knowing our Gloria, more like on her back!"

Two strikes – one more and I really will have to consider not inviting her to the wedding.

"Seriously though, you make it sound like all these allegations are true?" I say as I put another crate of Algerian champagne into the trolley.

"Easy does it," she says as I drop a third one in, "I can't afford all that."

"It's okay," I say with a wink and pat my right trouser pocket. She smiles and breathes easy again. "You can pay me back later. Now, about these awful press stories…"

"I guess they had to come out sooner or later," she says with a shrug. "We always knew Gloria didn't get all that money from the Social Security."

I nearly drop my crate of Archers when those words leave her lips.

"You didn't know?" she says after what seems like eternity.

My mouth goes dry at the thought of such depravity. How can I have Gloria as a mother-in-law now? Could she be trusted to behave at the wedding? What if she started trying to drum up business by coming on to *Hello* magazine photographers? There would be no other option but to get security to eject her if they spot her trying to gatecrash our happy day.

Linda starts rambling some more, but by now I'm not listening. I have to get Donna away from the nest of vipers she calls a family as quickly as possible. Perhaps the two of us need to get out of the country altogether? Hollywood is of course the logical destination.

Linda wants to get some food to go with the champagne, but I tell her I'll sort the food out later. I imagine Donna could do with being taken out to a classy restaurant in Ruislip for lunch; it might take her mind off things.

"Are there any good restaurants around here?" I ask Linda at the checkouts.

"Not really," she replies as she pays by debit card.

"Pity," I say, "we'll have to go to the West End."

"Ooh, that'll be nice," she says with a smile.

Yes it will, but you're not coming. By the looks of you, you've eaten more than your fair share of hot meals.

"Here, use my clubcard," I say obligingly as I hand her my in-store card. I can get a lot of points for this lot.

We leave the supermarket and head back to my car. I move the box of Donna's possessions out of the boot as Linda loads up. She'll have to have it on her lap during the ride home. Half an hour later and we're back at her front door and I'm finally about to get things sorted with Donna.

"Hi, Don, I'm back!" Linda yells up the stairs as she dumps the bags of drink down in the hallway – she'd better not have broken any of the bottles. "Guess who I've got with me?"

No answer – she's probably still in the bath.

"Donna? You up yet?" she calls again. Still nothing, but I'm not concerned as it gives me time to check my appearance in the hallway mirror. The shades really do highlight my distinctive cheekbones. I look round, but Linda's gone.

I venture into the lounge and survey my conquest. It's drab and the curtains could do with a clean, but I suppose this is to be expected in a council place. I look at the pictures on top of the television set. I see Linda in them with various inbred mutants who I assume are her family, but my eyes are drawn to a recent Polaroid of her and Donna in a pub. I smile to myself as I'm pleased Donna's managing to enjoy herself in these dark times.

"Would you believe it?" Linda shouts from another room. "She's gone out again – left a note saying she's just popped out to get some booze, but shouldn't be too long."

Yes, thank you, I will wait. While I listen to her clattering around in the kitchen, I spend my time looking through the drawers in the sideboard and seeing what little keepsakes I can take. A few things catch my eye, but I'm drawn to some of the other photos around the room. Linda appears to have a very attractive relative.

"Who's the girl in the graduation photo?" I shout.

"Claire, my sister – she got a BSC in Geography – with honours you know?"

I know, I can tell she's clearly the intelligent one of the two. She looks a bit like Donna come to think of it. I can see her blending in well in the wedding photos. Maybe one day she could even do a photo-shoot with her cousin?

"I'm making tea, would you like a cup?" Linda yells from the next room.

"I'd prefer a drop of that champagne," I reply. After a pause she agrees. "And would a sandwich be out of the question?"

Another pause, but she seems to like the idea of making food. She's obviously had a lot of practice.

I look about the room for other signs of Donna. What I'd really like to do is go up and see her bedroom, but for now I'll settle on the sofa while I wait for my meal.

"Oh, hello," a gentle voice says from the doorway. I look up to see Claire standing there in only a fluffy pink towel wrapped around her wet tanned body. Her brown hair hangs loosely around her shoulders and she stands there leaning against the door looking down at me.

"And you must be Claire?" I say.

"That's right," she giggles as she sits down opposite and hurriedly fixes her hair.

"The name's Morrell, Doug Morrell. I expect Donna's mentioned me," I say confidently as she eyes me up.

"Oh, yes," she replies and I think she blushes slightly, "she talks about you all the time."

Of course she does.

"Doug?" another voice says, and I look towards the door to see big Linda standing there with a sandwich that has been cut at the wrong angle. "Who are you talking to?"

"My agent," I say as I take out my mobile phone, but the damn thing starts to ring.

"Aren't you going to answer that?" the fat one asks as she puts my plate down, "it could be important."

"Hello?" I say into the phone, "no, you idiot. I said Johnny Depp for the lead role, not Tom Cruise. He's so last year – didn't you see Oprah? Goodbye."

I switch off the phone and reassure Linda that me being here is far more important than getting the right leading man for my motion picture.

"How long will Donna be?" I ask as she almost manages to fit an entire baguette into her mouth in one go.

I watch the crumbs spring from her lips as she chews her pate and lard sandwich while informing me that Donna won't be back till later this evening. After I tell her I'm not married, she actually has the nerve to suggest that we perhaps find a "nice little pub and get a bite to eat". I decline – naturally, then tell her I'll come back later and catch up with Donna, and maybe Claire if she's back.

"Aren't you going to leave her stuff?" she asks desperately as she practically chases me to the front door.

"I need to give it to her in person," I reply. How could I give it to this walking pudding now, after she had the nerve to try and ask me out when I'm already bequeathed to her cousin?

I turn my phone back on when I get home and sit in the front room to watch an old episode of *Voyeur*. No sooner have I put my feet up than it bleeps to tell me I have a voice message. Begrudgingly I listen.

"Hello, Holster, guess who?" cackles Doctor Death. "You'll never find Ms Trayhorn before me. As we speak I have an entire legion of my finest troops combing Acton, Ickenham and even Uxbridge! And what was that about Tom Cruise?"

I ignore his idle threats and keep my eyes fixed on the TV. If it wasn't for the fact it would cost me good money to phone him back, I'd have a good mind to tell him I'm never returning and going to live in Hollywood with Donna. But I don't – I'm too hungry. I haven't eaten all day as that sandwich of Linda's was disgusting.

But before I can see where Mum is hiding, my damn mobile goes off again.

"Trayman Bob!" a voice says. "It's Raptor here."

Yeah, like I didn't know that from the display on my phone flashing "Raptor". And did he just call me "Trayman Bob"?

"Yeah?" I say, dubiously.

"What have you got for me?"

Talk about obsessed. The man has a one-track mind.

"I've been with Linda all day."

"Yeah, and?"

"She's okay, if you like that sort of girl – bit fat though for my liking. She works in a call centre for Tele-linx and has a few good friends."

"That's nice. That's made my day that has."

Is he being sarcastic?

"Can I ask you something, Trayman Rosie?" he says, in a more threatening tone.

"What?"

"Is this fat chick dating Justin Timberlake?"

"No," I say, confidently, "she's actually just been dumped by a chiropodist."

I can't tell what he shouts next as I'm forced to hold the phone away from my ear. About twenty seconds later, his tone lowers to a suitably respectful level that I feel comfortable listening to again.

"...look mate; I gave you one hell of a big advance for this scoop. I want something back, got it?"

"I'm picking Donna up later on."

Silence – that's shut him up.

"Picking her up?"

"Yup, I'm meeting her at her cousin's place at eight o'clock."

"Well, why didn't you say?"

I could go into details, but I don't see why I should justify myself to vermin.

"Oh and one more thing, Doug," he says, coldly, "I received no less than three parking tickets in the post this morning."

He trails off, as if expecting me to say something. I don't.

"I don't suppose you know anything about them, do you?"

I tell him I'll be in touch before tomorrow morning and hang up. Does he really think I'm going to pay for parking on a car that isn't even mine?

Chapter 20: All Roads
Lead to Ruislip

After dinner I check my hair. I'm pretty sure the baseball cap I've been wearing all day has actually thickened it, but just to be on the safe side I comb it forwards.

I've bought new clothes for my date with Donna and booked a table in a local eating venue that I'd heard some of the guys at work talking about. I know she'll be pleased to see me and will no doubt be delighted with the bottle of champagne I took from one of the crates Linda bought.

Sadly the best laid plans of mice and celebrities often go to waste.

I step out of my front door at seven and head down to my car – it's been clamped.

Apparently because I hadn't moved my resident's parking permit from my own car to the Audi, some over-zealous little parking Nazi had taken it upon himself to slap a bloody great boot on the front wheel.

I get mad so quickly I bung tissue up my nose to stop it bleeding all over my new shirt. Then I dial the number on the sticker that's plastered on the driver's side window.

It's ten minutes to eight and I'm sitting with my feet up on the sofa watching an old episode of *Voyeur* – the one where Donna throws up in the Box Room while talking to camera. Normally this would be the highlight of my day, if it wasn't for the fact that in only ten minutes I should be seeing her in the flesh.

I check my mobile phone again – no missed calls. I've been sitting here since seven waiting for the clamp removal man to come. He told me he'd be here within the hour. I knew that would mean two. He eventually arrives at twenty past eight and I'm on my way by half past.

I speed through the streets faster than I've ever driven. If I wasn't so frantic about missing Donna, I might even crack a smile about how if I delivered parcels this quickly I'd be done by noon.

I pull up outside Linda's, but just by looking at the place, my hopes aren't high. There are no lights on and my gut tells me everyone's out.

It's nearly nine and I did say to Linda that I'd come by later on to give Donna her stuff. I knew I shouldn't have trusted that lump to pass on my message. I'll bet she was so jealous I turned her down, that she's taken Donna out herself.

I stand at the front door and try the handle. It's locked.

I take out the set of keys I found in Linda's sideboard drawer earlier and try them. The sound of the lock clicking as it turns is music to my ears. The smaller Yale key offers an equally pleasing noise as the door creaks slightly before swinging open to reveal the hallway.

"Hello?" I shout as I take a step into the house. "It's Doug! Donna, are you home?"

No answer. I had a feeling there wouldn't be, but it pays to be polite.

I check the lounge, but there's nothing new in there. However, this time I do make sure I get some photos for my site. The kitchen displays signs that some sort of takeaway has been consumed; I can just picture Linda with her snout in a box of noodles. I'll have to wait for Donna in her bedroom.

I return to my car and get her valuables and take them upstairs. I find her room immediately, almost like I'm drawn to it. It's the one filled with dozens of cardboard boxes containing carefully packed mementos from her glittering life. I place my box on her bed and look inside the wardrobe.

229

I can barely believe my eyes as I find I'm confronted by a selection of her dresses, skirts, tiny tops and hot pants – each carefully hung on wire hangers which dangle invitingly above at least twenty pairs of platform shoes on the wardrobe's floor.

One hanger has been put in the wrong way round, so I do the only responsible thing and correct this. Then I decide it would be a nice touch if I aligned her shoes next. Once the wardrobe is in order I stand and look at the piles of boxes around me. Some of them are almost touching the ceiling. I want to almost roll around in the feeling of success that's sweeping over me, but I know that if I do, I may well burst into tears of sheer joy. I need to keep myself busy until she returns.

I get a grip and start looking through boxes. She obviously hasn't had the chance to sort them out, so I guess it's up to me to take charge of her life. I open them one by one and start categorising them according to what's inside. All clothes boxes are meticulously placed by the window after I've emptied them and refolded the garments correctly.

While going through her clothes, I realise that some of her stuff might actually need a wash. She's obviously been too upset with all this negative publicity to give the laundry to her staff. So I find myself unpacking the boxes I've just packed and going over them all again. I give each item a thorough examination, first checking for dirt, then sniffing to check for perfume residue.

With the boxes now restacked, I move on to make-up and personal possessions. I reorder the contents according to what the application is, its size and how much I feel she needs to use it – personal and sentimental effects stored at the bottom, with sanitary products nearer the top.

Hours later every box is sorted and every garment either folded or ready for a good clean. I sit on her bed holding a small white teddy bear. He looks old and worn, with a rip where his spine would be. I'm certain that this bear – and I call him "Little Doug" – is her favourite. Undoubtedly he's stood by her through thick and thin, but of course she doesn't need him any longer, as she has me now. I sit here stroking Little Doug's furry head and try to come to terms with my surroundings.

I feel a little overwhelmed as part of me still can't believe I'm actually sitting on her bed – Donna Trayhorn's bed. It may only be the bed she's sleeping in before moving to Beverly Hills, but it doesn't matter as I'm finally here

I can feel tears welling up in my eyes as an even bigger wave of emotion washes over me and I swallow hard and blink to stop water rolling down my cheeks. I always knew we'd be together. The moment she gave me that cheeky look from the Box Room in *Voyeur*, I knew she felt the same way too. Now, in only a few short hours, she'll be back and we'll finally be together.

It's not just the physical aspect of our relationship I'm looking forward to; it's the bonding of two compatible souls. We've both strived over adversity to get where we are today. It's like the world is a giant chess board and fate was constantly moving enemy pieces in our way, preventing our love from blossoming. Now the game is almost over and the king and queen were about to live happily ever after.

And what a battle it's been. She fought her demons on live TV and came out stronger with a career to be proud of. While she braved the tabloids' slings and arrows, I fought on a different front: petty-minded bureaucrats and psychotic traffic wardens.

This isn't just a victory over the media; it's like me sticking two fingers up at everyone who has ever stood in my way. I imagine the front pages of the tabloids and glossy magazines over the next few days. The people I went to school with will be waking up to headlines like "Successful Author Dates Singer",

231

and they'll see what I've become and realise how wrong they were about me. How they'll wish they had treated me better. I can even see a few of them crawling out of the woodwork and trying to get back into my good books. Then they'll try to bask in my reflective glory and tell everyone they know a celebrity. I can hear them knocking at my door now.

"Doug!" they'll say with a false smile, "it's so great to see you again! I'm so sorry we lost touch. Maybe we can hang out some time and I can introduce you to my friends who I've told all about you and the fun we used to have!"

But before I slam the door in their face I will point out that I don't forgive people who used to refer to me as "the fat Moomin" so easily. Then I'll get my armed security guards to escort them off my estate.

And it won't only be the little demons I grew up with who will finally be put in their place. It will be every girl who's turned me down because they felt I was too intellectually intimidating. Not to mention every traffic warden who has moved me on and of course Henry, Matt and that bitter little Nazi doorman with the long face. The two of us have beaten them all. Together we are strong and there's nothing we can't achieve.

I look at my watch and it reads one minute to midnight. I take a deep breath and smile, knowing it won't be long before Donna comes back to me. I hope she hasn't had too much of a wild evening, as we may be up all night talking things over.

I can see her now, standing in the bedroom doorway, looking at me lying on her bed. I can tell by the expression on her face that she's amazed I've come to see her – it's the most delightful surprise of her life. She runs her sultry eyes over my toned body and flowing locks, while her mouth falls slightly open showing her moist pink lips. As she stares at me open-mouthed, she's dressed in leather trousers and a low cut black top with no back to it. The words "*COME GET SOME*" are written across the front in sparkly silver italic writing and her lovely flowing blonde hair hangs down on her bare shoulders.

Doug Holster glanced down at Doctor Death's severed head lying on the floor of Ms Trayhorn's apartment. The battle was over and the war was won. He listened to Ms Trayhorn in the en suite shower room making herself even more beautiful for him.

They were due to be married in the morning and he had thought about having Death's head stuffed and mounted as a marital gift.

Then as his deep and knowing eyes moved to the doorway, he saw his bride-to-be standing there waiting for him. Her virginal white summer dress rippled slightly as her eyes ran up and down the man she adored with all her heart. With one final act of restraint, she held back from running towards him with her arms outstretched. She tried to remain calm on the eve of the happiest day of her life. She wanted to wrap herself around his muscular physique so much and thank him for everything he'd done for her and her career; not to mention saving her from Death's clutches on numerous occasions.

Finally she could resist his bewitching masculinity no longer and opened her mouth to confess her undying love for the most heroic man in the universe.

"Who the fuck are you?"

I blink a bit and take stock of my surroundings once more. Donna is indeed standing in the doorway staring at me. My mouth goes completely dry.

"Linda!" she screams, not taking her eyes off me, completely captivated by my presence, "there's some fat, balding geezer in my bedroom!"

Chapter 21: Cross

"Watch your head, Sir," the policeman grunts as his rough palm pushes down hard on my scalp as I'm shoved in the back of a squad car. "You don't want to lose the rest of your hair, do you?"

"I heard that!" I snap. "That's discrimination that is. You wait till my lawyer hears about this! He'll have your badge for breakfast! I know people at MI5, I do! When they find out what you've done, they'll…"

I see Donna looking out of the upstairs bathroom window.

"Donna!" I shout. "Tell these imbeciles you know me! You told me to join your fan club! I was only bringing you your stuff back! Tell them, for God's sake."

"Now, now, Sir. Don't you think you've pestered the young lady enough for one night?" says the sarcastic copper as he starts the engine and pulls away.

What does he know? He's only this cocky because I'm in handcuffs and he's five foot nine. If I was as big as him it would be a completely different story. Plus he's got cross eyes. I'll bet he's only doing this job because he was bullied at school.

"What about my car?" I ask him as we leave Linda's street.

"We'll send someone to get it for you," he says, casually, "it'll be waiting for you at the pound."

The damn thing can stay there for all I care. All I want to do is get this huge misunderstanding cleared up as quickly as possible.

An hour later I sit in interview room eight. By all accounts it's the smallest of all the interview rooms at the police station. I don't know why I'm in this pokey little place as rooms one through seven don't appear to be occupied. It's obviously not a busy day for Ruislip's police constabulary.

The door opens and a detective walks in. He has a moustache that wiggles when he speaks.

"Now, Mr Morrell," he says as he sits opposite me, "can we get you anything before we begin?"

"You can get me out of here for a start!" I say, firmly.

"I was thinking more along the lines of tea or coffee," he replies and my nose begins to tingle.

Later on the doctor finally finishes giving me the once over and is confident my bleeding nose isn't merely a "ploy for attention" as the moustache sarcastically called it. I'm back in interview room eight with a glass of water, a tape recorder and the moustache sitting opposite me. He's quickly joined by another plain clothed officer, with yet another moustache, this time a ginger one. Don't you have to shave any more if you want to be a police officer?

"Now, you know why you're here, don't you?" Ginger says, patronisingly.

"Well, no actually," I say, loudly, before taking a breath as I've only just removed the bung from my right nostril. "All I did was return some personal possessions to an old friend and I end up here! Is that what you do to good Samaritans these days?"

"Yes, about your relationship with Ms Trayhorn," Ginger goes on. "When we spoke to her, she claimed she'd never seen you before in her life. What do you have to say to that?"

"Deflection," I point out.

The moustaches look at each other as they realise I'm not just another brain dead street punk. I have a clever calculating mind that won't bow down to their verbal dexterity and manipulation.

"And what do you mean by that?" one of the moustaches says. I don't see which one as I'm too busy smiling with the knowledge I am clearly operating on a high level. I suppose I

235

have to come to terms with the fact that Donna has enough press intrusion in her life, without adding stories about her seeing me.

"This is no laughing matter, Mr Morrell," the other one says. "You're looking at being charged with breaking and entering, harassment and theft."

"Theft?" I cry, amazed by what I'm hearing, "I didn't steal that box, I was bringing it back! How many times have you heard of someone breaking into a house to put something back?"

"So, you admit you broke into the property?" The non-ginger one says and I now realise that as well as having unsightly facial hair, he hasn't trimmed his nose hairs. This therefore gives the impression that his silly little moustache has grown right out of his nostrils.

"I didn't say that," I say, smugly.

"I think you did," Carrot-top retorts.

"Oh, no I didn't," I say, and fold my arms, before looking away.

"Oh, yes you did," one of them scoffs.

It's now becoming light outside and I'm still stuck in this tiny interview room with a furry carrot and a man who's never heard of nose clippers.

"I keep telling you," I begin again when I finally get a word in edgeways, "you've got your wires crossed. For the last time, I didn't break in – I had a key. Secondly, how can someone harass someone else when the said someone else is also claiming in the same statement that she's never heard of the accused someone? And finally, I – being the said accused someone – did not steal the bloody box of papers – pardon my French."

"Papers?" hairy says. "If we can get a word in edgeways, you might consider that we're not actually talking about the box of rubbish you dug up from somewhere…"

"Returned to her," I interject.

"Shut up!" the other one says. I clearly have them on the ropes as he's turning into the proverbial "bad cop".

"We're talking about this!" shaggy says as he slaps one of those plastic evidence bags you see on *Inspector Morse* down on the table. Folded up inside is a red negligee from New Look.

"That's mine," I say. Starsky and Hutch look at each other as they're about to use the one about "it won't fit me". I can almost feel my sides splitting. "I bought it for her."

"Did you?" Ginger says, sarcastically.

"Yes, I did actually," I say, then go on to explain how I'd bought it for her months ago and had it delivered to her previous management agency. Then, when I came across it at the bottom of a box in her room, I could clearly see it needed a good wash and iron. Therefore, the only reason it was in my trouser pocket when they searched me, was because I was taking it home for Mum to clean.

They look at each other again. They know they have nothing on me and I feel it's high time I started playing hardball with Cagney and Lacey.

"What are you going to do?" I ask as I sit back in my chair and cross my legs confidently, "charge me with laundering underwear?"

They don't answer and I know I'm in control now.

"I want my phone call, right now."

The ginger furry-faced one switches the tape recorder off and I'm escorted to the phone in reception.

"Hello, Raptor?" I say to the answer phone on his mobile. "It's me, Doug. Where are you?"

"There he is!" a man's angry voice shouts from behind me.

I turn round and just about make out Raptor being marched down a corridor by two policemen.

"...I tell you it was him driving, not me!" was about all I could make out from his expletive-ridden rant.

237

I hang up the phone, realising I'll have to speak to him later. The desk sergeant looks at me strangely.

"Do you know him?" he asks, suspiciously.

"No," I reply. "Never seen him before in my life. What's he in for?"

The officer checks the register-like book in front of him.

"His car was spotted going through six speed cameras last night."

"Joyriders, eh?" I say with a tut and he nods in agreement.

And to think that tourists are ushered round Alcatraz for ten dollars a time. Little do they know its dreadful secret about how Doctor Death was using it to stash away his captives while they were cloned and used for his evil ways.

But no cage was ever going to hold Doug Holster and by morning he had killed the ginger guards and blasted his way out of the island jail using a gun he fashioned out of a plastic fork and the Daily Sport.

As he looked back at the flaming hellhole he'd spent the night in, he realised his work was not yet done. Death was still out there. The man he had killed was merely a clone, as was his bride-to-be Ms Trayhorn. The real woman he loved so much was still out there waiting for him. He knew she was still alive because if she was no longer part of the human race, he would have no reason left to live.

I catch a taxi home and go straight to bed as work is right out of the question. Some people might think I'd find it hard to sleep, what with only being released "pending further investigation" as they called it. Not me, I go out like a light. I know it's all some hideous misunderstanding, started by that fat cousin of Donna's. She didn't want me to meet up with her last night, so she took her out to some sleazy bar and got her

238

plastered. Was it any wonder she didn't recognise me when she saw me in her room? Linda must have been force-feeding her so much alcohol she wouldn't have remembered her own mother! Then how was she supposed to see who I really was after she'd locked herself in the bathroom screaming?

I wake up mid afternoon and part of me would like to drive round to Linda's and have it out with her. But Raptor's car has been impounded and I'm certainly not going to shell out on the petrol to get there myself. Plus the idiot copper who showed me out of the station said I wasn't allowed to go near either Linda's house or Donna's family home. That annoyed me, but it was I who ultimately got the last laugh by tucking three biros up my sleeve from the front desk. Let's see that miserable desk sergeant fill in his soppy forms now.

On a nice sunny afternoon like this, I really should update my website and upload the photos of Donna's new digs. But the police have "hung on" to my camera while the investigation is in progress.

An hour later I leave my apartment to go to the shops to get today's magazines and papers. As I near the newsagents my mobile rings and it's Hannah.

"Yes?" I say.

"Doug?" she says, making it sound like a surprise that I've answered my own phone. "Is everything all right?"

"Er, yes," I say, sarcastically.

"Oh, right," she says, as if expecting me to pour out a list of my problems the way she seems to always want to do. "Are you sure everything's okay? Matt told me you'd been arrested and…"

"What were you doing talking to Matt?" I shout. "And I was merely helping police with their enquiries!"

She doesn't answer and I'm very tempted to hang up.

"Look, I don't want to go into all that again," she says. "But a reporter was waiting for me after I finished work. He wanted to talk about you."

"I hope you didn't tell him anything," I say, quickly. If an artist wants to maintain true credibility, he must remain obscure and not enter the media-feast of soundbites and misquotes. "He could have been an agent, trying to find out about my book! I've told you how they work!"

"Yes, Doug," she replies. "You never used to stop going on about that. But I think this one was definitely a journalist."

"But how do you know?" I reiterate as I get closer to the newsagents. "That's how they work, they lull you into a false sense of security and before you know it, they're running off with your entire synopsis!"

"He didn't ask about your book."

"He didn't? What did he want then?"

"He wanted to find out what it was like knowing a real life stalker."

The word alone would have stopped me in my tracks, yet what makes me freeze on the spot is something completely different. Now only yards from the newsagents, I read the headline on the sandwich board outside its entrance.

Local man stalks reality TV star.

I feel sick and my nose starts to tingle. My legs begin to wobble and I suddenly find my lungs have stopped working. I start to fight for air as my head spins. I think I'm dying and can just about make out a woman's soft voice calling my name. I look up for a bright tunnel of light leading to heaven, but only the sun glares down on me. I look again at the sandwich board and read it over and over again, while the woman repeatedly asks if I'm all right.

"Auntie Eileen?" I stammer. "Is that you? Am I dreaming?"

240

"Doug! Doug!" Hannah shouts and I look down at my mobile phone which now lies on the pavement. "Are you all right?"

I find enough strength to pick it up and switch it off. I tear my feet from the pavement and forcibly move them towards the shop window. Inside I can see the rows of newspapers. Not only the local ones carry the story.

Real-life Celebrity Voyeur is written on the front of the *Daily Mail* with a picture of none other than me underneath! It's the photo I have on my work ID badge and it's not even a good likeness – I blinked as the flash went off and they said it wasn't worth using up more film taking another one. That stupid camera Human Resources has is useless; it makes me look weird – not just because my eyes are closed and my mouth is slightly open, but the flash was too bright. You can see right through my hair and I look bald at the front! Who the hell has given it to them? How can they put it on the front page?

I try to get a look at some of the other papers further away, but I'm not wearing my glasses. Then two old biddies chatting nearby makes me turn around. They're looking at the sandwich board and shaking their heads.

"Apparently he lives near here," one of the senile old witches mutters to her sidekick.

Doug Holster was being framed. This whole thing reeked of a set-up and he was being made a patsy for a crime he didn't commit. There was no way he was going to take the fall for this one. He knew Death was behind it – so mortified at being thwarted at every turn, he has decided to discredit Doug and turn the public against their fearless hero.

"Colonel? Come in." Doug said into his communicator. "There's no way I'm going to let them do this to me, you hear me? No way!"

241

"Doug," his friend, boss and mentor said robotically. "I'm your friend, boss and mentor. You must trust me and hand yourself in. Everything will be all right."

God damn them! They've got him too.

Doug was alone. Death had taken Ms Trayhorn from him and now they had run him out of the Secret Service. But if they thought he was beaten, they were wrong. For Doug was stronger than the Government and Doctor Death's army put together! He would fight against injustice single-handedly and find a way to clear his name. They hadn't counted on how the man with nothing left to fight for could be the most dangerous and resolute of opponents.

I throw up, right there and then. I haven't got a clue what I should do. Would the press be at my flat? They already got to Hannah and my work colleagues. What if they started questioning Mum? She thought the *X-Files* was a documentary; who knows what inaccuracies she might spill about me.

I consider skipping town and going on the run to find allies who will fight alongside me; then return in a blaze of glory with my own army to crush all those who oppose me. But I haven't got a clue where to begin looking for people as pure of heart as myself. Would they reside in the suburbs? Perhaps Slough, Bracknell or Hemel Hempstead would be my sanctuary?

I could use underground contacts to obtain a false passport and driver's licence and change my name to Douglas Trayhorn to throw MI6 off my scent.

Even though I'd walked to the newsagents in only a few minutes, it takes me over an hour to get home. I use a back route across a couple of fields; then duck through some woods next to the park where I saw a couple of men in suits. I swear they're secret services. I did get pretty close to my flat about twenty minutes ago, but in order to get to the garages, I would have had

242

to climb a fence and I was already out of breath from trudging through dense foliage in Hillingdon's mountain district. This was a technique I had long since perfected from walking home after school and dodging my fellow classmates.

I've been hiding behind a communal bin for the block of flats opposite my own for nearly half an hour. I'm sure the coast must be clear by now. I break cover and commando roll across the courtyard and head to the door to my block.

But the problem with now having to fight your own side is that they're equipped with the same technology as you. As soon as I step into the communal hallway, a platoon of turncoat agents deactivates their cloaking devices and appears out of nowhere.

"Mr Morrell, how can you justify stalking an innocent woman?" says one man, while thrusting a Dictaphone in my face. I grab his weapon and pull him off before hurling him over my shoulders with a well practised judo throw.

"Excuse me," I say, casually, as I block another agent's feeble attempt at taking me down and move on to face the next armed assassin, brandishing a microphone.

"Why did you choose to stalk Donna over more successful celebrities?"

"I'm not a stalker!" I shout at him as I break his nose with a fast jab that sends him crashing back into the rest of them. "You are!"

"Can you tell us what the charges were for then, Mr Morrell?" another one cries as he runs at me with a notepad. I block, then counter and finally finish him off humanely by snapping his neck like a twig.

I step over the bodies of the human garbage I've rid this fair world of and head up the stairs to my flat. Not only have my years in the Secret Service saved me, but also my time at school.

243

"Ignore them and they'll go away," I say, confidently. "Once they see it doesn't get to you, they'll find someone else to pick on."

"This isn't the first time you've faced these charges, is it, Doug?" crows a lycra-clad female assassin with greasy hair and a clipboard.

"Death couldn't bring me down then and he won't succeed now!" I cry, defiantly stunning them into silence. "What's the matter; hasn't David Beckham changed his hair today? Haven't you got anything else to write about?"

They can see I'm a force to be reckoned with. I look from one sneering rat-like face to the next. They're all silent and I take the opportunity to leave this party early and march up the stairs, unlock my front door and slam it behind me.

"Mum!" I shout, "could you give work a ring? I think my upset tummy has come back!"

Chapter 22: Cigarettes
and Moustaches

I stand with my back leaning against our front door. My personal secretary has obviously been recalled by MI6 and I can see Mum still hasn't put away the breakfast tray I left on the hallway table a few days ago.

Maybe while I'm here I should pack my bags? Perhaps I could use Hannah's place as a safe house. I'm sure she wouldn't mind me popping by with a few suitcases. Seeing as the press have already been there they might not expect me to go back. Or maybe we could go away somewhere? She must have a bit of money tucked away; we could hide in some little hotel on the coast until all this dies down. I'll call her after I've loaded all my *Voyeur* videos into my case.

"Mr Morrell?" says a man's voice as someone opens the letterbox behind me. "We'd like you to come back to the station please."

The two police moustaches have found me, but if they want me to go quietly, they'll have to lead me out the back. They agree, and for a moment I actually think I'm dealing with two real members of the human race, but as soon as the handcuffs are on, they decide they can't be bothered marching me all the way round the back as they're parked out front.

Now I recall the events, I suppose I had the last laugh: at least I thwarted the media's attempt to get pictures of me. I borrowed one of Mum's old shawls to put over my head as Holmes and Watson escorted me through the crowd.

Slightly over three hours later and I find myself back in Death's underground Alcatraz lair (the bit I didn't blow up when I escaped last time).

This has not been a good day. I haven't checked my website and I don't know what's being posted on my message board. I had thought about using my "one phone call" to ring someone to check that no one's rejoined that I've already banned. Sadly, I don't know any of the phone numbers of my more trusted members.

Then there's the police brutality I've had to suffer since I was recaptured. Luckily I'm strong enough not to break while they attach electrodes to my ears. Even when they resort to using names like baldy, fatty and Mr Toad I still refuse to talk. All it does is remind me of being back at school. I can put up with their mental torture, but it would be nice if the desk sergeant would bring me a copy of today's papers like I asked. Yet all I keep getting are cups of tea that have been spiked with truth serum.

I should have thrown them right back through the security flap in the steel door. But instead I choose to remain civil and dignified in the face of such brutality, merely leaving the three cups by the foot of the door. If my executioner happens to trip over them and scold his feet when he comes in, then that's not my fault.

I should ring Hannah. I know she's been less than good to me, but I still don't like to think of her being hounded by scandal-hungry journalists. Besides, I may need an alibi or someone to break me out. But of course only guilty people need alibis, but then I have to call into question the integrity of today's police force – what might they plant on me just to bump up their "solved crimes" statistics?

What I'd give for my collection of *Voyeur* videos right now. How often do I get such unadulterated time on my own to sit back and do something constructive? I could have watched almost two entire episodes while I've been here.

What the police canteen classes as "lunch" arrives at four minutes past noon. It soon joins the cups by the door, which no officer has had the courtesy to remove. I'd hate to see the state of their homes.

Half an hour later I find myself frogmarched to interview room six like a common criminal.

"So, do you know why you're back here?" the one with the nose hair says.

"No, actually!" I shout. I know I shouldn't raise my voice, but by now I'm getting very hungry and my request for Mum to bring me a proper lunch seems to have fallen of deaf ears.

"What do you mean – no?" the hairy one shouts back, "how many more times do we have to tell you?"

He slumps back in his chair, seemingly cracking under the strain.

"Well, I understand the words," I say, with a shrug, "just not the charges."

"We know what you do," sighs one of them. "This isn't the first time you've been down here, is it?"

I've been held in more of Death's dungeons and torture chambers than these two have had hot dinners! And I've escaped from every last one.

"You were hauled in and warned about harassing women over at Ealing, weren't you?" he goes on. I knew it. Here come the lies that he hopes will damn me. "You made that woman's life a living hell, didn't you? What was her name, Caroline Gibney?"

Doug Holster recalls Caroline Gibney. She was the love of his life for a while. Yet he couldn't save her. The temptation of the dark side was too great for the poor weak willed girl and she succumbed to Death's seductive charms.

But she was ancient history as he only had eyes for Ms Trayhorn now.

"Caroline is a venomous slut!" I declare.

"That's not what you said on your *MSN* weblog about her a couple of years ago," Bristles goes on. "You said that after she'd won *Strictly Come Cooking* you and her were going to the Bahamas to get married!"

"And we would have," I scoff, "If it wasn't for the hate campaign against us!"

"Right," my adversary continues slowly. "But she was almost about to take out a restraining order on you. And what about Hannah?"

"What about her?" I ask, as I mask my annoyance at them finding my safe house.

"She came here a while back to ask us to get you to leave her alone," he went on.

"All lies!" I say as a shake my head.

"She was about to get a restraining order out on you too, until you disappeared for the eight weeks while *Voyeur* was on and set up your so-called website…"

"Excuse me, but what do you mean by so-called?" I exclaim – the hunger now getting worse. "I bought that domain name fair and square. You can't have it."

"We don't want it," butts in ginger. "What we want is for you to explain what you do outside Gloria Trayhorn's house every day."

"And what you were doing in Donna Trayhorn's flat," continues his partner.

I don't answer. Not that my silence proves my guilt, I merely don't understand what this has to do with anything.

"You're not exactly a master criminal, are you?" Ginger sneers.

248

"I am not a criminal," I say, with a slightly spontaneous laugh.

"You have over two thousand digital photos on your website, each one you've even gone as far as to label with the time, date and relevant changes to the building."

"Yeah, so?" I ask.

"So… we'd like you to explain to us, what possible reason you have for being there!" Ginger says through gritted teeth. I have him so completely on the ropes.

"I was there visiting Donna." I sigh. I've lost count of the amount of times I've had to reiterate that seemingly simple fact.

"You don't bloody well know Donna!" he shouts, before hairy-nose puts his hand on his arm to hold him back. You can tell when someone's losing the argument – they resort to obscenities.

"Then why did she ask me to join her fan club?" I say with a smile, "and why has she been emailing me?"

"You're talking about her newsletter again, aren't you?" says Hairy, under his breath.

"It had my name on it," I remind him yet again.

The conversation continues in this vein for quite some time. As the hours go by, part of me even begins to enjoy the situation. I feel like it's a challenge. As a media commentator, I have always tried to tell it how it is. It's the duty of people like me to educate the masses and let them know what's really happening. I've had far more heated discussions than this one on many a message board – ones where I desperately try to pound simple logic into empty minds. Of course most of the time I don't succeed, but that's not my fault; it's down to the sub-standard education system that's produced such poor deluded creatures. Then of course there are the times when my debates are cut short by some little sneak going to a moderator and having me banned.

But that was then, and this is now. Now, I am having a debate face to face. There is no "block" button they can click to get rid of me and I have to get my point across.

My cause isn't helped by Ginger keeping popping out for a cigarette every five minutes. I ask Hairy if we can go on without him, but he says that there has to be two officers in the room for an interview, blah, blah, blah. It's now getting dark outside and we still haven't got much further. I'm on the brink of suggesting to Hairy that perhaps he should put in an application for a new partner, as his ginger friend clearly isn't up to the job.

While carrot-head is out of the room on what must have been his thirtieth fag break, I'm yet again left talking to his hairy counterpart.

"So, why don't you watch reality TV then?" I ask, trying to make polite conversation to pass the time.

"Look, I've told you this before, I just don't," he replies.

"I know, but I can't understand your argument," I say. "Give me an example of why exactly you don't like it."

"It's not that I don't like it. It's because on top of working twelve hour shifts here, I also have three young kids which means I don't have the time to watch *Voyeur: Live and Unleashed*."

"*Voyeur: Live and Unplugged*," I correct him. "Anyway, you don't have to watch it live. You can just watch the highlights every evening!"

Then Hairy joins his colleague for a cigarette, leaving me alone in the room. I keep myself busy: I stroll around the seven by eight foot room, then borrow Ginger's pen that he'd thrown at me earlier and even try the door. To my amazement, it's unlocked! Hairy had actually forgotten to secure it when he stormed out. I could make a break for it – if I needed to, but I don't. I can tell when I'm winning.

After possibly the longest cigarette break in history, they return and take their seats. I notice Hairy has developed rather an alarming twitch, but I suppose that's what having kids does to you.

"Right," says Ginger as he inhales deeply, "let's try this again. You have been invading the privacy of an entire family…"

"Are you talking about a few photographs?" I ask.

"Yes, but…" Ginger begins.

"You just don't understand, do you?" I say, as I sit back in my chair and decide that it's time, yet again, to put my side of the story across.

"Have you ever been in love?" I ask without waiting for an answer. "Well I am. And I'm not talking about a little crush, I'm talking about destiny and the true merging of two souls – like Romeo and Juliet or Charles and Camilla – I know that me and Donna are meant to be together. Now I'm not judging the two of you, but I know for a fact that at least one of you doesn't watch reality TV, and this leads me to believe that you don't exactly have your finger on the pulse as far as current affairs are concerned. Well, I do. I'm a media commentator with my own website and a select, but dedicated group of individuals who regularly log on to hear what I have to say. I provide a service: I don't take those pictures to embarrass or intrude into Donna's life, but to share it with her supporters – the people she has given herself to. She entered the public domain through her own free will, and by a fantastic chance found me – her soul mate. Now, you call me a stalker – quite unfairly I must point out – but would an alleged stalker let his alleged victim live her own life so freely? I'm a twenty-first century guy; I don't want a woman tied to the kitchen sink. I respect her and her career too much. She lives her life and I live mine, then, when she's ready to settle

251

down, we'll get together. That's love you see, something I have a horrible feeling you two gentlemen know very little about."

I sit back and observe their reaction. They are indeed speechless.

"There's just one problem, Mr Media Commentator…" says the hairy-twitcher.

"And what's that?" I ask with a confident smile.

"You don't bloody well know her!" he shouts, which I must confess does take me aback.

"That's where you're wrong," I correct him once I have my breath back, "you know her, I know her, billions of people all over the world know her. Again, your lack of media knowledge lets you down: once someone steps into the spotlight, they become public property. We – the people – buy their music, watch their TV shows, go and see their films; therefore we have a right to know about them. You see…"

"You don't know her personally!" Hairy interrupts, emphasising the word personally.

"If he's going to keep shouting at me," I say to Ginger, "I'm going to have to email your superiors."

Ginger pats his partner on the arm and steadies him.

"It's all right, Graeme," he says, softly. "You can have one of my fags in a minute."

I'm too busy shaking my head and sighing to fully make out what Hairy mutters, but I think it was along the lines of "what about the drugs in the evidence room?"

I decide it's time to end this once and for all.

"I know her personally," I declare, to which they both turn and look at me. "You don't see the way she looks at me."

"When?" mutters the ginger moustache.

"While she was on *Voyeur*," I reply.

Chapter 23: The People Have Spoken

I suppose I should be grateful that old Crockett and Tubs let me leave the interview room and get some sleep. After a cold breakfast and no word from Mum or Donna, I'm back in interview room six awaiting the return of the two moustaches for "round two".

They don't come. I hear from another officer that the skiving pair of layabouts had both developed tummy upsets and wouldn't be in today. No wonder crime is reaching such astronomical highs when front line officers spend half their time developing fake afflictions.

After waiting nearly an hour on my own in the tiny room, two new officers enter. Both wear the dullest grey suits I've seen in my life, but at least they seem to know how to shave this time. I decide to christen them "Detective A" and "Detective B" as I don't think it's worth trying to remember their names. "A" has dreadfully over-dyed black hair for a man who had obviously gone grey prematurely, while "B" simply has a squint, which seems to draw my attention every time I look at him. Together, and in that patronising way police do, they explain that I'm going to be formally charged with harassment and unlawful entry and would I like to call my solicitor?

"I don't have a solicitor," I inform them. After all, I don't need one – anyone with an ounce of common sense only has to take one look at me to see that I'm innocent. Besides, I know exactly how much they charge after I tried to sue Walkers crisps for not using Donna in their last advertising campaign.

"A duty solicitor can be appointed for you if you don't have one," Popeye says, while I try not to look at his funny eye – I may just throw up if I concentrate on it for too long. I consider his offer.

"For free?" I say, cautiously.

"Yeah," says the walking advert for Just For Men.

"We suggest you take his advice," continues Squinty.

Oh, God, I looked at him by mistake. He's hideous, but I reluctantly agree to see the duty solicitor.

And with that I find myself once again in a room on my own while I wait for him to arrive. I'm beginning to wonder if anyone is ever on time for anything these days. Half an hour later an old man comes in. He's bald and he keeps propping his little round spectacles up on his nose.

"Mr Morrell?" he asks.

"Yes," I sigh. "My name is Morrell, Doug Morrell. Are you going to get me out of here?"

"I'll do my best," he says with a smile that I'll bet he uses on everyone then props his glasses back on his nose. "To be honest, I think we can have you out of her in a matter of hours."

"You do?" I say, genuinely surprised, "how come? Don't you have to ask me about the case? Find out what my defence is?"

"That won't take long," he says with a knowing smile that I find almost a little unsettling. "Can we just go over one thing?"

"Certainly," I say.

"You say Ms Trayhorn – loves you?"

"Yes, but she's far too clever to admit she's got someone while she's trying to promote her music," I say, amazed that a supposedly intelligent man of the law knows so little about the way celebrities work.

"Quite," he says. "And she told you this…"

He trails off, replacing words with peering over his little round glasses.

"…I could just tell, okay?" I say to him, while trying not to get too annoyed at his poking his nose into my personal affairs.

He doesn't say anything. What's he waiting for now?

"I see," he says slowly, but doesn't continue. He sits there looking at me as if I'm some mystical equation that has to be solved. Is he waiting for me to say something? Neither of us speaks as I'm not about to confide in a total stranger. I'll let him go first. The seconds pass and he must be feeling pretty uncomfortable by now. Finally I win and his resolve cracks under my willpower.

"You see, what I'm getting at is, when did you first know that she loved you?" he says, "Can you remember the exact time?"

Well that's an easy one. Why didn't he ask me that instead of all this eyeballing?

"When she was on *Voyeur*," I say firmly.

"The television show?" he asks.

Please don't say we have another person who doesn't watch it. Maybe I should record myself explaining the sociological and political impacts of the programme and its contestants.

"Yes, the television show," I say, being as patronising as I can.

"I see," he replies. "Now, as I understand it, this reality TV show – *Voyeur* – aren't the contestants shut inside a house with absolutely no contact with the outside world whatsoever?"

Oh, thank God. I sink back in my chair and almost let out a little sigh of relief on finding out he does know about it. Perhaps this funny little man with the ill-fitting glasses might be of some use after all. If he's a true *Voyeur* fan, perhaps he'd like to come round and watch my tapes of last season? Or, better still, he could become a moderator for my site. I could do with a second-in-command who can actually spell.

"That's correct," I say, with a smile.

"I see," he says again. I wonder what exactly he keeps seeing. "So – and don't take this the wrong way, but – how did you know she loved you when she was inside a purpose-built studio set, surrounded by television cameras, which monitored her every move for the entire three weeks of her stay?"

I'm impressed. He knows Donna was only in there three weeks. I'm sure I can get Mum to go out when I have him round. I would see if he wanted to meet up for a drink sometime and chat about Donna, but he's a bit old and people might think I was a bit funny hanging around with a coffin-dodger. Better to keep him out of sight.

"The way she looked at me," I say with a knowing smile that matches his.

I can still see her smiling and pouting up at me from the television screen to this day.

That evening I was home. My solicitor Mr Darling – if you can believe that's his real name – did indeed get me out. I now lie on my bed looking up at the posters of Donna on my ceiling wondering if he really is the kind of man I want as a friend.

After our little chat this morning, I returned to my cell out of choice as I had a lot to think over – his advice to be precise.

"Take the insanity plea," was what his years at law school had taught him.

Yes and why don't I stick some socks on my ears and claim to be the reincarnation of Lou Reed while I'm at it? I would have told him where to go there and then had it not been for my nose starting to bleed. While I was in the toilet cubicle with a bung up my nostril and an officer waiting outside in case I tried to fit through the twelve by six heating vent, I had time to mull it over.

Obviously I'm as sane as the next man, so suddenly claiming I'm some sort of nutter would be ludicrous. Yet at the same time I'd had enough of those feeble-minded cops and their loose grip on reality. The quicker I was out of there the better.

So, I swallowed my pride and started making strange whizzing noises on the spot. The policeman standing outside my toilet cubicle had to kick the door down and found me cuddling the toilet seat and flapping like a bumblebee.

"Admitting you have a problem is for your own good," said Darling as I lay on the toilet floor. "This act – is not."

I had to go and see the police doctor again, who was very interested in my nose. He thought that a second nose bleed while in police custody meant that I'd been subjected to police brutality. So I made a formal complaint about the officers slamming my head in a door and not allowing me anything to eat until I confessed. Then I got back to playing along with Darling.

"I think you need some of these," said Dr Frankenstein.

"Fish! Rabies! Banana!" I shouted, hilariously.

"Stop that now," whispered Darling and I was forced to tone it down a little.

"What are these then?" I asked as the quack handed me some pills.

"Medication, Doug," he nodded. "I think they'll help."

"I don't do drugs!" I declared.

"I think the court will take a far more lenient view of your case if you look like you want to change," whispered Darling as he put his hand on my shoulder.

I don't need to change as I'm perfectly happy as I am. I noticed he didn't have a wedding ring on his bony finger and shook his hand off. I then swallowed a tablet with some water.

"Well done, Doug," the doctor smiled. "Take your medication."

I was released within the hour, or rather ejected come to think of it.

Once outside, Darling said I could stop purring now as I didn't want to overdo it, and start concentrating on remembering to turn up for my hearing at the local magistrate. I obliged. I have to say I was getting quite into the whole "mad" thing. I suppose I found it interesting to see the way people looked at me once they thought I was a loon. It even gave me an idea for a future book: a study into the public's attitude to nut-jobs.

The desk sergeant told me to sign to say I understood the terms of my bail, to which I clucked like a hen before scattering his pens all over the floor. It took three officers to pick them all up while I tried to lay an egg in the waiting room, plus I even managed to stick a couple of biros up my sleeve for later.

So, here I am on my bed: officially an insane stalker. It's no wonder the world's in such a bad way, if this is what you get for trying to help the ones you love. I'm not allowed within fifty feet of any of her properties, or was it a hundred? I couldn't remember as I was too busy foraging for truffles in the waste paper basket. But they didn't say anything about emailing her! God bless the Internet.

I go into my *Hotmail* account and dash off an email to her that says not to worry about the other night and would she like to meet at a Harvester to talk things over?

After I'd sent it, I realise it was woefully too short and lacked feeling. So I send a few more in case she didn't get the first. Then I check my site to find yet more abuse.

This is just what I need right now – ignorant people believing that because something has been written in a newspaper, it's automatically true. Haven't these people ever bothered reading the many "apologies" that the tabloids are forced to print. I hate it when they cross the line from helping celebrities publicise their work to lying to sell copy.

Wait till the papers get a call from Darling, that's all I can say.

I delete all the scandalous posts from my message board, although, once they're erased, part of me says that I should have left them there as evidence. Darling could have traced their IP addresses and I could have sued them.

I phone Hannah, but her mobile is off, even though it's now Friday night and there's no way she can still be at school at eleven in the evening. I sit in the lounge and comfort myself with some old tapes of Donna on *Voyeur*. I have to say that even with her being so career minded, she's the only woman in my life who's stood by me.

I watch *Voyeur* into the small hours and fall asleep in front of the television. Those pills I'm taking have made me sleepy.

"I've got sweets for you, Willie!" Auntie Eileen says while trying to hug me.

"My name is not Willie!" I tell her over and over again.

"You're going to stay with your Auntie Eileen forever!" she says in a voice that is way too happy.

I wake up in a cold sweat the next morning and find Mum hasn't bothered to cook me breakfast again. I'm not in a good mood, as I failed to dream about Donna. I seem to remember also dreaming about trying to sign a giant egg with a pen, but every time I leant forward to write on it a giant llama appeared, sneezed on me and ate my biro. I should probably lay off these pills. If I am insane, I think they're to blame!

Doug Holster was holding up in one of his many luxury penthouses. He knew that as he owned so many, Death's forces couldn't possibly monitor them all at once. He thought about going to see Ms Trayhorn, but on the off-chance they were watching his movements, he wasn't about to lead them straight to her doorstep.

Things were bad and in these desperate times even good men think bad thoughts. He didn't want to lead the enemy to Donna's door, but he considered going round to her brainwashed cousin and putting the thumbscrews on her. It wouldn't take more than a few removed fingernails to get her to confess all the lies she'd told about him. No one calls Doug Holster a crazed lunatic and gets away with it.

He pressed the button in his fish tank that rolled up the bullet proof shutters and gazed across the serene morning skyline. His photographic memory combined with his designer glasses took in the occupant of every parked car in and around his building.

"Scum," he hissed as he could tell that every last one was an enemy agent. They all looked like giant gerbils, apart from one that looked like Gloria Hunniford in drag.

They were lying in wait for him, setting the old "plain sight ambush". He knew exactly what their game was. They wanted him to come out all guns blazing and take half of them down in a hail of bullets. But when he did, they would make sure a busload of schoolchildren was released into the firing line and then blame him for the carnage.

There's no way I'm going out there, not for the love of Donna, not for revenge towards Linda and not even for Gloria Hunniford.

I spend my weekend watching old *Voyeur* and checking my emails for some word from Donna. Nothing yet, but I expect she's waiting for all the heat to die down. Hannah rings Saturday night, but I cut her off before she can speak. If she can't be bothered to talk to me when I want to, why should I bother answering her calls?

I get Sunday's papers delivered and this is the first time ever I'm actually dreading reading what might be in them.

I'm relieved to find I'm not on any of the front pages. Luckily some American socialite has filmed herself having sex again. Normally I would condemn the self-publicising harlot for her blatant attempt to hijack the media to promote her cable show. But seeing as she's bumped my story down to page eight of *The People*, I'll let her off this time. I must remember to search for her new video on Google and see if I can download this one for free as well.

There's not too much about me, not unless you count the awful photo from my work badge. I swear some clever dick in the docklands has gone and touched up my hair to make it look like it's thinning. Sometimes Adobe Photoshop 6.0 can be a curse if it falls into the wrong hands. I read the article, which as usual, is nothing more than a catalogue of lies.

Loser [Excuse me, but what exactly have I ever lost?] *Doug Morrell, 34* [I'm thirty-one], *was caught hiding under his security blanket* [I'm going to sue over that one: I haven't needed my security blanket since I was nine and Mum is a witness to it.] *when the police led him away from his council flat in Hillingdon* [it's still in Mum's name], *four days* [three actually] *after being accused of stalking* [she never called me a stalker, the police did] *reality TV reject* [they always have to bring that up] *Donna Trayhorn, 21.*

This move makes a rare change from his normal location [spending one hour out of twenty-four does not make it someone's "normal" location], *which, judging by the photos on his website, is parked outside Gloria Trayhorn's Acton council house* [why are they obsessed with a property being council-owned or not?] *Although the balding* [only in their airbrushed photos. If the kid with the Photoshop editing software had coloured my skin blue, would they call me a Smurf?] *Mr Morrell cannot be prosecuted for "outing" a string of suburban sex perverts* [hearsay – the newspaper was not inside the house with these people, therefore they cannot possibly know what went on in there] *who visit Gloria even more than he does, a police spokesman has confirmed that tubby* [I'm suing] *little* [I'm only one inch shorter than what I read on the Internet was "average for a man" – see earlier comments about legal action]

261

Morrell has been charged with breaking and entering, harassment and theft [they didn't charge me with theft – that one got dropped].

A close friend [in other words no one, as I don't have any friends] *says that the short-sighted* [since when has wearing glasses been a crime?] *delivery driver* [my official title is "Load Distribution Executive"] *has been obsessed with the life of Ms Trayhorn ever since she was booted* [how many more times do I have to explain, she was not "booted out", she was evicted, and it's worth noting she survived the two previous evictions, therefore the public decided to save her twice!] *out of the Voyeur house after only three weeks* [the series only lasted eight weeks – she nearly managed to stay for fifty per cent of the duration].

If the case is due to go to court, Mr Morrell can probably expect to be let off with community service. A police source has also confirmed that Morrell, who lives alone [apart from my mother obviously] *may be trying to get off on an insanity plea. The People says: Page 12* [I don't care what *The People* says].

It also has a bit in it about my brother being unavailable for comment from his US home, but I couldn't see what that loser has to do with it. Reluctantly, I turn to page twelve.

Although we can all laugh at the pathetic antics of self-titled "media commentator" Doug Morrell, this case does raise the dangerous issue of obsession the general public are developing with celebrities. This time it was just a sad, lonely man, but next time it could be someone with more sinister intentions. And for what it's worth, Mr Morrell, we at The People strongly advise you stick with your insanity plea. There probably isn't a court in the land that wouldn't buy that one. After all, you did choose to stalk Donna Trayhorn of all people.

Chapter 24: Strength of Character

I don't sleep much and when the clock reaches five in the morning, I decide to put my work clothes on and head in. Not that I really want to be in a depot with people who think I'm some sort of nut-job.

But I take a deep breath, suck my stomach in, hold my head up high, and fix my gaze on my van as I walk inside. I can't tell which other drivers are already there as I make a point of not looking anyone in the eye. I'm pleased to see my van has been parked the right way round.

"Doug?" an annoyingly familiar voice says from behind me. I ignore it and open the door of my cab, "hey, Doug?"

A hand taps me on the back and I'm forced to admit that it would be rude to just ignore pin-headed Matt, so I turn round.

"Are you all right, mate?" he asks with fake concern. "Hannah tried phoning you to see…"

"I'm fine," I state, observing how his face looks like a tiny sheep's head. "Is that your stuff in my van?"

"Uh, yeah," he says guiltily. And well he might, he's left all sorts of pointless paperwork and forms all over the passenger seat. He'd better not have stolen any of the pens I keep in the glove compartment.

"I didn't – well, we didn't know when you were coming back," he stammers while withering under my steely gaze. "…today I mean. We didn't know you were coming in today."

"And why wouldn't I?" I ask with one eyebrow raised like a better looking Roger Moore.

He shuffles nervously from foot to foot, still not daring to make eye contact. I suddenly feel like it was worth coming back just to see him squirm like a worm on the end of my hook.

"I see you've been using my cab?" I ask rhetorically.

"Well, I've been doing a bit of overtime and…"

"All right, Doug!" another voice yells from across the depot.

I turn to see that arse Frank swaggering across the loading bay while grinning inanely as if something is hilariously funny.

"How's Donna, eh?" he shouts.

A roar of laughter erupts from other drivers who are illegally smoking slightly inside the loading bay doors.

"Don't let them get to you," Matt says, quickly.

"Let them get to me?" I say in amazement. "They don't get to me. No one gets to Doug Holster! I don't need your pity!"

My verbal raid on his meagre mind stuns him into silence and knocks him back. He stammers like a simpleton and I move in for the death blow.

"And while we're on the subject, I wonder who it was who sold my work ID badge to the papers, eh?" I hiss at him while repeatedly jabbing him in the stomach with my finger. He tries to say something, but I'm like Mastermind – I've started, so I have to finish. "How much did they pay you for that picture? A hundred, two hundred, or did you hold out for a nice round thousand?"

"I didn't…" he mumbles pathetically; he must think I'm a fool or something. Did his tiny, tiny mind not realise I left that pass behind the sun visor in my cab? Who else has been using my vehicle while I've been off?

"I wonder where my pass has gone then?" I say firmly as I unfold the visor to let it plop down onto the seat. Shit. "Oh, so you had the courtesy to put it back did you?"

"I didn't…" he begins again.

"Liar!" I scream. I shouldn't have raised my voice, but his Judas-like attitude is enough to bring on a nosebleed in the Pope.

Of course the other drivers love that. I know I shouldn't let myself get worked up as I'm playing into their hands. They make sarcastic "wooing" noises, before bursting into laughter. Now a couple of the office sluts come out on the gantry to see what the fuss is about. How strange they look in high heels, miniskirts and sheep heads. I'm about ready to tell them all where to go, when the theme tune to *Voyeur* starts blaring out from one of the other vans parked in the loading bay. A driver who I only know as "Nobby" climbs out and joins his cohorts. They cheer and slap him on the back.

"Look," Matt says quietly, "it'll all blow over when…"

He's not destined to finish whatever supercilious offering he's going to bestow upon me. I'm about to cut him dead when another voice beats me to it.

"That's enough of that," Death's shrill voice cries down from the gantry above. Just as well he called his attack dogs off otherwise they'd be joining the giant kennel in hell. "Let's all get back to work now."

Reluctantly the typing slappers are forced to slink back to their desks – how they must hate it there as no one can see their precious legs. The music is turned off and the drivers start loading their vans. I look at Matt, who is still reeling from the scolding I've given him.

"It'll be okay," he says as he pats me on the arm and walks off. "If you want to talk, you know where I am."

If I want to talk, I'll ring the Samaritans. I look up at Doctor Death, who actually thinks he has Doug Holster beaten. He must think he's God up there, surveying all below him. He looks down on me and gestures back behind him towards his office.

The psychotic Doctor presses a button on his computerised throne and the door behind Doug Holster slams shut as he enters his lair. Doug has tracked him down to his hideaway across the rope bridge over the lava pits. Now can feel the eyes of Death's minions burning right though him. Now he knew how

265

Jesus felt as he was carrying the cross through the crowds on his way to be crucified.

"Please, Holster," Death says. "Sit down before you fall down."

Doug looks at the swivel chair opposite Death's own. It has arm and leg restraints built in. Does this supervillain think he's going to fall for that one?

"I prefer to stand," Holster replies as he folds his muscular arms.

The super spy's strength of character takes him aback and he, like Pin Head, doesn't know where to look.

"Er, okay," he says. "You know why I've brought you here, don't you?"

"This isn't the end," Doug says defiantly. "You and me aren't over until the fat lady starts singing. And unless you're hiding Dawn French in your utility belt, I'm going to follow you to the ends of the earth to destroy you."

I know that by law he has to give me two verbal warnings, plus two written ones before he can sack me. To date, I only have the verbal ones and one written report of unsatisfactory behaviour. There's no way he can fire me. I allow myself to smirk as I win the argument before it's even begun. Yes, I am sorry Herr Doctor, so sorry for ruining your day before breakfast. I guess Doug wins again and I'll be taking my van out after all.

"I'm not going to fire you," Henry says slowly. "Are you sure you don't want to take a seat?"

"Why would I want a seat?" I ask defensively.

"Well," he says. "I just thought this would be a good opportunity for us to sit down and have a little chat about things. I won't pretend I don't know what's been going on, not that I read the papers much, but I do hear what's been happening. And I'd like you to know how sorry I am."

"What about?" I ask as I cautiously slide into the chair opposite.

"Well, I know you've had a rough time since your mother died and..." he begins.

"She's not dead!" I scoff. Although you might think so what with the lack of cooking and cleaning she does around the house!

"Okay," he says slowly. "But about what's happened recently then. The first I knew about it was when Charlotte from payroll was overhead talking about selling the photo we keep of you on file to a guy from a newspaper and..."

"Charlotte?" I interrupt.

"Yes, Charlotte, and I can assure you she has been dealt with severely for that breach of our contract as an employer. We've let her go."

"You fired her?" I ask.

Doctor Death nods solemnly – advantage Doug Holster. I lean forward slightly, allowing my shoulders to curl round a bit and stoop downwards. I hang my head slightly and look up at Henry; I think I can squeeze out a couple of tears if I try.

"Did you," I stammer in my softest voice. "Did you hear what they were saying about me down there?"

Henry nods again.

"I did," he says firmly. "And I can assure you this company takes bullying very seriously. I shall be talking to all of those involved later today. Was it anyone in particular?"

"Matt," I say in a whisper.

"I see," Henry says. "I'll talk to him first. I would like to assure you that your job is in no danger whatsoever in light of your current – troubles."

"It isn't?" I say, forgetting even to add a slight sob.

"No," he replies, "not at all. We understand that you're experiencing certain emotional problems in your private life. This must be a very traumatic time for you and we would never want to be accused of kicking an employee when they're temporarily down – especially not one with your long-standing service record."

Today was meant to be the end. Today was meant to be the final standoff between good and evil. Yet with all Death's plotting, it was Holster who emerged victorious yet again.

Doug allowed himself a rare smile as he marched out of Death's lair. He could see the faces of all the minions around him. They had expected him to be leaving in a body bag. Yet it was Death's concubine, Charlotte, who had found herself floating face down in a shark pit.

I stand in the payroll department in full view of all the little tarts. They manage to stop emailing their mates for a few seconds and look up at me. I spy with my little eye – an empty desk.

I saunter over and look at the dusty nametag that's half buried under a few old bits of paper. All of the office staff have these – presumably because they're too stupid to remember each other's names – I pick it up and read the name "Charlotte Pritchard".

"Such a shame," I say as I tut and shake my head, "she didn't mean any harm."

Then I take the pens from the dead woman's desk and leave the office to load up my van. This could be a good day after all.

I drive round outer London delivering the odd parcel here and there, but I'm in a bit of a daze. It's like I have this feeling that I should be somewhere else. I pass Donna's mum's street and every fibre in my body tells me to pull up outside. Instead I

268

put my foot down and speed past in a fit of rebellion. I should be given a medal.

Later I drive back to the depot and see the usual suspects milling around. I pick up the odd look here and there, but don't take any notice.

I get out and start slinging the parcels back on the conveyer belt. If Matt's so desperate for overtime, he can load them onto his little van tomorrow. Oh, talk of the devil.

"Doug, you got a minute?" he says.

"Of course," I reply with a smile. "Had a chat with Henry have we?"

"Er, yeah," he says. "He's spoken to all of us."

I don't reply. Instead I smile back – righteous in victory. He shuffles from side to side again and I use the opportunity to stare past him at the other drivers. Not one of them dares to look in my direction. I am truly victorious.

"I just wanted to say sorry about everything," he finally says. "Sorry about how everyone's been. You know what people are like when they get an idea in their head?"

"I know what some people are like," I say emphasising the word some and keeping my eyes fixed on his smarmy friends. He looks back at them guiltily, and I tell him I have to be getting along.

"Yeah, sure," he says. "Have a good one, okay?"

I don't answer; instead I stride past the gaggle of defeated idiots. I glare at each one in turn, daring them to look at me back, but they can't bring themselves to.

Frank's among them. I slow down to a snail's pace as I pass, keeping my steely gaze on him at all times. Finally he plays right into my hands and sneaks a quick peek. His eyes meet mine and I read defeat on his face. I have you now.

"I'm surprised to see you're still here," I say confidently as I stop right in front of him and look at his averted gaze.

He doesn't respond immediately and this gives me the chance to check out the others' reactions. I feel enormous satisfaction seeing his fair-weather friends slink away like shadows disappearing into the night. He's on his own now, and he knows it.

"Yeah, well," he begins, still finding it impossible to look at me. "If it wasn't for that stupid cow selling your picture, you'd be gone by now."

"And what's that supposed to mean?" I ask, amazed at his sheer lack of backbone.

He doesn't answer. Instead he picks up his coat and wanders off to join his rapidly vanishing clique.

"I asked you a question!" I say in a commanding voice which stops him dead in his tracks.

"If you can't see it, mate," he begins. "I ain't going to be the one to tell you. Goodbye, Doug. Don't forget to take your meds."

Then he leaves in disgrace, and good riddance.

Chapter 25: The Owl Is Not What It Seems

"Five hundred hours community service and a restraining order of no less than a hundred blah, blah, blah…"

And to think I have to refer to him as "your honour". I am certainly not honoured to be in his presence. I knew I was in trouble from the moment I set foot in the courtroom and heard his name was "Stewart Martins". I've never got on with people called Stewart, right back from when I was at school – the whole lot of them are moody sods who are constantly out to get me.

As for my defence, against my better judgement I pleaded something along the lines of "diminished responsibility". Then my defence made out I was some sort of social leper, desperately seeking a life that was completely unobtainable. Looking back on it, I'd rather have said I was simply mad; although I'm beginning to think the only truly insane thing I did was stick with Darling and his loose-fitting glasses.

I even have to question what kind of solicitor he is exactly. I'd shown him umpteen copies of *The People* and all the others who had printed inaccuracies about me. You'd think a real solicitor would have jumped at the chance to represent me and cream off a juicy slice of the libel payout. Sadly Mr Short-sightedness turned out to be the most timid, under-motivated man I've ever met. All he could say was that I could try launching a private prosecution, but he didn't want to advise right now. Maybe if he had the foresight to pick up my case he could afford a pair of glasses that fitted properly.

He said I should sue my own firm instead, but I couldn't understand why. I think he was simply too scared to go after the big fish and kept going on about work related breaches of confidence. But if truth be known, I've been enjoying work recently. The people I deliver to are still as rude as ever, but back in the warehouse, things are a different story. No more dirty looks, no more sniggering behind my back, no more shouts of "here comes the Weeble". Everywhere I go people treat me with dignity and respect for the first time. Not one of them has said a word to me in weeks. Only Henry talks to me when it's work related and although Matt has tried, I basically refuse to acknowledge he even exists.

Still, none of that helped my case. Everyone totally ignored my cries to call Donna as a witness and get her to put the record straight. It seemed I was hung, drawn and quartered before I even entered the pokey little courtroom. I was destined to be the sacrificial goat and take the fall on behalf of Donna. I imagine she's out there somewhere plugging her album and doesn't want the adverse publicity. I fully understand this and know I have to back off until it's all died down. She's a survivor and she'll bounce back, just like me.

"Have you anything you'd like to add?" asked moody Stewart.

I politely said no even though I had plenty to say, but I figured I'd save it for my website, or perhaps an autobiography.

I like to think I'm an optimist, so I decided to dwell on the positive side of "being made an example of" as Stewart put it. The way I saw it, that was merely yet another example of how suited me and Donna truly are. We have both suffered knocks at the same time, both been the victim of a callous hate campaign by an insidious media.

Plus the courthouse was literally awash with pens. Every other table and desk seemed to have them lying around for the taking. By the end of the three days, I'd almost amassed a small stationery cupboard of my own.

So I spend the weeks biding my time before I launch my comeback: I go to work, check the newspapers and gossip magazines and come home again – all the time ignoring Hannah's calls and that text message about it not being Matt's fault.

There hasn't been a mention of Donna in the papers for weeks now, or me for that matter. Never did I think becoming "old news" would be such a relief. Sure, there was a bit in the local papers, but once the nationals realised I'm not the next Jack the Ripper, they lost interest in me.

I'm pretty sure Donna hasn't read my mail yet, as the last thing I did read about her was from an online news service. It was only a short piece about her checking into some clinic in the Midlands, but it didn't elaborate. I hope she's having a good time up there, as if anyone needs a break from it all – besides me – it's her.

In the meantime I've been emailing Metropol Industries after a technical glitch seems to have meant that her website has been taken down. I keep getting that annoying "this page cannot be displayed and it may return if you refresh your browser window" message. That's a lie, I've been clicking the refresh button for hours and it still hasn't come back. I'm therefore a little concerned that she might not have received any of my emails.

I finally decide to use the old-fashioned method and put pen to paper and write her a letter courtesy of Metropol. Sadly it was returned four days later with a hand-written note saying that "Ms Trayhorn can no longer be contacted through Metropol Industries". I think this must be some sort of clerical error, so I try and contact them directly, which proves to be a mission in itself. Like all big companies, they have decided to have their call centres abroad.

When I do get through to someone who sounds like they vaguely know what they're talking about, the moment they find out what I want, they suddenly remember the person I need to speak to is "not at his desk".

I phone back numerous times, yet not only would no one at Metropol give out their direct extension, but it seems like their staff don't actually sit at their desks in the first place! I try calling them from the phone in the loading bay at work as all the other drivers wander off the moment I come in, but still no one takes my calls.

How I want to write a harsh email to the company's boss Peter Carter and tell him exactly how unhelpful his staff are, but I don't want my actions to reflect badly on Donna. So, once again, being the model of self-restraint, I bite my lip and concentrate on delivering an ugly ornamental flamingo to lovely old Mrs Jones for her precious garden.

A few weeks later I'm on the Internet looking at old posts when my mobile phone rings.

I can't even remember where I put it as it hasn't rung in days. I don't rush over to answer, as I'm sure it'll only be Hannah again begging for forgiveness. Instead, I go to bed, as I have work tomorrow.

It's not until the following day when I'm sitting outside the newsagents browsing the papers that I bother to check my answer phone.

Hi there, this is a message for Doug Morrell. My name's Belle Warren, I work for Metropol Industries – I take it you've heard of us – I was wondering if you'd give me a call back for a little chat. Thanks, bye.

This is a turn up for the books and it goes to show that persistence does indeed pay off. This is the first time I've ever been given an actual name and number for a Metropol employee.

Belle Warren – where do I know that name from?

Then it comes to me: she's one of the production team on *Voyeur*. I dial her back immediately, but my hopes are dashed when I find she's not at her desk. However, this time the girl I speak to – who I assume is her assistant – is surprisingly helpful when I mention my name and books me in to see her the following day at Metropol Towers itself.

Once upon a time the two towers which make up Metropol Industries' head offices were merely a landmark on the London skyline, but today they're right in front of me. Belle even paid for a cab to take me past that nice guard at the gates and up to the main entrance. I still have no idea what she wants and I can only assume she needs advice on an upcoming series of *Voyeur*. Perhaps I could be a pundit?

"Mr Morrell," says the smiling guard at the front door, before stepping aside and holding the door wide open, "go right through, please."

I thank the handsome man and do just that. Before I know it, I'm inside the main entrance hall of one of the two Metropol towers. I'm somewhat in awe of the marble floor stretching out in front of me leading towards a fountain next to the main desk. There isn't any need for artificial lighting as the black glass which covers the building all the way to the fortieth floor is actually a two way mirror. I look back through the tinted glass at the world I've left behind. I've finally made it inside Metropol Towers, the home of *Voyeur*, and also Donna. Now I can find out why I can't reach her via these offices.

I watch people rushing back and forth around me. They are indeed as beautiful as I'd always imagined. Every one of them has a clipboard under one arm and dedication in their eyes. A little part of me feels like I've returned home after a long, hard journey.

"Doug?" a polite woman's voice says. "Glad you could make it."

I cast my eyes down from the hypnotic, glistening chandelier high above me to a woman in her twenties. She has

275

dark blonde hair tied up in bunches and dresses in deliberately hippie-like clothing, set off with trendy designer glasses. I can see she's classy, while at the same time being sharp as a razor.

"Not at all, Belle," I say like we're old friends. "It's wonderful to be here."

"Huh? What? Oh, right, yeah," she replies. "You should try being here every bloody day…"

"I'd love that!" I exclaim, quickly. "The hustle and bustle of a career in the media, rubbing shoulders with the great and good. I feel like I could be a real addition to this place."

Belle looks at me, obviously impressed with my enthusiasm.

"Be careful what you wish for, Doug," she says with raised eyebrows, "come this way."

I watch the car park below my feet getting further and further away as we take a glass elevator out of reception. I feel like Charlie from *Charlie and the Chocolate Factory*, as we ascend higher and higher into a magical world of dreams and mysteries. During the lift ride, I point out that along with being a life-long fan of her work on *Voyeur* and an accredited media commentator, I'm also a successful writer. Perhaps while I was here I could drop in on the publishing side of Metropol's empire.

"Don't worry, Doug, I know all about you," she says with a sly grin. My heart jumps a little at the thought of finally being acknowledged as a heavyweight presence in the media. "But we had something else in mind for you."

Then it comes to me: the new series of *Celebrity Voyeur* is starting up soon. She must have been one of the few people who bothered to listen to my courtroom defence. She must have heard when I spoke about my skills as a commentator on celebrities. That's a point; in all my excitement, I haven't even mentioned her yet.

"Is Donna here, by any chance?" I ask.

"Who? Oh, of course, Donna. No, she's not here right now."

"Oh, that's okay," I say. "It's just I'm not allowed in a hundred yards of her – if you can believe such a thing."

"Yeah, I can," she nods, "don't worry. Donna's not with us any more."

"She's left Metropol? But why?"

"Oh, she only had a short-term contract with us," she replies, "with er, some people it's best not to offer them anything too – long term – if you know what I mean?"

I didn't. Metropol Industries are always quick to back up and coming starlets. I couldn't see why they'd part ways.

"With a new season of *Voyeur* starting," she goes on, "we figured the public would lose interest."

"I didn't!" I point out, still a bit confused at what she's getting at.

"I know," she says, slowly. "But she knew what she was getting into when she signed up for *Voyeur*; she had quite a good run really. But now her fun's over, and it's time to let the next lot have their fifteen minutes. Did you know Kat has just released a fitness video?"

I don't care about that heartbreaker.

"Oh," I say. "So what's Donna doing now?"

"Last thing I heard she checked into some rehab clinic," she muses as the lift slows down. "I'm sure she'll be okay. We knew she was on her way down when we released the story about pirates downloading her tracks illegally via the Internet and…"

"Scum," I snap, "taking advantage of hard-working artists."

"Yeah, right," she laughs. "But in this case they never did – we just leaked it to the press in the hope it would stir up a bit of interest in her flagging career. Maybe generate the sympathy vote – anyway, it didn't work. Ah, here we are."

The lift stops and I catch sight of the luxurious corridor stretching out before me through the doors. Belle's face is reflected in the glass and I suddenly become aware of just how thick her glasses are; they make her eyes look way too big. Still, I'm here now; I should try to put up with her oddities at least until I find out what she wants.

We step out onto plush black carpet and I follow her into meeting room one hundred and one. Inside is a boardroom-like glass table with a giant window overlooking London.

"Take a seat please, Doug," she says as she pushes a well-stocked trolley in my direction, "anything to drink?"

I pour myself a glass of mineral water and take a few bottles for later.

"I expect you're wondering why you're here," she says. But I'm more taken with her huge eyes; I think she's a giant owl.

"Not really," I quip, "I'm sure it's got something to do with the new series of *Voyeur*, am I right?"

"Spot on," she says through her beak, clearly amazed at my perception.

"I knew it," I say, "I take it you've seen my website?"

"I have, it's…"

"And you do know I've been offering commentary on the last eight series of *Voyeur*? It really is the best reality TV show of the lot. I don't watch any of the others while it's on."

"That's nice, Doug, but it's actually about *Celebrity Voyeur*," she says as she uses her beak to pluck a rogue feather from her underbelly.

"Yes, I watch that too. Would you like me to be a pundit?" I ask politely, while she lifts up a glass of water with her right wing.

"No."

"No?" What does she mean, no? Why has this monstrous bird dragged me to her nest then?

"We'd like you to be on it."

Now that the sunlight streams through the giant windows on to us and I'm sitting directly opposite her, I realise her eyes aren't as big and owl-like as I'd first thought; she's actually a very pretty girl again.

Chapter 26: Just Like Heaven

That was the second greatest moment in my life (The first being when I realised I was in love with Donna). I am officially a celebrity.

Apparently it was Belle herself who had put my name forward for the next series of *Celebrity Voyeur*. I knew she was an astute woman the moment I laid eyes on her. She felt that an up-and-coming author like me had something new to offer the public, and I couldn't agree more. I signed with Metropol right away. I can't believe I'm actually being paid to appear on television. For twenty pounds a day I'm going to be given my own soapbox to educate the masses with. For the first time, a series of *Voyeur* will have a credible contestant, one who will say things without adding "you know what I mean?" at the end of each sentence.

People will see how a decent human being behaves, as opposed to the fame-hungry idiots who are normally selected for the public to laugh at. I think to the best of my knowledge, this is the first time I've heard of an author being selected for a series of *Voyeur*. I suspect the supposed literary heavyweights like JK Rowling and JRR Tolkien would consider a reality TV show too lowbrow to participate in, but that's their loss.

Not only will it be an excellent chance to showcase my literary talent, but also to plug my website. Once the press see how much Donna and I mean to each other, they'll start taking back all of those inaccuracies. Only the little matter of my job stands in the way of my crowning glory. Belle's given me a letter asking my company to let me have the time off, but I think I'll be writing my own note instead.

"It's over, Death," Doug laughs as he bursts into the mad Doctor's lair and puts a gun to his head.

"No, please don't kill me!" his arch enemy begs, but Holster has heard it all before.

The theatre of their little war was about to have the curtain pulled for good. Holster was about to add another supervillain's name to his tally of those he'd saved the universe from.

"I've had it up to here with your petty rules and regulations. You can take your forms, your signatures and your useless satellite tracking devices and stick them where the sun doesn't shine! I don't need this job," I say, triumphantly. Let's see how he likes that.

"Well," Henry says slowly. "We still need you…"

"But I don't need you!" I interrupt as I laugh loudly, making sure all the office can hear.

"No, please, let me finish, I was going to say we still need…your mobile phone back. It's company property."

"My mobile?"

How typical of the cheapskate. I work here for all these years and the first thing he does when I say I'm leaving is ask for my phone back. How am I supposed to make calls now?

"Fine," I say bitterly as I slam the stupid old Nokia down on his desk, deliberately dislodging some of his precious paperwork.

"We'll be very sorry to see you go," he lies through gritted teeth.

I wait for more bile to spew from his bitter and twisted mouth, but he's clearly too shocked that one of his supposed underlings has finally had the guts to stand up to his tyrannical ways.

"Good luck then," he adds and gestures to the door.

I stand there smugly, hammering home my point that I no longer need him and his little delivery firm any more. I'm a celebrity and that's official.

"Was there something else?" he sighs, desperate for me to leave and end this awkwardness.

"I don't need this job!" I say.

"Yes, I gathered that by your previous comments," he replies. "Now, if you'll excuse me, I still do have a job and the work that comes with it."

He's so mad, it's unbelievable. He can't even bring himself to ask why I'm leaving after all this time.

"Aren't you going to ask me where I'm going?" I say victoriously.

"No. That's your business now, Doug."

"I'm going on TV," I say, watching his face drop as the words sink in.

"Oh, right," is all he can say to that. "I'll be sure to watch out for you then."

His phone rings, probably someone telling him to get his drivers to fill out yet another pointless form.

"Excuse me, I have to take this," he says as he picks up the receiver.

Doctor Death never knew who was on the other end of the line. The next and last thing he ever heard was the sound of Doug's twin pistols sending bullet after bullet through his evil and twisted old body.

Once again, the world is safe. Once again, the fearless and unstoppable Doug Holster has saved the day for humanity.

He poured petrol over his ex-nemesis and flicked a cigar butt at him, engulfing his corpse in flames. This was the way he chose to dispatch all supervillains just in case they came back the next day.

With Death vanquished, his underlings were free. As Doug strode out of his lair, he listened to the cheers coming up from all the people the mad Doctor had enslaved during his reign of terror.

"Twat!" I hear one of the junior slappers mutter as I saunter through the typing pool thinking how light I was on Doctor Death. I – accidentally of course – knock her in-tray onto the floor as I pass.

I leave via the loading bays, as I might as well say goodbye to Matt and let him know he used to know someone famous.

"Hi, Doug," he says in his usual over-cheery manner.

"Goodbye, Matt," I say with a smile and can almost see the question marks above his confused little head. "I'm leaving this dump and everyone in it and the next time you'll see me, I'll be on the telly."

Before he can answer, a couple more Neanderthal drivers prove their level of maturity with some cheering before lumbering off.

"Seriously?" he says, probably still high from whatever he's been smoking.

"I'm afraid so," I say loudly so all the other cavemen can hear, "I'm a celebrity now!"

"Well done, mate," he goes on, consumed with jealousy, "what you going to do?"

"It's hard to say where my career will take me, but…"

I'm cut off by one of the other drivers shouting something particularly unfunny about "as long as it's anywhere, but here". They all laugh, but I'm not bothered. It only goes to prove how many levels I've risen above them.

"I'm going now, Matt," I say with a smirk aimed at him and his companions. "You certainly will never be seeing me again."

With that I turn and leave, ignoring his last-ditch attempts at pleasantries and depart that cursed loading bay forever.

I return ten minutes later to get my pictures of Donna from my cab. Unfortunately the other drivers are still there and I'm forced to ignore the jeers.

The next two weeks drag by like no others in my life. Normally, if I was off work, I'd be with Donna by now, but what with the police and all that, I figure I'd better not. I did drive to her mother's street once, but I saw undercover policemen posing as postmen, so I sped off.

I text Hannah and say her and me aren't working out any more and not to bother contacting me again. When was the last time you saw a celebrity hanging out with a primary school teacher? She texted back saying we only ever went out twice and that was over a year ago, but that's women for you.

I update my site, but sadly Belle said that if I mentioned online I'm appearing on *Celebrity Voyeur*, it would invalidate the contract and they'd have to use the back-up contestant. As I've proved on many an occasion, I can be the model of self-restraint. There was no way I was going to let some eighties children's TV presenter and his duck puppet take my place.

I consider advertising for another moderator to look after my site during my absence. Over recent weeks I've been so inundated with crank members – or brainless sheep who believe everything in the newspapers – that I've added the words "stalk" and "stalker" to the list of expletives that are automatically banned from my forum. At least that's gone some way to limit the amount of slanderous posts about me.

I thought Friday night would never arrive, but after what seemed like an eternity, I find myself sitting in the back of a limousine a few streets away from the studio house. Belle has advised me personally on what I should wear. I had considered appealing to the common man by wearing those trousers with pockets half way down the leg, but Belle said no. I then put forward a suggestion that perhaps I should try and sex up my image a bit with one of those "figure-hugging" men's T-shirts in the Metropol wardrobe, but again, she said that wasn't a good idea.

So here I am, sitting in the back of my limo wearing what she described as "something that suits my personality". And, to be fair, I feel she's done her job admirably as the sky-blue turtleneck jumper heightens my chiselled jaw line and raises my charismatic profile. I must say that the beige corduroy trousers feel a little funny without my mobile phone in one pocket and my wallet in the other. No matter, I'm banking on my wallet becoming a lot fatter once I leave the show.

"Okay, all the others are in now," a woman's voice crackles through the radio next to the driver. I think that must have been Belle. "Bring the last one round."

My heart skips a beat as the car moves closer to the studio. The cheering gets louder and I can make out the show's presenters Ray and Ford keeping the crowd amused while I make my grand entrance.

You'd think I'd be used to handling screaming fans after all my showbiz bashes, but as the ovation gets louder, my stomach starts churning.

"Oh, please God, don't you dare throw up," I say out loud.

"You'll be fine, mate," the driver laughs as security guards pull back the barriers to allow us to pass through the legions of fans.

"You think so?" I say, nervously.

"I know so," he replies confidently. "You lot always are."

I want to ask him what he means by that, but two words boom through the car's walls which freeze me to my seat.

"Doug Morrell!"

I don't know whether that was Ray or Ford as most people can't tell them apart at the best of times. Either way, a suave minder opens the car door and I catch sight of what seems like a thousand eager young faces clamouring to catch a glimpse of me. The security guard gestures for me to come out.

I take a deep breath and leave my vehicle's womb like interior. Immediately flashbulbs go off all around me and an almighty cheer goes up that lifts my soul. I hold my head high and allow myself the luxury of savouring the moment. I look from one adoring face to the next along the rows of youngsters lining the barricade. They obviously know who I am as they turn to each other and discuss my shock inclusion to the show.

"No one knows young Doug Morrell better than our very own Donna Trayhorn…" either Ray or Ford says over the microphone. That's my cue; when they start reading my profile I'm supposed to walk down the road between the crowds and towards the house. Did I feel like throwing up now? Was my nose about to start bleeding?

Not a bloody bit of it!

Who needs drugs when you have fame? And the respectable crowd adheres to Metropol's request not to ask for autographs. Granted I don't see many of them cheering, so it's impossible to tell which ones are rooting for me.

While Ray and Ford continue their patter, I give the nearest bunch of girls a wink and a wave as I stride past. The crowd loves me: they laugh at my witty gestures and pretend shock at their admiration. I can't even make out what Ray and Ford are saying about me. I did give Belle a script I wanted them to read and she promised to look at it and make any necessary adjustments. I hope she left the bit in about Jack Nicholson and my film script.

As I reach the final part of the road before I enter the house, I run to another group of girls and give the prettiest one a kiss.

She bursts into laughter and blushes before her friends hug her and try to wipe her cheek – obviously amazed I should single her out for such affection.

The press pack waits before my final security check – time to let my humorous side shine through. I stage-dive into the crowd, but the metal barrier is more sturdy than it looks and I bounce off and land hard on my back. At any other time I might feel the pain as my head hits the tarmac, but not now. The crowd roars with laughter as they obviously like a bit of slapstick. So I spring to my feet and do a little dance, before doing a Roger Moore pose for the press who snap away like they'd never seen a celebrity before.

"Raptor – my man!" I yell into the pack of photographers.

He doesn't reply as he's too amazed to see me there. He just stands among them dumbstruck – the only photographer not taking my picture. Slowly he lifts his hand and points at me in sheer disbelief. I wink at the journalists – they love me too.

Before I let the last security guard search me, I turn and hold my hands above my head as if I'd already won the series. The crowd laughs louder and I hear a hearty cockney voice booming over the microphone.

"That's enough, Doug – the show only lasts eight weeks!"

It was Ray, looking down on me from the stage where he and Ford are doing their piece to camera.

"Good one, Ray!" I shout back and wink.

Then I force myself to leave my fans and let the bouncer search me before I enter the doors to the house. Just think, this will be the last time these people will be able to see me in the flesh for eight whole weeks.

"I'm Ford," Ford replies dryly, to which the crowd laughs even more.

What a rapport I have with celebrities – perhaps the three of us could form some sort of comedy double act once I've won?

The bouncer takes all three pens from my inside pocket.

"I will get those back, won't I?" I ask quietly, but I forget I'm wearing a microphone.

The crowd laughs, I turn to look at the sea of smiling faces. It suddenly hits me what natural comic timing I have. Sometimes I can be funny without even trying.

"Don't worry, Doug," the one I believe to be Ford says. "I'll look after your crayons personally while you're in there."

I breathe a sigh of relief at his comforting words. I'm sure a recognised TV personality will take good care of my possessions, especially now he's promised to on live TV.

Silence.

I look around myself and think I must have died. I'm standing in a long white tunnel, leading down some steps into a set of white sliding double doors with a giant "V" logo on it. But I'm not in heaven yet, although I imagine this must be what it looks like – a giant reality TV studio in the clouds. I look round to see the house's doors have slammed shut behind me and my supporters can no longer help me. I am alone with nothing more than my natural wit, charm and sophistication to entertain and educate the masses for two months.

A rotating dome-camera tracks my movements as I walk down the stairs towards the inner bowels of the house. I'm about to meet my new housemates. Nine other stars, all experts in their chosen fields, will be my new companions. At last I have made it into the inner circle and can mix with a better class of people. Not like those miserable customers who complain when I'm late with the second hand CD they bought from eBay. But of course the people who await me are not really people, but rivals and I feel an invisible outer shell forming around me as I go over the battle plan in my head.

They may be famous, but I will have to stab every last one of them in the back to make it to the final. I reach the bottom of

288

the stairs and the second set of double doors slides open and I take in my nine enemies. One by one they eye me up, probably assessing my strengths and weaknesses. Little do they know what I'm capable of; they haven't got a clue as to what's about to hit them.

Chapter 27: Beer and Tears

I survey my prey as they stand in the lounge basking in their ignorance. I smile – this is going to be easier than I thought.

"The name's Morrell, Doug Morrell" I say as I thrust my hand out towards the nearest person who I haven't the faintest idea who he is.

He looks at my hand as if it's diseased, then back at my bronzed face.

"Who?" he says at last.

Now you might think I'd be offended by his lack of knowledge, but not a bit of it. I haven't got a clue who he is, so the feeling is more than mutual. Plus I'm happy being the underdog – if there's one thing I know about popular culture, it's that the public like to see the little guy make it big.

"I'm an author," I say, politely. No need to give him the tongue-lashing he so richly deserves just yet.

"Oh, right," he says. What a bland person he is.

"Rick, Rick Street," he states as if it's supposed to mean something. I think he picks up on the fact that I'm still none the wiser of his origins and so elaborates. "Twisted Fantasy?"

I look at the other housemates to see if I'm the only one who thinks he's speaking a foreign language. I'm bolstered by the fact they all look as nonplussed as me. Wait a minute; is he wearing make-up?

He goes on to give us an impromptu rendition of what I have to assume is a song called "Twisted Fantasy". As he croons to some lesbian weather girl with his pelvic thrusts, an old bloke called Mike Sparks, who was a DJ back in the seventies, whispers to me: "This got to number four in 1982. He's never had a top ten hit since."

As Rick launches into the third verse of his only hit, I suddenly realise why the edited highlight shows of *Voyeur* are so popular. Does he really think people want to listen to this?

"Thank you, thank you," he says as he pauses for air and we applaud politely in the hope he's finished. "I could go on!"

"Yeah," I say, "or, you could not!"

The lesbian weather girl cheers and a couple of the other women titter. Rick shrivels to the back of the group like a slug taking a salt bath. They're like lambs to the slaughter.

I don't bother introducing myself to the other men. Mike seems okay, but I knew there's no point in me getting friendly with him as he's elderly. And, as we all know, old people are quickly evicted from reality TV shows. Instead I concentrate on the women. If reality TV has taught me one thing, it's that the public are obsessed with the prospect of two people getting together on screen. Of course I wasn't going to do anything that might upset or distress Donna. After all, I know exactly how helpless she must be feeling with me trapped in here and her on the outside. I felt that way when she was in here.

I'm pretty sure Sarah Richmond is giving me the eye, but then she's a bit on the old side too. She's turning forty soon and fed up with only getting acting parts on stage, so has turned to reality TV to try and put her name forward for the small screen.

Then there's Amber Brown, who also seems to have taken a shine to me. Perhaps all those stories about her and that female anchorwoman were exaggerations?

Naturally Abi Glasgow is all over me, but then she would. She's not a celebrity at all so I don't know why she's even in here. All she does is sleep with footballers then sell stories about the size of their manhood to the Sunday papers. I'll be damned if she's going to do that to me!

Once the introductions are out of the way, *Voyeur* ushers us to the dining area to have our "welcome dinner". I quickly find out that this means beer – lots of beer. It's like the producers are deliberately trying to get us to act like a bunch of drunken idiots. For some that will come easier than others.

Glamour model Soho Star and some ex soap actress called Wendy Turner, who failed to crack Hollywood sit either side of me. I can tell there may well be some tension between the two of them as to who gets the lion's share of my affections.

But the obligatory "romance element" of the show would have to wait for now – there were more important things afoot.

"Is this it?" I declare as I survey the alleged banquet before us.

"What's up, man?" says the mandatory American contestant, Brett Large. "You limeys won't eat anything apart from fish and chips soaked in tea!"

I was about to point out that there were no such things as ghosts; therefore how this man claimed to be a professional "ghost-buster" was beyond me. He should have stuck to being a priest, even if he did look more like Elvis. Plus the stupid yank has only gone and turned up in full ceremonial robes.

"At least we eat healthily!" Sarah shouts at him.

"And we're not all fat!" continues Wendy. "Do you know how many models and actresses are out there abusing their bodies in pursuit of what Hollywood has declared beautiful?"

Hmm, she's not bitter about all those wasted auditions in LA then.

"Look…" begins Brett, before being cut off with some more anti-American outbursts. It seems I've put a little strain on our special transatlantic relationship.

"Americans always think they can tread on people," states some indie musician guy from a band no one's heard of.

"I've been to Australia!" chimes in Soho from my right-hand side.

Cue world war three.

Once again, my comprehensive knowledge of reality TV saves me from making a mistake. If there's one thing that gets you nominated for eviction, it's starting rows – not that I meant to start one, I wasn't even referring to the food. I was talking about what there was to drink. I hate beer! I was hoping for some Archers and lemonade.

I get up and leave the table, which is just as well, as a chair flies across the room at Brett, thrown by the indie guy. He really was overdoing the whole "rock-and-roll" thing. If there was a TV in the house, I'll bet he'd have thrown it out the window.

Soho bursts into tears and as I approach the Box Room to speak directly to *Voyeur,* I leave behind shouts of "the power of Christ compels you!" from Brett.

"Hello, Doug. How are you finding your first evening under the gaze of *Voyeur*?" says the overly polite voice of whoever is manning the console in the production booth.

"Not bad," I muse. "I was wondering if there was any chance of getting a proper drink?"

"*Voyeur* has provided the group with enough beer to last the weekend."

"I don't like beer. I only drink Archers and lemonade."

Dramatic pause while the person on the other end of the microphone has to run off and check with his superior whether he can grant my request.

"*Voyeur* is about trying new experiences. We suggest you try some of the beer that has been laid on for you?"

"Thank you, *Voyeur*," I say through gritted teeth, then get up and bang on the Box Room's door to get out. I know there's no point in arguing with them, not unless I want to make myself look stupid. They never give in – they know if they stick to their guns, there's not a damn thing we can do about it. And why *Voyeur* must always refer to itself in third person is beyond me.

I return from talking to the screen to find that things have calmed down a bit. Most of the group are eating dinner and swigging from beer cans which have had the labels removed to avoid advertising bias. Amber is "comforting" Soho with one arm round her shoulder and the other down her top. It seems Brett and the indie guy have both left the dining area and are nowhere to be seen.

"Has Father Ted sorted out his differences with that other guy?" I ask the group in general.

Before anyone can answer, we all hear some muffled shouts of annoyance, before the toilet flushes. The door to the bathroom opens and the musician marches out holding Brett's sunglasses in his visibly wet hands.

"Bloody Americans," he mutters to himself as he picks up his can off the table.

Soho bursts into tears again.

Later that night we get set our first task by *Voyeur*. We're supposed to formally introduce ourselves and say why we're famous and how.

"I was born the day Elvis died," begins Brett. "But the King's soul wasn't going to lie down and roll over for the reaper and got carried into me. Now I exorcise Satan's minions every Tuesday night at eight on Fox."

Shameless plug for his already cancelled show.

"Men just seem to find me irresistible!" says Abi.

Well, if you set your standards low enough. Besides, I'm still finding it hard to believe that she's in here to begin with. It's not like she's even a proper celebrity!

"Three words," begins Rick. "Stock, Aitken and Waterman. Their record label practically launched itself off the back of me. Need I say more?"

Well, yes please, and by the way, that was four words. He doesn't elaborate on his boast and it becomes Amber's turn.

"Where would the British be without weather?" she says with a smile. Everyone waits for more. After an uncomfortable pause, she continues, "and since I came out as gay, the tabloids seem to follow me around like a cloud."

"Thousands of people woke up with me every morning during the seventies – but don't tell the wife!" says Mike, trying to be funny and failing miserably.

"I'm an actress!" chimes in Soho.

No one says anything. If acting involved taking your clothes off in front of photographers all day and falling out of nightclubs at night, then maybe.

"I am!" she insists.

You can almost hear the wind whistling outside. She then bursts into tears and the task is called off for now.

When we've finally persuaded Soho to unpack her suitcase and not to leave the show after only five hours, the game continues.

"Rock and roll!" screams the indie guy as he jumps to his feet and punches the air.

Perhaps we're supposed to swoon at his Adonis-like manliness, or maybe just sing along with one of his hits – if anyone actually knew any of them. Either way no one does, but I take the opportunity to pick up Sarah's cigarette lighter and wave it slowly in the air. Everyone laughs as it's really funny. I'll bet that's the sort of thing the producers are looking for and I'm sure it'll make tonight's highlights.

"I've just finished a gruelling three-month stint as Lady Macbeth in the Wyndam theatre in London."

"Cool," replies Soho as she nods. "What's that? Like a gig or something?"

The game is once again paused while I explain that Macbeth is actually a play.

"Ooh," she says, "cool. Did you write it?"

"Yes." I say with a straight face. Again, everyone laughs, including Soho for some reason. I'm at my best in front of a camera. I should easily get my own show after this. Finally I put her out of her misery and explain that I didn't really write the play, it was a gentleman called William Shakespeare who wrote it long ago.

"Even before you were born!" I add.

"No way!" she gasps.

"As you all know," Wendy says when it comes to her turn, "I was in *Cul-de-sac* for three years when I thought – hey I've had enough of this, I don't want to be doing soaps forever – so I went to Hollywood."

"Where's that?" Soho asks.

Cue another lengthy pause while I give a brief geography lesson. As it happens, Abi didn't know "where in Britain" that was either.

"Was *Jaws* made there?" Soho asks.

"Yes," I say slowly.

"Cool! What about *Ghost*?"

"Yes," I sigh, "that too."

"No way!" she exclaims, "what about *Star Wars*?"

"That too," I say, before asking the others whether we can just move on before she lists every film ever made.

Soho bursts into laughter.

"You're winding me up again," she says, before calming herself down with another beer, "half of that was filmed on another planet!"

On Wendy's insistence, we skim over the bit about how many films she starred in while she was over there and finally finish the game.

"What about you, Doug?" the indie guy says. "I haven't heard of any of your books."

"Have you even read a book?" I retort.

Everyone laughs and he shuts up. Then I offer to get another drink for Amber as she had the good grace to laugh the loudest.

"Seriously though," says Brett as I get up off the sofa. "Which books have you written?"

All eyes are on me. Why do I suddenly feel uncomfortable having nine people looking at me when there are a further nine million out there watching me?

"You ever heard of Donna Trayhorn?" Rick sneers.

"No." says Brett.

"Exactly," laughs Rick, "hardly anyone has. I remember this guy now; he's stalked her ever since she left this show!"

"Well, you know how the producers like to stir things up by putting a non celebrity in among everyone else," sneers the indie guy.

I look at Abi, but she doesn't seem to be upset by his snipe at her. All eyes are on me and I think hard how I'm going to phrase this without embarrassing Donna. What do other A-listers do when the pressure mounts? A public apology where they don't really apologise.

"I'm here to clear my name," I say with grace and dignity as I hold my hands together as if at confession. "Things have been said, mistakes have been made and my name has been linked with some scandalous accusations. I'd like to take this opportunity to put my side across."

"And what is your side then?" asks Rick.

Yeah, thanks for that.

"That I'm innocent," I say defiantly. "And that I'm merely a victim of an unwarranted and callous hate campaign by a twisted and unscrupulous media."

I finish talking and finally allow myself to take a breath. I look around at the nine blank faces. I think I've put my case across succinctly and maturely.

297

"What?" asks Soho, after her brain has had time to digest the longer of the words.

"Press in-true-shun," I say, breaking it down for the poor dear.

A volcano of appreciation erupts around me as verbal lava spews in torrents from the mouths of my fellow housemates.

"The Sunday papers called me a slapper!" Abi shouts. This was followed by cries of "rubbish" and "they never" from Soho.

"And they said I was a fake!" complained Brett, to which those nearest him recounted their own experiences with the undead.

"Were they at any of the auditions I attended in Beverly Hills?" asks Wendy to everyone and no one. "Do they know how many I went to? How can they call me a failure?"

Naturally everyone agreed that simply setting foot in Hollywood was an achievement in itself. And it didn't matter if the only part offered to her was "third swamp-creature on the left".

"And they said I was unintell... unitele... inuntold..." begins Soho.

"Thick?" asks the indie musician, who I find out is called Terry Butler.

After Soho has been suitably comforted and the wailings have died down, a new sense of peace falls over the *Voyeur* household. I never even considered I had anything in common with these so-called celebrities, yet it seems that they all have their own gripes with the press and, like me, have decided to use the media against itself.

For a split second, it feels like we are one: one giant famous organism, breathing and moving together. Perhaps this is what it must be like to be at the pub with a group of people you actually like? For now I'll play along and laugh, joke and make out that I'm their best buddy. What a shame that I'm going to have to knock them off one by one. Then Terry suggests the media is only interested in good-looking young people, which offends Mike, who then raises his voice point eight of a decibel, which in turn makes Soho start to cry again.

Rick tries to comfort her, but Amber stops him by leaping across the room to get there first. I watch Rick slink away dejectedly and make a mental note that he dared to claim no one had heard of Donna.

"Nice make-up," I say to him when the noise has died down.

"What's that supposed to mean?" he snaps back.

Touched a nerve there, have I?

"Nothing," I say innocently.

"You obviously never heard of the New Romantic movement," he says patronisingly.

"I've heard of the gay movement," I scoff, to which the others laugh.

"I am not gay!" he shouts, before bursting into tears and storming off as his mascara starts to run.

I decide it's time to leave the room and go to bed as I've won the battle. It seems Amber and Sarah are above all this too, as they obediently follow me into the bedroom. Amber makes sure Soho comes with us in case she needs more "comforting". I have followers under my spell already.

The weekend passes without further incident. And when I say that, I mean without anything happening that affects my chances of winning. There are one or two hundred more rows caused by clashes between either overbearing Elvis-impersonating, American paranormal priest Brett Large and Terry. Or, Terry versus single-minded, New Romantic, one-hit-wonder Rick "I'm not gay and those stories in the tabloids are all lies" Street.

All three will do almost anything for attention. Brett wants his old show – which the Fox network dropped in America – picked up by a British station. Rick will sell his soul for a new recording contract and surly Terry just keeps sticking their heads down the toilet. By Sunday he's already on his second warning from *Voyeur* about indulging in physical violence against fellow contestants.

With the three guys too busy hating each other and Mike being way too old to be considered attractive, I find I have the pick of the women. I spend my days engaging the ladies in some witty banter on the sofa – when the sofa isn't being hurled across the room by Terry.

"Oh, Doug, you are a one," Amber says after I regale her with my story about dealings with Johnny Depp. She pats me on the head and strokes my thick hair. I can only imagine what the press are saying about us on the outside: "Morrell turns gay woman straight".

"I try," I say with a smile.

"You're like a helpless little puppy dog, aren't you?" she goes on.

I'm not sure what she means by that, but I scan her voice for any trace of sarcasm or venom and there's none detected.

"Woof!" I reply and everyone laughs hysterically.

Then Soho starts barking like a dog for the next ten minutes. It's not until Terry pours a can of beer over her head that she finally shuts up.

Amber takes the opportunity to "console" the blubbing glamour model, before storming into the bedroom to hunt down and destroy the miserable musician. Meanwhile Soho makes mewing noises – if there's one thing to be said about her, it's that she does bounce back quickly.

I take the opportunity to strike up a conversation with Wendy.

"Funny, isn't it?" I say. "Normally there's at least one gay man in the *Voyeur* house?"

"Yeah, that's true," she replies.

"What?" screams Rick from the kitchen area, "why's everyone looking at me?"

Note to self: if bored, mention homosexuality around Rick and stand well back.

Monday comes and brings the first round of nominations. I vote for Brett and Terry as during one of my many late-night chats with the girls, Wendy drunkenly stated she found the two of them attractive and would consider going to bed with them if they "weren't such arses".

It occurs to me that although the two men look like Tasmanian devils that had been hit with bricks, the camera may portray them differently. Some impressionable youngster might not see how hideously unattractive they are and actually fancy them.

Luckily their constant rows gave me the perfect excuse to vote them out, and I suspect others will do likewise. When the nominations are announced the following day, I'm again proved correct. Their names are read out and they will to be put to the public vote, the loser being evicted this Friday. Soho starts crying when she hears who faces the boot.

"Why can't we all just stay here and get along?" she mumbles between wails.

"Because then the show would never end," I sigh and everyone laughs again.

And lo, the moment their names were read out, the almighty god of reality TV came down and touched blessed Brett and Terry, making them into completely different people. Strange how the second someone finds out they're up for eviction they suddenly become everyone's best friend.

Brett and Terry then find time for a "serious talk" in the bedroom. When they come back, they tell us they've worked through their problems and sorted everything out. Brett offers to make everyone a cup of tea and Terry organises a game of charades. How appropriate.

Friday evening comes and white noise is being played into the house to mask the cheering crowd amassing outside. Brett and Terry have both repeatedly mentioned to everyone who would listen that "they were ready to go" in a pathetic attempt at a double bluff.

Terry is evicted, but my original prediction of Mike leaving on the first week would have been right, had it not been for Brett and Terry's constant arguments. I'm now putting my money on him going next week.

"That's okay," Terry says as he fights back the tears. "I've done what I came here to do."

"You could have started fights in a pub," I remark to all of us non-losers.

They laugh and Terry scowls at me, but what do I care? It's not like he can nominate me any more.

He says his goodbyes as Ray and Ford call for him to leave the house. He even manages to shake hands with Brett and avoid punching him when the ex-priest starts flicking holy water and blessing his "safe exit".

Later that night, when the glorious boos die down for our departed rocker, we sit on the couch and discuss the day's events.

"I think they kept me here because I'm honest and up front with people," Brett declares, probably more to try and convince himself than us.

"Are you saying you didn't vote for him in the Box Room then?" I ask casually.

He shuts up and we get back to drinking, or at least they do. I feel like I'm on some sort of detox – I've been on nothing more than tap water for the last seven days and I'm starting to feel the strain. I hate beer – I always have – yet right about now I'd drink a pint of Guiness laced with Tequila just by way of a change.

"You want a drop?" asks Abi.

I look up and realise I've been staring at someone else's pint glass for what must have been ages.

"Um, er…" I flap. I do want some. I do, but I don't. Oh, I don't know.

"Drink, drink, drink!" everyone starts chanting.

I hate this sort of pressure. Now I remember why I don't go to pubs. I don't know why, but I look at Amber. Perhaps I'm looking for an ally?

"Go on, Doug, just a little sip – take your medication," she grins at me.

Et tu Brutei?

I sigh and take a swig from the glass. Oh my god it tastes worse than it looks. I almost want to spit it across the room, preferably at Rick.

An almighty cheer goes up and I feel hands slapping me on the back. I look up at their smiling faces and wonder whether merely drinking liquid is worthy of such accolade? I think about all the pubs, bars and clubs up and down the country where this sort of immature social bonding is happening every night. Do I really want to sink so low?

"Now that's a real man!" declares Abi as she plants a peck on my cheek.

I look at the empty glass. Did I really just drink what they commonly refer to as "a half"?

"Give him another!" shouts Brett. Before I can do anything about it, I find my glass ominously full again. Another cheer goes up and I begrudgingly make this one follow.

303

I have to go to the toilet, but find there's a gnome sitting on the bowl and he gives me such an evil look that I'm forced to leave him there and use the ladies'. When I come back, I find as per usual the conversation has turned to sex in my absence. I hate this kind of talk. I don't want to share my most private and intimate details with a bunch of strangers. Fortunately Soho is quick to take the lead.

"I slept with two women the week before I came in here," she chirps.

I watch Amber's eyes light up before realising someone's filled my glass again. I don't want to seem rude, so I drink.

"Okay," begins Wendy. "If you had to sleep with one other person in this house, who would it be?"

Oh, please don't ask me that.

"Abi?" continues Wendy allowing me to breathe a sigh of relief.

"Everyone!" she shouts.

Yes, I could believe that.

"Amber?" Wendy says, turning the question to her.

"Soho!" Amber says spontaneously, to which Soho rolls around on the sofa in a fit of giggles while Brett and Mike cheer.

"No, no, no," laughs Wendy, "men only!"

Silence falls as Amber ponders Wendy's lewd question. Amber looks at Brett, who makes the sign of the cross – how cliché, then passes Mike by completely as she obviously isn't into necrophilia. Rick's out of the running completely as he's gay, plus he's currently passed out from excessive alcohol consumption. No doubt the selfish man will be keeping me awake later vomiting. Finally, her eyes rest on me.

"Aww," she says, "it would have to be Doug."

I can hear the wolf whistles and cheers, but I'm not sure who's making them. I try to work out if I actually have a muscle in my face that I can tense to prevent my cheeks from burning a scarlet hue.

"Oh, bless him, he's blushing!" I think comes from Wendy.

"No I'm not!" I say loudly, "it's just very hot in here."

"I'll make it even hotter," says Amber seductively, before marching over to my seat and planting a long, lingering kiss on my lips.

Chapter 28: Apology is Policy

The next morning I wake in a bed. My eyes are still closed, but I can feel a duvet on top of my skin. Skin, why am I not wearing the flannel pyjamas I brought in?

What the hell did I do last night? I try desperately to cast my mind back to the previous evening's events. Terry kicked out – check. Soho crying – check. Rick accusing Abi of stealing his make-up again – check. Mandatory sex talk – check. Wait a minute; did Amber kiss me?

I lie here and ponder whether my mind is playing tricks on me until another thought occurs to me: why can't I remember anything after that kiss?

Before I can consider it any further, I feel a leg brushing against my own. I spring upright in bed as if waking up from a hideous nightmare.

"What am I doing here?" I say, shocked.

I'm not in my bed – I'm in the double one. The one the producers put in every series in the hope that contestants will actually have sex on TV. To my left I have Amber, who is beginning to stir after my outburst, and on my right Soho.

"Morning, stud," Amber says, still with her head on the pillow.

I have a funny taste in my mouth and my throat is dry as a bone. I don't answer, as I've suddenly come over all light-headed. I stagger to my feet, trampling over Soho as I climb out of the bed.

"Oh, please leave me the covers, Daddy," murmurs Soho.

"Going to get us breakfast in bed?" smiles Amber, now sitting up.

She says something else, but I don't hear. I'm too taken aback by the fact that my eyes are drawn downwards to her breasts – her naked breasts. I'm looking at a pair of real life naked breasts. I don't know what to say as my mind goes blank. I've only ever seen them before in magazines and now I have two of them staring me in the face, no wait – make that four!

Soho rolls over to reveal she's stark naked as well! I feel sick and while Amber shouts something about the duvet, I use what little strength I have left to lurch into the dining area where Mike, Brett and Rick are cooking.

"Touchdown!" shouts Brett as he makes an American football gesture.

"You sly old dog," says Mike with a wink.

"What?" I ask, still reeling from the shock.

"You've got a nerve," Rick says bitterly from a bowl of cereal.

"What?" I ask again.

They all laugh, apart from Rick.

"Congratulations, darling," Sarah says from behind me, and I spin round to find her arms hanging something around my neck.

I look down at what appears to be some sort of makeshift medal. It's the belt from a dressing gown attached to a piece of corn flake packet with a giant "3" on it.

"Well done, you're a record breaker," she goes on, before pouring herself a cup of coffee. "I don't think the bookies had you down for that!"

I don't know what to say. After all, I can't remember a thing about last night. How am I going to get it out of this sniggering bunch of backstabbers without looking like a complete idiot? This is a wind-up, surely?

"Doug," *Voyeur's* voice booms into the house via the loudspeaker. "Can you come to the Box Room, please?"

I oblige.

The thing I hate most about sitting in this tiny room staring into a miniature camera is that they keep you waiting so long before they speak. I've been in here for nearly three minutes.

"Good morning, Doug," a male voice finally says. "How are you today?"

"Well, I'm a bit confused actually. Why, what have I done?" I reply honestly.

"What do you think you've done, Doug?" *Voyeur* answers.

I take a deep breath, trying not to get too wound up by the person on the other side of the camera thinking it's hilarious to answer a question with a question.

"I don't know, *Voyeur*," I say, suppressing the urge to shout at them. "That's why I'm asking you!"

Oops, I shouted. I didn't mean to shout. What will the public think?

"You had unprotected sex with a lesbian and a glamour model, Doug," the voice says after a pause. "Doug? Doug? Did you hear what *Voyeur* said to you? Doug?"

I think I'm going to cry.

"Doug? Are you okay, Doug?"

I nod.

"Do you want to see a doctor, Doug?"

I think hard. At first I'm not sure what I've been asked. A doctor, why would I want to see a doctor?

"Sorry, *Voyeur*?" I stammer.

"Your nose is bleeding, Doug."

A little while later and I'm in the toilet. I thought I was past hiding in toilets when I left school, but I never figured I'd be hiding in one on national television.

I know there's a camera over my head, but from what I've seen on past episodes, they rarely show what happens in here, unless a couple are kissing or...

"Ughh," I say out loud as I think back to the night before.

At most, they'll use a three-second shot of me sitting here. I don't want to face the others. I can't. I still don't really believe anything happened.

Someone knocks on the door.

"You all right in there, mate?" Mike's voice says from the other side.

"Fine," I reply, "please, I just want to be on my own."

Actually, I think I want a long hot soak in a bath while I scrub my skin clean off and get that weird taste out of my mouth.

"But you've been in there for nearly five hours, mate?"

"I'm just a bit constipated," I lie. And please stop calling me "mate" – you're not on the radio now and haven't been for over a decade.

"*Voyeur* asked me to ask you if you needed some laxatives?"

"Well, you can tell *Voyeur* from me..." I begin, before trailing off – show no anger, show no anger, the public don't like anger. "...that I'm okay, thanks – mate."

He goes away and I continue to sit on the loo pondering what I've done, or rather what I might have done.

It's not that I don't like the prospect of having intercourse with a lady as much as the next red-blooded male and, as I understand it, the prospect of having two of them at once is a positive bonus. So why do I feel like this?

I suppose it's mainly because of Donna. I'm sure if I've done what they say I did then it will be all over the papers this morning. God I hope Mum comes down with a migraine today and doesn't find out. The shock would kill her.

But what will Donna think of me? The moment her back's turned, I seduce the first woman, no, make that two women I meet. I suddenly have the urge to get out of here as quickly as possible and sort things out with her.

309

Maybe I won't be in here long now anyway. The two golden rules of reality TV are: don't fight. If you fight, you get nominated by your fellow housemates, and the public don't like you because you're dubbed a troublemaker. I had that rule sussed from the start. Whenever a fight breaks out, I get out of there as soon as possible. But what about the second rule: don't have sex.

Yes, I know Britain is supposedly part of Europe, and in almost every series of *Voyeur* on the continent people are having intercourse left, right and centre, but not here. The great British public likes a bit of romance and maybe some mild flirting, but everyone who's ever been "overly sexual" has been booted out pretty damn sharpish. I could be gone by Friday night. I think it's time for another apology:

Soon I sit in the Box Room's comfy chair awaiting *Voyeur* to "get back to me". Again, they make me wait.

"Yes, Doug, how can *Voyeur* help you this afternoon?" a woman's voice says.

I knew it would be a woman. I'm going to have to bare my soul to the tea girl.

"I have made a mistake," I say slowly, making sure I have my head suitably cast downwards while adding a slight sniffle. "I don't normally drink alcohol and last night I feel my good nature was taken advantage of."

"Do you regret becoming the first person to have a threesome on *Voyeur*?"

"Yes, I do," I say, continuing the solemn tone. "I would like to apologise to my family, my friends and above all the general public, for my lewd and thoughtless actions. But at the end of the day it was Amber and Soho's fault for getting me drunk."

"Is this the first time you've had sex, Doug?"

It suddenly gets very hot inside the Box Room and I insist that they stop playing silly games and turn the heating down.

Luckily I don't have to answer that most ridiculous of questions as I suddenly get another nosebleed.

I spend the weekend avoiding Amber and Soho. With Soho it isn't too hard as she doesn't seem to be able to tell when someone's talking to her or not. Unfortunately Amber corners me in the shower.

"You've been quiet recently?" she says with a smile.

I don't answer.

"Are you blushing, sweetie?" she asks. "Oh, don't worry. I promise I won't rip your Y-fronts off again without asking."

"I could have you done for rape," I say in my most serious of tones.

"Oh, Doug, you are a one," she says. "You didn't mind for the three minutes it lasted!"

"I don't remember doing anything!" I protest. "Honestly!"

"Want a reminder?" she asks as she flutters her eyelashes.

I try to get past her, but she blocks my way.

"I'm sorry," she says. "I didn't mean that. But what's the problem? It's not like people have never done what we did before. I'm sure the viewers enjoyed it, even if you didn't."

"I thought you didn't like men!" I say, trying to mask the fact I shouted.

"I don't – really," she says. "But you're hardly, well, a proper man."

I'm about to answer, even though I don't quite understand what she's getting at, when something she said a moment ago suddenly sinks in. She said "the viewers would enjoy it". I see it all now, so that's her little game. She only did it to try and make herself more important to the household's dynamics. I think another trip to the Box Room might be in order, where I can point that out to the more gullible viewers.

"Sleeping with you is kind of like being with a woman," she adds.

311

I have no idea what that means, but I take it as a compliment. But just in case it's not, I play for sympathy and hang my head slightly.

Tuesday becomes my most nerve-racking day in here to date. I sit on the sofa awaiting the results of our nominations. I can't look at Soho or Amber after what they did to me. Obviously I had to vote for them to go the previous day: I told *Voyeur* how Amber was blatantly using sex to keep her in and – although I had inadvertently become sucked into her sordid little game plan – my eyes were now open to the scheming harlot and I wanted nothing more to do with her. I voted for Soho because of the same incident, but I didn't want to admit that to *Voyeur*, so I mentioned the time when she asked me whether I starred in *Twins* with Arnold Schwarzenegger.

"The results of this week's nominations are in..." begins *Voyeur*, with the typical dramatic pause that follows.

What seems like a lifetime later the voice goes on to say Abi and Amber.

Somehow Soho has slipped through the net, but better them than me. Soho still manages to steal the limelight by bursting into tears again. No wonder she's so damn thin – she must get rid of half a stone in water a day out of her eyes.

Friday night comes and we watch Amber packing her bags. I reluctantly let her give me a goodbye kiss on the cheek before watching her march up the steps and out of the house for good. I had considered I might find it difficult to pretend like I was sad to see the losers get kicked out, but since I've been in here, I'm finding it easier and easier to stab them in the back.

We're nearly deafened by boos from the crowd as she leaves. Soho bursts into tears and declares she loved her, but no one bothers to comfort her. I did try the other week when she threw a fit after mispronouncing the word "egg" six times in a row, but I ended up with her make-up all over my turtleneck.

During the night I lie awake pondering whether my apology and blatant distancing from her will have made the public aware that I am not allying myself with the silicone enhanced one anymore.

Throughout the next week I spend more and more time with the older housemates: Mike and Sarah. I know that to some viewers it may look a bit funny, me being a youngster and still choosing to hang around with fuddy-duddies. But I know that Mike is too old and past it to argue with anyone and that even if I got drunk again I'd never be desperate enough to sleep with Sarah on account of her age.

I use my new-found alliance to generally freeze Rick out. The man is a cretin of the highest order. He thinks he's something he isn't, but I know that if I bitch about him to the others, and to the viewers, it would look like I was trying to influence nominations. Instead, I make sure he isn't included in anything. It's not too hard, as he doesn't fit in with my two old workhorse colleagues and he's too up himself to try and bond with the kids.

Sure enough he's nominated this week along with Wendy. She really does think she's Cameron Diaz the way she struts around the house. Pity she doesn't get evicted on Friday. Instead, Rick is sent packing.

Another advantage in keeping tight with Mike and Sarah is that I'm in no way worried about them being competition. Mike is old, and oldies never win. Besides, I'm far wittier than him and my accidental night with Soho and Amber may well have put me above him in the tabloids. Sarah won't win either, again: too old. Plus she's posh and the general public never like "the posh one" in *Voyeur*.

While Wendy is suitably booed upon leaving the house, I shake my head and along with everyone else say things like "how terrible". Actually, I couldn't think of anyone who deserved such a scathing from a crowd. Perhaps Rick, or maybe my old mate Matt – I'd like to see him publicly humiliated.

Young Soho has survived an eviction now. I can only think her looks are keeping her in, that and the fact she's as thick as the complete Lord of the Rings in Braille. People must like hearing her gaffes. It probably makes them feel better about themselves when they can watch a girl who – when questioned about what she'd do about crime and punishment if she became Prime Minister – answered, "Fly Batman over from Gothic City."

We laughed, but sadly she was serious.

Fortunately the next two nominations almost nominated themselves: Soho and Abi. Three weeks after crying over losing "the only woman who's made me feel like a man", Soho ends up sleeping with Abi. What was worse is that they kept me awake all night making strange sloppy kinds of noises.

Another rule of *Voyeur*: no woman should be, or act like she is, sexually liberated or independent. I think Donna taught us all that. Acting like it's okay to have wild sex equals being a slut in the great British public's eyes.

When Friday comes, Abi goes. Some might think this means Soho is fast becoming the favourite as she's now survived more than one eviction. Fortunately when *Voyeur* reads her name out, she's booed almost as much as Abi when she left. Tragic.

The next week, it's Brett versus Soho. Brett has been trying to fly below radar for too long, hence it was time he got picked off. As it happens, just when I set my sights on getting rid of him and his stupid blue suede trainers, Soho finally goes. She gets booed too.

And now there are four – four that are about to become three.

314

I know people will be studying the last set of nominations carefully as it is plain even for someone like Soho to see, that me, Sarah and Mike have formed an alliance. Therefore, the public will be expecting Brett to be up for nomination, but who against: Sarah or Mike?

When the results are announced, I'm half right. Brett is indeed up for eviction again. I knew my little monologue about him using too much hair gel to keep his quiff in place would sign his death warrant. Sadly, and to my utter amazement, neither Sarah nor Mike is up for eviction. I am.

Chapter 29: Exit Strategy

I knew this day would come sooner or later and I tell everyone I'm completely fine with it. I mean, what kind of idiot comes on this show and doesn't expect to get nominated? That would be mad. I'm ready to go now – really I am; after all, I've had a good run, participated in lots of new experiences and made some good friends. What more did I come here for?

I think Brett is a worthy chap and decide that I've possibly been spending too much time with the other two and not exploring his obvious charms. Interestingly enough, he feels exactly the same way. We've barely spoken the entire time we've been here, yet strangely, during this penultimate week, we become virtually inseparable.

I find he has a certain honesty about him that the other two don't share. They've become too cliquey in recent weeks and now I look back on my time with them, I feel I knew this all along, but didn't like to admit it for fear of offending them.

From Tuesday to Friday, I try to put myself in the place of the voters. Who would I vote for? After much careful consideration, I decide that although Brett is a worthy opponent and I will be very sorry to see him go. If I was the public, I'd vote for me to stay. After all, Brett is an American.

I find myself again sitting on the sofa with good old Brett on a sunny Thursday afternoon. I don't know what the other two are doing, and quite frankly, I don't care. He's telling me about the time he banished a class nine demon out of an old lady's hamster, which is absolutely fascinating. Naturally I don't believe a word of it and the guy quite clearly has no grip on reality, but he is still a most interesting lunatic.

We then decide to engage in some playful wrestling. We've been doing a lot of that since Tuesday – wrestling and water fights. I normally let him win these "male bonding" sessions as I'm anxious to get them over as quickly as possible. The producers will probably not use more than a few seconds anyway, so no point in prolonging the gayness. Besides, the material his robes are made from brings me out in a rash.

We stop growling at each other and return to the sofa, but don't stay there long. He goes over to the kitchen area and fills up a bottle of water; I expect he's going to suggest throwing it over Sarah again. Cue water fight number six thousand and twelve.

I hurry to the bathroom and put on the shower cap I requested from *Voyeur*. The problem with water fights is that under the bright lights inside the house, having wet hair makes it look like I'm thinning on top. I snap the cap around my head and quickly change into something that I don't mind getting wet – maybe one of Brett's spare robes? No, wait – the rashes. I hear a splash of water, followed by a woman's scream. That gag never seems to lose its originality for Brett.

It's Friday evening and I'm sitting on the sofa with the others. We can hear the crowds cheering, but I'm not sure whether it's pre-recorded or not.

Brett is out there right now, giving his exit interview to Ray and Ford. Typical isn't it? Your fiancée gives birth eight weeks prematurely and you're called out of the *Voyeur* house to attend the delivery. Personally I'd have said "that's what home video cameras are for" and hung on in case I was saved. After all, we're only in here for another week and he's got the rest of his life with the kid. Mind you, I didn't even know he had a fiancée, I had sort of come to the conclusion he was gay. Must be that priest's dress he wears all the time. Either way, I wished him all the best as he left the house yesterday and was very flattered when his last words to me were:

"If it's a boy, we're going to call him Doug."

317

I have to say, that almost brought a lump to my throat. What this world needs are more Dougs.

Now that the evictions have been cancelled for the penultimate week, I suddenly have the desire to rekindle my friendship with that wrinkly old pair Mike and Sarah.

Over the next week not much happens. I would like to say that the final Friday soon came around, but it didn't. We're at that dead stage in a reality TV show where everyone thinks they have a chance at winning. None of us are stupid enough to start a row or throw a table, as we don't want to scupper our chances. Naturally this must be making pretty dull TV and *Voyeur* has done its best to upset the apple cart. We have an unlimited supply of booze, none of which I touch on account of what happened last time. Mike on the other hand is a different case, especially on Wednesday night.

"You know what I hate?" he mumbles after about his fifth bottle of wine.

"What's that, dear?" says Sarah, who hasn't had as much yet.

"Black people," he slurs.

Well that is that – his chances of winning gone in two little words. We are left open-mouthed as a tirade of racial abuse flows from his nasty mouth. It turns out that he always had a bit of a problem with alcohol. Over the years he had spent more than his fair share of time in "drying-out" clinics second-rate celebrities go to when their careers hit rock bottom.

Anyway if he's a bigot, that's his own funeral, but there's no way I'm going to let that one slide. This is the perfect opportunity to show the world how completely "un-racist" I am.

"You're well out of order, you slag!" I shout while jumping to my feet and pointing my finger down at him accusingly. I feel like someone out of a Guy Ritchie film.

He doesn't answer. In fact, I don't even think he knows what he's said. I'm about to dig the knife in deeper, when that crafty cow Sarah leaps on the bandwagon.

"I'm shocked you could say such a thing!" she comes out with.

I hope the camera can pick up the insincerity I hear in her voice.

"I don't think you deserve to be in here with that sort of attitude!" I cry as I fold my arms and turn away from him.

I then repeat that line with a few slight variations so the producers would definitely have a take they could use. I want to put my point across to the viewing public to vote him out as soon as possible.

"Some of my best friends are from ethnic minorities," Sarah blatantly lies, to which Mike can only mutter something about "political correctness gone mad".

Damn the sly old witch; she's really trying to boost herself to the public. I need to counteract and fast.

"And I work with loads of them," I say honestly. "They're just like the rest of us, only a bit darker. There's – Abdul and – Saddam, and…"

Oh, Christ, why to they have such stupid names? I can never remember them when I need to.

"I played opposite one of the most talented black actors in the world when I was in Othello at the Old Anne Theatre in Tottenham Court Road," boasts Sarah.

How was I going to better that one?

"I do a lot of work helping famine victims in South Africa," I say casually, before turning to Sarah. "Do you?"

Silence – perfect – just the reaction I was hoping for. That's shut the lying old bag up. She decides to try and go for round two with Mike, but we both realise he's passed out in his chair, so we go to bed and talk about how we never liked him since the moment we met him.

Friday comes round a lot quicker for me and Sarah, but for some reason, Mike isn't too keen on leaving. It could have had something to do with the tennis balls that are constantly being shot over the high walls of the garden. The ones with death threats attached to them and the Photoshop mock-ups of Mike in a Ku Klux Klan outfit hanging from a tree.

As the three of us sit on the sofa, a multitude of boos ring out all around us – Mike must be on the screen outside. It's not surprising when Ray and Ford read his name out first. I can't wait to see the footage Mum's taped of his exit interview – if he's still alive.

Only me and Sarah left. She looks across at me and smiles – Judas. Sure enough, while Mike gets hung, drawn and quartered on stage somewhere beyond the walls of the house, she comes over and sits next to me on the couch. She's about to speak, but I don't let her.

"I hope you win," I say sincerely. "You deserve it."

I watch as the thunder is stolen from her lips.

"No, no, no," she cries desperately. "I hope you win, you've got so much to gain from winning here."

Dammit, I wanted to use that one.

"Yeah, but seriously though, I'm only an author. No one knows who I am, whereas you're a serious and very talented actress – you need to get your face out there," I say to the actress who's so talented, she's hardly ever been seen on TV.

Twenty long minutes later and Mike's interview has probably finished, or he's dead – either way I don't care. I reckon they're out there waiting for the adverts to finish so they can get rid of Sarah. All this time we've been reminding each other of the many and varied achievements we've accomplished

320

while being in here and how really, when it comes down to it, we're both winners.

It's not that I'm worried about being evicted. Like I've said before: if you don't expect to be nominated, you're on the wrong show. It's more that I feel I belong in here – under the gaze of television cameras, knowing there are people out there hanging on my every move. I now know how some prisoners feel after they've been released from serving long sentences: they get institutionalised.

Finally the crowd noise goes silent and Ray and Ford's microphones are directed into the house.

"We can now reveal…"one of them says.

"…that the winner of *Celebrity Voyeur* is…" the other one continues.

Sarah and I have time to huddle up together on the sofa and look like we want the other to win.

"Doug."

My mouth goes dry and my mind is blank. I can't even remember saying goodbye to Sarah when she leaves the house. I suspect I must have kissed her and said something along the lines of, "Oh no, it should have been you. Really, it should."

I am alone. The last to enter is about to be the last one out. While I sit on the sofa in this now eerily quiet house with its gentle lighting and white walls, I'm sure I can make out the crowd outside, over the now deafening whirring sound coming from the rotating cameras above my head.

I think I float out of the house on pure air, like my feet are being lifted up by angels. I seem to skip up the steps to the exit to be greeted by what feels like a billion flashbulbs and an almighty cheer.

"Doug! Doug! Doug!" chants the crowd as I glide gracefully down the stairs towards the main stage where Ray and Ford are waiting to interview me. I see banners everywhere, ones with slogans of appreciation, even quoting my vast repertoire of witticisms and one which reads:

"Never mind the spiders!"

People lean over the barriers to touch me and beg for an autograph. It's only then do I remember that the security guard took my pens on the way in. As a slight wave of anger creeps over my body, I touch my nose out of sheer reflex. Is it about to bleed?

My nose is dry and to celebrate, I lift my head high to pose for the press pack.

"Doug! Doug! It's Raptor!" a familiar voice screams from among them, "just a couple of quick shots for old time's sake?"

I turn away. There were far more deserving and hardworking paparazzi on the other side of the barrier who need me. Finally Ray and Ford escort me to the podium and I sit down, ready to take my rightful place as the ultimate celebrity.

"Calm down, mate," says cheeky old Ray – or Ford, I'm too charged to tell which is which.

"Sorry," I say, "I'm just so excited to be here."

"Hey, hey, don't you go getting all excited on us, little man," says the other cockney presenter. "We've seen what you're like when you get like that!"

I think I can make out a multitude of "oohs" and wolf whistles from the crowd. I hope I'm not blushing.

"It's okay," continues Ray, "we're not going to show that mini episode again…"

"…yet!" says Ford, finishing his colleague's sentence.

I must be blushing by now.

"Aww, he's gone all red!" one of them shouts to the crowd. Yeah, thanks for pointing that out. At least I get a round of "ahhhs".

"So, seriously, Doug," says Ray, "did you really expect to be here all those weeks ago?"

Of course I did. The other lot were a bunch of nobodies and losers.

"Not at all," I say. "You wouldn't believe how…" insert dramatic and emotional pause while I let out a slight sniffle, "…deeply humbled and honoured I am that the public has given me this platform with which to reach out and embrace – well, all of them."

The crowd laughs – they love me.

"That's great, mate," says Ford, "and why do you think they chose you over all the others?"

Perhaps because I'm the only one with talent?

"I really don't know," I say with a shrug. "I guess I've always tried to be – well – myself. You know – what you see is what you get."

Another round of applause. My god, they'll buy anything.

"Some people said you shouldn't have even been in there at all," says Ray. "What with you not really being a celebrity."

I'm not really sure I understand that question, if indeed it was a question.

"Oh, I can completely understand," I say. "But I won."

"You sure did, Doug," says Ford. I know it's Ford now as I've just noticed he's got a name badge on. I should have taken my glasses in with me. "Would you like to look at some of the headlines while you've been away?"

No, not really. Mum should have kept them all for me anyway.

"Sure," I reply, "I'd love to!"

The first one reads "Celebrity Stalker Let Loose on Celebrities!" which is completely unfair, if you ask me. Unfortunately more follow in that same twisted vein.

"Oh, dear," I say with a shrug. "I guess you can't please everyone all the time."

"Do you know what turned things around for you?" asks Ray.

The fact it was obvious I was better than everyone else from day one?

"Haven't a clue!" I laugh.

Ford produces yet more headlines, some of which really do take me aback a bit. The first reads "Male Rape!" while others say things like "Used and Abused" with a particularly unflattering screen-grab of my face looking terrified. I must mention that at no point while I was in there was I scared at all – it's just the way the cameras caught me.

"Do you want to tell us your side of that night?" asks Ray, as he leans forward and puts his hand on my knee, the way Michael Parkinson always does with guests.

"I was drunk," I say immediately, "I don't remember a thing."

The crowd laughs, or do they cheer – it's a bit hard to tell. Ray and Ford laugh too. I must have said the right thing. I try to catch a look at the content in the papers under that last lot of headlines as I could have sworn I read "Doug the Pug" in one. But my eyes fail me again and the print blurs into one.

"You know something, Doug?" Ford laughs. "You were voted most helpless man in Britain!"

"Congratulations!" shouts Ray.

What on earth is that supposed to mean? The crowd laughs again. I laugh too.

"Great," I say.

"That's right, mate," Ray goes on, "it seems you're the man who brings out the mothering instinct in people."

"Great," I say, before realising I've just said that. Dammit, I must keep the material fresh. Quick, say something deep and meaningful: "I feel that my winning *Voyeur* is a vindication of my innocence."

324

"Yeah," grins Ford while he grabs yet another newspaper from behind him. "Or as *The Mail* put it: stick it to the Z-listers and cast a protest vote for Morrell!"

I don't quite know what they're getting at and for a split second there's dead air. Ray quickly fills the silence.

"So, you and Amber Brown – are you going to see her again?"

What kind of stupid question is that? I can see her now; she's sitting about twenty yards away from me with all the other losers. While I try and formulate a suitably polite way of saying that I never want to see that whore again, the crowd goes halfway to answering my question by letting out a colossal "boo" at the mere mention of her name.

"I don't think so," I quickly say, to more cheers.

I watch Ray and Ford look over at Amber.

"You shouldn't have taken advantage of the poor man!" Ray says jokingly.

"Haven't you ever heard of date rape?" Ford goes on.

I watch as a man with a boom mike lowers it over her head. Why would they want to give her air time during my interview?

"I only chose him because I knew he was the only man in the world I'd never catch anything from!" she laughs, "a girl can spot a virgin a mile off!"

Don't bleed, don't bleed, don't bleed. I must concentrate on looking hurt rather than ramming that boom mike down her throat. I put on my "puppy-dog" eyes and bite my tongue. It must work as the crowd boo her again. Ray calms the mob down and they both turn back to me.

"Water under the bridge, eh?" he jokes. "So, Doug, you think you won because the audience took you to their hearts?"

"I think they saw me for what I really am," I say wistfully. "There's been a lot of unfair things written about me in the press, and I just wanted the opportunity to let people know what I'm really like."

"You're referring to the stalking allegations?" Ford asks.

I really hate that word. People seem to brand you with it without having a clue what it means.

"I'm not a stalker," I say firmly, but with a hint of meekness about it.

Ford leans forward and puts his hand on my knee.

"You know what, Doug," he says. "We believe you."

I scan that sentence for sarcasm, but find none. I look at Ray, who's nodding in agreement; then the crowd bursts into rapturous applause.

"You know that *Voyeur* sees all, right?" Ray says.

I nod.

"And that we, your family, your friends and most importantly the public, have been watching your every move for the last eight weeks?" Ford continues.

"Uh-huh," I say with a slight nod.

"Well, I think I speak for everyone when I say that when you first came on the show, you were dubbed a creepy, sinister, celebrity stalker and I for one I didn't know what to expect…"

There's that damn word again. I don't say anything, just let him continue.

"…but after watching your performance, I think we can all say that without a shadow of doubt, you are – the most – unthreatening man we have ever seen in our lives!"

"You couldn't hurt a fly if you tried!" chimes in Ray. "Let alone stalk anyone!"

The crowd cheers and I feel exonerated. My name has been cleared by trial through media. Who needs the courts and judges called Stewart when you have reality TV?

"Well, our time's almost up…" adds Ray, "…but there is just one more thing I think the world would like to know before we call it a day on this series of *Celebrity Voyeur*."

"What's that?" I ask expectantly.

"Who is Auntie Eileen?" they say together in well rehearsed unison.

The crowd laughs and cheers, so I assume I've inadvertently cracked another joke. Ray and Ford stand up and Ray pats me on the shoulder.

"Don't worry, mate, we all talk in our sleep. We'll let you keep your fantasies to yourself."

Then they turn away from me towards the camera.

"That's all we've got time for," Ray begins, "but be sure to tune in for a completely new series of *Voyeur* which starts in only eight weeks time!"

The crowd cheers – cheering for me.

"Doug, come up and join us!" Ford shouts, and I do just that. "I think it's only fair that the last word is yours. Is there anything you'd like to say before we sign off?"

I don't have time to think, but then that's just me – I'm a creature of impulse.

"What d'you think of me now – Matt?" I scream as I charge right up to the lens.

The crowd cheers and the credits roll.

Chapter 30: Joining the Club

My life is a whirlwind. Since leaving the show last week, I've barely had a chance to log on to the Internet and check my old site, let alone browse any new publications.

Metropol Industries have appointed me my own agent: Richard Graves. Apparently he's worked there for years and specialises in "new and upcoming talent". I like the sound of that.

My progress is monitored closely by Belle Warren and me and Richard have frequent meetings with her between book signings. Right now we're in my luxury hotel room in Newcastle. I sit on the bed surrounded by the white walls of my suite while we talk to her via videophone.

"You have a book signing in Waterstones until lunch," she goes on as she reads from an itinerary I can't see. "Then afterwards you'll be stopping off at Geordie FM for an interview and after that…"

I think Richard is taking notes, at least I hope so because I've started to tune out again. It's no joke getting up at five in the morning to be in make-up by six, then dazzle the nation at eight with a gruelling breakfast TV interview. I've hardly had a moment to myself.

"…have you got all that?" she says.

I look at Richard, but he's already looking at me.

"I said: have you got all that, Doug?" she repeats.

"Huh?" I say to either of them.

"Richard," she says in a stern tone, "the press have done another story about phone-rigging in the *Voyeur* call centre."

"Not another whistle-blower?" he asks.

"We've put it down to – disgruntled ex employee runs slander campaign," she reassures him. "Either way, make sure

Doug points out just how fair and above board the voting system is on all our reality TV shows."

"Got it," he replies.

"Er, Belle," I say, "about all these book signings…"

"What about them?" she says while flicking through her notes.

"It's just I've been signing copies all week and – well – I wondered how much I'm getting paid for all this?"

She looks from me to Richard, who suddenly averts his attention to something on the wall.

"What's the matter?" I ask him.

"Oh, er, nothing," he mutters. "There's a spider on the wall – that's all."

"Get it out!" I say sharply.

"Right you are," he says then quickly telephones down to one of my entourage.

"Richard has the details, Doug," Belle says as she prepares to switch off her end of the video conferencing system. "Speak soon."

"Wait, wait, wait!" I say, positioning myself on the part of bed furthest away from the eight-legged-fiend. "About the book signings, I was just wondering if I could sign one of my own books for a change."

"You haven't written anything," she says, far too sharply for my liking. "You signed the contract to come into the *Voyeur* house which ties you to us for a period of one month pending your eviction, departure or victory. Then we decide whether we want to extend that contract at the end of every subsequent month. I explained all this to you before and how it was non-negotiable."

"No you didn't!" I say.

"It was in the small print," she mutters, "it's not my fault you didn't have a solicitor run through it before you signed it.

Either way, it doesn't matter as you have to attend the book signings and plug the official *Celebrity Voyeur* compendium, okay?"

"Okay," I say reluctantly, as one of the make-up girls comes in with an empty glass and a piece of cardboard to evict the spider. "Don't capture it! Kill it!"

She puts the glass down and rolls up a magazine.

"And don't make a mess on the wall this time!" I remind her. "You know what I mean?"

She looks at Richard and he nods. I think I caught him rolling his eyes.

"Look, Doug," Belle says from the screen, "I have to go..."

"Yeah, but what about payment?" I say quickly.

"The limos you drive in, the five star hotels, your entourage, the crates of Archers and lemonade you've stashed under your bed..."

"You know about those?" I say defensively.

"Yes, Doug," she goes on. "And the six hundred pounds worth of pens that have mysteriously joined them since you left the show. All these costs – and more – have been borne by us since you won. Do we ask you hire your own make-up artist?"

Reluctantly, I don't reply.

"I take it that's a no then?" she continues. "Now get out there and smile. We didn't pay for you to have your teeth whitened for nothing!"

The video phone switches off and I hear the clatter of rolled up magazine meeting arachnid. I look at Richard.

"What?" he says.

"Look," I say to him, before adding: "mate? You're supposed to me my agent. Can't you put in a good word for me?"

He looks at me blankly.

330

"You know?" I go on, "get me out there using my fame to highlight some of my other skills?"

"But you're a reality TV contestant?" he says.

I know that. Why do so many people keep saying that to me?

"But you see, now that I've been on TV, I'm different from everybody else," I point out. "I'm famous – yeah? Important – you know what I mean? Since everyone knows me, everything I do is newsworthy. I'm a cultural icon. I can use my prestige to endorse products."

"I don't think so," he says, as he gathers up another crate of *Voyeur* Annuals that I expect I'm going to have to sign in a matter of hours.

"Why not?" I ask indignantly. "You think I can't act or something? I was in my school's drama group for over a year!"

"Really? Who did you play?"

"Okay, so I was a lighting technician, but that's not the point. I hear there's good money to be made doing commercials."

"Oh, yeah, I agree," he says as he nods, "but no credible company would want to use a reality TV star to endorse their product. Wrong image, see?"

I don't see.

"What about a book deal?" I ask, "A proper one – one that's not connected with *Voyeur*. I don't want to always be known as *Doug from Voyeur*, do I?"

Richard doesn't answer and I can see he's thinking it over.

"Okay, I'll speak to Belle later," he finally answers. "And I'll see what I can do, okay? But right now we've got to get to that book signing. Then there's a new Costcutters opening down the road – you're expected to cut the ribbon at two."

The following day comes and I find myself in Liverpool. I'm sitting in the back of another limo with Richard. I ignore the

331

complimentary champagne in favour of the Archers and lemonade I'd told him to get for me. A noble security guard opens the car door for us as we pull up by a sports field where I'm supposed to be picking the winning entry in a school raffle.

"Get that, will you?" I say to Richard, as I gesture towards the untouched champagne. I can sell it on eBay when I finally get home.

Doug Holster had been on the road for nearly three years after his heroic struggle with Doctor Death. It seemed that after his knighthood everyone wanted a piece of him.

The Colonel had suggested that he would be a good ambassador for the Secret Service and now that he'd saved the universe, little children looked up to him. Apparently parents all over the world were being told "I want to be like Doug" by their offspring.

But Doug Holster was not a man who would settle for a life of luxury. He craved the thrill of adventure and the taste of battle on his brow. He kept Death's eyeballs in his wallet as a souvenir of the life he had been forced to leave behind.

"Doug," a man's voice said from his communication device. It was the Colonel. "Can we talk?"

"Go on," Doug replied bitterly.

"I just wanted you to know how sorry we all are for ever doubting your integrity," he confessed meekly. "I hope you know that it was the others who wanted to reel you in and hang you out. I tried to stop them, I really did, but..."

"I know, old friend," Doug nodded, showing how big a man he really was.

"I'm so glad you feel that way," sighed his boss. "It's just...I've always thought of you as the son I never had and It wanted to tell you how much I love you."

"I love you too, old man," Doug replied.

"No, I really love you, Doug," said the Colonel bashfully. "An amazing guy like you just does things to a man."

Doug ended their communication there and then. Sometimes there was too much love in the world. Sure, he was now loved. Loved by everyone, yet the one woman who he truly wanted was still as far away from him as she ever had been. The war with Death's forces had taken their toll on Ms Trayhorn and all she could do now was await her man's key in her door.

Doug received a rapturous reception that reverberated round the room as he got up to speak at a high-class charity do in aid of some starving foreigners.

"Number four-hundred and forty-two," I say as I pick the ticket from the sack. I remind myself to look pleased as six-year-old Sophie comes running up to the stage in the school's drama hall to collect her box of chocolates. But from somewhere, I begin to question the direction my new life is heading.

I get a cheer from the crowd as I draw the raffle – that's nice – but seeing as I've been getting cheered everywhere I go now, it's all getting a bit repetitive. All I do is sign autographs, then bugger off back into the limousine and put the complimentary pen inside my pocket.

I had hoped that by now I'd be well on my way to getting a proper book deal with Metropol Publishing, not judging the "Glamorous Granny Competition" at Pontins next Thursday. Either that or perhaps becoming some sort of goodwill ambassador for the United Nations like Angelina Jolie did. After all, celebrities are as close to superheroes as you can get in real life. I should be using my new-found powers to help those less fortunate than me. I've seen Bob Geldof and Bono in action: they fly out to a desert for five minutes then come home and get invited to Downing Street for drinks with the Prime Minister. Granted I wouldn't go to Number Ten as I didn't vote for him and I'd be too tempted to tell him what I think of his slimy Government, but still, a token of appreciation would be nice.

"Oh, God, I'm exhausted," I say to myself as the limo takes us back to the hotel.

"Yeah?" says Richard, sounding surprised. "You don't want to hit a club with me and a few of the guys later on?"

"Are you kidding?" I say. "About the only thing I want to hit is my pillow, and possibly that little kid with the runny nose who took one of my pens. How do you have the energy to go clubbing?"

He grins at me, before clicking his fingers at the driver – who has obviously been listening in.

"Cheers, Ian," he says as our driver – who I didn't even know had a name – passes back a small container. Richard opens it up to reveal small bags of white powder and what looks like an entire bottle of Aspirins.

"You want some?" he says, completely seriously. "They'll give you a lift – take your mind off the pen."

I bite my lip and politely decline as there's no point in firing my management yet.

"Go on, Doug," he whispers. "Be a good boy and take your medication."

I decline again, but allow him to mix me an Archers and lemonade and I drink it in silence during the ride home.

As I sit in my hotel room I suddenly find I can't sleep. I'm not sure how this has happened as I was completely knackered all day. But now I've got the chance to doze off, my legs feel like they're tingling and I have a strange urge to dance. I had considered phoning Belle and report Richard's dodgy little bag of pick-me-ups. Yet now I stand next to the phone, capable of destroying the man's career, I suddenly feel warmly towards him. He's not such a bad bloke after all. And today was quite fun really.

Before I get a chance to call her, there's a knock at the door. It's him.

"Are you feeling better, Doug?" he says with a smile as little coloured orbs dance around his head.

As it happens I am; I feel very good about myself. I almost feel like running a marathon.

"Groovy!" I say with a smile.

"Thought you would," he says with a nod. "Me and the rest of the team are hitting one of the bars. You sure you don't want to come? There are some pretty tasty women out tonight."

My legs seem to think they could dance all night and my head has started buzzing. A little voice inside me that I've never heard before tells me I should go, but I don't. I remind first myself, then my manager that the club scene just isn't me. He's okay with that. He's a good bloke really, a bit like my mum in many ways – I miss her – and Hannah. I wonder what they're all up to.

"Oh, and here's something that'll give you an even better high," he says just before he leaves. "I spoke to Belle about a book deal – your autobiography hits the shops in three weeks."

I realise how right I was to refuse his offer of a night out. Three weeks to sum up my whole life – how am I supposed to do that?

Within minutes I phoned the hotel staff to bring me a laptop and I sit at the desk in my room preparing to write.

It's three in the morning and I stand on the opposite side of the room to my computer. I've yet to write anything but my full name, and then I can't decide between Doug Morrell or Doug Holster. It's not that I have nothing to say – I could write ten chapters on how much I hate Matt – it's that I've spent the whole night walking up and down my room fiddling with things; I don't know what's up with me. I think I may be coming down with something, as when I ran into the bathroom for no reason at all, the lights were so bright, they hurt my eyes.

My alarm goes off at five in the morning and I haven't slept. This seems almost impossible as I've felt so tired for the last few days. Richard starts knocking at my door and doesn't appear surprised to see me up and ready to go.

"Ready to leave?" he asks. "We're hitting Manchester today."

"Aye-aye captain!" I say with a smile.

By midday I feel like death. Not only have I bitten the heads off my PA, my make-up artist and my stylist, but I'm supposed to be handing out prizes at some company function. My cranium's been thudding all morning like someone has smacked me repeatedly across the temple with a football boot.

"I can't go out there," I say to Richard as I sit doubled over in my dressing room. "They're a bunch of bloody morons! You know what I mean?"

"Sure you can," he laughs. "There's a whole hall full of businessmen waiting for you out there. You're just on a bit of a comedown right now. I can give you something for it if you like?"

"No thanks," I mumble through my hands. "I've taken some Aspirins, Paracetamol and even an Ibuprofen. Nothing seems to get rid of this fuzzy head."

"I was thinking of..."

"Oh, shut up, will you?" I snap. My god, this man's annoying. It's like I'm back home with Mum. I'm constantly being hounded day and night. Why can't people just leave me alone? And what's he laughing at now?

"Try some of these," he sighs as he takes out that grubby little box of narcotics.

"I don't do drugs!" I declare. "What sort of loser do you take me for?"

"You want to feel like this for the rest of the day?" he scoffs.

No I do not. But I don't want to do drugs. I'm above all that.

"Of course not presenting the prizes here won't look good to the people deciding whether or not to let you do your autobiography," he sighs as he shakes his head.

"I thought you said it was already sorted?"

"Oh, no," he laughs. "Nothing's definite in this game. Are you sure you don't want your medication? A couple of lines would cheer you right up."

Decisions, decisions, decisions. I finally have the prospect of finally getting my autobiography out there to inspire and educate the world, but only if I stick a load of what looks like washing powder up my nose. I try to weigh up the pros and cons, but the aching in my head almost stops me thinking.

"Are you sure this will help?" I ask.

He nods and slides a razorblade across the dressing room table towards me.

A few hours later and we were back on the road again. Finally our whistle-stop tour of the north has come to an end and we're heading back down south. As for the prize giving: I have to say it went fantastically well. I was on top form, laughing and joking with all the men in power suits. I could have talked on the microphone all night, but it was a pity I had to leave when they had dinner. All this excitement has given me a bit of a cold and I have to ask the driver to pull over into a service station to pick me up some more pocket tissues. I hate my nose: if it's not bleeding, then it's running.

By the time I return home it's eight in the evening and my headache seems to have come back with a vengeance. I'm finally standing back outside the old flat and only now do I realise how drab and lifeless it is after the brightly lit interior of the *Voyeur* house, then one posh hotel after another. Do I really have to spend the night in here?

I go inside and look for the video tapes Mum was supposed to have recorded of my performance on *Voyeur*, but to my horror I find that she hasn't bothered. I'm so disgusted I can't bring myself to spend another second here and ring Richard to get me a hotel.

"What hotel?" he asks.

"The one Metropol is going to put me up in until you can find me somewhere more fitting!" I snap as this headache is making me cranky again. "Doug Morrell doesn't stay in council digs!"

"No problem, Doug," he says as he realises who really calls the shots. "Also you're sounding a little tense…"

"Who wouldn't be when confronted with this dump?"

"Yeah, yeah, yeah. Look, don't worry about things, I'll sort it out. It looks like you're due another dose, eh?"

"Well, I think I am!" I practically spit down the phone. "And make it quick, will you?"

Later I watch a man load all my magazines, videos and posters into a Metropol van, making sure he doesn't crease any.

"Bye, mother," I say to the flat window as she can't even be bothered to see me off. She's held me back all my life; does she really think I'm never going to fly the nest? So typical of her not to want me to go and fulfil my destiny. If she had her way, I'd be married to someone like Hannah by now with two screaming kids. Besides, she seems to have allowed a giant cream pastry to move in while I've been away. It tried to shout something at me while I was in the kitchen, but I ignored it. I hope the two of them will be very happy together.

I finally relax as I lie back on the king-size double bed in the Hilton. I'd like to sleep, but I can't as it sounds like security are dragging other guests up and down the corridor all night. I

338

ignore the screaming and the thumping and decide to ask the little people who work here to get as many back issues of newspapers and magazines sent up to my room as they can. It's hard to believe I haven't picked up a periodical in almost three months. Every time I've suggested it to Richard or Belle, they'd change the subject or find me another bingo hall to be a guest caller in.

I take great pride in the fact that there's nothing about that reality TV reject Kat and her hairy eyebrows in any of the papers. Only a "Where are they now?" article regarding last season's contestants. Kat and her mono-brow received only three out of ten stars for "keeping her career alive" – as I predicted.

Then the words "Sexually Dysfunctional" leap out of the Sunday papers at me. A national publication actually has the nerve to try and suggest that I have some sort of hang-up regarding intercourse. I read on, anxious to find out where they dug up this baseless and unfounded allegation.

"Ex girlfriend Hannah Mathews reveals all."

What more needs to be said? I'm amazed no one at Metropol spotted this one. It's as if they've let this slander slide unnoticed. I have a good mind to ring them up and get our lawyers down on her like a tonne of bricks. How dare she say such a thing? It's not as if we even did anything like that in the first place, so how can I be dysfunctional?

I ignore the strange stories about the moral implications of people with psychological problems being paraded on TV for the public's entertainment. Those must have been about a different show to the one I was on. Instead my eyes are drawn to the phrase "Weird Loner" that seems to be repeated over and over again when referring to me. I know it's a lie straight away as the person who'd allegedly said it is referred to as "a close friend" and we all know what that means. Unless of course…

"Open up!" I yell as I bang on Matt's flat door. "I know you're in there!"

He opens up wearing only a T-shirt and boxer shorts, then blinks at me.

"Doug?" he mumbles. "It's three in the morning. What are you doing here? I thought you'd been put into a…"

"Did you call me a weird loner?" I demand to know as I push the newspaper into his face.

He scratches his head and I'm about to repeat the question, when a familiar woman's voice stops me in my tracks.

"Who is it, Matt?" she says and I see Hannah behind him wearing a dressing gown that shows off her legs from the knees down. "Doug, what are you doing here?"

I'm speechless. In only a few months the cheeky little strumpet has hopped from my bed into this stoned layabout's squat.

"Oh, I see it all now," I say as I look them up and down. "What, the two of you cooked all this up together, huh? So, you're supposed to be my – close friend at work, are you? Well, friend, how much did they pay you for these sordid little stories?"

"I never even spoke to the press, Doug," he lies. "For the record, it was Frank who referred to you as a weirdo. If you want to go and talk to hi…"

"Oh, don't waste your breath!" interrupts Hannah as she puts one arm around his shoulder. "He's not worth it! You're too kind to him, Matt. I don't know why you even bother talking to this idiot. You know the shit he's put me through!"

Matt doesn't know where to look and I must say I'm a bit taken aback myself. I've never heard her swear before.

"Look, Doug," she begins. "When will you ever understand? You and me never had a bloody relationship!"

340

"It doesn't say that in the press!" I snap, demolishing her feeble lies with my wrecking ball of truth.

"They came to see me and I just said we went out a couple of times and never did anything else. They made up the rest!" she cries. "And do you know why I even agreed to go out with you in the first place?"

I'm about to say something along the lines of because she knew I'd be rich and famous some day, but rudely, she doesn't give me the chance.

"It was because your mum had just died and you needed a shoulder to cry on. And I tell you, that's the last time I feel sorry for the sad, loner of the pub! Do you know what you've put me and my family though with your constant phoning and texting?"

"Well, how do you think I feel?" I yell, as I point at Matt's head, which has now completely disappeared from his neck. "You left me for him!"

"What, a real man who cares for me and listens to what I have to say? Someone who makes me laugh and even takes me out once in a while – I don't ever want to see you again! And what the hell is up with your eyes, they look like saucers!"

"Well," I say when she finally runs out of breath. "If you don't want to see me, then you'd better go around with your eyes closed and your fingers in your ears. Because I'm part of the celebrity elite now, and I don't need you either! I've got a book deal in the pipeline and by Christmas I wouldn't be surprised if you saw me and Donna conquering Hollywood!

Ha! That's shut her up. While Matt stands behind her still unable to look me in the eye, she gives me a strange look. At first I think it's anger, but then as her face relaxes again, it's a different look altogether. I wonder what's she thinking?

"Doug," she says. "For a start, you're not a celebrity – you're just obsessed with fame and you see reality TV as some

341

sort of route – or escape – to your weird fantasies. And do you know what the ultimate irony is?"

I'm about to tell her more about my book deal, when I realise the question was apparently rhetorical.

"You have no concept of reality whatsoever," she says while shaking her head. "You're so far gone, you don't know who or what is real any more."

"I'm famous!" I remind her.

"No," she says softly while shaking her head patronisingly. "No you're not. Go home, Doug, watch your TV shows and above all, just keep taking your medication."

And with that she shuts the door leaving me out in the cold night. Something clatters around the bins and at first I think it's a reporter. They're lying in wait for me everywhere trying to get a scoop – then I hear a cat meow. But what if the cat is a journalist in disguise? I bark like a dog to startle it before heading back to my hotel, but then the moaning starts.

I stand outside Matt's block of flats watching them staggering out from behind the recycling bins: their flesh hanging down from their decaying faces, dropping down on their white uniforms as they come at me. The undead shuffle closer, hands outstretched, ready to tear the very ideas from my head. I draw my sword and prepare for the onslaught.

Later I find myself back in my luxury hotel room – alone. I take the pens from the desk drawer and put them in one of my boxes, then put a video of Donna on. I miss her – she'd never leave me for a delivery driver.

I watch a couple of hours of old *Voyeur*, but I can't sleep. I feel that there's a little piece of me missing somewhere deep inside. God I feel low.

Chapter 31: From Zero to Hero

Exactly eighty-three minutes later I'm no longer low. Why? Because I'm reminded about what being famous is all about. One two-minute call to my manager and a young lad drops a few little parcels to my room. I'm getting quite good at cutting the white powder with my Tesco's clubcard.

My legs want to dance again and I feel the dubious tasting powder trickling down the back of my throat while the synthetic smell fills my nostrils with confidence and vigour. I should write my autobiography now. I should, but seeing my clubcard again has reminded me I still have some old Tesco's receipts to get the points put on.

After a phone call and short limousine ride across London to the nearest all night Tesco's, I'm standing at the Customer Services desk talking to the completely un-famous girl behind the counter doing the graveyard shift.

"The name's Morrell, Doug Morrell," I say proudly.

"I know," she yawns. "Nice slippers."

"Thank you," I say as I hand her the piece of paper. "These are the old receipts I wish you to put the points on for me. You can have an autograph if you like?"

"No thanks."

"What do you mean, no?" I say, amazed. "Why don't you want my autograph?"

"No, I mean no, I can't put points on them, because they're not receipts. One's a sweet wrapper and the other looks like a piece of toilet paper with "AUNTIE EILEEN MUST DIE!" written over and over again on it."

I squint down at the things I've put on the counter before her. Why do they make the lights so bright in these huge megamarkets? I can barely see a thing. I could have sworn they were Tesco's receipts.

"Didn't you stalk a *Voyeur* contestant?" she says cautiously from behind her tatty desk.

I'm about to remind her who I am, but for some reason I don't. Do commoners still think that of me? Even after they voted me their favourite celebrity? I need to talk to my agent.

The next day I'm back at Metropol Industries in a much smaller boardroom than the one where I first met Belle. She's sitting there talking to Richard when I arrive.

"I have a great idea!" I declare as I take a seat. "Can someone get me a drink of Archers?"

"Later, Doug," says Belle. "Before we get on to your great idea, we need to talk to you about the dates for your book signings – don't worry, not that *Voyeur* compendium again – your autobiography. Then we can get the dates put up on your official website."

"You mean my Donna Trayhorn site?" I say, slightly confused.

"Don't be silly, Doug," she smirks, "your official website!"

"But I don't have an official webs…" I say, before getting cut off.

"We made it for you," chimes in Richard. "Your fans can log on and find out what you're up to. You know? Subscribe to your newsletter and stuff. Find out where you're going to be signing your autobiography."

"Oh, right," I say eagerly, relieved they've actually listened to me for a change. "You do know that I haven't quite finished it yet?"

"That's okay," says Belle. "We've written it for you."

And with that, Richard slides a copy of my "autobiography" across the shiny desk. I flick through it and sure enough, it's about my life. Well, something that sort of resembles my life. I scan a couple of paragraphs.

"I never had sex in a cable car in Greece!" I say aghast.

"You have now!" says Richard with a grin. "Relax, we employ ghost-writers all the time. All you have to do is turn up and put your name to it."

"But," I stammer. "I can't very well go on Parkinson plugging a book I didn't write!"

"Don't worry," says Belle. "I don't think there's any chance of that happening."

"We were thinking of getting you on some sort of daytime TV show to promote it, or maybe one of the cable channels," says Richard, to which she nods in agreement. "And probably local radio?"

"I don't want to do local radio!" I shout.

I ignore their matching smirks.

"Really?" yawns Belle. "And what did you have in mind?"

"Well," I say. "What about a more credible show that suits my natural wit and ability to commentate on popular culture? What about *Room 101*?"

"Probably not a good idea," says Richard as he inhales deeply. "While you were on *Voyeur* Chris Morris actually nominated you to go into *Room 101*!"

"You what?" I say, aghast. "I hope the presenter told him where to go?"

"Um, not exactly," he says guiltily as he changes into a giant cockroach wearing a bow tie. "Still, any publicity is good publicity, right?"

"Right!" chips in the owl who tweaks one of his antennae.

"I beg to differ!" I shout, "I've finally got round to looking at what was written about me while I was in the house!"

"Oh," mutters Belle. "I hoped you wouldn't have to see that."

345

"You shouldn't pay any attention to what's written in the papers," says the cockroach casually. "They're rubbish – the lot of them!"

"Half of it was written in publications Metropol own," I point out. "Why is it they keep banging on about the only reason I won was because the public have become so sick of celebrities trying to reinvent themselves on reality TV? And a vote for me was some sort of protest vote?"

Neither of them answers and Belle flies up to a tree in the corner of the room and hoots.

"And the non-Metropol owned papers keep saying that *Voyeur* is rigged anyway!" I carry on.

"That's nonsense!" They seem to say at exactly the same time. "Join us! Let go of your feelings!"

"You won fair and square," Belle says as she pats my arm with her wing and offers me half a mouse on a silver tray.

"You feeling a bit wound up, mate?" Richard asks softly as he becomes a puddle of water with arms.

Oh, well done for finally noticing. He doesn't seem to realise what pressure people like me are under – constantly in demand and always having to stay one step ahead of the vile paparazzi.

"You want to…" he continues. "Pop to the executive toilets? They're just down the hall."

A small pot of pills floats through the air and comes to rest in my outstretched palm. Belle turns her head completely round the other way while her wings write gibberish down on her notepad. I want her pen.

"I'm a famous celebrity, you know?" I remind them.

"Yes, of course you are," says a man sitting where Richard was. "Take your medication and come back to us."

"Thank you," I say sharply as I take the packet and leave.

Ten minutes later and I bound back into the room. Belle and Richard are looking gorgeous as they wait patiently like good little underlings. I reward them for their hard work by getting my personal trainer to pour them both a glass of Archers and lemonade to celebrate my book hitting the stands.

"I've had a fantastic idea!" I say as I sit back down with them.

"That's wonderful, Doug!" she says, delighted with my enthusiasm. "Sign this."

I sign something and quickly pass it back to Richard. These two really want to hear my idea.

"I want to marry Donna!" I say. "Can you believe people still see me as some kind of crazed stalker?"

"Yes!" says Belle with a smile. "Admitting it is the first step to curing yourself."

I knew she'd think my idea was amazing.

"Nice idea, mate," continues Richard. "But, we were thinking of setting you up with a celebrity girlfriend. Just for a few pre-arranged paparazzi shots. Don't worry, you don't actually have to spend any time together once the cameras have got what they want."

The former owl slides a leather-bound book across the table towards me. I open it to see various photos of other Metropol-contracted starlets.

"There," she says as she points to a blonde haired girl. "That's Nina, she's twenty-four and from Essex, she's a page three girl and I think you two would go great together."

"But what about Donna?" I ask.

"There are other girls in the world apart from Donna. What about this one," says Richard as he turns the page. "She's Brandi, twenty years old and makes up one sixth of a new girl band called Turbo. See, she's nice?"

"I want Donna!" I repeat.

"Donna Trayhorn?" Belle says with a look on her face which makes her appear as if she's just swallowed a lemon. "But why? She's completely washed up. Last time I heard, she was in some drying out clinic up north."

"I want Donna," I say, hoping this time they can see I'm serious.

She looks at Richard. He looks back her.

"We won't be a moment," she says with a smile, before she leads my manager out of the room.

About five minutes later they return.

"Go back to your room, Doug," she grins at me.

"I'm a star!" I point out.

"Yes, Doug, a big star and you're going to conquer Hollywood!" Richard agrees.

"Don't feed him," hisses Belle before turning back to me. "You can't entertain the love of your life in a hotel, can you? I'll get our people to move you into a nice little flat in Clerkenwell for the time being."

"I'm meeting Donna?" I say, slightly amazed it was that easy to get through to them.

"Sure," says Richard. "You're going to be taking her out to the best restaurant in London tonight; then of course what you do afterwards is entirely up to you!"

"We have a make-up team and wardrobe advisor standing by for your date," adds Belle. "Richard, have you seen my pen? I could have sworn I left it on the desk."

That night I sit at a table in a restaurant so upmarket that I can't even pronounce its name. The chair opposite me is empty, as it will be for the next – I look at the Rolex watch wardrobe gave me – seven and a half minutes.

I'm right by the window and I feel a bit on view. Why couldn't Belle get me a private booth at the back?

That van is still parked across the street. It was outside my flat as well. Can you believe the person who had moved into Donna's old flat had just moved out when Belle happened to need it for me! I swear they're paparazzi in that van. God only knows how they found out I was living there. I thought it was just me, Belle, Richard and about thirty or forty of my entourage who knew I'd moved there. I'll bet it was my dietician who tipped them off. I'm going to have her fired first thing tomorrow.

Six minutes to go before Donna arrives and I'm so nervous, it's unbelievable. I have just enough time to nip to the toilets and have a little pick-me-up before she gets here. I don't want to lose my nerve before the big moment.

One minute to go and I'm back at my table feeling absolutely amazing. My whole life has been leading up to this moment: the woman I'm going to marry must be almost here and I'm on top of the world.

A flash goes off from somewhere outside, then another.

I crane my neck to look out the window and I make out the grizzly shape of a press pack following someone down the street. Only it's not merely someone, it's Donna! She hurries through their ranks and bursts through the door. She looks amazing. That health spa must have done her the world of good. She's wearing a sky blue minidress with a white apron-like front, rounded off by a red cross-like logo on the front. Her matching white stilettos make her well over five foot five. The waiter goes straight over to her.

"No," she says handing him a piece of paper, "I'm not looking for McDonalds: I had a Double Whopper before I came. I'm meeting some bloke."

The waiter turns round to me, then back to her, then back at me again with a funny look on his mug. I wave at her and she waves back.

"Is that him?" she asks the waiter.

"He's on the table reserved for you," he mutters and she comes over.

"Oh, Donna, it's so good to see you," I say as I stand up to hug her. We embrace and she feels warm against my skin. I hope I haven't died and gone to heaven. She sits down opposite when I finally force myself to let her go.

"I've been waiting for this moment all my life," I begin. "You wouldn't believe how long I've been waiting for this moment – all my life!"

"Cool, do I know you?" she says.

"I'm Doug, Doug Holster," I remind her.

She looks at me and rolls chewing gum round her beautiful mouth.

"I think I've heard of a Doug," she muses. "Have I slept with you?"

"You told me to join your fan club," I say. "I run an online site to keep your supporters up to date with your career. I've been doing it ever since you kept looking at me while you were on *Voyeur*."

"I don't remember you in the house?" she remarks. "Where have I seen you before?"

"I was wrongly accused of stalking you," I say resentfully. "But don't worry about that."

"Oh!" she cries. "That Doug, I remember now. I thought you got locked away?"

"Only inside a TV studio," I mutter. "The important thing is that people think I used to stalk you, when I didn't, did I?"

"I can't remember," she says blankly. "I've been spending my time in this clinic in some place where they talk like, really weird – you know what I mean? And they won't let you do drugs – can you believe that?"

"That's a bit harsh," I say. "It's not like we're addicts, is it? We're famous!"

350

"That's what I kept telling this guy up there, but he wouldn't let me out," she says as she puts a fork into her handbag. "If it wasn't for Belle getting me out of there, I wouldn't be here."

"She said we'd be good together," I say confidently.

"Yeah, I know," she says as she pops the bubblegum between her teeth and slides a dessert spoon into her bag. "The bitch dumped me without so much as a thank you; then rings me up out of the blue going on about a free dinner date. You know, I heard a weird statistic the other day: did you know more people get killed by napkins, than by sharks?"

"I want to marry you!" I blurt out, hoping I haven't played my trump card too early.

"Oh," she replies. "Are we supposed to be going out then? It's just the last time Belle set me up with a guy, we only stayed together while we were coming out of clubs and stuff – we never actually had to go out to dinner. Of course, I slept with him a couple of times anyway. Will I have to sleep with you when we're married? Oh, and do you know what would happen if we ate ourselves? Would we double in size, or just disappear?"

"So, you'll marry me?" I ask again. She didn't say she wouldn't – is that legally binding?

"What?" she says, too busy looking at a fork on the empty table next to us. I'm about to pluck up the courage to repeat the question when she beats me to it.

"I don't suppose you've got any…"

She sniffs and rubs her left nostril. I smile like Doug Holster and slide a packet across the table when no one's looking.

"I never stalked you, did I?" I say with a grin.

I watch as her face lights up.

"Nah!" she giggles. "You're a cuddly little sweetie!"

351

Nine minutes go by and finally I see her come bounding back from the bathroom. She sits back down at our table with a huge grin on her face. She removes a fork from her cleavage and puts it into her bag.

"Look what I got from that old couple's table over there!" she whispers.

"Feeling better?" I ask. "Have you – you know…"

I make a gesture for her to give me back the rest of Richard's stash.

"What?" she says blankly. "No, it's – gone."

Jesus Christ, she's got a healthy appetite. I've seen Dyson vacuum cleaners hoover up less than her!

"Oh, I'm so glad to be out of that place in Wales," she says dreamily. "Sorry, what was your name again?"

"Doug Holster!"

"The stalker!" she laughs.

"No, your husband to be," I remind her.

"We're getting married?" she asks.

"Oh, yes, Belle's sorting out the arrangements as we speak," I say confidently.

"Are you famous?" she asks strangely, "because you don't look famous?"

"I've just won *Celebrity Voyeur* and my autobiography comes out in a matter of weeks," I state, before adding "and by night I slaughter waves of evil undead zombie-agents."

"Oh, my god, that's like so cool," she says open-mouthed, "I've been trying to get a real celebrity boyfriend ever since Metropol stopped returning my calls and threw me out of my flat. But I didn't have an agent and Richard wouldn't answer his phone."

"Your search is finally over," I reassure her. "We're getting married as soon as the press releases go out to all the major publications."

"Wicked! I love weddings! I want kids! Do you want kids? Because I do. Would it be illegal if I call our daughter Tiramisu?" she splutters. "Do you reckon we could get our wedding into *Heat* magazine?"

"Belle's got a deal with *Hello*," I inform her.

"*Hello*?" she gasps. "Oh, my god, I've never been in *Hello* before. You really think we'll make it into *Hello*? Hello! I just love saying hello! Do you like saying hello?"

I don't get a chance to answer.

"Will there be photographers there?" she goes on with raised eyebrows over her wide black eyes.

"Yes!" I cry, hoping the other diners don't all look over. "When two famous celebrities like us get together, everyone wants to know!"

"Oh, I can't wait," she goes on as she literally bounces up and down in her chair. "I haven't been in the papers for weeks! It's like, they don't want to know me any more – you know what I mean? Hello! Did you hear me say hello just then?"

"Oh, they'll want to know us now," I laugh heartily as I put my hands on hers. "Belle says she wants us to do a fitness video!"

"I love videos. Oh, my god I can't believe all this; it's all happening so fast. We'll be like Ginger Spice and David Beckham!" she muses.

"Posh," I correct her.

"Yeah, I'm well posh – know what I mean, Dave?"

"Doug."

"What?"

"My name's Doug, remember?" I say gently.

"The stalker!"

People in the restaurant look round.

"No," I say through gritted teeth, "just Doug the celebrity author, superspy and media commentator."

"Is that like, one of those guys who talks while the football is on?"

"No, look, I'll explain on our honeymoon," I say, anxious to turn the conversation back to our wedding plans. "What about Hollywood? You know, get a feel for the place if we decide to live there one day?"

"What about Brazil?" she asks. "I love the nuts, see? Do you reckon they call Brazil nuts Brazil nuts in Brazil, or just nuts? Hello!"

"I don't know," I say blandly. "Metropol will only pay for us to go places they have studios where we can do photo shoots. Maybe we can pop down there; we're only being given a fortnight."

"That's like, a week isn't it?"

"No – fourteen days," I correct her.

"A whole month?" she exclaims. "Oh, my god, I've never been away for like, a whole month. How many pairs of underwear should I take for fourteen days?"

I think the drugs are wearing off as I can see that her upper lip hair needs bleaching.

"Um, darling," I say casually. "Are you sure you don't have any of the you know…"

I tap my nose inconspicuously and am relieved when she smiles.

"I was just playing with you, I've got your medication right here, Doug," she says with an endearing smile which melts my heart. "It's time for your next dose now."

I take the small bag and hide it in my inner pocket with my pens then discreetly make my way to the toilets. Before I push the door open, I find myself smiling for no reason. I like feeling like this and I turn to look at my fiancée from across the restaurant.

From our table, she smiles back and mouths the words, "Take your medication, Doug". I'd be a fool to go against such a beautiful woman's wishes. As she sits there smiling she almost looks like an angel, or maybe a nurse.

THE END